The
Sword of
Dalmar

The Sword of Dalmar

Charles Ebert

Trebe Books
Durham, NC

To Dorothy E. O'Brien, because a boy should always dedicate his first novel to his mother.

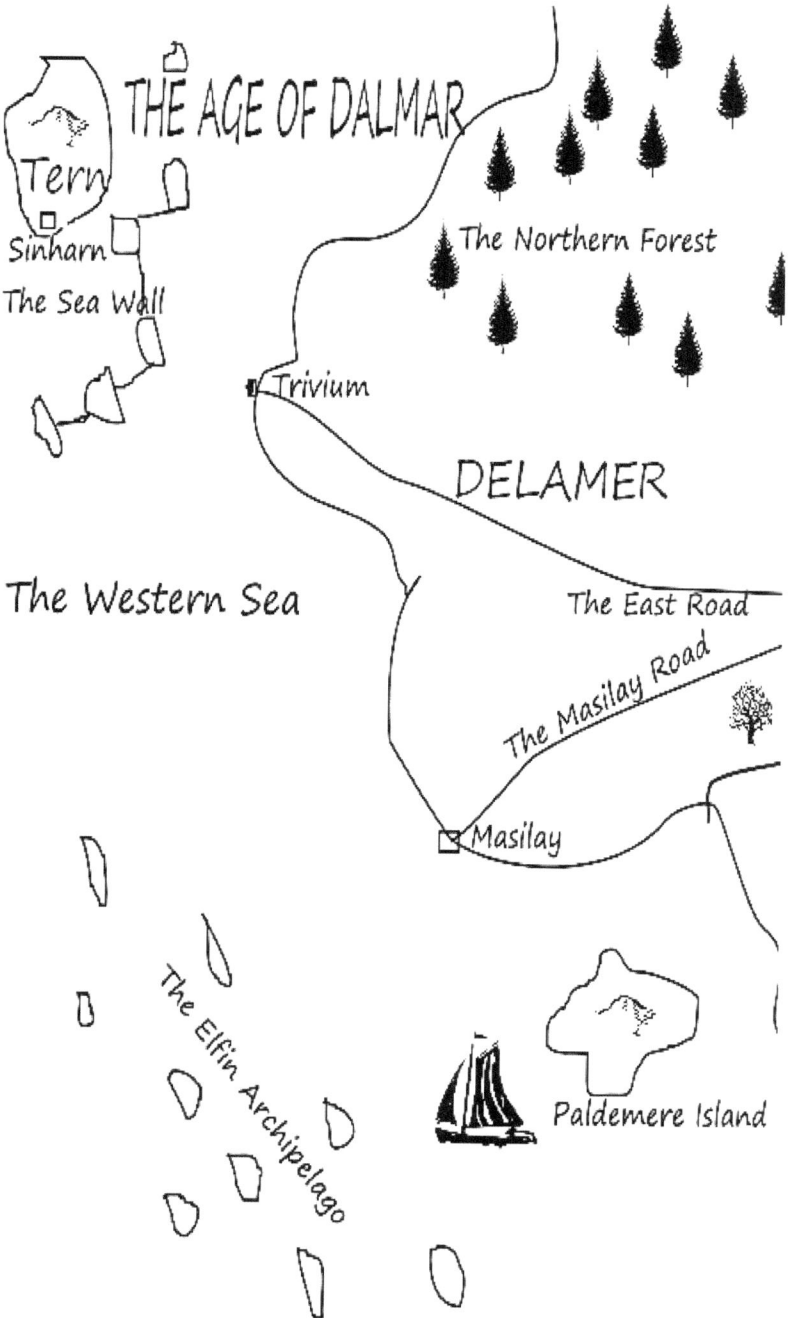

THE AGE OF DALMAR

Tern

Sinharn

The Sea Wall

Trivium

The Northern Forest

DELAMER

The Western Sea

The East Road

The Masilay Road

Masilay

The Elfin Archipelago

Paldemere Island

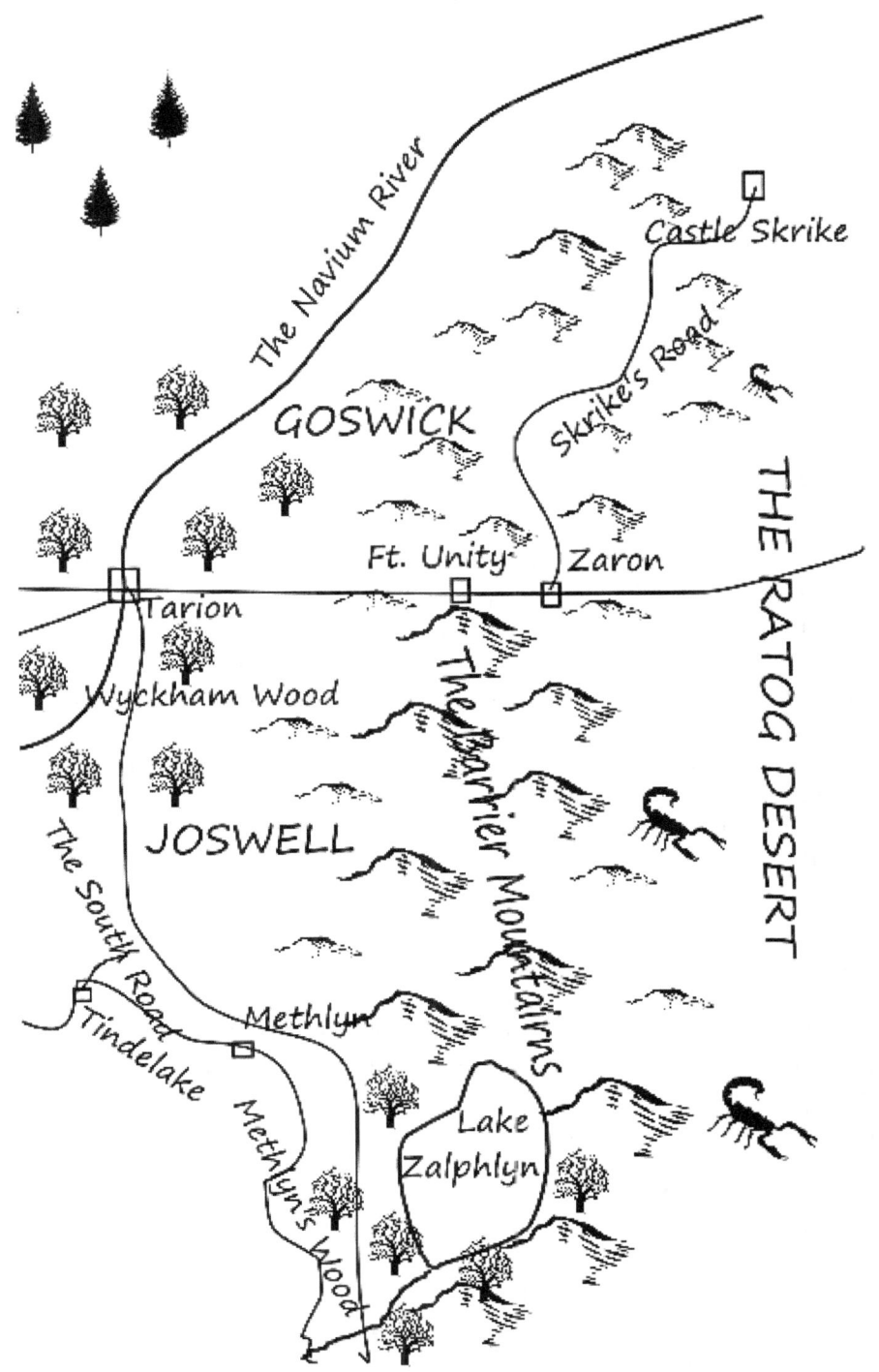

Prologue

His eyes fluttered open and then snapped shut against the blinding sunlight, the first he had seen in a hundred years. When he tried to move, he was rewarded with pain shooting up and down his body. It took a few minutes of massaging muscles and joints before he could get his limbs to work. When he could sit up, and his blood felt like it was flowing again, he looked around. The cave was as he remembered it. It was the size of a tomb and about as featureless. It would have been as dark if it weren't for the gap at the top of the pile of stones that blocked the entrance. Outside he could hear the muffled sound of the surf and he could smell the salt in the air.

His stomach growled and he decided it was time to move. When he tried to stand, the result was a brief flurry of arm waving and then a painful and undignified flop onto the stone floor. He closed his eyes and breathed in the moist sea air. When he could feel the power, he cast a strengthening spell over his legs. He stood and stumbled to the opening in the cave entrance. Grabbing the edge of it, he stood on tiptoe and took a deep breath of fresh air. This is bliss, he thought, feeling stronger with every passing second. The saltiness of the air he took in made him think of food.

As was the way with his people he cast his mind into the crowded seas of thought. And when he hauled it back in, he knew the situation had not changed. The sword had not been found and his dark cousin still ruled in the desert and still had ambitions for more. In the west, men were preparing to defend themselves. He and his kind were obligated to interfere. He sighed. He was not the only one of his people to find such meddling distasteful. But the final word was that his cousin Skrike was a Tenaryan, and his transgressions were their responsibility.

Anyway, it wasn't all bad. His task kept him here on the island out of danger. It was a pleasant place with fresh water and abundant plant life. Besides, he loved sea food.

He looked down at his body, grown thin during his long sleep, and clicked his tongue in disgust. He was never meant to be thin. It would take a long time to fill himself out to the point he felt nature intended him to be. His stomach growled again in anticipation and his mind raced, planning menus.

With skeleton arms, he began to widen the hole until he could crawl out of the cave.

Two hours later he sat on the beach, his tongue jammed into a crab leg, trying to capture the last morsel of meat. When he got it, he sighed and tossed the leg on the pile next to him. He wished he had some wine to wash it down. But such amenities would have to wait. He lay back in the sand to watch clouds.

The sky was a dark blue, broken only by a couple of friendly cumuli. These fluffy travelers were borne eastward on the same gentle breeze that tousled his ringlets of brown hair and fluttered the blades of beach grass and the palm trees behind him. The sun cast the scene in a warm glow.

If he had been a human, he'd have taken a nap. He'd always envied them that pleasure, possibly the only one he couldn't indulge in. The ability to pass away long hours in unconsciousness fascinated him. Especially since many humans he had known claimed it was an agreeable experience. But he wouldn't have had time for a nap, even if he could have taken one.

He sat up, his task drawing him onward. According to his captured thoughts, he had only a short amount of time. And he knew the task ahead of him was complicated. He stood, feeling the sand between his toes. Taking one last whiff of moist air, he set off to find a place to start.

Pity, he thought, it was such a nice day.

He searched the edges of the island for a suitable spot. Most of the eastern shore was low sandy beach, where gentle waves lapped at the island. Not high enough. To the north were rocky shoals and reefs. Nowhere to stand comfortably. Only on the south and west sides of the island were there suitable spots for his purposes. He finally

5

settled on a short cliff facing the sea. About six feet below him, the water churned against the rocks. This was a perfect place to start. Once his skills were sufficiently developed, he'd move to one of the higher cliffs on the west side of the island and then finally to the highest peak in the center.

Standing straight on the cliff, he held out his arm and made a scooping motion with his hand as if he were brushing a speck of dust off an antique mantle. A spout of water shot out of the ocean, and a puff of cold wind chilled him through the rags he wore. At his feet landed a silver fish which flapped its two foot length on the stone cliff, spraying drops of oily water.

"Ah," he cried in delight. Instantly, his mind raced. He'd seen some berries on one of the paths down to the eastern shore. Ground up and heated with a little water and some spices, which he knew were common on these islands, they'd make a great sauce for fish, especially when broiled. If he wrapped it up in leaves, lightly dusted with...But no, there would be plenty of time for that later. Events were moving quickly on the mainland and his mother needed his help. He picked up the fish and wrapped it in palm leaves. Then he turned to the sea.

1

Someone pounded on the door of the manor house, sending echoes rolling off the walls like the thunder from the storm rolled over the estate. That, thought Buckle as he threw off his covers, was that. Between the battering of the rain, the booming of the thunder and now a visitor, and an insistent one at that, sleep was impossible. Usually, Methliana was such a peaceful place. When the doorkeeper tapped at his chamber door and entered, Buckle sat up, swinging his feet over the edge of the bed. He looked up at Yarrel with unfocused eyes.

"Forgive me sir," said the doorkeeper, "there is someone at the door to see Lord Roduct."

Buckle massaged the back of his neck. Nagging pains scampered up and down his spine. Yarrel held a lamp in his hand which cast yellow light on the walls and on his face.

"What does he want?"

"He claims to have a message for the Lord."

Fierce white light shot through the shutters on Buckle's single window, followed by a deafening crash of thunder that shook the house. Somewhere down the hall a shutter came loose and started banging in the wind.

"Great Dalmar," said Buckle, "that was close."

"Yes sir, the storm seems to be getting worse."

Buckle nodded. "I've been listening to it all night. I doubt anybody can sleep." He rubbed his eyes. "A message you said?"

"Yes sir,"

Buckle sighed. "Prepare a room for him and tell him the Lord will see him tomorrow."

7

Charles Ebert

"Forgive me sir, I offered him accommodations but he refused. He insists that his message is important and that he must see Lord Roduct tonight."

"Has the Lord been informed?"

"No sir, I thought it best to talk to you first."

"Very good. Where is the visitor waiting?"

"In the front parlor, sir."

Buckle stood up and stretched. His back complained bitterly. "Don't awaken the Lord yet. I'll go down and talk to the stranger. Light the candle on my bed chest before you go."

"Certainly sir." With his withered hands, the old doorkeeper put the lamp's flame to the wick of the candle. Then he retreated from the room. Buckle yawned and lifted the candle in order to open his bed chest and retrieve a pair of breeches and a tunic.

It was possible that this message was as important as the visitor was insisting. For the last year, Roduct had been trying to convince the other Lords on the Delamerian council to unite their forces against the Sarondakis and bring Delamer into the war. The ancient enemy was awakening from a three hundred year slumber and looking westward again. From what Roduct had told him and from sitting in inns, gathering news for himself, Buckle knew that they were making raids into eastern Goswick and Joswell, and by most accounts, raising an invasion force. These activities had sent a flood of refugees heading west who brought chilling tales of atrocities with them

Goswick and Joswell were already calling upon their Lords to raise a force to supplement their standing armies. Every man who could hold a sword or a pike was being conscripted.

And yet in Delamer Roduct was having a hard time overcoming complacency. People, especially most of the Lords didn't want to hear about war. And deep down Buckle had to admit that he would hate to see good hands taken out of the field and sent away to the east. The last thing the country needed was for the harvest to be disrupted this fall.

But a good steward supported his lord in any way he could and if this visitor's message was from the capitol, Roduct probably should hear it.

Buckle pulled on his boot and then stood up to force it securely onto his foot. He ran a hand through his graying curls in an attempt at straightening them. He felt the stubble on his cheeks. "No time to shave," he murmured aloud. "It can't be helped. If people will pound on our door in the middle of the night, they must expect to be waited upon by an unshaved steward." He left his chamber and walked down the hall. Somewhere that shutter was still banging. He'd have to mention it to Yarrel.

When he arrived at the parlor, Yarrel was there, his back to the slightly open door. A band of yellow light cast from the parlor striped his face as he peered through the crack.

"Listening at doors again, Yarrel?" whispered Buckle, "That's hardly hospitable."

"Forgive me, sir," he said, "but this stranger bears watching."

"What do you mean?"

"You'll understand when you see him, sir."

"I see," said Buckle, wondering what was making Yarrel so suspicious. "I'd better see what he wants." He reached out to push open the door but Yarrel stopped him with a discreet clearing of his throat.

"Perhaps I should come in with you, sir?"

"Why?" said Buckle.

The old servant looked down at the floor and coughed delicately. "You may find it...comforting to have someone with you."

Buckle wrinkled his brow in puzzlement but nodded his head. "Keep discretely to one side."

"Certainly, sir," said Yarrel and they entered the parlor.

Standing by the fireplace was a huge figure, dressed in a black cloak which dripped water onto the wood floor of the parlor. A hood covered his head. The figure was studying the tapestry which covered one wall of the parlor. It depicted Dalmar's siege of the Castle Skrike three hundred years ago. The blond haired hero could be seen scaling the castle walls with Methlyn, his lady, right behind him. In the distance could be seen the Sarondaki armies retreating from the west, pursued by the armies of Goswick and Joswell, Dalmar's compatriots in the rebellion. The Sarondakis caught Dalmar before he could secure the castle and massacred his army. The two other armies hesitated when they got to the Barrier Mountains and were too late to save Dalmar. The fate of Dalmar and Methlyn was unknown. Roduct, a member of the long-lived Sarondaki race had been in Dalmar's army, a scout who had been lucky enough to be on patrol during the final battle. Many Sarondakis who had been stationed in the west in those days had joined in the revolt against Skrike. All of them had been given land as repayment. Roduct was the only one left alive now.

"You are not Roduct." The voice was harsh, grating, with an accent that after three hundred years, Roduct had not been able to completely lose. This was a Sarondaki warrior standing before them. It was no wonder Yarrel was anxious.

"No, Lord Roduct is asleep at the moment," said Buckle. His heart pounded and he could feel his chest tightening. "I am his steward, Buckle."

"Where is Roduct?"

"Well," said Buckle, "as I said he's asleep."

"Awaken him now."

"I understand that you have an urgent message for him. Perhaps if you let me hear it..."

A loud thump interrupted him. The Sarondaki pounded his fist on one of the parlor tables. "Bring the traitor Roduct to me." he shouted.

Buckle took a step back. Instinctively, he glanced over at Yarrel who looked equally alarmed.

Obviously, this message was not from Tarion. Buckle rubbed the stubble on his chin, trying to decide what to do. He probably could be stubborn and insist that the visitor wait until morning for an audience. There were close to twenty men on the estate's garrison, most of them being the field and stable hands who could all handle swords or pikes. Also this was a Sarondaki in the middle of Delamer, far from home. The rain was a factor too. Sarondakis were dependent on fire magic for their strength and longevity. Rain weakened them, not fatally, but enough to make them uncomfortable. Buckle knew that Roduct always walked stiffly when it rained and was even more taciturn than usual. In fact Roduct had once admitted to Buckle that he was in constant pain even when the skies were clear.

Still, it was hard to ignore that dark presence. The visitor leaned forward, his fist pressing into the table. Buckle couldn't see the warrior's eyes but he felt them boring into him. Could the pain brought on by the weather cause the warrior to forget where he was and send him leaping over the table? Buckle swallowed with some difficulty, noting that none of the garrison happened to be in the room at the moment.

"If you will just calm down, sir, I will have Lord Roduct sent for."

The warrior relaxed and so did Buckle although he retreated a few steps away toward the far wall of the parlor. Yarrel exited to have Roduct awakened and informed about the visitor.

After an awkward silence, Buckle cleared his throat, and said, "Perhaps I could take your cloak?"

"No," said the visitor, who turned back to the tapestry.

Buckle sighed and tried to lean against the wall without seeming to. The parlor was unbearably stuffy and Buckle could feel sweat forming on his forehead and neck. His legs were shaking so bad, it felt like he would collapse if he were forced to stand for another minute. Just when he had decided to ignore politeness and go ahead and sit down, Roduct entered the room, followed by Yarrel.

Buckle watched as Roduct's eyes scanned the parlor. His gaze stopped at the visitor who had turned to face him. Roduct and his visitor were of much the same build, tall, wide-shouldered and deep-chested. Roduct had dark hair, cropped close to the skull and eyes which were so brown they were almost black. He had the high cheekbones which marked his Sarondaki heritage. He was dressed in everyday breeches and tunic which were wrinkled as if they had been slept in.

"My staff tells me you have a message?" This to the visitor who jerked his head toward Buckle and Yarrel.

"Yarrel, Buckle would you please wait outside?"

"But Lord..." said Buckle. Roduct cut him off with a gesture.

"I can take care of myself, now go. Wait in the hallway. I'll call if I need you."

"But Lord Roduct," said Buckle, walking up to the imposing nobleman, "he's a..." Buckle hesitated. It wouldn't have done to inform Roduct that his visitor was a Sarondaki. "Very well, Lord. We'll be in the hallway if you need us."

Roduct nodded, his eyes fixed on the visitor. Buckle and Yarrel left the parlor.

The hallway was cooler than the parlor and draftier. The lamp Yarrel held fluttered until he cupped his bony hand around it. Flashes of brightness from the lightning outside forced their way through the door frame. The air had a damp musty smell. All around them loomed the dark wood of the staircase and the wainscoting.

Buckle rubbed his eyes and felt the coolness of the foyer penetrate his skin. "This has been a very long day."

"You look very tired, sir, if I may say so."

11

"Yes, Lord Roduct and I have been up late the last few nights going over the estate's finances. And now this storm and the visitor. I'm afraid that I am no longer young, Yarrel. This is too much excitement for me."

A hoarse shout cut through the air. Then from behind the door came a crash and several loud thumps. Buckle and Yarrel rushed into the parlor.

The first thing Buckle saw was that the window was open. Wind and rain were blowing the shutters to and fro, and a puddle of water was accumulating on the floor. The table was in shambles and beside it laid Roduct. "Lord Roduct," cried Buckle, as he rushed to his side. Buckle watched in apprehension until he saw the lord's chest move. A growing puddle of blood soaked the floor and was seeping into the rug.

The visitor was gone.

Roduct groaned and tried to turn over. Imbedded in the back of his left hand was a small funnel or shunt, originally white but now painted red with blood.

Out of the corner of his eye, Buckle saw Yarrel rush toward the open window. He looked through it and shouted for the guards to ring the alarm bell. In a second, it could be heard but only just barely above the din of the thunder and rain.

"Don't let him get away," whispered Roduct. "It's important."

"We're raising the alarm now, Lord."

Roduct sat up. When Buckle tried to stop him, he was motioned away. With a grimace Roduct grabbed the shunt in his hand. The bleeding renewed as the barbed point was worked out of his leathery flesh.

Buckle picked the linen cover out of the wreckage of the table and tore off a strip of material. He grabbed Roduct's wrist and started binding the wound.

"I'll awaken Sora to tend to your wound," said Yarrel.

"No," said Roduct, "I'll be all right. Bring Bertam."

"Bertam, Lord?" asked Yarrel. Buckle was puzzled himself. Bertam was his older brother and Roduct's solicitor.

"Yes, Bertam," said Roduct, his voice rising.

"Yes, Lord. Right away, Lord." Yarrel scurried away.

Roduct pushed himself up on his feet with Buckle's support.

"Perhaps you should sit down, Lord?"

"Yes." He eased himself into a chair by the fire. His face looked pale in spite of its natural dark coloring. He looked down at the bandage of his hand. "I don't know how much blood he got before you came in, but I think it was enough."

"I don't understand, Lord," said Buckle. He squatted beside Roduct.

Roduct shook his head slightly. Buckle was worried. This was the first time he had ever seen Roduct shaken.

"Forgive me, Lord," said Buckle, "but can you tell me what happened?"

"He attacked me," said Roduct.

"Why?" The Lord shrugged and looked down at his boots. "What was the message?"

"There was no message. That was a ruse to get to see me. This was an assassination attempt...of sorts."

"Assassination?" said Buckle. "But who would..." As soon as Buckle said it, his mind came up with several names, political enemies both local and in Tarion. "Do you think it was Erklin?"

Roduct looked thoughtful for a moment. "I don't think our sheriff has the connections to recruit a Sarondaki warrior. And then why would he? No, I'm afraid it's much worse than that. He looked up at Buckle. "If we can't find the visitor I may have to leave Methliana."

"Leave?" said Buckle.

"Perhaps only for a short time." said Roduct, "There will be other 'messengers' and they may not be so easy to spot."

"Excuse me, Lord," said Yarrel, standing in the doorway. "But the guards say that the stranger has escaped."

Roduct looked down and clenched his teeth. Buckle sank back on the floor. "Very well, Yarrel. Is Bertam here?"

"I'm here, I'm here," said Bertam, who stepped into the room and stood beside Yarrel. "What in Skrike's Hell is going on here?" His eyes were wide with indignation and his hair was gray and tousled. On his chin was an iron gray stubble that gave the lower half of his face a metallic look as grim as his permanent frown.

"Bertam," said Roduct, standing up, "we must rewrite my will."

The old solicitor squinted at him. "Right now, I suppose. Hell of a thing! Well, it's up in your study isn't it? We'll have to trudge all the way up there, assuming my bones don't collapse or I don't trip over something in these infernally dark halls." The old solicitor was still grumbling as he turned and led the group through the mansion to Roduct's study.

Once they arrived, Buckle sat in a chair by the windows, listening to the rain. Dimly, he was aware that Roduct was pacing the floor, dictating while Bertam wrote down every word. Buckle's mind rebelled when he tried to think of it. This was highly irregular. The planting season was no time to be leaving the estate to go off on mysterious errands. There were still vital decisions to be made about crops and personnel. Methliana had done well in the last few years but not well enough for its lord to disappear at such a crucial time.

But Buckle knew that the financial condition of the estate wasn't what was bothering him. He hardly dared to put his suspicions into words even in the privacy of his own thoughts. Roduct was in this very room dictating a new will. Why would he do that if he intended to come back?

Finally Buckle noticed that Roduct was talking to him...

"...do you understand all that, Buckle?" Roduct was staring at him, expectantly. Bertam was busy scribbling.

"I'm sorry," said Buckle, stammering, "my mind...that is I..."

Roduct's expression softened and he lowered his head. "It's all right, Buckle. Bertam can explain it to you later. The gist is that you are in charge while I'm gone."

"Me, but..." Buckle shook his head, "I still don't understand."

Roduct looked away.

"Very well," said Buckle, "if you must go, I'll see to arranging a wagon and some guards..."

"Yarrel will make the arrangements. I'll be traveling alone. All I need is a horse and two week's provisions."

"Then you'll be back in..."

"That's all I can carry. I'll need to move quickly. I leave tonight."

"Tonight? But..."

"As soon as Bertam finishes writing up my new will, I'll go."

"I'm working, I'm working," grumbled the solicitor.

"Why so soon?"

Bertam finished writing and turned to face Roduct and Buckle. He held out the revised will which Roduct took. "I know Methliana will be in good hands."

Roduct signed the paper, and was gone.

Outside the storm raged in unabated fury.

When Zabeth was sure that Belvica was asleep, she eased herself off the pallet they shared and then crouched on the cold floor, waiting to see if the motion would awaken her fellow drudge. But Belvica didn't stir, despite the thunder and rain that clashed so loudly outside and the clanging of the alarm bell earlier in the night. All the other girls were up. Zabeth could hear their voices through the paper thin walls, no doubt trying to comfort each other and succeeding only in making themselves more scared. Belvica though, could sleep through anything which was why Zabeth had worked so hard to room with her. She knew this night would come.

But did she pick the right night to run away? With the storm, hardly anybody would be asleep. The chances of her encountering somebody in the halls would be greatly increased. But at the same time the racket would cover her footsteps and discourage any pursuit. She bit her lip, wondering what the correct choice was. She could see advantages and disadvantages on both sides and couldn't decide between the two. Finally, she thought about Legothin, the man they were making her marry. He was stupid, cruel and conceited. They were barely engaged and the man had already hit her once. If Sora hadn't been there, Zabeth would have killed him. She always kept a dagger hidden in her bodice. To her credit, Sora almost killed Legothin herself, or would have if words could kill. But she didn't call off the wedding. Zabeth loathed him and worse, couldn't think of any other men on the estate who were better. The wedding was in a week and Zabeth intended to be a hundred miles away by then.

With new resolve, she stood up and retrieved her possessions, which were rolled up in a blanket and securely tied. She had hidden them in a dark corner behind an old bed chest, its wood gray and rotten. Then she tip-toed across the chamber to the door. Carefully she opened it, wincing as it squeaked, and peered into the hallway. It was almost pitch black.

A candle, sitting on a table just down the hall had either burned out or had been blown out by a draft. That was good, she thought, as she ventured out of the chamber and grabbed her worn boots by the door, anybody, up and walking the halls would be using a candle which would give her plenty of warning.

She padded down the hall toward her first stop which was the toilet. The halls were drafty and Zabeth wore only a thin shift, but she refused to shiver or complain, even to herself. Halfway down the hall from her destination, she stopped and bent over to see if she could see a light shining underneath the door. It was dark, so she crept up to it and gently pushed it open.

Unoccupied. So far the plan was going well. She slipped inside and pressed the door closed, lowering the plank that locked it. Then she threw her bundle down on the wood floor.

The toilet was cold and drafty. Rain poured through the window which had no shutter in order to cut down on the smell. It was cruelly cold in the winter and flies were a problem in the summer. Two of the five holes were thoroughly soaked.

By the light coming through the window, she untied her bundle and took out a knife. With her thumb she checked the sharpness of the blade. For a few moments more she held the knife, biting her lip. Once past this part she'd be committed. She drew a sharp breath and then brought the knife up to her blond hair and started cutting. A handful at a time, the hair came off and was thrown down one of the holes. When she was done she had about a half inch of fur covering her scalp. She inspected it with her fingers to be sure it wasn't uneven and also to feel the strangeness of it. Already her head felt light and cold.

Then she pulled off her shift and that followed her hair down the same hole. Naked, she stood in the breeze that blew through the window. Several small drops of rain made it across the room to land on her bare skin like tiny pin pricks.

She was about to reach for her bundle when she heard footsteps in the hall. They were heavy and getting closer. She stood perfectly still, not wanting to betray her presence in case whoever it was didn't want to use the toilet.

The door rattled. "Aw, damnit," hissed a voice from the other side of the door. It was male. "Who's in there?"

Zabeth bit her lip. What should she do? She couldn't pretend she wasn't there because the man would figure the door had blown closed and the plank had fallen into its latch, locking the door. He'd just break the door down or take it off the hinges.

"Occupied," said Zabeth, trying to disguise her voice and yet still sound feminine. If another man had been in here or if the person wanting in had been a woman, Zabeth would have been expected to open the door and share the facilities. She knew that in some of the smaller, more remote estates people were not even that modest.

"Oh," said the voice, "I'll wait."

Zabeth thought fast. "It could be awhile. I'm not feeling very well."

"You want me to fetch Sora?"

"No, no," said Zabeth, a little too fast. "I'll be fine as soon as...you know."

She heard a chuckle. "Yeah, I know. I thought that chicken we had for supper was a little gamy myself. I'll sneak over to the west wing and use that one." Then she heard his footsteps walking away.

Zabeth wiped a drop of sweat from her forehead and resumed breathing. She reached into her bundle on the floor and pulled out some strips of cloth. These she wrapped over her breasts and tightened them until her chest was flat. Her breasts were not very big so it wasn't too uncomfortable. Then she took a tunic and some breeches she had stolen from the laundry. She slipped into these and then re-rolled the bundle. She had a spare length of cord which she used for a belt. The knife she placed in this.

After making sure no one was in sight, Zabeth stepped into the hall. Somewhere above her she could hear floorboards creaking as somebody made their way along the hallway upstairs. Damn, she thought, fighting the panic rising inside, tonight was a mistake. Everybody was up and the storm didn't keep her from hearing those footsteps one bit.

Treading as lightly as she could, she walked down the hall toward the kitchen. Expecting at any moment to see Sora whipping around a corner or charging out of a doorway, Zabeth could feel her pulse in the back of her throat. The hallway seemed unreal to her as did the sound of the storm. Even the familiar musty smell of the servant's wing seemed alien. She could see her fingers brushing against the wall but couldn't feel them.

It seemed like hours before she came to the door of the pantry. It too was dark and Zabeth could hear no stirring within. With a look both ways down the hall she pushed the door open and went in.

The pantry had no windows so once she closed the door total darkness enclosed her. She held out her left hand until it touched the shelves. Then walking forward she counted the shelf sections as her fingers brushed them. At the fifth one she stopped and knelt. Carefully, she took the urns full of lard off the bottom shelf and laid them on the floor beside her. When the shelf was clear, she reached in and with her fingernails pulled up the plank from the floor and then laid that beside the urns.

She took a ragged breath. What if it wasn't there anymore, she thought? A year was a long time, what if somebody had discovered it? She'd have heard, a more reasonable part of her contended. She'd have probably been punished for stealing it, since everyone would have known what it was and who it had belonged to. And who would have been most likely to want to keep it for herself.

Her hands shaking, she reached into the slot below the shelves. Her fingers found it and carefully wrapped themselves around it. The blade, even though wrapped in oilskin, was razor sharp.

Zabeth rocked back and set the sword on her lap. Through the covering her hand caressed the familiar pommel and memories of Grazzle surfaced in her mind. At an early age just after she had arrived at Methliana she had sneaked into his combat classes disguised as a boy, much as she was now. Of course she'd fooled no one, least of all him and the first thing he had done was to try and wash her out. He had her wrestle the biggest boy there, thinking to discourage her. But ten year old Zabeth knew a few things even then. Things her father had taught her before he died. When the boy had run at her, she had stepped aside and tripped him. Then she jumped on his back and twisted his arm until Grazzle had declared the fight over.

Throughout that session the tests had gotten tougher and tougher but Zabeth had passed them all. But at the end when all the boys had left, Grazzle kept her after and told her not to come back. He couldn't have girls in his combat class. When she complained that she had beaten every boy in the class he remained unmoved. When she showed up for the next days' class he sent her away. The next day, he did the same and informed Sora who whipped her. The next day, he whipped her himself. But on the fifth day, he relented and told her that he would privately tutor her if she finished her chores for Sora and attended every one of the cooking and sewing classes she was assigned to. Zabeth eagerly agreed and although it meant fourteen hour days sometimes, she never missed a private session with Grazzle and she quickly surpassed the boys.

Zabeth felt along the blade of Grazzle's sword to see if she could feel any rust through the oilskin. Her private lessons with Grazzle, had of course, stopped when the old man's heart gave away and he'd died. Sora wasted no time in making Zabeth a drudge, since she was useless for anything else. Cooking and sewing bored her. She hadn't been allowed to touch a sword in all that time. But the drills and exercises could be done with a mop handle in one of the upstairs halls when nobody was around.

They buried Grazzle in his best tunic and breeches but they were never able to find his sword. Zabeth now held that sword. Finally deciding that she had to see it right away she set it aside and got up. She found a candle sitting in a holder on the shelf beside the door. Beside it were flint and steel. When the candle was lit she carried it back to the sword and sat cross-legged on the stones. Pulling off the oilskin she hissed in pleasure to see it again. Its steel surface winked at her in the candle light and looking down its length to check for bending, she could see its keen edge. She held it close to the flame and frowned at a spot of rust near the cross-piece. She scraped at it with her fingernail.

When she first saw the sword, in her second year of sessions, she had imagined that it was the legendary sword of Dalmar. Grazzle had laughed, saying that, no it was merely an ordinary fighting sword. Of the best manufacture to be sure, Goswick steel and craftsmanship but there wasn't a whiff of Tenaryan sorcery about it. But to Zabeth the sword was pure magic. On the rare occasions that he'd let her exercise with it, it seemed to sing in her hands. The blade cut clean and moved more swiftly than the rusty practice swords she usually used. And when she had grown to her full height and weight, she found that the sword was the perfect length and weight for her. Grazzle saw it too and on his deathbed he told her to take it and hide it until she needed it.

During his life, Grazzle helped her all he could. He customized his instructions for her, emphasizing speed and accuracy over brute strength, although he had her build up her strength in certain areas like her arms so she could draw a bow. But he was also frank about her chances. No army would consider a woman as a soldier nor would many estates want a woman for a guard except maybe a small struggling one in the interior. And that was Zabeth's plan: to escape and make it to a new estate struggling to establish itself and short on manpower. Among the items in her pack were a couple of letters of introduction written by Grazzle, outlining her qualifications. His name might be enough to get her foot in the door and allow her to prove herself.

The door to the pantry flung open and the room brightened as another candle was carried in.

"There you are, young lady," said a voice from behind her. Zabeth stood and wheeled around to see Sora standing in the doorway, her face menacing in the flickering light. In spite of herself, Zabeth backed away from the diminutive estate cook. She watched as Sora's eyes moved from her clothes to her hair and finally to rest on the sword.

"Where did you get that?" Her voice was high and rough. As Zabeth watched, Sora's face turned bright red. "That's...that's..." she sputtered.

Zabeth grabbed her blanket roll and dashed out the door, shouldering Sora out of the way. Once in the hall she darted to the right toward the servants' entrance. She didn't see the figure shambling down the hall until she was almost upon it. And then it was too late. She collided with it. There was a grunt of pain and she felt the sword slip from her fingers and clatter to the floor. Overbalanced, she would have fallen but the figure grasped her by the arms and held her with a tight grip. She tried to spin away but was held fast.

When Sora arrived with the light, Zabeth looked at her captor and saw that it was Bertam, Roduct's solicitor.

"What have we here," his voice creaked. He examined her with his rheumy eyes. "Why you're that girl..."

"She's a thief," spat out Sora, grabbing Zabeth by the arm and pulling her out of Bertam's grasp. "She's the one who stole Grazzle's sword. Look, there it is." Sora's bony finger pointed to the weapon where it lay on the stone floor, glittering in the lamplight.

The old man glanced at the sword and then back at Zabeth. "Where did you get that?"

Zabeth looked from one of them to the other. "Grazzle gave it to me," she said, her chin jutting out.

"Oh nonsense," said Sora. "Why would Grazzle give you a sword?"

Bertam waved her to silence. "You realize young lady that sword constituted a significant part of Grazzle's estate."

"He gave it to me," said Zabeth, her voice growing colder.

"Humph," said the old man and he walked over to the sword and picked it up, grunting as he bent over. He examined the blade with a critical eye. "At least it's undamaged."

"Of course it is," barked Zabeth. Sora savagely yanked on her arm.

"You don't talk to Master Bertam like that young lady." Zabeth tried to shrug out of her grasp but couldn't.

"It's my sword," she hissed between clenched teeth.

"I don't suppose you can prove that," said Bertam. Zabeth lowered her head. "I thought not. This is a serious crime, young lady. We would be entirely justified in contacting the sheriff."

"Then do it," spat Zabeth. She was rewarded with another yank on her arm.

"Don't tempt us," said Sora.

Bertam held up a hand to stop her. "What are you doing, running around the halls at night?"

"I'm leaving," said Zabeth.

"Such nonsense," said Sora. "With your wedding one week away."

"That's why I'm leaving," said Zabeth.

Bertam shook his head as if to clear it. "You know we can't let you do that. Not only are you a woman and it is dangerous for women to travel alone, but Lord Roduct is your liege. You are tied to this estate."

"I can't stand it here anymore," blurted Zabeth. This time she pulled away from Sora's grasp. "I won't marry that bastard, Legothin, I won't."

"You'll do what I and Lord Roduct tell you. That's a woman's duty," said Sora.

Zabeth rounded on the older woman.

"I don't want that life," shrieked Zabeth. "To be at the beck and call of man who's not half as smart as I am, little better than a slave."

Sora pursed her lips and her eyelids contracted over her eyes. "That's not a bad life, and as a woman it's the best you can expect. Certainly better than anything you can find out there." She flailed her arm toward the shuttered window at the end of the hall. Brilliant white light forced its way through the slats and thunder boomed so loudly Zabeth could feel it in her chest. The shutters rattled in their hinges.

When the noise of the thunder passed Bertam said, "She's right, Zabeth. Most of the women I knew during my years in Tarion that weren't attached to an estate were drudges or maids in inns, much more difficult work than what you have here. Or else they were...ah, well...camp followers." He said the last words in a low embarrassed tone of voice.

"Not me," said Zabeth. "I'd die first."

She saw Bertam's eyebrows arch upward. "I'm sure you would. But why should we send you out into the world to die?"

"I can take care of myself," said Zabeth between clenched teeth. She reached into her blanket roll and pulled out a leather pouch. Out of this she retrieved three documents the old Captain of the Guard had given her before he died. "Here," she said, waving them in front of Bertam. "Letters of introduction from Grazzle. They say I'm as good a warrior as any man he ever taught."

Sora's bony hands snatched the documents out of Zabeth's grasp. "Grazzle may have been a great warrior back east when he was younger, but during his last few years here, I don't think he had all his wits about him. He did you no favors by encouraging you like he did, young lady." She eyed the documents with disdain. "Well I'll take care of this right now." She held them to the flame. Zabeth watched in horror as the dry paper ignited.

"No," she shrieked. She charged Sora, grabbing the letters and almost knocking the candle out of the old cook's hand. Zabeth frantically waved the papers in the air and blew on them until the flame went out. Then she looked up at Sora. The old woman's image was filtered through the blood boiling in Zabeth's brain.

"Why you..." Suddenly Bertam was in front of her, holding his hands out to catch her if she bolted forward.

"Now Zabeth," he said softly, "perhaps you should think carefully about your next action. You're in enough trouble as it is." Zabeth ground her teeth and glared at Sora but then relaxed. She concentrated on putting the letters back in the leather pouch.

"I say we send for the sheriff as soon as the storm stops," said Sora.

"I'll have to talk to Buckle about that," said Bertam. He looked down at his feet. "I'll do it tomorrow. He has a lot on his mind tonight. As for now Sora, lock her in one of the store rooms."

"I certainly will, Master Bertam." She grabbed Zabeth's arm and pulled her down the hall.

"I will take charge of this," said Bertam. Zabeth turned her head back and saw him heft the sword and then turn and walk away.

2

Buckle was awakened the next morning by a sudden increase in light. When his eyes fluttered open, he saw Yarrel standing beside the window, his hand on the open shutter. Buckle had spent the night sleeping in Roduct's desk chair.

"Forgive me, sir, I didn't realize you were there." The ageless doorkeeper bowed slightly and started to close the shutters again.

"No, no that's all right," protested Buckle, rising woozily, "I should get up anyway." He limped to the window, his back crooked and sore from a night spent in the chair. He pushed the window further open, letting the cool air wash over him.

Morning had dawned through a crystalline blue sky. The rays of the sun glittered and sparked through traces of moisture in the trees. The yard was bustling with activity. One of Sora's drudges strained under the burden of two full milk pails, which she carried to the kitchen. A few hands were rummaging through a wood pile beside the barn. In the corral, ponies were playing as the stable hands cleaned out their stalls and cleared out the stable in order to assess the storm damage.

Buckle glanced at the sun which had just cleared the roof of the stable. "Oh Dalmar, How long did I sleep."

"Given the night you had last night sir, I don't think anyone can blame you for sleeping in."

"Perhaps so, Yarrel but I should still be out there. There's bound to be storm damage and..." He stopped short, remembering the previous night. His hand went up to an amulet he wore around his neck.   It was a brass representation of Roduct's seal.   The lord had presented it to him on the day he'd become steward.

"No need for concern, sir.   Everything goes as it did when Lord Roduct was here."

"Do any of them even know?"

"The lord's horse is gone, so they know the lord must be also. But as for details they have none and are probably at this moment making them up."

Buckle looked up at Yarrel.   "Perhaps you're right.   They should be told.   I'll do it at the midday meal.   See that everybody available is there, will you, Yarrel?"

"Of course sir, will that be all?"

"Ask my brother, if he's up, to join me here."

Yarrel nodded and said, "I believe I saw Master Bertam walking the grounds earlier this morning.   I'll dispatch someone to find him, sir."

Buckle watched as the doorkeeper's aged hands pulled the door shut behind him.   Then he was alone.   He collapsed into the desk chair and cradled his head in his hands.   His mind was finally beginning to work.   Buckle didn't have a grasp on the specifics but he knew that if Roduct was gone for a long time, he would abdicate his position as lord of Methliana.   Succession laws in the west were murky at best, the old noble families of Dern having been eradicated during the Sarondaki rule.   Only now was a noble class beginning to emerge from the hardy peasants who went into the forests to reclaim the old Dernian estates.   But Methliana was an established estate, having been founded by Roduct three hundred years ago.   Buckle suspected that a new lord would be chosen by the council from among the pool of second sons of the families running other established estates.   Which meant that the futures of Buckle and the other members of the staff were in question.

Buckle had lived at Methliana ever since he was four years old. He remembered the day he came.   Bertam, young then and ambitious had led him by the hand into the manor house where they were greeted by Roduct who looked exactly the same as he did now.   Their mother had just died on their small farm in the wild interior of Delamer.   So Bertam, fifteen years older, had arranged with Roduct for Buckle's care and then had left for Tarion to become a solicitor.   Roduct provided well for Buckle, good room and board, and as good an education as could be provided.   When Buckle began to show an aptitude for organizing things, Roduct started grooming him for the job of steward.

Now Buckle felt like his four year old self again, facing an unknown future.   What would happen if a new lord took over and wanted to bring his own staff?   Buckle knew he was probably too old to find another position.   He didn't have the energy or courage to go off by himself and try to reestablish one of the old Dernian estates like his father had tried.   Besides his experience with that lifestyle wasn't exactly positive.   Mostly though, he would miss Methliana.   This manor house was his home and he came near to panic at the thought of leaving it.

He turned at the sound of the study doors opening.   Bertam, wearing his usual sour expression, entered the room.   His craggy face hung on his skull like an old sack.   The alarms of last night could be read in the slightly darker shade of purple ringing his eyes.

Me in fifteen years, thought Buckle with an inward sigh.   But as soon as he thought it, he knew it wasn't true.   The lines on Bertam's face had been etched there by city living, the sedentary yet hectic lifestyle of a Tarion solicitor.   Too many expensive meals at fancy inns; too many extra cups of wine, and too many bowls of tobacco not balanced by physical activity had worn Bertam out before his time. The life had led to the irregular palpitations of his heart, which had forced Bertam into semi-retirement here at Methliana as Roduct's solicitor.

"Brother, how are you this morning?"

"Terrible, between the storm and that business last night, I couldn't get any sleep at all.   You know one of the drudges tried to run away last night?"   He lowered himself into a chair.

"Which one?"

"The girl old Grazzle took a liking to, Zabeth."

Buckle nodded.   "As I recall, she took the old man's death pretty hard.   We're going to have to do something about her.   Isn't she to be married in a few days?"

"Why do you think she tried to run away?"

Buckle nodded.   "Is there much storm damage?"

"Yes," Bertam replied, waving the unpleasant thought away, "the whole place is a mess, debris everywhere, shutters pulled off their hinges.   Lost about a half dozen hens, I'd guess."

"Roast chicken for dinner tonight."

"Yes, and chicken stew for at least two weeks or until they rot too much for even Sora to cook them." He eyed the carpet in bitter expectation of upcoming menus.

"Um, about last night Bertam..."

"You want to know what was in the will."

"Well, yes," replied Buckle, sitting up in his chair. "But what I really want to know is...why did he leave?"

"He told me less than he told you." Bertam waved the question off and then stopped, looking at Buckle's crestfallen expression. "I'm sorry Buckle. But this matter is a mystery to me. What happened last night?"

Buckle related the events of the past night up to the point where Bertam entered the study.

"You're sure this visitor was a Sarondaki?"

"As sure as I can be, having only seen one Sarondaki in my entire life."

"Hmm," mused Bertam. "It could be Soowooli."

"Sarondaki mind control?" asked Buckle.

"Yes. What happened to this shunt you mentioned?"

"I don't know. I can ask Yarrel."

"Do that. It could be important."

Buckle nodded. "What about the will then?"

"Lord Roduct has made you legal caretaker of Methliana for a period of a year at which time, if he has not returned, he will be declared legally dead and the entire estate will go to you."

Buckle's stomach dropped about a foot. "To me, everything?"

"Yes, even his seat on the High Council."

Buckle decided to ignore the implications of that last part for now. "Can he do that?"

"Of course, despite the airs some lords put on, there isn't anybody with a drop of noble blood in them around anymore and everybody knows it. The only basis for holding land is making it productive. No one can doubt your ability to do that."

"But I..."

"Look Buckle, I don't know why Roduct up and left. I suppose he had his reasons but from where I'm sitting, it looks like a foolish move. But he did do one smart thing: He left you in charge."

"Maybe so," said Buckle, springing to his feet to pace, "but this business about leaving everything to me if he doesn't come back..."

"Well who else?   The man never married.   There are no bastards that we know of.   You have to know he was planning to leave it all to you anyway."

Buckle stopped halfway across the rug.   "I...I suppose I never really thought about it.   I guess I just can't imagine him dying."

Bertam's body groaned in protest as he lifted himself up and stood beside Buckle.   "Well, considering his Sarondaki blood, he may not die in our lifetimes."

Buckle walked to the window and looked out at the still busy yard.   Suddenly the kitchen bell rang and the hubbub increased as people rushed to finish their chores and get to the dining hall.

"I'm going to tell the staff what's happened over dinner.   I want you there to explain some of the legal aspects."

"If you wish."

The staff took the news better than Buckle had expected, but thinking again, he realized there was no reason they shouldn't take it well.   Roduct's departure would mean little or no change in their routine.   The lord had always relied heavily on Buckle to run the estate.   Now it was just going to be official.   If anything, the help seemed happier at the idea of working for the personable Buckle rather than the standoffish Roduct.

They don't understand, thought Buckle, as he helped a few of the stable hands clear the debris from the yard.   If Roduct doesn't return in a year, I'll assume all his responsibilities and I won't have time to do things like manual labor or even eat my meals with the hands. I'll become just as aloof as Roduct.   Buckle inwardly cringed at the thought of spending three months out of every year in Tarion; giving speeches in High Council, making deals and hobnobbing with the landed gentry that ruled Delamer.   There was a whole other set of duties Roduct performed of which Buckle knew nothing.

"Great Dalmar," he muttered, "I hope Lord Roduct makes it back."

"Do you think any of this can be saved?" Yazzle, a large blond stable hand was examining a fairly big piece of the barn roof that had blown off during the storm and was now sitting in the middle of the barnyard.

Buckle squatted beside the debris and gave it several good raps with his knuckles. "It seems sound enough." He stood, brushing the knees of his breeches. "Is there any room for it in the barn?"

Buckle walked into the barn with Yazzle in tow. About a third of the roof had blown off. Silhouetted against the blue afternoon sky, what was left hung in tatters. Cross beams and shingles littered the floor just like in the yard outside.

"Wow, that was some storm," said Buckle.

"Pretty strong for the first of the season, sir."

"It sure was. Has the carpenter seen this?"

"I saw him in here this morning, sir," said Yazzle.

"Good. Well let's get started, Yazzle," said Buckle, walking to the wood pile. They sorted out various planks and two by fours, keeping the ones which might be useful and tossing the rest aside.

"This one, Master Buckle," asked Yazzle, holding out a six foot plank in his huge hands.

"That may be long enough, keep it."

The blond giant tossed the plank on to the keeper pile and continued rummaging.

"Where do you think Lord Roduct went, if you don't mind my asking, sir?"

"I couldn't tell you, Yazzle. But my guess is that he went east."

The big lad gave a visible shudder. "Nothing but bad news come from the east lately." He heaved an eight foot plank onto the pile. The only wood left was a door sized plank which was adhered to the wall by time and the press of the wood pile. Most of it was half visible in the murky light of the barn but a beam of sunlight shone through the ravaged ceiling, casting a bright pool of light on part of the plank.

"It can't be as bad as all the stories suggest. Here, help me with this," said Buckle, grabbing an end of the plank. Yazzle grabbed the other end and together they pried it away from the wall.

On the wall where the plank had been stuck, and visible in the shaft of sunlight, there was a slimy stain. Buckle got a good whiff of the mold and staggered backward, dropping his half of the plank. He could feel his chest closing, as if someone were tightening a vice around him, and the more he tried to force air in, the tighter it became. He stumbled again, falling on the packed dirt of the floor. His vision darkening, he crawled to the wall.

"Are you all right, Master Buckle?" Yazzle squatted beside Buckle, his face distorted with worry. Buckle leaned back against the wall, trying to force air into his chest. Weakly, he motioned Yazzle away.

"Help, help," cried the big hand, running out of the barn. "Master Buckle is sick." In an instant, the barn was full of people, crowding around each other to get a look at their ailing steward. Buckle closed his eyes, trying to ignore them. But the din created by people talking and shouting at him and each other refused to let him relax.

Suddenly the press flew away like chaff. "Get away from him, give him air," screeched Sora, pushing her way through the crowd. "Haven't you got work to do," she bellowed at a hand twice her size while pushing him toward the door.

The barn was cleared in a few seconds time. Sora knelt beside Buckle, placing a hand on his shoulder. He could feel the muscles relaxing under her touch. "You're having another attack, aren't you?"

Buckle nodded his head.

"Well, let this be a lesson to you. You're not twenty years old anymore. You should stay away from the physical labor. What do you think we hired all those hands for? Not their brains, surely?" She sprang to her feet and walked to the barn door. "Yazzle, get your empty yellow head over here."

"Yes'm."

"Get over to the kitchen and tell Ruyca I want some jimsonweed and a pipe, you understand, jimsonweed."

"Yes'm." Yazzle hesitated and then asked, "Will Master Buckle be all right?"

"Not unless you hotfoot it to the kitchen right now," she said, raising her hand in a universal gesture the estate help knew and feared. Yazzle scurried away on his appointed errand.

"Worthless dunderhead, probably come back with oregano."

Buckle coughed.

"Don't cough. Makes it worse."

"Mphmph," mumbled Buckle.

"Don't talk." She grasped his shoulders with strong hands and forced him to lay flat on the floor. 'My baby brother used to get attacks and Mama always knew what to do." She put her finger into his lower abdomen about an inch below the belly button and pressed down slowly. "Out."

Buckle exhaled and the finger let up. "In." He sucked in breath.

"Easy, easy," she said, "You'll just pack all that stuff in there tighter. Relax your shoulders and lie flat."

Buckle did his best to comply, but spots were beginning to form in front of his eyes. He looked up at Sora and she placed her free hand on his chest. "We've gotten through these things before, Master Buckle. If your attacks were going to kill you, they'd have done it long before now."

Buckle closed his eyes and concentrated on breathing. Soon he could feel his chest loosening, allowing air to flow freely. The panic drained away and was replaced by sleepiness.

"Ma'am?" Yazzle's hushed voice came to his ears. "Here's the jimsonweed."

"Well you took so long in getting it, we don't need it anymore. What did you do, stop off to see some relatives in Tarion on your way back?"

"Sorry Ma'am, the estate's in a mess. There's some kind of disturbance up at the manor house."

"The disturbance was last night. That storm."

"No Ma'am, visitors. Important ones by the look of their horses."

"So that's what you were doing. Spying down at the manor house."

"No Ma'am, I..."

"Excuse me." It was Vald's voice. He was one of the more experienced hands on the estate. Buckle, who had been half asleep, perked up. "Sora, Master Buckle is needed at the manor house."

"Well, he's not available. He's..."

"It's all right, Sora," said Buckle, rolling onto his side to view the trio standing in the doorway, "What's the problem, Vald?"

"Constables sir, at the manor house. There's been a murder on the main road and they're looking for Lord Roduct."

Buckle raised his hand to him. "Help me up."

3

Buckle lightly kicked the flanks of his pony, urging it forward as fast as its stubby legs could carry it. The road was soft but quite passable, which was a miracle, considering the storm the night before. One thing the Dernians knew how to do was build roads. The track leading from the estate house on Methkana to the road was a river of mud.

On both sides of the road now, were the outermost fields of Southwinds, Lord Ferkle's estate. By the look of it, Ferkle had done much worse during the storm than Roduct. His corn was flattened in places. Buckle thought he could almost trace the path of the storm by the trail of ruined crops. Which reminded him, he had yet to inspect his own fields. He wanted to see the crops for himself, even though his men assured him the damage was minimal.

Up ahead he could see the backs of the constables as they plodded along on their big stallions. The leader, a huge man named Torkle, looked back and whuffed in exasperation. He reined his horse around and galloped back to where Buckle was riding. Clods of mud sprayed off the stallion's hooves as Torkle approached.

"Your mount seems to be failing," he said, reigning in and falling in step beside Buckle's pony. "Perhaps we should give the poor beast a rest."

"You want to stop," asked Buckle, glancing at the sun which was well past midday. "I thought you were in a hurry."

"No, what I actually meant was you could ride on the back of my horse. We'd make much better time." He clipped his words short,

31

making each one fit precisely into the sentence like a carpenter making a cabinet.

"What would I do with poor Quist here," asked Buckle, leaning over to give his pony an affectionate pat on the neck.   Quist nickered in response and continued his plodding progress.

Torkle answered with a low growl.   "Well, we're almost to the East Road and Scarver's is only a short distance from there."   The constable had thick features.   His block-like jaw was unshaven and his nose had been broken several times by the look of it.   Consequently he breathed through his mouth and Buckle could see many missing teeth and the remaining ones were yellow or black.   Oily black hair peeked out from under his dull steel helmet.

"So when was this body found?" asked Buckle, as lightly as he could.

"Last night."

"During the storm?"

"Storm was last night wasn't it?"

They rode on in silence for a while before Buckle tried again. "And you say Lord Roduct was seen..."

"Look, Erklin will explain all of this to you."   He leaned sideways on his horse, bringing his face close to Buckle's.   "I will say that it won't look good to the sheriff that Roduct couldn't come."   He righted himself, a wicked smile on his face.

Buckle swallowed hard and gave up on trying to pump Torkle for information.

The sun was approaching the western horizon when Scarver's Inn came into sight on the right side of the road.   Standing in the middle of the road, as if he owned it was another constable.   His mouth was worked into an all-day frown, and no matter how hard he tried to keep a properly stoic constable stance, he still rocked back on his heels, impatiently waiting as Buckle urged his pony down the road.

"Ho, Torkle," said the standing constable, "Where in Dalmar's name have you been?"

"Ho, Chernal.   Came as fast as I could," replied Torkle.   Then motioning toward Buckle, he said, "Civilian."

Chernal glowered at Buckle, who calmly returned the man's gaze, "Erklin's mad enough to eat a barn, nails and all.   Better get them over there."

"Where is he?"

"Over by the stables."

Torkle turned in his saddle to face Buckle, "Do you think your horse can make it?"

"Yes sir." His smile was forced but it was there. Twenty years of dealing with Erklin's constables had taught him that the path of least resistance was always the best.

"Very well." Torkle clicked his tongue and turned, spurring his horse toward the inn's stables. Buckle followed as best he could.

Scarver kept a clean inn. The sides were freshly painted and they glowed in the noonday sun. Discounting the storm debris on the grounds, they were well kept up. The building itself was a sprawling affair, almost as big as the main house on Methliana. The guest rooms were located in an ell wing that extended alongside of the road. There was a large common room in the front and stables off to the side.

A group of men, most of them constables were assembled in front of the stables. Buckle recognized Sheriff Erklin by his bald head. Beside him was Scarver, almost as tall as the constables, who were all recruited for their size and fighting ability, but thin. Under his receding hairline hung a dour face which seemed incapable of mirth. He stood beside the sheriff with his arms crossed, staring balefully at a wagon parked along the eastern side of his stables.

As they approached the stables, Buckle could see a tarpaulin spread over a man-sized object in the wagon. Swarms of flies buzzed around it.

"Are you almost finished with your investigation, Erklin," said Scarver, "That thing's stink is beginning to drive away customers." He waved distastefully toward the wagon.

"Sorry Scarver, but this is official business," growled the sheriff, "These things can't be hurried."

He looked up and saw Buckle and Torkle. "By all the Sarondakis in Hell, where have you been," he bellowed at Torkle.

"Sorry sir, I hurried him as much as I could."

A threatening growl emerged from Erklin as he turned to face Buckle. His head then swiveled around in confused agitation. "Where in Skrike's Hell is Roduct," he shouted.

"Lord Roduct was...unavailable," explained Buckle. "He sent me in his place."

Erklin eyed Buckle closely, as if sensing a lie. Buckle thought he was about to object, when instead, he said, "Well, as long as he understands that we'll need to talk to him eventually. As it happens, I need to question you too, Buckle."

"Of course, sir," said Buckle in his most placating voice. "That's why I'm here."

"Humph. Well let's get this over with." He motioned Buckle off his pony.

Once on the ground, Buckle turned to the cadaverous innkeeper. "Scarver, my pony needs a brush down and some feed. And if you could get me some dinner after my business here, I'd appreciate it."

Scarver shifted his eyes in all directions before answering, his head bent as if being pressed down by some burden. "All right, but I want payment in advance. Two silver pieces."

"What? You don't think I'm good for it?"

"A lot of strangers in these parts nowadays. Can't trust anyone."

"But I'm not..."

"Pay him," croaked Erklin.

Buckle looked up at both of them. A nasty smirk was forming on Erklin's lips. Scarver stood with his hand held out, staring deep into his palm.

Buckle shrugged, "Very well, but it's a sad thing when neighbors won't trust each other." He pulled a money purse out of his belt and handed Scarver two silver coins. The lanky innkeeper made a motion, and stable hands led the horses away.

Erklin snorted silently and said, "Now that the amenities are over with, let's get to business." He repeated all that his constables had told Buckle, namely about the body and Scarver's identification of Roduct standing over it.

"I was in the stable," explained Scarver in his monotone, "trying to settle the horses. They were riled because of the storm. One bolted, kicked his stall open and damn near took off my head off. He ran into the courtyard, with me following like a fool in all that rain and wind. I caught up with the beast about right where we're standing. He was kicking and carrying on, screaming like the dead in Skrike's Hell. I grabbed his reins and tried to hang on. Just then, the sky lit up brighter than I'd ever seen. Lightning must have hit out in the field there. The thunder was deafening. But during the flash I happened to be looking over that way." He pointed to a ditch by the road, about fifty yards from where they stood. "And I saw Lord Roduct standing on the road, looking into the ditch. I called his name, but got no answer. Well, I finally got the horse settled down and maybe an hour or so of sleep.   But when my men were out this morning looking for damage, they found that poor soul lying in the ditch."

Buckle squinted at the faraway ditch.   "You mean to tell me you can recognize someone from fifty yards, in a torrential rain, with less than a second of light?"

"The lightning hit very close and like I said, it was very bright and Lord Roduct is rather distinct in his appearance, being bigger than most men, like a...an Easterner."

"Hmm," said Buckle.   "Sheriff, Scarver's identification of Lord Roduct is, at best, tenuous.   Do you have anything else?"

"Why yes I do, Master Buckle.   I would like you to view the body."

"What?" Buckle swallowed.   "Why?"

"For one thing we don't know who he was.   We're asking everybody to try and identify him.   Also..." Erklin stepped in front of Buckle.   "One of my constables talked to Nunsy this morning.   He said a stranger came into his inn last night, asking about Lord Roduct. Nunsy gave him directions and he left for Methliana."

"So?"

"So, that man was a stranger.   My corpse is a stranger.   They could be the same stranger."

"There's lots of strangers around.   That inn is full of them."

"And all of them are accounted for," put in Scarver with a venomous look at Buckle.   Erklin nodded agreement.

"Yes we did have a visitor last night," said Buckle, his heart pounding.   How much should he say?   He wished Bertam were here. "But even if it is the same stranger, I wouldn't be able to recognize him.   I never saw the man's face.   He wore a hood the entire time."

"Indulge me, Master Buckle," said Erklin, motioning with a sardonic gesture to the cart.

"All right, but this is a hell of a thing to do just before dinner."

Buckle was not sure he would have recognized the body even if he had seen the stranger's face the night before.   Between the flies and the awful pallor of the skin, the body didn't even look like a man.   It certainly didn't smell it.   But the man was big enough to be the stranger, and his cloak could have been the one the stranger wore. Buckle admitted as much to Erklin.

"All right," said the Sheriff, motioning to a constable who pulled the burlap tarp back over the body.   Buckle was the first to turn and walk away on unsteady legs.

"What were this stranger and Roduct talking about last night," asked Erklin, catching up with Buckle.

"I don't know.   I'm not privy to Lord Roduct's private conversations."

"I don't believe that for a moment," snapped Erklin. "But if you say you don't know...I'll of course need to talk to Lord Roduct right away."

Buckle stopped and looked at the ground.   "You can't talk to Lord Roduct."

"And why not?" Erklin moved in front of Buckle.

There was no way out of it.   He sighed in resignation. "Because Lord Roduct is gone."   The constables murmured in amazement.   Erklin just stared at Buckle, realization growing on his thick features. "He left last night, and didn't say when he'd be back."

Erklin almost laughed out loud, he was so happy.   "Well that's it then.   Open and shut.   The stranger came to Roduct's estate.   They argued.   The stranger left.   Roduct followed and caught up with him and killed him."

"You can't prove that," said Buckle.   "Your evidence is inconclusive.   I can't recognize the body and Scarver's identification of Lord Roduct is suspect at best.   Bertam would shred your evidence if you brought this to trial."

"Oh, but there won't be a trial.   We can't try Roduct if he's not here.   What I can do, is seize his property until he returns to face the charges."

"You wouldn't do that," cried Buckle but he knew that Erklin would.   "I'll talk to my brother about this."

"You do that.   But if Roduct doesn't contact me in three days, I'm taking possession of Methliana and there ain't nothing your Tarion solicitor brother can do about it." He poked his finger into Buckle's chest, an angry gesture, but there was a trace of a smile on his face. One of Scarver's drudges ran up to the innkeeper and whispered in his ear. "I believe your dinner is ready, Master Buckle," said Erklin.

"Suddenly," said Buckle, "I'm not hungry anymore."

4

"He can do it," said Bertam, scowling at the pages of a leather-bound book entitled County Law of Delamer.

"How?" asked Buckle. They were sitting in Roduct's study, Bertam at the desk and Buckle on the edge of the window sill.

"Just the way he said. If a suspect in a murder runs away, the sheriff can seize his property as compensation to the county after three days."

"Then we'll lose the estate."

"Don't sink into your stockings yet, Buckle," said Bertam. He flipped a few pages in the book. "There might just be a way to stop him and I can certainly slow him down."

"How?"

"Somewhere here is a...yes, here it is." Bertam pressed the pages of the book flat and squinted his eyes to look at the small print. "There's a provision for pursuit. What that means is as long as there's still an effort being made to catch Lord Roduct and bring him back to the county, Erklin can't take control of Methliana."

"So as long as there's someone chasing him, the estate is still ours?"

"Well it would be put under the control of a temporary caretaker which a magistrate would select. However, both we and Erklin can suggest candidates and if he doesn't know what we're doing, he won't think to recruit someone and we can get our man appointed."

"But it won't work," said Buckle, standing up. "As far as Erklin is concerned, Lord Roduct has escaped. He'll never send out a search party."

"He couldn't anyway. Lord Roduct is undoubtedly out of the county by now. We can send someone. As long as he is being sought, the pursuit rule holds."

"How long," asked Buckle.

"Please?"

"I can't believe we can stall Erklin forever."

"No, after a year, if Lord Roduct isn't found, Erklin can take over."

"Then how is this going to do us any good?"

"If you let me finish, I'll explain it to you. Now if you'll recall, the will Lord Roduct signed was dated yesterday. One year from yesterday the estate will be yours. The soonest Erklin could take it would be one year from today. And that will be too late. It won't be the property of the suspect anymore. So what we do is send out some people, tell them to stay away for a year, and then the estate will come to you one day before Erklin can seize it."

"And this will work?"

"Well," said Bertam, dragging his hand through his hair. "It's possible that a magistrate, especially one under Erklin's influence would declare Lord Roduct's will void. But I think I could fight that." He shook his head and exhaled. "I just can't think of anything else. This is, in my opinion, our only chance."

Buckle paced to the window. "I'd rather find him."

"Buckle," said Bertam, shifting in his chair, "I don't want to upset you, but there is a very good chance that Lord Roduct is guilty."

"What?" Buckle turned to face him.

"You know what happened last night better than I do."

"Lord Roduct wouldn't do something like that."

"Under normal circumstances, no," said Bertam. With a groan he lifted himself to his feet. "Listen, Buckle. Was that shunt you mentioned ever found?"

"No, Yarrel said the drudges looked all over but they couldn't find it. Is it important?"

"Those shunts are used by the Sarondakis to take blood for Soowooli. If we had the shunt we could prove that Lord Roduct's actions were in self-defense."

"But Soowooli isn't murder."

"It's worse, and Delemerian law recognizes it as such. Sarondakis in Delamer are allowed to kill in order to keep from coming under its influence."

38

"But we need the shunt to prove this?"

"Yes, and probably Lord Roduct.   All this would have to come out in a trial."

Buckle turned back to the window.

"Another thing you need to consider, brother," continued Bertam, "is that even if Lord Roduct is innocent he may very well be found guilty anyway.   Erklin is powerful in this county, and Lord Roduct is unpopular.   It may be best for him and you if he remains unfound."

Buckle put his fingers up against the windowpane.   He tried to see past his reflection and into the darkness beyond.   Out past the stables a few campfires burned in the fields where some of the hands were watching the horses which were spending their nights outside until the stables were repaired.

"Do you remember our father, Bertam?"

"Of course I do, I was sixteen when he died.   Terrible man.   If I had the energy I'd go out and find his grave and dance on it."

"You see, I don't."   Buckle took a breath, and turned to face his brother.   "I'll send out a party to search for Lord Roduct on two conditions.   It must really search for him.   Not...," he said, holding up his hand, "to necessarily bring him back but I want to know why he left."

"I think you're setting yourself up for heartache."

"And the second condition is that I lead the expedition," said Buckle.

"Now just a minute," cried Bertam.

"I want to find out from Lord Roduct himself why he left."

"You're needed here."

"Whoever we choose as caretaker will be in charge.   If we choose carefully, we won't need to worry.   Besides I don't want to stay around here and watch someone else run my estate."   Buckle pulled the cord to summon Yarrel.

"Damnit Buckle," cried Bertam, grabbing his brother's arm. "It's dangerous.   Never mind the usual hazards of travel, you're talking about going east boy, and there's a war brewing back there.   What if you don't come back?"

"You want me to make out a will?"   There was a discrete tap at the door and Yarrel walked in.

"I don't want to make out two wills in two nights.   Besides, it doesn't matter.   If you don't come back the place'll be Erklin's."   He threw up his hands and stalked back to the desk. "Is there something in the air around here that makes people do foolish things?"

"Yarrel, another late night I'm afraid," said Buckle. "Get somebody to bring the cart around. How much salted pork do we have?"

"Only a paltry amount is left over from the winter, Master Buckle."

"We'll take all of it, and I'll need a supply of cash to get more provisions once we're out of the county. Get someone to pack some of my clothes...rough stuff, no finery. And...well I'm sure you're aware of the necessary preparations for a journey."

"Of course sir. I'll attend to it immediately." He turned to exit.

"Oh, and one more thing, Yarrel."

"Yes, sir?"

"Get one of Lord Roduct's dirty shirts from the laundry and pack it also. Make sure you wrap it in a clean cloth."

"One of the Lord's dirty shirts. Certainly, sir." The old doorkeeper kept the puzzlement out of his face and turned to leave the room. Bertam stopped him with a hand on his arm.

"At least take some men with you."

"We can't spare many people with the growing season coming up. But you're right. I'll need a guide at least."

"You'll need more than that. If you took all the men on the estate, you wouldn't have enough to travel safely in the east right now. But I have an idea."

"What?"

Bertam rubbed the stubble on his chin. "Let me see what I can arrange. If it works out, I can supply you with one man-at-arms and not deplete the garrison."

"All right, I'll take whoever you have in mind and one other. Yarrel I want a volunteer. Smart, strong and able to keep his mouth shut. We'll leave as soon as we can."

"Yes sir," said Yarrel. He turned and left.

"Why tonight," asked Bertam.

"Lord Roduct's trail is getting colder as we speak. I wanted one of his shirts so that if we find a witch, we can pay her to track him. But his trace will fade. Even that sort of magic wears off eventually."

"If Erklin finds out you're gone he may figure out what we're planning."

"Then we'll have to make sure no one sees me when I leave. If he comes looking for me in the next two days, tell him I'm in Tarion on business. I think we can rely on the estate staff's discretion until you can reveal the truth." Buckle opened the door to the study and looked around the room perhaps for the last time. Surely this wasn't what he'd intended? "Besides I should go right away or I may change my mind."

Zabeth's candle had gone out hours ago, leaving her in complete darkness but by then she didn't need light. She was thoroughly acquainted with the five steps it took to pace across the storeroom. She knew every crack in the floor, every pile of dust that ground under her soles as she waited for something to happen. At this point anything would have pleased her. If the door opened and Erklin himself stood there, ready to take her to the gallows, she'd have gone with him willingly just to relieve the boredom.

The first thing she had done when Sora had locked her in here was to search for ways to escape. She tapped every inch of the walls, searching for weak spots she could punch through. She inventoried the contents of the shelves, looking for a tool or a weapon. But the walls were solid and the stores consisted solely of sheets and tablecloths. The shelf units were solidly built so Zabeth couldn't pry them apart. The door was stout oak with the hinges on the outside. And when the drudge came in to deliver her meals, a guard accompanied her with his sword out. Zabeth smiled grimly at that. Sora, despite her talk, had that much respect for Zabeth's abilities.

Zabeth spun around when she heard the bar being drawn from the door. By her calculations it was the middle of the night so this couldn't be a routine visit to bring food or take away the chamber pot. Zabeth pressed herself against the wall beside the door.

She knew Sora and Bertam wouldn't cause her to come to harm, but there were several men among the hands who, if they thought she was alone, unarmed and asleep might try and take advantage of the situation. Briefly, she thought she might take advantage of the situation herself. Grazzle's sword was gone and they had taken her dagger and blanket roll as well. All she had left were her men's clothes and Grazzle's letters of introduction which they couldn't pry away from her. But the blanket could be replaced from the very store room they'd locked her in and if the person opening the door had a knife or better yet a sword, then she'd be all set.

The door creaked open, letting in the wavering light of a candle. Zabeth swallowed, hoping her instincts would guide her. Whoever it was, held the candle up so that it lit as much of the room as possible and cautiously peered inside.

"I'm still here, Master Bertam," said Zabeth as she relaxed.

Bertam started, almost dropping the candle. "You wicked child. Don't fright your elders so. How would you have felt if I'd keeled over dead, which could very well have happened with my heart?"

"One less witness," said Zabeth, crossing her arms and leaning against the wall.

Bertam peered into her face and sniffed in contempt. "You don't fool me, young lady. You may be a killer but you're not a cold hearted one."

Zabeth frowned and shifted her position. "What do you want?"

"'What do you want,' she says. That's your problem, young Zabeth. You have no respect. I remember when young people..."

Zabeth pushed off the wall and walked over to the pile of blankets she had heaped up, intending to use them as a bed.

"What are you doing now?" said Bertam.

"If this is going to be a long lecture, I thought I might get comfortable," she said, sitting down.

He narrowed his eyes at her and it seemed to her in the distorted light of the candle that his face folded in on itself. All but the underside of this jaw and the tip of his nose were in shadow.

"I don't have time to lecture you, as much as you might benefit from it. Assuming of course you listened which you wouldn't anyway. I'd be wasting my breath and I haven't got that much to waste anymore."

Zabeth sighed loudly and dragged her hand over her hair. She looked off to the side with a carefully constructed look of boredom on her face. She didn't clearly see what she had to gain by making him angry but she knew in a fight it was a useful tactic. Angry opponents make mistakes and take stupid chances.

This wasn't a fight though and it wasn't likely to become one. Zabeth didn't care to attack a lone old man. That went against almost every idea of honor she possessed. Also a bitter memory came to her of the night before when she had been unable to break Bertam's grasp. She reflected that he might not be as easy an opponent as he appeared.

"Do you still have those letters?" he said. Zabeth bristled, sensing that somehow he knew her strategy, such as it was, and was turning it back on her.

"You're not getting them," she said.

"I don't want them. But you may need them yet."

"Why? Are you going to let me go?"

He thought about the question for a second and then waved it off. Then he set the candle on one of the shelves and leaned against the doorjamb.

"I should have brought a chair. I'm too old to stand for long." He looked at her, his eyes glinting in the light. "Grazzle used to talk about you."

Zabeth looked sharply at him, interested in spite of herself.

"He and I struck up a friendship towards the end of his life even though we had nothing in common except we were both old men. He'd come to my chamber every so often and we'd swap tales over some ale or wine." Bertam's face fell and suddenly Zabeth could see all of it in the light, from the lean grizzled cheeks to the tousled gray hair. "I think you were kind of a daughter to him. He was always exceedingly proud of you and bragged incessantly about your progress. I must say I never really believed him."

"Grazzle didn't make a habit of lying."

"Oh, I know that," said Bertam, petulantly. "But in this case he was hardly objective. In the end, he could refuse you nothing. That's why he had me draft those letters."

"You mean you..."

"He told me what he wanted to say and I wrote it out and applied my seal to all three copies." Zabeth thought about the small wax seal at the bottom of each of the letters. Grazzle had said that they would assure people that the documents were genuine.

"I'll have you know that I tried my best to talk him out of doing it, but he was firm. Such was your hold on him."

"The letters were his idea, not mine," said Zabeth.

Bertam made a sour face and waved the comment away. "It didn't matter back then. He was near death and you weren't old enough yet to take advantage of them. I had hoped your enthusiasm for this sort of thing would pass before you tried to leave and ruin Grazzle's good name."

"I won't ruin..."

"Will you please stop interrupting?"

"I have a question," said Zabeth.

Bertam pursed his lips in consternation.   "Very well, what is it?"

"Did he tell you anything about the sword?"

"Yes," said Bertam, looking at her.   "He said he wanted it to go to you."

Zabeth sprung to her feet.   "Then why wasn't it given to me?"

"For one thing, some damn fool hid it and we thought it was stolen."   Zabeth bowed her head.   "And for another, he had no will and verbal requests are not binding."

"But why didn't you stand up for me last night with Sora?"

"Why should I help you?" he said.

"Then why are you here?"

For the first time the old man looked uncertain.   He shifted his eyes and ran his hand across the back of his neck.   "Because I love my damn-fool brother and I can't keep him from doing foolish things." He explained to her about Roduct's sudden departure and Buckle's determination to follow.   "So what it comes down to is we can't spare many of the hands to escort him.   But if he's going east toward the war he'll need a...er...man-at-arms."

"I'd say he'd need at least twenty, and even then I wouldn't like his chances."   Zabeth shook her head.   "No, it's suicide, and besides my plans don't include going east."

"Fine," said Bertam, standing up straight.   "We'll send a messenger to the sheriff first thing in the morning.   It'll probably be a few days before he'll come pick you up..."

"But you said that Grazzle wanted me to have the sword."

"I can forget that.   I've forgotten a lot of things in my life."

"But that's not fair," said Zabeth.

Bertam turned around and looked at her.   "Excuse me.   Are you laboring under the belief that the world is fair?   If the world were fair Lord Roduct would be upstairs in his chamber right now and my brother would be sound asleep in his bed."

"You don't even think I can do this."

"No, but as I said, it's either you or we deplete the estate's work force.   I'm taking a chance that Grazzle's opinion of you wasn't clouded by love."

A thought suddenly occurred to Zabeth.   "I'll do it," she said.

He looked at her, one eye wider than the other. "Why?"

"I have no choice."

"Sure you do. You can say yes and as soon as you're out of sight of the estate house you can abandon Buckle and go your own way."

Zabeth started. That was pretty much what she was planning.

"I thought so," said Bertam. "Well if you want the job, you'll have to take an oath."

"An oath?"

"I know, I know. It sounds antiquated; like something they'd have done in old Dern. But I've given this some thought," he said, reaching behind him for something in the hall. He retrieved a long object wrapped in burlap. He let the burlap fall to the floor, revealing Grazzle's sword.

"Now," he said, "Lord Roduct isn't here so you can't swear to him, and the old gods of Dern have forgotten us as surely as we've forgotten them. That leaves this." He held the sword with the pommel towards her. "Grazzle's sword."

"Hardly a sacred object," said Zabeth.

"It is to you," he replied. "What object could be more sacred? When you swear on this, you'll be swearing to Grazzle, himself."

"And if I don't swear?"

"Then it's Sheriff Erklin and the gallows I'm afraid. Your choice." He proffered the sword.

Zabeth bit her lip, indecision building into anger. Then all of a sudden, she smiled. "I don't believe you," she said.

"Excuse me?"

Zabeth crossed her arms and leaned against one of the shelves. "I've seen the way this estate is run. Nobody's ever flogged or physically punished in any way. Lord Roduct and Master Buckle don't even like the sheriff. I don't think you would turn me over to Erklin, knowing that he'd hang me."

"Well, if you want to take that chance, stay here and find out." He leaned over with a small groan to retrieve the burlap sack. "I would remind you, however, that Lord Roduct is no longer here, and Master Buckle is preparing to leave."

"Wait," said Zabeth. He paused. "I'll do it."

"Of course, now that I'm all the way bent over," he said, straightening up. "You couldn't have stopped me a second earlier?"

He held out the sword and Zabeth put her palm flat on the pommel. Then he asked her to repeat the oath.

"I swear upon this sword to protect my lord's Steward, Buckle to the best of my ability until he returns to Methliana." She was bound now as Bertam no doubt knew she would be. With every stroke, every riposte he taught her, Grazzle emphasized that her honor was more important than life.

"Very good," said Bertam. "You may keep the sword and your other gear is in the hall."

Zabeth took the sword and attached the scabbard to her belt. "Master Bertam?" she said softly, looking at him.

"Yes."

"Would you really have turned me over to Erklin?"

He shook his head. "Of course not. What kind of a monster do you think I am?" Zabeth thought she saw him smile. "But I would have let Sora marry you off to that fool, Legothin."

As they walked out the door, Zabeth said, "I think I would probably have preferred Erklin."

5

It was too light, thought Buckle, staring at the cloudless star-speckled sky, somebody's bound to see us.   He urged the horses onward.   The ground had dried sufficiently to provide swift travel, but it was still soft enough to muffle the sound of the horses.   Vald and Yazzle had tied bits of velvet cloth to every metal piece of the two horse team's harness assembly to dampen sound and cover reflections. The cart axles had been thoroughly greased and it now rolled more silently than Buckle could remember.   But this damn starlight would be the ruin of them.   Luck had been with them so far; they were almost to the East Road and they hadn't seen anybody yet.

Buckle heard two sharp whistles and he stopped the cart.   That was the signal from Zabeth, who rode about fifty feet ahead.   She must have caught sight of the East Road.   So far the girl had done admirably well.   She had picked out one of the best horses on the estate and she rode the mare with confidence and ease, far better than Buckle could have.   Grazzle's sword looked incongruous on her hip but she wore it like she knew what to do with it.   Buckle was impressed with her.   But of course she hadn't been tested yet.

She appeared and reigned in her horse beside him.

"What's ahead," asked Buckle.

"I saw the East Road," Zabeth said.   She stared in that direction as she talked.   "There's a lot of tents set up for refugees. Scarver's let them overflow into the road itself.   The constables are patrolling the camp.   There's no way we could get through unnoticed."

"So the road isn't passable?"

"No, sir."

Buckle slumped in his seat. "Well, maybe we can backtrack and take another road."

Zabeth cleared her throat.

"Yes?" said Buckle.

"Nothing, sir."

"If you have a suggestion, I'd like to hear it."

"Well, she said, bowing her head. "When I rode past the inn, I noticed a small path leading east just before I got to the road. I followed it a little ways and it runs parallel to the road and goes behind the inn."

"Where is it? Can I see it from here?"

"Yes. It's about thirty feet to the right." Buckle squinted his eyes until he could see the path. It was almost a rut, about five feet across and deeply grooved with the passage of countless vehicles.

"Is it clear?"

"As far as I could see."

"It sounds like a good plan."

Zabeth paused, biting her lip. "Sir, I think Yazzle should drive the cart at this point."

"Why?"

"Because the path goes right past Scarver's back door. You should be in the back of the cart, hiding, in case we're spotted."

"What difference would that make. They'd just see Yazzle or you."

"But we're not as well-known as you are."

The object of their debate pulled the tarpaulin off himself and sat up, poking his head into their conversation. He yawned, having been awakened by the mention of his name.

"Another good idea, Zabeth. Take the reins, Yazzle." Buckle stood up and climbed into the back of the cart while the huge field hand clambered into the front.

Zabeth pulled her hood forward, and turned her horse toward the road. Yazzle clicked his tongue and slapped the horses with the reins and they were moving.

Buckle peered down the road and thought he could see some campfires along the East Road.

"Master Buckle?"

"Yes."

"How long do you figure we'll be gone from the estate?"

"I don't know Yazzle, if it's more than a year, we won't have an estate to come back to."

Yazzle turned the horses onto the access road.

"I'd sure miss Methliana."

"We haven't lost it yet, Yazzle."

Buckle looked at the young hand, as he drove the horses along the path. When Yazzle first came to Methliana, he had been an awkward and strangely shy lad but obviously strong and he had claimed to know everything there was to know about working on an estate. He said he had worked on a large establishment in the north; too far away to check. His first time plowing a field, he'd removed his shirt and Buckle saw the huge welts on his back. That had explained Yazzle's closeness. Whips had a way of doing that to a man. Neither Buckle nor Roduct believed in the lash. The closest things to whips on Methliana were the riding crops, which were only used on livestock and then gently.

"Excuse me, Master Buckle," he said, "but you'd better get under that tarp."

"Quite right," said Buckle. Up ahead, he could see Scarver's back door, illuminated by a single lantern, hung on a hook above the porch. There was a row of young trees lining the access road and Buckle could see Zabeth silhouetted in the light. She had dismounted and was standing beside her horse, studying the porch. She whistled twice and Yazzle stopped the cart.

Buckle pulled the tarp over his shoulders but kept his head above the side to see. A surly looking man came out of the door, carrying a slop bucket. He heaved the contents off to the side of the porch and set the bucket down. Then, leaning against a post, he pulled a bag of tobacco and a pipe out of his belt. He proceeded to fill the pipe.

"Let's hope Scarver doesn't allow his drudges to take long breaks," sighed Buckle, turning around to put his back to the side of the cart. The sight of the man enjoying a smoke made Buckle wish for his own pipe. He had spent many hours sitting on the grand front porch of the estate house, watching the sunset while puffing away on his favorite clay pipe. His favorite blend of tobacco was grown in the south. It had a hearty tobacco smell with just a trace of exotic southern spices.

Buckle put aside the daydream. It might be a very long time before he could smoke on the porch again, if ever. Realization of what he was doing was beginning to dawn on him. He had left his home, really the only one he'd ever known. And he'd done it voluntarily. What was more, he was heading into an adventure that even the most insane gambler wouldn't have given him a chance of surviving. There were so many unknown factors. Where was Roduct? Where was he going? And most importantly why? Even if they did catch up to him, Buckle had his doubts that he could talk Roduct into returning with them. His resolve was dissolving in a sea of doubt. Common sense told Buckle they'd be gone the full year and maybe longer. He wasn't sure he could go that long. Already, not two hours into his quest, Buckle could only think about smoking on his porch.

"Forgive me Master Buckle," whispered Yazzle, "The man's gone inside again and Zabeth is motioning us on."

"Right," said Buckle. He lay down in the bed of the cart and pulled the tarp over his head. Along the side he found a knothole in the wood and watched as the trees, colored a silvery blue in the starlight, marched past him.

The cart which had seemed so silent a minute ago, now thundered in his ears. The vibration of its passage threw Buckle back and forth. He grabbed the edge of the boards that made up the side and held on until all the blood drained from his knuckles.

"Halt," said a voice from up ahead. It was familiar to Buckle. He had heard it recently. The cart jerked to a stop.

"What are you doing here, boy?" It was Torkle, Erklin's constable. Carefully, Buckle eased forward, trying not to make any noise and peered out the knothole. They were in the glow of the lantern. Buckle could only see a small circle cut out of the scene and none of it had any action.

"I'm just passing through, sir."

"Just passing through? Why aren't you on the East Road?" There was a pause. Buckle could imagine Yazzle sitting up in the driver's seat, scratching his head, trying to think. "Well?"

"The road was, uh, too busy."

"You in a hurry?"

"Uh, yes. I need to get home."

"And where's that?"

"Well, ah...I..." They were in trouble. Yazzle knew little of the villages and estates to the east of them.

"Don't you know where you live boy?" Someone laughed; a second man. Buckle moved to put his eye up to the crack between the side of the cart and the front. His foot hit a bag in the cart and knocked it over.

"What was that?" demanded Torkle. Buckle froze, unable to see anything now.

"There's someone in the back, Torkle," said the second person.

"All right, boy, step down." Hoof beats thudded down the road and then came the sounds of a struggle.

Buckle moved back to the knothole and got his eye smacked when somebody was thrown against the side of the cart. Shadows obscured the view and then cleared. Buckle saw a gray hooded figure thrown to the dirt. With the impact, the hood came off to reveal Zabeth's blond hair.

"Wait a minute. I know you. You work on Methliana. Freg, go get Erklin."

Buckle could hear footsteps running up the porch stairs and through Scarver's back door. Zabeth sprang to her feet and pulled out her sword. She circled out of Buckle's view.

"All right, wench," said Torkle. "Put the sword down and I won't hurt you." There was a clang of metal.

"Hey."

Another clang.

"All right, if that's the way you want it."

Most of the fight was invisible to Buckle who wanted to raise his head above the side of the cart but didn't dare. All he saw was the occasional flash of metal in the lantern light and the dancing silhouettes of the fighters when one of them crossed his limited field of vision. He could hear grunts of effort from both of them and a few of surprise from Torkle. The cart jostled every time a fighter was thrown against it. Every so often his view was blocked as one tried to pin the other against the cart.

A sword chopped directly over Buckle's head, biting into the wood and showering him with splinters.

"Damn." It was Zabeth. Torkle, visible only from the shoulders to the knee walked slowly to where Zabeth stood. Her frantic efforts to dislodge her sword rocked the cart violently.

"You little bitch," said Torkle, his voice heavy. "If you think you're going to live to brag about this to your friends, think again." He advanced, his sword raised.

51

"Mister, you can't hurt Zabeth." The cart's movement doubled as Yazzle jumped out of the driver's seat. Buckle couldn't help it now. He scooted forward and peered over the side of the cart.

"Shut up, boy," sneered Torkle, who turned and threatened the field hand, "or I'll carve you a new bellybutton."

"Yazzle, get my sword," cried Zabeth. She dropped to the ground, rolled and kicked. The kick landed right on the side of Torkle's knee. There was a crack and Torkle crumpled into a heap, screaming in agony.

"Shut up," yelled Zabeth as she stood up. Yazzle circled around the fight and wrenched her sword free with one try. She motioned for it. Buckle didn't like the look in her eyes.

"Yazzle," said Buckle, standing up. "Give me the sword and go round up Zabeth's horse, hurry." The lad did as he was told with no small relief. Torkle, his face contorted in pain, looked up at Buckle.

Zabeth glared at Buckle as he clambered onto the driver's seat. "Get in," he said.

"But Torkle..."

"Get in."

She slammed the side of the cart with her fist but climbed in and Buckle slapped the horses into motion. Secrecy was unnecessary now. What was needed was speed. Buckle whacked the horses' rumps until they were galloping. The cart jumped and sailed over the bumpy path so much, it was all Buckle could do to stay in his seat. Even Zabeth in the back hung on for dear life. About sixty feet past the inn they stopped and waited for Yazzle, who they could hear scrambling to catch up. In his hands he held the reigns to Zabeth's horse which trotted behind him. They could still hear Torkle's screams and curses as he rolled around in the dirt. Scarver's back door slammed several times and a handful of men gathered around Torkle as he frantically waved them in the cart's direction.

Yazzle came up alongside the cart, holding out the horse's reins. "Get on your horse, Zabeth," ordered Buckle, "We don't have much time."

"He saw you."

"Let's get going."

Zabeth jumped on the horse and galloped ahead. Yazzle leaped into the bed of the cart and Buckle urged the horses into flight. When they got to where the access road curved northward to join the main road they kept going straight, cutting through the cornfields until they felt safe enough to angle toward the main road.

6

For four days all Zabeth could think about was the fight. What a glorious feeling! Drills and exercises couldn't compare. Even the occasional bouts Grazzle would set up for her paled in comparison to the real thing. After a shaky start, all he had taught her suddenly fell into place. The thrusts, parries and ripostes she did without thinking, leaving her mind free to think about strategy. And towards the end of the fight, she was actually several moves ahead of Torkle, manipulating him into position for a disarming thrust. If only she hadn't made that ill-advised overhead cut and buried her sword in the cart. That was when she lost control. Torkle's threats had infuriated her. He couldn't accept that he had almost been bested by a woman. He would have killed her. Zabeth had no doubt about that. But whenever she tried to remember how she had felt, she failed. Her rage had sent her into a kind of fugue. Would she have killed him? She didn't know the answer to that question.

At first, she had tried to tell herself that it would have been best if she had killed Torkle. He had, after all, seen Buckle and would have relayed that information to Erklin. But the other constable, Freg had seen her before he left to get help. Erklin wasn't so stupid that he couldn't have figured out what was happening. The secret was ruined. There was no need to kill Torkle.

Zabeth rode her mare about fifty yards ahead of the cart. Buckle's attempts at conversation bothered her. She had never been one to discuss the weather, or crops and she certainly wasn't about to tell him anything about her past. The man knew most of it, anyway. He'd been steward of Methliana for as long as she'd been there.

The only thing he hadn't brought up yet was the fight.

Zabeth had to admit she was worried about that. Never had she seen Buckle angry, nor heard about him being angry. But that night he was furious. He didn't seem upset now, but Zabeth didn't really know him. For all she knew, he was planning to leave her with some innkeeper once they got to Tarion. An inn would be easier to escape from than Methliana but Zabeth wasn't sure if that would release her from her oath.

Knowing she couldn't avoid it much longer, she turned the horse around and galloped back to the cart. Buckle was sitting on the bench holding the reins. He looked tired. Zabeth knew that he hadn't slept well since the trip began. He was used to a nice bed with feather pillows, and the ground, even in spring was cold and hard. And every night, he would be up with one of his attacks, wheezing and coughing. With shaking hands, he'd put the jimsonweed into his pipe and draw the smoke into his lungs. Eventually the wheezing would stop and he'd sleep for a while but never for very long.

"Sir," she said as she halted her horse by the cart. "I saw a marker over that hill. We're about a half mile from Tarion."

"Good," said Buckle. He looked behind him at the western sky. "We should make it before dark. And maybe even before this storm hits."

Zabeth followed his gaze. A purple mass was just visible on the far edge of the western landscape. It was hard to tell from this far away but the storm looked worse than the one five nights ago.

"Sir, maybe I should ride ahead and reserve a place for us."

Buckle rubbed the bridge of his nose. He had always seemed old to her, but the bags under his eyes made him seem ancient. "We've got some time yet. From what I hear they have a lot of good camping space outside of the city."

"Well, I thought we might try for a room tonight, sir. You look pretty tired."

Buckle smiled. "Even at the best of times, the price of a room in Tarion is exorbitant. I'd hate to see what they're charging now. No, we'll camp in the tent city. I'll be all right."

"Yes, sir." She started to kick her horse's flanks.

"You know I saw you fight once on Methliana," said Buckle. "It was one of those tournaments Grazzle set up occasionally with his students."

Zabeth remembered. Grazzle had thought the competition of those contests kept his fighters sharp, as well as providing entertainment for the rest of the estate. They would use wooden swords and leather pads instead of armor. Once in a while Zabeth would be allowed to compete.

"You fought Vald, as I recall," continued Buckle. "He gave you more trouble than Torkle did."

Zabeth hesitated in commenting, sensing that she was on shaky footing. "Vald is good with a sword."

Buckle nodded. "Was the other night with Torkle your first fight? I mean in earnest?"

"I've had some dust-ups with some of the hands that turned pretty serious. But that's the first time anybody ever tried to kill me."

"Or you them?"

Zabeth bowed her head and sighed. "I wasn't going to kill him."

"What were you going to do?"

"Knock him out so he couldn't raise an alarm."

"I see," he said, staring at the road ahead. "Why didn't you explain that back then?"

"There wasn't any time."

"Of course." He nodded. Zabeth could tell he knew she was lying and was going to let her get away with it. Briefly, she thought of confessing, and suddenly, she very much wanted to. His face had a hurt expression on it that she would have given much to erase. But she couldn't do it. Even though this position as escort wasn't exactly what she had envisioned, it was a job for a warrior. She liked it, and wanted to keep it. What was more, she felt confident that she could do it at least until they got far enough east that the odds against them would be so high that an army wouldn't have been sufficient.

But she was a woman, and she couldn't be sure that he shared that confidence in her. She didn't have the luxury of being able to make mistakes.

"Well Zabeth, my only complaint about you so far is that you make lousy conversation."

"That's not something either Sora or Grazzle covered."

Buckle laughed. "Really! Well, no matter, I can teach you."

Zabeth studied Buckle's face again. His mouth was curled into a smile and his eyes were sparkling with humor as he lectured her on the art of conversation. It was amazing. He had to have been worrying about a dozen different things, from where they were going to camp tonight, to what was going on back on Methliana. And yet here he was making small talk and laughing.

As the threatening clouds rose up on the horizon to devour the setting sun, Zabeth interrupted him. "Excuse me, sir, but I really think I should find a camp soon."

Buckle twisted around to look at the western sky. It had gotten dark quickly. "Yes, you're right, Zabeth. Ride ahead. We'll see you in about an hour."

"Yes, sir," she said and galloped up the road toward Tarion.

Buckle watched Zabeth as she raced away from him. He hoped she felt better now. At first he had thought it was best to avoid the subject of the fight with Torkle altogether. But when she continued to be close-mouthed and almost hostile, he decided to let her know that he didn't blame her.

Of course it could have been that it wasn't the fight that was bothering her. She was, after all, here against her will. If that was the case, there was nothing he could do about it. If nothing else, the fight had proven that she was more than up to the task of protecting him. He needed her.

Tired of thinking, Buckle watched the landscape roll by. The soil around here was poor. He could see that much at a glance. Most of the land lay bare, stripped of its trees to build the great city. It lay naked and ugly in the gray air. The road was lined with stunted scrub and grass, as well as the few scraggly remains of the forest that had once covered most of Delamer and still engulfed much of Goswick. Buckle looked at the beeches and elms, and was reminded of the huge shade trees back on Methliana. The two elms nearest the estate house were taller than the highest roof. They blocked the harsh afternoon sunlight from the front windows and made those rooms cool on summer evenings.

Some time later, the cart topped the final hill and Buckle saw Tarion. Nestled in the bottom of the river valley, the Delamerian capital was already cloaked in twilight. Lights in the taverns and wharf side inns were lit, their images copied and inverted by the gently flowing Navium. Buckle could see the Tarion Bridge, strung with lanterns, spanning the river into the eastern half of Tarion and the East Road continued on its journey across the world.

"Great Dalmar." This came from the back. Yazzle had awakened and had sat up in the cart bed. His wide eyes took in the splendor of the world's largest city. To him it must have looked as if some stars had descended to rest here beside the river and twinkled their mysterious light as repayment to the earth for its hospitality.

Buckle had been to Tarion a few times on business. There were some nice inns there that were comfortable and served a good meal. But to Buckle the city was just too crowded. He didn't like the noise, the smell, or the fact that one had to watch one's purse when walking the streets. He had never understood why Bertam had liked living here. Still the view from this hill was impressive.

Behind them, they heard the faint booming of thunder and Buckle tore his gaze away from Tarion and looked back to the west. The purple clouds had grown into a dark line of thunder heads. Another gift from the Western Ocean. Usually they broke apart before reaching this far inland, but looking at the advancing front, Buckle could tell it was strong enough to reach them.

"We'd better get going," he said, urging the horses down into the valley. "I'd hate to miss Zabeth in the dark and rain."

By the time they had set up their camp in the middle of the tent city, it was raining. The wind kicked up from the west, driving the rain so hard that each drop felt like a nail being hammered into them. Yazzle had tried to start a fire but couldn't even get a spark in the wind and the wet. So they ate cold salted beef soaked in rain water to wash most of the brine from it.

After eating, Buckle couldn't decide what to do. The usual routine had been to eat, and then he and Zabeth would split up and wander around whatever tent city they had stopped in, looking for clues that Roduct had passed through. The last few nights had been clear and warm, so Buckle had had no trouble finding a gathering of people around a cooking fire, exchanging news, stories and songs. Even homeless refugees clung to each other's company and somehow managed to find joy in their disrupted lives. In spite of his lack of success in finding any word of Roduct, Buckle had found himself enjoying these outings.

But this night he couldn't believe anybody would brave the inclement weather just for a little human contact. He wasn't sure he wanted to venture into it either, even though he had a more compelling reason than most. Zabeth had eaten her dinner, rinsed off her plate and left without a word.   Yazzle sat at the edge of their tent, keeping watch.

Buckle decided to go.   He walked past Yazzle and patted him on the shoulder.

"I'll be back in a couple of hours."

"Master Buckle, you can't go out in this."

"I have to.   We can't miss any opportunity to find information about Lord Roduct."   And with that, he waded into the rain.   Within seconds, he was soaked.   His feet were heavy with mud and he had to shield his eyes from the driving rain.   He slogged through the ankle high muck, until he came to a point where the path between the tents forked.   Stopping for a second, he looked around him, hoping to spot a fire.   Off to his right, he thought he caught a yellowish flicker.   He waded toward it through the mud.

On the edge of the tent city, near the road, Buckle found the fire.   It belonged to a small group of refugees.   There were eight of them, an old man, four women and three children who slept fitfully under the cart that helped support the tent.   When Buckle stooped just inside the tent and asked if he could come in, they welcomed him. One of the women pushed a cup of ale into his hands.   He tried to pay her but she refused.   Later, when no one was looking, Buckle laid a few coins in the bottom of their cart.

Over the past four days Buckle had seen many such families: Sturdily built Joswellians or Goswickians with curly black hair and dark complexions.   There were very few men on the road, most of them being back east, trying to protect their lands, so the women traveled in groups, made up of sisters and neighbors.   They were sent west with the children and the aged in hopes of finding safety.

Many told horrifying stories of Sarondaki atrocities.   Whole farms and ranches had been burned, their inhabitants slaughtered after the women had been raped.   The attacks came first at night but as the ineffectiveness of the defending armies became known, the invaders grew bolder and soon there was no time of the day or night that was safe.   And now Sarondaki raiding parties reportedly roamed freely over the eastern third of Joswell and Goswick.

Buckle had almost finished his ale and was about to start asking questions, when a figure stumbled into the tent.   It lay shivering on the ground before the fire, a heap of wet muddy burlap.   Finally a head appeared from the pile and Buckle saw the figure was a young man.

He surveyed the ring of faces surrounding him, and tried to smile. A woman handed him a cup of ale.

"Thank you Matron. It's a terrible night."

"It is indeed," said the woman, a gray haired matron with a face like an ax. Under the cart, the children were fully awake and watching the man with wide eyes.

"Have you any food," asked the man, simply. He wasn't begging but at the same time he turned his eyes to the ground.

"None to spare."

"Not even for a soldier?"

"A soldier," cried a younger woman on the other side of the fire. She glared at him.

"Hush Dennith," snapped the matron.

"But Mareth..."

"Hush, I said." But the old matron's gaze echoed the younger woman's.

"I'm in the Barrier Scouts, I swear to you." The man shifted his body to sit cross-legged. He hugged his cup of ale to his chest, as grateful for the warmth as for the drink. "My comrades and I were on leave when the Sarondakis started crossing the Barriers. When we got the news, three weeks had already gone by. We were ordered to move out the next day but the night before I..." He looked around at all the faces in the tent, Buckle's, which was carefully neutral, and everyone else's which were hostile. His gaze returned to Mareth. "I tripped and hurt my ankle." He winced at the giggles and snickering that surrounded him.

"How long ago was this," asked Buckle.

The man shifted to look at him, his face brightening a little. "About two months ago, good sir."

"Why haven't you moved on? Surely your ankle has healed by now?"

"Indeed it has, sir. Good as the day I was born. But I can't get my horse out of the stable until I settle with them. I owe for a month's upkeep now and I haven't got anything. After tomorrow, they'll sell her."

"Matron," said Buckle, digging into his pouch. "Please give this man a meal and I will give you enough money to more than replace what he eats at the next inn you pass."

Mareth looked at the coins in his palm and then at the unfortunate soldier. She had a disdainful look on her face but when she swallowed, Buckle could see a little pride slide down her gullet. She took the coins and motioned to one of the women who grabbed a wooden plate and began dishing some beans onto it.

"It's not that I'm stingy by nature," said Mareth, "but times are lean. We've been on the road for six weeks."

"I understand. In hard times we must look after our own first." The soldier was handed his meal and began wolfing it down.

"You're a good man, sir," she said, her eyes still not meeting his.

"I wish you nothing but good fortune in the west."

She hung her head and turned away. He turned to the soldier, who incredibly, was just finishing the meal.

"Thank you, sir," the man said. He stood and looked around, gauging his chances for seconds. The closed expressions on the faces of the women answered his question and he reluctantly laid his plate on the cart and extended his hand to Buckle. "My name's Bindle."

"Buckle. So you've been in Tarion for two months?"

"Yes, sir." Bindle sat on the ground, next to Buckle.

"I wonder if you've seen a friend of mine." Buckle described Roduct.

Bindle looked at the ground for a minute and bit his lower lip. "You know, I may have seen someone like that."

"Yes," said Buckle. His insides swelled with hope.

"About two days ago, I was working at a tavern, doing drudge work. I've had several menial jobs, trying to save money to get my horse. Anyway, I was taking my break in the alley behind the tavern when a rider came by. He looked like a Sarondaki as you said."

"How tall was he?"

Bindle shook his head. "It's hard to judge a man's height when he's on a horse. But this man did seem taller than average. He was in a hurry. That's why I noticed him. He was galloping through the alley and constantly looking behind him."

Buckle was sitting on the edge of the rude stool the women had given him. This was it, he thought, his first clue.

"Was he wearing a black cloak with red trim?"

"I'm sorry, it was dark."

Buckle looked at the man, remembering the wistful look he got on his face when talking about his horse. He said, "Was the horse black, about eighteen hands high, with a splash of white on the left forelock?"

61

"Yes," said Bindle, "That's it exactly."

"Then it's him. It has to be," cried Buckle. The women looked up at his exclamation. "Two days, you said?"

"Yes, sir."

Buckle stood up and looked out at the raging storm. The wind blew tendrils of rain that reached underneath the tent and brushed against them.

"And was he heading east?"

"Yes, he was."

"Hmm." Buckle rubbed his chin in thought and eyed Bindle. "You say you're a Barrier Scout?"

"For five years. I serve under Renwick."

"Do you know the land from here to the mountains?"

"I grew up in Joswell."

"Bindle, if you'd care to brave this weather and follow me, I may have a job for you."

"Would you loan me enough to get my horse out of the stable?"

"Certainly, I'll even let you work the debt off."

The soldier stood up and said, "I'm your man, sir."

The two men ducked outside and ran as fast as they could through the mud back to Buckle's tent.

7

"What is it?" snapped Marduct.

The warrior in the doorway to Marduct's rooms quaked. He was just a lad, barely of age. In fact, Marduct wondered if this boy's was one of the many initiation trials he had witnessed in the past month as the tribes prepared themselves for war. Marduct shook his head. It didn't matter. If the boy had shown any promise he wouldn't be here, serving as clerk.

"This dispatch just arrived for you, Warlord." The smooth un-calloused hand offered a scroll, sealed with the mark used by the spy cabal in Tarion. This was important.

"Lay it on the desk," said Marduct. He watched out of the corner of his eye, as the youth's shaking fingers put the scroll on the smooth wood of Marduct's desk.

A desk! And an office! Was this how a warrior fought? Marduct sneered at himself. He'd enjoyed some of the benefits of Skrike's rule as much as any warrior, but this indoor living was making him and his top chieftains soft. Castle Skrike was, by western standards, cold and inhospitable but compared to life on the high desert it was the lap of luxury. Even after all this time, most chieftains only spent part of the year here, and Marduct found he could only stand being locked up in this cage for six months at a time. Then he had to get back to the desert. Not only to renew himself on the forge of desert life, but also to maintain his position as leader of the Eastern Tribes. That was the only reason Skrike let him go. He needed his Warlord and second in command to keep his traditional position of power. If Marduct ever slipped from that pinnacle, no warrior in the desert would have accepted him as Warlord, no matter how much Skrike threatened them with Soowooli.

He looked up. The young clerk still stood by.

"Is there more?"

"Yes, Warlord. Deruct is waiting outside to see you."

Marduct sat back in his chair and sighed in frustration. "Who has he killed now?"

"Beltuct is the name I've been hearing, Warlord."

Marduct hammered the desktop with his fist. Several blasphemous and heated oaths clamored in his thoughts, demanding to be let out first. Instead, Marduct took a deep breath and said, "Show him in."

Marduct snatched the scroll from the edge of his desk and snapped the seal in half. He then pressed the document flat upon the desk and read.

More bad news. Marduct scowled as he read the dispatch which described how the Delamerian Lord, Roduct had disappeared. The agent they had sent to take his blood hadn't reported back and was presumed dead. Marduct had known Roduct from the last war in the west and the occupation before. He had turned traitor like many other Sarondakis serving in the west. He had even broken Soowooli to do it. That was something only a few warriors had ever done. The rest of the traitors from that time had already succumbed to the weather or Sarondaki assassins. Apparently, after three centuries in the humid west, Roduct still had the strength to eliminate their spy before he could take his blood and enslave him.

Marduct seethed. He had been planning to use Roduct and his position as senior member of the Delamerian council to delay Delamer's entry into the war. Now the risks of the coming campaign were higher.

Marduct's thoughts were interrupted when a tall, proud looking warrior strode into the room. He carried himself with casual arrogance. At his side, he wore a sword made of polished Kareezian steel.

Marduct looked at the black pommel of the sword and said, "What is this about, Deruct?"

"Warlord, I have come to inform you that I have slain Beltuct in honorable combat and do hereby claim his possessions, his women and his position in accordance with ancient tradition."

Marduct's chair squeaked as he leaned back. "As for his possessions and his women, they're yours. The position is not."

"But Warlord, the ancient tradition..."

"May be superseded in time of war. Beltuct's tribe is to play a very important role in the upcoming invasion. I need someone I know and can trust to lead it."

"But..."

"There is no time to acquaint you with the details of the invasion plan. No, I'll install Narontuct as chieftain of that tribe. He has sat in on all the war councils."

"Narontuct," shouted Deruct.

"And if I hear that you've challenged him, I'll have you arrested and staked to the back of a scorpion, the biggest one I can find. Clear?"

The young chieftain bristled. "I'm a better soldier than Beltuct ever was."

Marduct slammed the desktop again. "Damn your insolence. Beltuct was a comrade of mine. We fought in the last western war together. He may not have been the most imaginative warrior among the tribes, but he could follow orders. The last thing I need out there is some young chieftain who is more interested in covering himself with glory than in doing what needs to be done to win the war."

"My exploits in Kareez are legendary."

"You were just a hetman of a small tribe. You've shown me nothing of what it takes to lead a tribe of Beltuct's size and importance into war. I'm assigning you to the new tribe I'm collecting at Zaron."

Deruct sputtered. "But that's made up of old men, boys and Soowoolis."

"It's that or return to patrolling the eastern border."

"How can I distinguish myself if you won't let me fight?"

"Following an order or two might impress me." Marduct leaned forward in his chair and pulled a fresh sheet of parchment from the pile on the corner of his desk. "I'll write up your orders right away. You'll have them by sundown. Tomorrow you'll start for Zaron."

A hand slammed the desktop, stopping Marduct's writing in mid stroke. Marduct looked up to see Deruct leaning over the desk. The Warlord set down his quill and folded his hands.

"Are you challenging me, Deruct?" The young pup's face paled most satisfactorily, and the hand slowly retreated from the desk.

Marduct regarded the young chieftain. Actually, he doubted that he could have survived a duel but fortunately Deruct may not have realized this. Marduct had a reputation as a fighter, mostly from his younger days, but it served to intimidate potential foes. And besides it was well known that Skrike would not look kindly on anyone who supplanted his Warlord, especially one as young and inexperienced as Deruct.

"No, Warlord," mumbled Deruct. "I wouldn't dare to challenge you. My respect for you is too great."

"Then I suggest that in a few days time, you be in Zaron, training your men."

"Yes, Warlord." Marduct didn't watch him go. Instead he finished writing out the young chieftain's orders and put them in the slot for his clerk to recopy and seal later.

So much for insolent young chieftains. At least for today. For the first part of the war, he'd keep Deruct well behind lines. The young pup would wile away his days, escorting prisoners and supply caravans. Only when there was nothing left in the west but mopping up, would Marduct let Deruct set one foot west of the Barriers.

Marduct gathered up some of the paperwork on his desk, including the dispatch from Tarion. It was time for his daily council with Skrike. Once again, Marduct shook his head in amazement at what he'd become. He was a bureaucrat like they had in the west, reading and writing reports, and going to meetings. How he longed to get back on the desert, or even better in the mountains, marching toward the west and the greatest plunder of all. Only a short time now, he thought, a couple of weeks and the invasion would begin.

"Great Dalmar, but that woman's angry," said Bindle as he rode back to the cart where Buckle was seated. The young soldier had a leering smile on his face, and his eyes were wide with excitement and speculation. Buckle shook his head in wonder. Ever since he had brought Bindle back to the camp three days ago, Zabeth had treated him with nothing less than acid animosity. She had ignored him, insulted him, even had taken a few swings at him, and far from being discouraged, Bindle seemed to thrive on it.

Buckle could barely see Zabeth, riding about fifty yards ahead. She had not taken the news that Buckle had hired Bindle as a guide very well. When Buckle told her she had muttered, "fine," and rolled over in her blankets.   She didn't sleep though.   Buckle listened to her all night and at no time did her breathing become regular like a sleeper's.

For his part, Buckle hadn't slept much either.   Between the excitement, the rain and the damp moldy earth they had been camped on, he had had a serious attack.   About an hour before dawn he finally had broken down and used some of his precious supply of jimsonweed.   It had grown depressingly small.   They had tried to buy some at every inn they came to, but the herb apparently only grew in western Delamer, and most innkeepers didn't understand what Buckle was asking for.

By morning, Buckle was so groggy from the effects of the herb, he had sent Zabeth out with Bindle to retrieve the soldier's horse. When they had returned a half hour later, they were in a furious argument.

"Master Buckle," she had said, "do I have to take orders from this...this?"

"What do you mean, Zabeth?"

"I was with you before him.   Do I have to do what he..."

"You're a woman," said Bindle.   "Of course you do."   This comment was followed by a flurry of insults and oaths.   In the middle of it Bindle had given Buckle an impudent smile.   He was having fun.

Buckle, who had been sleepy and sick from the night before, just walked away from them.   When it looked like they would argue all day, he sent them ahead to scout the road.   That had been two days ago.

"I still can't get over it."   Bindle shook his head.   "When you said you had an escort, I never dreamed it was a woman."

Buckle felt himself rising to the man's tone.   In his mind, Zabeth had proven herself.   What was more, she was from Methliana. Who was this stranger to criticize?   "Grazzle used to say she was the best warrior he ever trained."

"Grazzle trained her?"   Bindle looked at Buckle in amazement. "Grazzle of the Foothills?"

"I believe that was what he was called before he came to the estate."

"He commanded a company in the Barrier Scouts, oh...about twenty years ago now.   They still tell tales about him."

Charles Ebert

"He was quite fond of her. But she puzzled him too. He'd look at her and say that a man's spirit must have been trapped in a woman's figure."

Bindle looked down the road at Zabeth. "There's nothing manly about that figure." He looked back at Buckle with a smile. "And nothing womanly about her spirit."

"Bindle, I'd keep clear of her for a while. She can be dangerous when she's upset."

Bindle laughed and spurred his horse ahead. He spent the rest of the day pestering her and suffering her abuse. Buckle sat in the cart with Yazzle snoring in the back. He daydreamed and watched the scenery go by.

They were the only group heading east. When they were still in Delamer, there had been some local eastbound traffic. But once they crossed the Tarion Bridge the only people they saw were refugees. They crawled westward, carrying their possessions in any manner of vehicle, two wheeled or four wheeled, or even on their backs. As they trudged onward, past Buckle and his band, they would stare, most in disbelief. Some looked as if they wanted to warn him, but then bowed their heads and pressed on. Better to mind your own business in these times.

Buckle worried about them. Where would they go? Delamer could only support so many of them and after the storms of the last couple days, that number would be even less. And Delamerians were notoriously contemptuous of their neighbors to the east, using the folklore of Dalmar as an excuse for assuming moral superiority and prejudice. Somehow, Buckle couldn't imagine men like Erklin and Scarver welcoming these people with open arms.

Late that afternoon, they arrived at yet another temporary tent city. In the middle of the expanse, like an island surrounded by a multi-colored ocean was a large inn. It was bigger than Scarver's and nicer, at least as far as Buckle could see from the outside. Two wings of rooms extended from a main entrance hall which was built of stone. The wings were brightly painted white with brown trim. The inn and the tent city were run by an enterprising innkeeper who reserved the best sites for those who could pay, but denied no one a patch of ground on his property. He was fat and bald but of good humor.

"I've got just the site for you, sir," he said to Buckle, as he led the cart through the city. "It's up on a hill, clean and dry, with a view of the wood. There's game there if you're catching your dinner. But

68

these days you'll have to go far into it. If not, we'll be happy to fix you a meal and I'll even have one of my boys walk it out to you."

Bindle, who was riding ahead with Zabeth, turned back and smiled at Buckle. He jerked his thumb at the oblivious innkeeper. Yazzle sat beside Buckle in the cart. The lad leaned over and whispered in Buckle's ear.

"We need provisions."

"I can do that," said the innkeeper, overhearing. "Just let me know what you need and I'll send it out to you."

Buckle nodded. "Yazzle here is in charge of provisions. He'll give you a list before you leave. Tell me," said Buckle, leaning forward, "Is there a witch in the camp tonight?"

They had been talking about using a witch to trace Roduct ever since leaving Methliana. Buckle had asked the same question at every stop.

The innkeeper paused a minute, scratched his head and said, "You know, I do believe there is a magic woman down close to the road." He waved his stubby hand in that direction. "But if you're going down there tonight, you want to be careful. I've had some pretty rough trade through here the last few nights. Don't you go down there alone. And I'd keep a watch posted at your own site. There are thieves and worse everywhere."

"Thanks for the advice," said Buckle.

"Well, this is it," said the innkeeper. The campsite was indeed as he described it. The ground was dry and covered with a carpet of pine needles. Buckle sniffed at them experimentally but detected no trace of mold. He saw Zabeth scowling at the woods, no doubt thinking they were too close for her comfort, but she didn't say anything. Bindle dismounted and examined the layout in much the same way as Zabeth.

Yazzle was talking to the innkeeper, listing the things they needed. The host stood with his neck bent, his ear cocked toward Yazzle.

"I don't know, sir," he said, massaging his scalp. "Never heard of jimsonweed."

Buckle walked up to them. "Maybe they call it something different in these parts. It's an herb that grows about four feet tall. It has dark green leaves with serrated edges and a bell shaped flower in the middle."

The man scrunched his face in thought. "I'll ask the wife. She does most of the herb gathering, but I can't promise you anything."

"I'd appreciate it." Buckle handed him some silver coins and the innkeeper went scurrying down the hill, talking to himself.

The tent city was packed and not just up on the hill where Buckle's band was but everywhere he looked, right down to the road, where travelers on foot were bivouacked. The innkeeper and his staff kept a few paths clear between the tents, but otherwise the tent city was a kaleidoscope of humanity. If just the people in the inn and on the hill were paying customers, Buckle could well imagine the portly innkeeper contemplating an expansion with the profits he was making from all this. Buckle hoped the man wouldn't over build. Once the war was over, traffic along the road would once again go back to normal. And of course if the west lost...Well, Buckle knew that three hundred years ago when Skrike and his Sarondaki nomads ruled to the sea, nobody in the west had made much money.

Yazzle had a fire going and dinner was well on the way. Bindle was brushing down the horses. And Zabeth was sitting on her haunches, watching the woods.

"I don't think the Sarondakis have penetrated this far yet," said Buckle, walking up behind her.

"You don't have to be born in the desert to have a Sarondaki heart." She recited the old maxim, tersely. "I hear there are outlaws in Wyckham."

"Yes, I've heard that too. I'm going into the camp tonight to find that witch. I'll need you as an escort."

"Can't Bindle do it?"

"I want you."

She cast a sharp look at him and said, "If you're doing this to make me feel better, don't bother."

"I'm doing this," said Buckle, leaning over her, "because I need an escort and that's your job on this trip."

She sprang up and paced for a minute and then sat down by her saddlebags. She didn't say another word.

Their new provisions came during dinner. They were delivered by a stout young man with the innkeeper's face. One of the man's sons, thought Buckle, as he examined the packages.

"He couldn't find any jimsonweed?" asked Buckle.

The young man looked puzzled for a second and then brightened. "Oh, that must be the herb you asked for." He pulled a loosely wrapped packet from his shirt and opened it. Inside was a purplish green mixture of crushed vegetation. Buckle took a pinch of it and carefully smelled it. "Mother never heard of jimsonweed but she says this is close to what you described. We call it dwale." He pulled part of a plant out of the pouch. "This is what it looks like."

Buckle took the plant and examined it. It wasn't jimsonweed; that was certain. The stems were the wrong shade of green and the leaves were the wrong configuration. But the resemblance was strong in other respects. Perhaps this dwale was related and did the same thing.

"Did your mother mention what this herb did?"

"Yes, she said it put you to sleep."

That made sense. Jimsonweed always made Buckle sleepy. "I'll try it. How much do we owe you?"

"For all the provisions, 15 silver pieces." Buckle counted out the coins and paid the young man. Buckle put the dwale in with his private bundles and then went to finish his dinner while Yazzle piled the rest of the provisions on the cart.

When Buckle finished his meal, he rinsed off his plate and walked over to the cart and got Roduct's bundled-up shirt. Then he stood at the edge of the camp, staring at Zabeth. She dallied by the woods, pretending to peer into the gloom between the trees. When she saw Buckle wasn't falling for it, she sighed dramatically and stomped toward him. On the way, she passed Bindle, who was hunched over his dinner. She gave him a whack on the head and said, "Watch the camp."

"Yes, Matron," he said, smiling and watching her as she walked toward Buckle.

Down in the tent city, Buckle clutched his bundle tightly in one hand and grasped his money pouch with the other. Even though she wouldn't speak, Buckle was glad Zabeth was there. Around him, in tents and gathered around fires was a mass of humanity. This tent city differed from the many he'd seen the last few weeks, both in its size and in the high proportion of males.

Women were still in the majority, but the men dominated the camp. They were young men mostly, dirty but fit enough to fight which, with their homelands under imminent attack meant they were either cowards, pacifists or up to no good. From the brawling and arguing going on around him, Buckle could see they were not pacifists, and he knew the other two possibilities were not mutually exclusive.

71

"I think it's over here, Zabeth," said Buckle, pointing to the right. They had asked several people, and had found out that the witch was in a tent by the side of the road, across from a tall evergreen. Buckle and Zabeth had been rushing to find it before the sun went down and their landmark disappeared.

Hundreds of campfires cast the tent city in a flickering orange and yellow light that was tinged with soot. It smelled too, and not just of smoke. The innkeeper had dug dozens of privies all through the campgrounds, but they were crowded and many chose to do their business on the ground like their animals. One had to be careful where one stepped.

Finally, Buckle spotted the tent and motioned Zabeth to follow him. Up close, Buckle could see that the tent was an example of faded brilliance. It had stripes which were embroidered with gold trim, and tiny bells hung from knots in the seams. Most of them were missing and the remaining ones were dented and worn, their coats of gold paint flaking off to reveal the cheap tin underneath.

Buckle poked his head into the entrance and said "Excuse me." Sitting cross-legged in the middle of the tent in front of a small but smoky fire was an old woman. Her hair, the color of cotton on which somebody had spilled black ink, shot out from her head like a dandelion gone to seed. Her black eyes stared at Buckle from within enfolding wrinkles. She wore a tatty feathered robe which was threadbare in places.

"Who enters here," her voice crackled.

"My name's Buckle, Matron." Buckle stepped into the tent. The smoke almost choked him. Zabeth slipped in after him. "This is my escort, Zabeth."

"Do you have money?" The woman's eyebrows arched and met each other in the middle of her forehead.

"Yes."

"Good." She motioned them to sit down. "What is it you wish from Matron Kareth?"

"We are looking for someone," said Buckle, sitting down and laying his bundle beside him.

"I see. I will need an article of clothing or jewelry owned by the missing person."

"I brought one of his tunics," said Buckle, offering the package.

The woman stared at him until Buckle laid the package down in front of her. Only then did she take it in her knurled fingers and open it. She pulled out Roduct's tunic.

"Finding magic is an ancient power. It is older than the immortal Tenaryans, who came to our world centuries ago. Such magic is intimately tied with elemental forces." The old woman chanted this while she held the shirt in front of her and swayed from side to side with her eyes closed. "I am a fire witch and my color is red." She waved the shirt over her head in one hand like a flag and the fire sprang up and turned a dark cherry red. Unfortunately, Buckle, who knew something about sleight of hand tricks, saw her throw some powder into the fire with her other hand. He looked at her in disappointment. She was a charlatan.

"He is a tall man and well-to-do, even rich," she intoned as her fingers traveled over the vast expanse of silky linen. She held the garment at arm's length and Buckle could see her eyes move as she examined the weave of the fabric and the cut of the tunic, which was of the western style.

"He is from Delamer," she said. "And he is headed east." It was almost a question. She stopped swaying.

The old woman stared at them. "Why are you searching for him?"

"He's in a certain amount of trouble at home." said Buckle, a little taken aback by the change in tone. "We need to bring him back to Delamer to prove his innocence."

"Hmm, why did he leave?"

Buckle shrugged his shoulders and said, "We don't know. A stranger came from the east and threatened him with Soowooli. He left right after."

"Yes, this could be it," muttered the old woman. She stood up. "You must follow me."

"What?"

"Come, Krinseth must meet you."

She shot out of the tent, pulling Buckle along by his sleeve. Zabeth followed. Her knife was out of its sheath.

The old woman dragged them to a large fire. A crowd stood around it. Someone had taken some logs and branches from the forest and turned a campfire into a bonfire. Others had helped by heaping garbage into the flame. As Kareth plowed into the mass, her head darted back and forth, obviously looking for this Krinseth she had spoken of.

"Wait here.   She is close." Then Kareth let go of Buckle's sleeve and disappeared into the crowd.

On a stump, in front of the fire, sat a bard.   He cradled a lute in his arms.   A crowd had gathered around him as he played the old ballad "Dalmar and Methlyn."

He had just strummed a final chord and was acknowledging the smattering of applause.   Buckle noted that the bard had omitted the last verse.   Actually, he thought, that shouldn't be surprising given where he was.   The verse condemned Dalmar's allies, Goswick and Joswell for hesitating at the edge of the desert.   That version was probably never popular this far east.

Dalmar's defeat had shaped the political climate of the west for three hundred years.   Two nations, Joswell and Goswick had been formed just to the west of the Barriers.   West of them was Delamer which was the Tenaryan name for Dalmar.   Because of the failings of the two surviving allies, the nations that bore their names also bore the responsibility of keeping the Sarondakis on the eastern side of the mountains.   A treaty to that effect was signed.   Buckle knew that it was a treaty that Roduct had always felt was unfair.   Delamer was by far the richest country in the west with more arable land than its neighbors and a strong sea trade.   This strange alliance had worked for three centuries, but in that time, it had never been seriously tested. Now that the Sarondakis were active again, the weaknesses in the alliance were beginning to show.   So much so that even the singing of a simple song, with the most offensive part excised, could incite an argument.

"Don't be playing that offal around here, boy," said a nasty looking man with matted black hair and a scar running down his cheek. He was big, half a foot taller than Buckle but much broader, with a barrel chest.   He was surrounded by equally dangerous looking types. They were all dirty and their clothes hung in rags.   They stood in a semicircle with their arms crossed and their faces contorted into smirks.

"I am sorry if it offended you sir," replied the young musician, "but it was a request and I play all requests.   Perhaps you have one?"

"Even if the story is true," said the man, stepping forward.   He weaved a bit on his feet.   "And I've noticed that these things never are. But even if it..."

"Are you doubting the truth of the legend of Dalmar?" said an older man with close cropped white hair and an indignant expression.

"Yeah," said the black haired man. "And I'll tell you something else. Dalmar was a coward."

This drew cries of protest from the crowd.

"You sir, are drunk." A third combatant stepped forward. She was a woman, middle aged but remarkably well preserved. Her face had high cheek bones that supported steel gray eyes. Her soft brown hair was pulled back into a loose bun, secured by means of two sticks stuck in the top. Her figure was hidden underneath her robe but Buckle guessed she was thin.

"Dalmar was, if anything, recklessly brave," she said, staring at the black haired man. He stepped back. "Taking on Skrike like that! Sheer foolhardiness!"

"But he won," pointed out the old man. He stepped out of the crowd. "Skrike was defeated."

"Only with the help of the Tenaryans."

"Zalphlyn and Methlyn," he said. "But surely you must agree that Dalmar's daring had a lot to do with it. According to the songs..."

"What good is it to moon over old songs," bellowed the black haired man. He shoved the old man aside and confronted the woman. "What do we do now to save the west?"

She looked at him, her face hardening like cooling molten metal. "For one thing, you can get all able-bodied men back east to fight."

He took a ragged breath. "What are you saying, hag? You think I should be back there?" He looked around at the crowd, which stared back, judgment in their looks. "I can't help it if I've got flat feet, carrying around all this weight."

"You seem to run pretty well," came a voice from the crowd.

"Who said that," cried the man, putting his fists up. "Come out here and back that up."

"Put your fists down, you bellowing ox," shouted the woman. She breathed in air and fire seemed to come out. "You're a bigger fool than Dalmar."

"You call Dalmar a fool," he bawled, forgetting that just a minute ago he had called Dalmar a coward. "I'll give you the back of my hand for that." He advanced on her.

"Hold it son." Buckle stepped in front of the black haired man. "I don't like what she's saying either, but they're only words and nothing to get violent about."

"Out of my way." The big man shoved Buckle with both hands. Buckle flew backwards and fell to the ground at the feet of the woman.

Zabeth darted into the fray, driving her shoulder into the black haired man's stomach. He bent over double. After a few nimble steps, she was behind him. Grabbing his arm, she bent it behind his back and drove him toward the fire. Buckle began to fear the worst, when he saw Zabeth's boot stick out and trip the bully. He fell forward, his face landing inches from the flame. Zabeth flopped him over on his back, placing her boot on his chest and put her sword tip at his throat. He stared up at her with wide, yellow eyes. She looked at his companions significantly. A small twist of her wrist indicated her intention if any of them tried to back up their friend. They didn't interfere.

"If you ever touch my master again," she said to the bully, "I'll kill you and it'll be slow and painful." She then applied the gentlest of pressure to the sword, forcing the man to scoot back and put his hair into the fire. He screeched and Zabeth stepped back as he leapt to his feet.

Dancing and hopping around the fire, he patted the top of his head which was smoldering. He bellowed for water which amused the crowd. Someone procured a slop bucket and emptied its contents on the man's head.

"You'll be sorry wench," he sputtered. "I'll have my revenge." He ran from the circle. His companions, not knowing whether to follow him or to stay and deliver the promised revenge, looked first at his retreating back then at the crowd and finally at the tip of Zabeth's sword and the look in her eyes. They chose retreat. The surrounding crowd broke into gales of laughter and applause.

Zabeth ignored them and ran to Buckle's side. Squatting, she said, "Master Buckle, are you all right? If he hurt you, I'll chase him down and skin him."

"Zabeth, I'm fine," he said, grinning.

"Why are you smiling?"

"I was thinking of my brother's face when I tell him about this. He thought I was going to have to leave you behind somewhere. He's such a good judge of people." Buckle laughed.

Zabeth bowed her head. "I thought you would after the fight with Torkle."

Shaking his head, Buckle said, "No, but I do wish he was here so you could give him one of your special haircuts."

He watched as Zabeth pressed her chin into her sternum. In the flickering light of the fire, the edges of her mouth curled up. She was fighting very hard to straighten them out. A strangled snort came out of her nose. Buckle pushed her shoulder, toppling her backwards on her rear end which jarred the laughter out of her. She wouldn't meet his eyes, as embarrassed about this loss of composure as she was about the fight in Delamer. But Buckle could see a lot of her anger draining away as she rolled over onto one elbow, still laughing.

"I take it you are all right, sir." It was the woman's voice. She stood over them with her arms crossed. Buckle looked up at her and smiled. She really was quite attractive.

"Good," she said, "it would not do for you to get permanently hurt in such a useless pursuit."

Zabeth sprang up, "Hey Matron, this man may have just saved your life."

"Hardly. On the contrary he probably saved the life of that oaf. I can handle my own affairs."

Buckle got up and laid a hand on Zabeth's shoulder as the young warrior opened her mouth to carry on the argument. "Matron, if I have trespassed into your business, I apologize. I did so with only the best intentions."

The woman nodded her head curtly and turned to leave.

"You're going to let her get away with that," cried Zabeth. "You save her life and then apologize for it? It's not fair."

"It's not important, Zabeth."

"But you could have been killed."

Buckle smiled at her. "Not with my escort around." He put his arm around her and turned her toward where they'd left Kareth. "Where did that old witch get to? What was her name? Kareth?"

"Kareth brought you?" said the woman, turning back to them.

"Yes," said Buckle, looking at her. "She said we had to meet somebody."

"That would be me. I am Krinseth."

"I think that's the name she mentioned."

"There will be more privacy in the tent. Please follow me."

"I don't like this, sir," said Zabeth.

77

Charles Ebert

"I don't either, but she may be some kind of real witch.   If she's willing to help us, she may be the only chance we have of finding Lord Roduct."   He and Zabeth followed Krinseth back to the faded carnival tent.

8

Inside the tent, Krinseth opened a flap in the roof and began waving away the smoke. She motioned for Buckle to leave the entrance flap open also. As she picked up some of Kareth's paraphernalia, she said, "Kareth pretended to be a fire witch." She pulled out two bags of powder, which had been shoved under the pillows upon which Kareth had sat earlier. She held them up with a significant glance at Buckle. "I've known a few real fire witches in my time. Couldn't abide them." She tossed the bags into the mud and filth outside. "I believe Skrike's power is fire based." She cocked her head and pursed her lips.

"Kareth seems like a decent sort, even if she isn't really a witch."

"Yes, she was of great help to me. Tell me why she wanted you to meet me."

Buckle related the story of their journey so far, leaving out the details of Roduct's legal troubles which Krinseth didn't seem to be interested in, anyway. She listened with growing interest, asking questions now and then. When Buckle was finished, she sat on the cushions staring at them.

"Roduct is a Sarondaki?"

"Yes. He marched with Dalmar."

"Hmm." She stared deeper into the fire.

"Is that significant?"

"I just thought that maybe I knew him from somewhere." She leaned forward and asked, "Have you the tunic?"

79

Buckle had left it in the tent.   He picked it up off the ground and handed it to her.

Krinseth took the shirt in her hands.   She licked the fingers of her left hand and held the fabric between them.   "He's on the main road about three days travel east of us."

It never occurred to Buckle to doubt her.   "You're the witch."

"In a way.   But I cannot be pestered with people constantly asking for fortunes, love potions or minor finding magic.   That is why I traveled with Kareth.   She was quite good at providing those services."

"How do we know you're not a bigger fake than Kareth is?" asked Zabeth, staring right at Krinseth.

"I don't suppose you can know that.   But what choice have you?   You can return west and lose your estate and Roduct's honor or you can continue eastward and maybe find him."

"We can't go back, Zabeth," said Buckle, "and it makes sense that he'd be on the main road."

"Which makes it a pretty easy prediction.   And she knew that Lord Roduct was two days ahead of us, the last time we heard."

"He is traveling by night.   Sarondakis need very little sleep," said Krinseth.

"Then how will we catch him?" asked Buckle.

"The foothills and the mountains have a way of slowing people down, and since Roduct is a Sarondaki he will need to hide from both his own people and the western armies.   This will slow him down more.   And once he gets to his destination, he'll stop."

"What's his destination?" asked Buckle, shifting in his seat.

"You mean you haven't thought about where he might be going; where you're going in fact?"   Krinseth gave him a reproving look.   "He is undoubtedly going to the Ratog."

Buckle looked at Zabeth, who was staring at Krinseth.   "Why would he be going there?"

"On that, I do not care to speculate.   And if I could read his mind, would there be any need for you to find him?"

"Then we'll have to travel faster, try and catch him in the mountains," said Buckle as he stood up.   "I don't want to go to the Ratog."

"You are wise.   But you may have to."

Buckle looked down at her.   The fire was burning low and the differences between the shadows and the lit parts of her face were becoming indistinct. He felt a wave of fatigue run from his shoulders down his body. Thoughts of home came unbidden to his mind: His bed made of fluffy down, the sound of the wind, rustling through the trees outside his window on summer nights. Things he might never experience again.

Buckle shook his head and drove those thoughts from his mind. "How much do we owe you for the consultation, Krinseth?"

"It is I who owe you, Master Buckle," said Krinseth, a smile playing upon her lips, "I have been traveling on this road for eighteen months, looking for someone like you. Your quest and mine are intimately related. I suggest we join them."

"I thought you were heading west?"

"Only until I could find a suitable quester. Now I am headed east."

"What is your quest?" asked Zabeth. She stood next to the exit.

"There is a magic growing in the desert, an evil magic. A fire magic." She looked at Buckle. "You've noticed the storms we've had this spring? They are a...reaction to this evil. They will continue growing in strength until one is powerful enough to sweep over the Barriers and soak the desert." She stood up. "I must be there when it happens."

"You are a water witch," said Buckle.

"My power comes from water."

"Get your gear."

Krinseth said, "All I need is what I'm wearing."

"Buckle, I don't trust her," said Zabeth.

"Good, you can keep an eye on her," said Buckle. "But at the same time I think we need her." He turned to Krinseth. "What about Kareth?"

"She will not be going," said the witch as she stepped past them out the tent.

Buckle followed, motioning to Zabeth, who came along reluctantly. "What about your tent, Krinseth?"

"Leave it. It's not important." Buckle shrugged and continued following her.

It was later now and many in the tent city were asleep, although most had left watches. There were a few bands of men, roving among the camps, looking for unguarded property or stragglers out alone.

Some were still at the campfires drinking and singing. But it was all much more subdued than before.

As they made their way past the fire where they had met Krinseth, Zabeth stopped. "Master Buckle," she said, grabbing his arm and pointing.

"What?" He strained his eyes to see what she was pointing at. Something lay in the darkness, just beyond the rim of light cast by the fire. "What is it?"

Zabeth ran into the shadows. Buckle and Krinseth followed. Lying face down in the garbage and mud was a body, wearing a feathered robe.

"Oh, great Dalmar," whispered Buckle when Zabeth turned the body over to reveal that it was Kareth. He bent down to listen for a breath. She was dead.

"Sad tidings, Krinseth," he said.

"She is dead, I know."

Buckle and Zabeth looked up at her from where they kneeled over the dead witch.

"Please do not think me heartless. She died six months ago. I shed plenty of tears then." Krinseth stood over them now, looking down on her former partner. "Since then I have been animating her with a part of my own power. Sarondaki magic, clumsily applied, using water magic, very distasteful to me and somewhat unpleasant for her. But necessary. She is better off now. Let's get to your camp."

"Shouldn't we bury her or something," said Buckle.

"No time. We should get an early start in the morning. There will be another storm tomorrow night. The innkeeper here is a decent man. He'll give her a better burial than she could ever have expected. Come." She turned and walked away. Buckle and Zabeth reluctantly followed.

When they reached the camp things were quiet. The fire had burned down to a few embers. Bindle lay on his bedroll, snoring lightly, while Yazzle sat in the cart, alert for any sound.

"Master Buckle," he said, once they had answered his challenge and had introduced Krinseth. "Did you find out where Lord Roduct is?"

"Yes we did, Yazzle. Krinseth here is a witch and she can help us track him." The giant field hand cast a quick glance at Krinseth. He had a peasant's fear of such things. "What happened while we were gone?"

82

"Not much, sir. Some people came by to talk and exchange news. Bindle caught one of them trying to steal some salted beef."

"Have you heard anything in those woods," asked Zabeth.

"No, Zabeth. A deer came out of it earlier, before the sun went down. Bindle wanted to shoot it but it was a doe and gravid too, I think. So I didn't let him. We got plenty of food."

Zabeth chewed her lip and nodded. "Yazzle, you keep watch until the moon clears the treetops on the other side of the road. Then wake Bindle. I wish I had somebody just to watch the woods."

"I'll watch the woods," announced Krinseth. They all looked at her. "I don't sleep. I'll just sit in the cart and watch the woods. You are very wise to be concerned about them, young miss. They are very old and very dangerous."

"Well, if your eyes get tired, wake me up."

"They will not get tired, and I will watch with more than my eyes." She climbed into the cart, and the rest unrolled their bedrolls and went to sleep.

In the middle of the night, Buckle awoke, unable to breathe. He sat up, but then forced himself to lay flat on his back and to draw breath from deep in his chest. It was blocked. He would draw in a breath and nothing inside his chest would move. It felt like a solid mass.

He pulled himself to his feet. His vision sparkled with red and yellow spots, through which he made his way to the cart. Halfway there he stopped and put his hands on his knees. Gasping for air, he was too blocked to even wheeze.

He looked over to see the dark form of Bindle beside him. "Buckle, you're having another attack?"

"Jimsonweed," Buckle managed to gasp.

"Jimsonwhat?"

"Cart," breathed Buckle, motioning to his destination. The back of his throat tickled so much it hurt. But he dared not cough. Bindle helped him to the cart. Krinseth looked down at them from her seat on the bench.

With tingling fingers, Buckle tore into one of the bundles and pulled out the sack of jimsonweed. There remained only enough for maybe two more doses. Considering, Buckle put the sack down and picked up the package of dwale. He opened it and grabbed a pinch of the herb and started packing the bowl of the pipe.

A hand grabbed his wrist and stopped him. Buckle looked up and saw Krinseth leaning over him.

"Let it go," she hissed. "It'll kill you." She smacked his hand, forcing him to drop the dwale and the pipe. Then she bounded out of the cart and took his arm. "Follow me."

"Hey," said Bindle.

"Out of the way." She drew him almost to the edge of the woods. By now everyone in the camp was awake. Buckle could hear Yazzle and Zabeth asking what was happening in sleepy voices.

"I don't know," said Bindle. "Buckle had another attack and she led him away."

"Trust me," whispered Krinseth in Buckle's ear. "Stop here and bend over."

Buckle did as she said. He then felt her hand gently travel up and down his back.

"Relax." She made her voice smooth and soothing in contrast to her regular harsh tone.

"Can't...breathe," gasped Buckle.

"I know, I know. Just relax. Loosen those back muscles."

Buckle tried to quell his panic and concentrate on loosening his back. The caressing hands of Krinseth helped. Then she stopped and placed one hand, which felt damp, on the small of his back. Buckle felt her push with a slight pressure. Then it felt like his chest exploded.

A tremendous force pushed out of his lungs and his mouth and nose erupted, mucus spewing out. Buckle cried and fell to his knees, coughing and spitting. After a moment of confused panic, he realized that he was breathing normally again. He looked up at Krinseth.

"Here, wipe you face," she said, offering him a rag.

Buckle accepted it and buried his face in it. He tried to stand but couldn't.

"What did you do?" asked Zabeth. The entire group was now standing around Buckle.

"A small moving spell and a relaxing spell."

With Yazzle's help, Buckle managed to gain his feet. He felt like a drained water sack, limp and damp. It seemed like he could sleep right there on his feet like a horse. But he marshaled his strength for one question. "Why didn't you let me take the dwale?"

"Dwale is nightshade, a powerful sleeping herb, not a clearing herb. It might have killed you in your condition."

Yazzle led Buckle back to his bedroll where he instantly fell asleep.

9

As the days passed, Buckle grew used to traveling, although he doubted that he'd ever like it. Lack of a bed and a clean toilet were the things he had always imagined were the worst about long journeys. But with Krinseth there to cure his attacks, he was sleeping better, and he found that after a while, even he could get used to a thin bedroll on the ground. Also, it had taken almost the whole of their time on the road so far, but Buckle had gradually grown accustomed going into the wild to relieve himself. As a result, he was much more comfortable.

Some things about it were positively pleasant. Riding on the cart and watching the trees along the side of the road was almost as relaxing as sitting on the porch of the manor house at Methliana. And when there was a blue sky and a soft breeze wafting the pine smell from the wood, Buckle was almost content.

Nothing was like home though. Guilt pervaded Buckle's thoughts when he imagined all the work he would be doing if he were on the estate. The corn would be about waist high by now and there was hoeing to be done. Worry knotted Buckle's stomach. Deep down, he believed that seeing to such things was his responsibility, and no matter how compelling his reasons for leaving, he had abandoned that trust. He had dreams of finding Roduct, only to be remonstrated for gallivanting around the countryside when he should have been home working. Most of these dark thoughts only came at night just before sleep. In the day, out on the road, Buckle could ignore them, having other things to think about.

For instance, over the last few days the traffic of refugees was thinning. They had even been able to stay at an inn once. An actual bed and bath had improved everyone's morale. The east was almost completely depopulated now. Every couple of days or so, they would pass through a deserted village or town. Doors and windows would be broken or hanging open, left that way by either their owners or the looters who came afterward. So far though, they had seen no sign of Sarondakis.

Western troops were becoming more common though. The most reliable news came from the soldiers they encountered, especially the ones headed west, away from the fighting. They camped one night with a company of walking injured, making its way to Tarion. The leader of the band of twenty or so was a constable named Nittle. His arm was in a sling and it caused him great pain. He had come to their campfire that night.

"If I were you folks, I'd turn back," he had said, holding a cup of ale in his uninjured left hand. Buckle, Bindle, Zabeth and Krinseth sat around the fire, listening to him. Yazzle was clearing away the supper dishes. "Fort Unity is under siege. They didn't give it more than a few days, and that was two weeks ago when we left the foothills. The entire eastern half of Goswick and Joswell could be overrun by the savages by now."

"My company was going to Unity," said Bindle, leaning forward. "Perhaps you know if they got there?"

"Who are they?"

"Renwick's company."

"I'm sorry, I didn't hear any word about Renwick," the soldier said, his eyes staring at the fire. "My unit was stationed out of Unity, but we were out on patrol when Marduct's army rolled through the mountains. It took us six days of fighting, hiding and running to regroup in the foothills with what was left of the rest of the western armies. We didn't dare face them in open combat. Their army is just too big. We're fighting a retreating action now, until we get the reinforcements from Delamer. That's how I got this." He lifted his injured arm and winced.

"How could this have happened?" Zabeth demanded.

"We're under equipped, undermanned and ill-trained. Desertion is high, rations slim, and you can just forget about pay. Everything that can go wrong with a campaign has in this one." He sipped his ale, looking down into the cup. "We just weren't ready."

"You broke the treaty," said Buckle softly.

The man looked up, anger flashing on his face. He glared at Buckle for moment, and then the fire went out. "Yes we did," he finally said. "The defense of the west was entirely the responsibility of Goswick and Joswell and we allowed ourselves to grow soft." He put his cup on the ground and put his head in his good hand.

"My master, Lord Roduct spoke many times in the Delamerian council in favor of sending aid and manpower to Goswick and Joswell." Zabeth and Bindle looked at Buckle in open surprise. Krinseth arched an eyebrow. "He told me once that he didn't think the armies of Goswick and Joswell could stand up to a full scale invasion by the Sarondakis."

"Your master is a wise man, sir," said Nittle. "But that was common knowledge in the east. What most in your country don't realize is that when the Sarondakis have defeated us, Delamer is next."

Buckle nodded his head in agreement. "At one time I didn't think so, but seeing the fear in the faces of those refugees...What they're running from frightens me."

"I've seen it, and it should. If Skrike's armies are as powerful as of old," said Nittle, "then all is lost. He will rule once more to the sea."

Everyone looked away, lost in thoughts of panic or despair. The fire crackled and spat orange sparks into the night sky. Buckle suddenly felt cold. He pulled his cloak tightly around his shoulders.

Krinseth sniffed at the air. "Do not despair. Tenaryans understand humans imperfectly. Skrike will almost certainly make a mistake. Not the same one as last time, but it will be just as fatal to his plans." She stood up. "There will be another storm tomorrow. We must get an early start."

"You're going on?" Nittle looked at them in amazement.

"We have no choice," said Buckle, standing up and stretching. "Who's taking the first watch?"

"My men will stand guard," said Nittle. "For Dalmar's sake, at least take my advice, and leave the main road at the first opportunity. Before long you'll get to our lines and they won't let you through, just for your own safety. That is, if they don't think you're spies. Or worse, you may run into the Sarondaki army."

The members of the troop looked at each other uneasily. "Come on everybody," said Buckle. "No watches tonight. Let's get a good night's sleep." If we can, he added silently.

That had been several days ago. They weathered the predicted storm and pressed as hard as they could without wearing out the horses. Yet every few days, when Krinseth traced Roduct, he was further ahead.

They now stood at a crossroads, the dust caking their clothes and bodies, trying to decide which direction to turn off the East Road. Trees towered above them, although the woods were getting sparser and the land hillier as they moved eastward. There stood a small house on the corner. The roof was missing and fire had charred the walls above the broken windows and doors.

"I say we go south," said Bindle edging his horse that way, "Joswell is more settled. There'll be better roads."

"If it's more settled, we're more likely to run into somebody," reasoned Zabeth. "If it's more prosperous there are liable to be looters, bandits and even Sarondakis. Let's go north and avoid all that."

"After all this time, everything will be looted out. Look around you, everyone's gone, north and south. At least in Joswell we can make better time."

"How can you be sure everyone's gone?" Zabeth gyrated her arms in frustration. "Can you see through these trees? Do you know for certain that those woods are deserted?"

"Can you say the same for those woods?" said Bindle, gesturing to the north side of the road. "No, both sides are a gamble. I say if we go faster, we'll put the odds in our favor."

"Lunkhead."

"Harpy," he replied, smiling. He still enjoyed the game, thought Buckle.

"Peace," said Buckle. They all looked at him as he sat on the cart next to Krinseth. "Bindle, do you know the roads to the south better than the north?"

"Yes, I grew up not far from here."

"Then we'll go south."

"But..." Buckle put a hand up to stop her.

"We'll post extra watches at night. Two people up at all times. You and Bindle will take turns scouting ahead. We'll set up a signal of some kind for you to tell us it's clear. Will that satisfy you?"

"Yes," she mumbled.

"Zabeth?"

"I'm all right, sir," she said, holding out her hands, palms out. "We'll go south."

"Good. I don't think we should stop for lunch. Yazzle," he said, turning to the lad who sat in the back of the cart, "break out some of that salted beef and we'll eat as we ride."

10

A few days later, another storm came rolling out of the west at about sundown. They had found an abandoned barn to shelter in just before the storm hit. Buckle stood in the doorway, watching the sky in the gray light of an obscured dusk. Rain pounded the ground with the force of hammers, splashing the water out of puddles and even digging up clods of mud in front of the yard. Lightning flashed across the sky, forcing Buckle to cover his eyes. The thunder followed a second later, so loud the barn shook and a little dirt from the rafters fell onto Buckle's head.

Buckle dragged his hand through his hair. "This is some storm. Stronger than that last one," he said, closing the barn doors. It was strange how these storms came one after the other, each a couple days apart. Krinseth had said they would grow in intensity, and she always seemed to know when they were coming in. Buckle wondered what her connection to them was.

I'm going out to check the grounds," said Zabeth as she walked up beside him.

"In this?"

"If there are any Sarondakis around, they'll want this shelter for the same reason we do, and I don't think they'd be willing to share."

"Yes but Bindle's scouted up to here. Surely he'd have left a sign if there was trouble?" Three days ago, Bindle had ridden ahead to scout the road. They had found his all-clear mark the day before.

"We haven't seen a mark today," said Zabeth. "Besides the man's a fool. He could easily miss something. I don't want to take chances."

Buckle shrugged and waved at her to proceed. He then turned to the fire Yazzle and Krinseth were building. "What do you need off the cart Yazzle?"

"No need to trouble yourself, sir. I can get to everything by and by."

"Nonsense, I want to help. And besides, I'm hungry. The more I help, the quicker I eat."

Yazzle looked at the fire, thinking hard. "If you could get the big bundle out sir, the one with all the foodstuffs, I'd be grateful."

"Sure," said Buckle, cheerfully. He grabbed the bundle and carried it over to Yazzle. "I'll unhitch the horses. We can put them in these stalls tonight." Buckle motioned to the empty horse stalls lining the walls. Then he looked up. "Maybe I can find some fresh hay in the loft."

"Sir, there's no need. I can do all that."

"Now settle down Yazzle," said Buckle, Putting a hand on the big lad's shoulder. "We go through this every night. We're not on Methliana anymore."

"Yes, sir."

"Didn't I always pitch in, even when we were on the estate?"

"Yes, sir. It's just that…" Yazzle stopped, grasping for words. "What?"

"It's just that I don't feel I'm doing enough."

"Not doing enough," laughed Buckle. He squatted beside Yazzle and looked at him. Yazzle was not handsome by any stretch of the imagination. His head was too big, his hair unkempt and he had an enormous jaw which gave him a look of melancholy stupidity. But after a month and a half with him on the road, Buckle knew that what others took for idiocy in the lad was shyness. He was actually rather sharp. Yazzle didn't say much or dare much but Buckle felt that he could be counted on.

"Yazzle, you're cooking for us and cleaning up and doing far more than your fair share of the manual labor. These things may not seem important to you but they are. This group would fall apart without you."

The lad looked up into Buckle's eyes, perhaps searching for confirmation of the last statement. "If you say so, sir."

"I do. You cook dinner, and I'll see to the horses." Buckle pounded him on the shoulder and walked to the cart. He glanced at

Krinseth and saw she was staring at him. When she noticed he'd noticed, she turned her eyes away.

There was some reasonably fresh hay in the loft. The horses, after being unhitched and brushed down, seemed calm or at least as calm as horse could be in such a storm. They stood in their stalls, munching on hay and staring at Buckle with dim gratitude. Buckle grabbed another bundle out of the cart and sat down next to Krinseth who was chopping strips of dried meat for the stew Yazzle was fussing over.

He opened the bundle to reveal Roduct's tunic. "Time for another reading," he said.

Krinseth looked up at Buckle and then down at the tunic. She arched her eyebrows and they carefully set down her knife.

"If he hasn't moved for the last two days," she said, snatching a rag and wiping her hands, "I don't think he'll have moved today. Nevertheless..." She licked the pads of her fingers and held the tunic. Her brow furrowed and she shifted her sitting position.

"Well?"

"In a minute. His trace is fading from this garment. In a few days it will be worthless. I just need to pick up a small trace and..." She squinted her eyes and inhaled audibly. "I see him. He hasn't moved." She threw the tunic back into Buckle's lap and resumed her cutting.

"Why hasn't he moved?" asked Buckle. "He gets to the Barriers and then he doesn't move. It doesn't make sense."

"The answer is obvious."

"Obvious?"

Krinseth turned to face him. "He's been captured."

"That's not the only explanation."

"It's the simplest."

"Maybe he's just reached his destination."

"Where would he be going in the Barriers?"

Buckle sighed, giving up. "Well, at least we're getting closer. If he's a prisoner, we'll rescue him." Buckle wrapped up the tunic.

"Even if we could find him, what could our group do to rescue him from a Sarondaki war party? Besides it may be too late by then."

"What do you mean?"

"Soowooli," said Krinseth.

Buckle had to admit she was right. If Roduct had truly been captured, then he was undoubtedly under their control. But, He

93

thought stubbornly, there were too many other possibilities to give up now.

He was about to say as much when the doors flew open. Zabeth, wringing wet, stumbled into the barn and fell to the ground. Buckle ran to her, grabbing her shoulders as she gasped for breath. Krinseth shut the barn doors again.

"Zabeth, what happened?"

She looked up at Buckle with blue eyes.   Her hair was dark with rain and plastered to her skull.   She gasped and shifted to a sitting position.   "The outside is clear.   I scouted about a hundred yards into the woods to the east."

"Now that was dangerous," said Buckle.   "You could have gotten lost in this weather."

"I know what I'm doing."   She gave him an annoyed look. "Anyway, I found this."   She pulled a hunk of tree bark out of her pack and handed it to Buckle.   Yazzle came over and gave her a cup of ale which she accepted with mumbled thanks.

On the bark was carved a circle with a dot inside it, Bindle's symbol of warning.   "I was following what I thought was a trail.   It's hard to tell in this rain.   I found this on the ground."

"Maybe it's an old marker.   Lots of people use this system when traveling," said Buckle, although he knew he was wrong.   The carving on the bark was fresh.   He handed it to Krinseth who stood by.   She looked at the bark and shook her head.

"Is it Bindle's," asked Buckle.

"Yes, his trace is strong.   He must have carried it for several hours before he had a chance to drop it."

"What do you mean 'had a chance to drop it?'" asked Zabeth.

"He's been captured."

"Great Dalmar," said Buckle.

"The idiot," cried Zabeth.   "Well I'm not risking my neck to rescue that clumsy oaf."

"You may have no choice."

"What?"

"Bindle and his captors are headed this way."

"Aren't they east of us," asked Buckle.

"Yes.   They probably passed this way earlier today, before the storm and noted the barn.   They are now caught in the rain, and are making their way back to use it for shelter."

"How far away are they?" asked Zabeth.

"About an hour."

"You're sure?"

"My power increases when it rains."

Buckle watched Krinseth in the flickering light of Yazzle's cooking fire and believed her. She seemed to positively crackle with magical energy, nothing visible, but Buckle could feel it like he had felt the air earlier, just before the storm. He helped Zabeth to her feet.

"What should we do Zabeth?"

"Are they Sarondakis?" she asked Krinseth.

"No, bandits." Zabeth nodded, drops of water falling from her nose.

"Let's eat supper. Then we'll dowse that fire and wait for them," she said with a very unpleasant grin on her face.

Buckle crouched in the stall nearest the barn door, trying to keep his chest clear and his legs from cramping. They had moved all the horses into the stalls farthest from the door in hopes that the bandits wouldn't notice them when they entered. Buckle gripped his old rusty sword in his hand. He had packed it almost as an afterthought. It was the sword he had used when he was a boy, and Roduct had taught him the basics of self-defense. Now Buckle crouched uncomfortably in the dark, trying to remember what he'd been taught. He didn't have much success, but it was better than the alternative, which was panic.

He went over the positions where Zabeth had stationed them. Yazzle crouched, much the same as Buckle, in a stall across the barn. He carried a large oak staff which they had found in the back of the barn. Buckle suspected it was a spare axle for a cart because it had grooves worn into it near the ends. Yazzle had been the only one could lift it comfortably, and he whirled it around like it was a twig.

Krinseth sat somewhere in the loft. Zabeth had tried to get her to wield a weapon. But Krinseth merely stated that she didn't need weapons and that she'd join the fray at the appropriate time. Zabeth, to her credit, bit back her anger and let Krinseth go. No doubt she wasn't counting on the witch's help. Zabeth never seemed to rely on anybody if she could help it.

She hid underneath a tarp in the cart which was still in the middle of the barn. The bandits couldn't help but see it. She was banking that they'd be curious.

Outside the wind howled. Rain, driven by the storm, forced its way into small cracks in the barn's walls and roof. A leak formed above Buckle, dropping a steady stream of water on his head. He shifted back a little.

The barn doors swung open with a clatter. Rain poured in, along with a scraggly band of about five dangerous looking men. They were soaked and they stumbled into the barn, leading their horses.

"Someone, light a fire," ordered one.

"Aye," said another. Buckle heard the rustling of hay being gathered and then a few clicks as whoever was making the fire struck this flint and steel. In a few minutes, the barn was lit by a fire.

"Damn this storm," said the first voice.

"And all the rest of them."

"You bastards," said a voice from outside. "Help me get this thing inside before the rain puts it out. And someone take care of the prisoner." The five standing in the barn rushed outside. They returned a second later, carrying an urn which was about three feet tall. It took two people to carry it. Smoke snaked out from tiny holes in its base.

From behind them, a man was thrown into the barn. His hands were tied behind his back so when he fell, his face jammed into the mud. Several more men came in, making a point of stepping on the bound man. Some even stopped to deliver a vicious kick or two. The bound man reacted to the kicks but made no sound.

A large man entered behind the group, which brought the number of bandits in the barn to seven. The men still standing in the doorway made room for him. He had black hair which peeked out from under his forester's cap. There was a nasty scar running down the side of his face.

"Pick him up," he said. The others scurried to obey. They held the bound man by his arms. His head lay limp at his chest. "Throw him in one of the stalls." They dragged the figure over to the stall Buckle was hidden in and threw the man into it. He almost hit Buckle who had to move slightly to avoid him. The man lay there, making no sound.

"Close this door," said the black-haired man. "Find some torches and check this place out." They hurried to obey his orders.

Once the torches were lit, they began poking around the corners of the barn. One saw the cart and walked up to it to investigate.

"Hey, Urgallo, this cart still has stuff on it."

"What's in it? Maybe there's some food."

The entire band gathered around the cart as the man grasped the edge of the tarp and held it up. With the other hand, he raised his torch to see what was underneath.

Steel flashed, and it the next instant, he stood transfixed by Zabeth's sword. The torch tumbled out of his hand and came apart on the ground. Embers exploded and landed the wooden floor.

Zabeth shot out of the cart and yanked her sword from the bandit's body. She downed one more before they had even drawn. Mustering all his courage, Buckle yelled and rushed into the fight. His rusty sword wheeled above his head and he slashed at the nearest bandit who blocked his cut. Distantly, Buckle could hear Yazzle roaring and swinging his staff in the great whistling arcs that ended in meaty thumps.

Fortunately for Buckle, his opponent wasn't very good at combat. Being a bandit, he probably wasn't used to much opposition. Indeed if Buckle understood the theory of banditry at all, these men spent most of their energy arranging situations where they wouldn't have to fight so it made sense that they weren't used to it. Also, his opponent was tired and water logged, for Buckle soon slipped past the man's guard and impaled his shoulder. He screamed and toppled to the ground.

Buckle leapt over him and scanned the scene, now lit by the flickering light of the fire which was beginning to climb the posts and walls. He could hear their horses stomping and screaming in their stalls, and the bandits' horses were running up and down the length of the barn, stopping to kick with their hind legs.

"Zabeth, we're got to get out of here," he cried.

Zabeth was too busy to answer. She traded thrust and parry with a bandit who did appear to have some skill. Still, Buckle could see that she was wearing the man down. Yazzle and another bandit stood before each other, weapons held out.

Four men lay on the floor. The two at Zabeth's feet were obviously dead. Buckle's still writhed in pain and Yazzle's lay in a pool of blood but Buckle thought he could see the man breathing.

Urgallo, the leader, crouched over the urn which lay near the doorway. He mumbled softly and made strange motions with his hands. Buckle gripped his sword tighter and ran toward him.

Before he got there, the doors burst open again. Fierce white light blinded him, and a chill wind blasted past him. Intermingled with the howling and whistling of the wind, Buckle thought he heard the word, "Fire."

Spinning around, Buckle saw the wind, which glowed white, twisting itself around the fire which quickly went out. The bandits' horses screamed and bolted out the open door. Buckle could hear their own mounts screaming, trying to kick down their stalls.

Fed by the flames, the apparition grew and twisted itself faster and faster, but now it whirled around Buckle and the rest of his group. Inside the heart of the white wind, Buckle thought he could see shapes. Nothing distinct, but he caught glimpses of a pair of fiery red eyes and the glowing outline of a battle-ax.

Buckle suddenly felt cold. His limbs lost their feeling as the whiteness encircled him, growing in intensity, even as he grew colder. His sword dropped to the ground. With an effort, Buckle managed to look at his two fellow combatants. They too suffered as he did. Frost was forming on their brows and their weapons lay at their feet.

Urgallo called out a few words Buckle couldn't understand and the apparition's motions ceased. It hung in the middle of the room until Urgallo motioned it into a corner. Its flickering white light was the only illumination.

The scarred bandit strode into the middle of the room. He was unaffected but his men were as frozen as Buckle, Yazzle and Zabeth. He cast a murderous look at the white apparition.

"I said only the enemy, you blasted demon." The implacable apparition did not reply. Buckle thought he could taste the hatred the thing emanated. "What's the use of being master of a wooliman if it kills friend and foe alike?" He leaned over the two bodies beside the cart. "Can't blame you for these anyway. That one there got them." He stood up and walked over to Zabeth, whose eyes followed him.

"A woman are you?" He leaned closer and wiped the frost off her face. "I know you. But I wonder if you remember me?" He took off his cap to reveal a bald head. Scars and burns marred the pate, and the uneven edges of the sides where hair grew, were still singed.

Urgallo was the man who had tried to accost Krinseth on the night they had met her. Somehow Buckle wasn't surprised to find out he was a bandit.

"Tell me, does look as funny now as it did back them?"

"Funnier," Zabeth managed to croak, little flakes of frost floating out of her mouth as she said it.

Urgallo slapped her with the back of his hand. She fell backwards like a block of ice, unable to break her fall. Buckle could see her struggling to move. Urgallo cursed and doubled over, holding his hand.

"By all the demons in Skrike's Hell you're going to pay for that." He looked at Yazzle and then at Buckle, whom of course he also recognized.

"Well if it isn't the gallant knight? You old fool. I wonder if you'll be so brave when you don't have a woman around to protect you?" He spat and then set to work.

He dragged the three Delamerians into the stall in which Buckle had been hiding and tied them up. Beside them lay the prisoner, who turned out to be Bindle. He was conscious and watched them with eyes that Buckle felt were trying to communicate.

Then the bandit built another fire and dragged his three remaining men around it to thaw them out. The apparition stayed in its corner, waiting. Buckle could see its flickering white light infusing the barn. It shone far brighter than the fire Urgallo had made.

Buckle eventually heard some noises from the bandits, muttered curses, the stamping of feet. One of them finally managed to speak.

"Damnit, Urgallo, do you have to call that thing every time we get into a scrape?"

"You were losing."

"We'd have had them," said another voice.

"Sure you would have. Fools, a band of soft Delamerians, and you were letting them beat you. I've lost two good men tonight already and Delmatin doesn't look good."

"The one in the cart wasn't soft," said the first voice. "She got two of us before we knew what was happening."

"Yeah, and you keep quiet about that. I don't want it getting around that Urgallo's band was almost beaten by a woman. Understand?"

The two voices murmured assent.

"What are we gonna do to them Urgallo?"

"Kill them eventually," said Urgallo. "I can tell you though, that girl gets it slow."

"Why didn't you let the...thing kill them?"

"Because it would have killed you two at the same time.   Not that I care about your miserable lives, but I don't want to haul that damn urn around by myself."

"I wish you'd get rid of that thing," said the second voice in almost a whisper.

"It's my source of power.   It'll make us invincible."

"All four of us?"

"More will come when they hear what power I command," said the bandit.   "That old hermit squatting in his hut on the lake didn't know what he had.   Only I saw that spirit's true potential.   Now the hermit is dead and I have the power to make myself king of the wilderness between the mountains and the sea."

"I think the Sarondakis might have something to say about that."

"Fool, not even the Sarondakis can stop a wooliman."

"If you say so, Urgallo," said the second voice.   "But I don't like that thing."

"You're a nervous woman."

"But what about the Delamerians?   Why keep them alive any longer?"

"Because I want to question them," said Urgallo.   Buckle heard him get up and pace.   Bindle stared into Buckle's eyes.   He too, was listening.   "Think about it.   They're Delamerians, fat, spoiled and soft.   Why would they be heading east when there's war brewing?"

Buckle could imagine the two bandits looking at each other and shrugging.

"There must be a reason and a good one.   I think that maybe they're after some treasure."

"Do you think so?" said the first voice.

"I just said so didn't I?"

Just then a wailing scream pealed through the barn.   The third man with the injured shoulder had apparently thawed out.   Buckle could hear the other three grabbing him and trying to stop his thrashing.

"Buckle," Bindle whispered below the noise.   "Don't talk.   It hurts until you're totally thawed out.   Can you move your head?"

Stiffly, Buckle nodded.

"Look up."   Buckle did so and saw Krinseth, sitting like a cat in the hayloft above them.   She regarded them impassively and put a finger to her lips for silence.   Outside the wind blew and thunder boomed.

11

Buckle was desperately uncomfortable and every time he shifted to a new position it grew worse. The rope bit into his wrists. His muscles had stiffened up, and he was soaking wet from the thawing frost that had covered his body. The storm had abated somewhat and was now reduced to a steady driving rain that pattered on the roof of the barn and leaked, drops of it falling onto Buckle's bound hands. The apparition had been banished to whatever hell it occupied when not fighting Urgallo's battles for him, so now the barn was dimly lit by the dying fire.

One bandit had been left on watch. He sat on top of the urn, which had been moved against the wall, and dozed. Buckle could hear him snoring lightly. He could also hear the breathing of his companions tied up in the stall. None of them could sleep either. He sensed Zabeth behind him. She was a tightly wound spring of tension. Her breath had a fierce edge to it and small nasty words of violence were imbedded in her exhalations. Yazzle, also behind him, shivered with cold and fear.

He could only see Bindle, who had been able to sleep off and on. During the time he was awake he explained to them in a soft voice what had happened. This was between furtive glances at the guard and long pauses precipitated by any sound in the barn.

Bindle had been scouting about a half a day ahead of the main party when he came across the bandits' trail. Following it, he eventually came upon them. They were arguing over their plans for the immediate future. Urgallo and his supporters wanted to keep heading east, while another faction, led by a man named Bedwickian rebelled against the idea of heading straight into a Sarondaki army. Urgallo claimed that he was scared of no army and patted the top of the urn they had been lugging around. Bedwickian called Urgallo a fool and the two bandits fought.

They were pulled apart by the other men and the decision was put off until the morning. Bindle climbed a tree and prepared to watch the company all night in order to discover if they were headed east or west.

In the middle of the night, Bindle watched as Urgallo sneaked over to the urn and made a few hand gestures over it, while whispering some words. Slowly the white apparition formed around his rival. It glowed and pulsated furiously. The other bandits, awakened by the light and sound of Bedwickian's screams, backed away from the spectacle and from Urgallo who was laughing and shouting at Bedwickian, demanding to know who the fool was now.

Bindle, figuring it was safe to assume the bandits were headed east, sought to remove himself as far away from the grotesque scene as possible, but in doing so lost his balance and fell from his perch, making a huge commotion. He hung upside down with his feet caught in the branches. His arms flailed about, making a lot of motion and a great deal of sound. The laughing and taunting stopped which scared Bindle more than the falling. He heard an unintelligible command from Urgallo and then the air surrounding him grew cold and white.

"They spent half of the next day trying to beat out of me who I was and what I was doing spying on them. Then they moved on eastward passing this barn and then backtracking to it when the storm hit."

"You dropped the warning marker?" asked Buckle.

"Yes, I had managed to scrape some bark off a tree and mark it with my fingernails. Then I dropped it in the soft undergrowth when they weren't looking."

"Idiot," hissed Zabeth. "Allowing yourself to get caught. If you thought I was going to save your worthless skin..."

"I didn't think you'd do anything. I didn't think of you at all. You never entered my thoughts. What do you think of that?"

"Oaf!"

"Harpy!"

"Silence, both of you," warned Buckle. "Do you want to wake up the guard?"

"Where is Krinseth, that's what I want to know," muttered Zabeth.

As if in answer to her question the witch appeared above them. Buckle couldn't tell if she was standing just beyond them in the stall or if she were suspended above them like a spider. But her fingers, damp with rain, worked quickly and efficiently at untying Buckle's hands. Her voice sounded faint but he could understand every word.

"Sorry I didn't help you in the fight but there are certain precautions that need to be taken when a wooliman is in the area. And then I needed to be sure they were all asleep."

"The guard?" asked Zabeth.

"He's next to the door where it's more humid. I'm certain he won't awaken. The others are too dry and my spell is weak. I'd counsel you to be quiet until things start happening."

"What things?" whispered Buckle.

"No time to explain. But I will say one thing. The urn is the most important thing. What I do will merely be a diversion. One of you must destroy the urn."

"How?" asked Buckle.

"Any way will do. Just smash it and make sure the fire in the bottom goes out. I may be of some help there." Buckle's hands were untied and he worked at getting blood back into his fingers.

"Buckle," she said. "Are you all right?"

Buckle looked up at her, a little surprised at her concern. "I'm a little stiff, and I hope I don't catch cold in this damp, but otherwise I'm fine."

"Good, I would be...displeased if you were injured." She looked at him a moment longer and then seemed to vanish. Buckle couldn't see where.

As he untied the rest of his friends, Buckle wondered at Krinseth's last words. He knew very little about women. In his younger days he had called on a few of the ladies on the surrounding estates but nothing had ever come of it. One reason was his nebulous situation when it came to class. At that time it was clear he was being prepared to be Steward of Methliana, a job traditionally given to the heir, so it wouldn't have done to have courted the daughter of a menial laborer, or at least that's what everyone on the estate was telling him. At the same time not being connected to any land by blood, he couldn't court the daughters of the local landowners. That was what the local landowners told him. So in typical fashion, Buckle backed away from the dilemma, figuring it would solve itself one day.

Consequently, he hadn't worried about women for years. His brain was rusty when it came to figuring out what they were thinking and what any particular action meant. So when in the last few days, he found Krinseth's hand on his, as they rode beside each other in the cart or he caught her staring at him pensively, he hadn't the confidence to interpret the signs the way he suspected they should be read.

Also he was unsure about how he felt. Krinseth was an attractive woman but she could be so cold. Although they had been traveling together for weeks, he felt he barely knew her because she was so reluctant to talk about herself. He didn't understand her or her closed ways. And, he asked himself, how can you love someone you don't understand?

Buckle shrugged the question off as he removed the last rope from Yazzle's wrists. The bandits had feared the giant and had put a few extra coils around him. Only Zabeth had gotten more. Now they were all untied but still lying down in the stall, flexing stiff muscles and waiting.

The fire was now out and they lay in complete darkness. The barn creaked and moaned as it settled. They could hear their horses nickering and stomping in their stalls. One of the bandits snored intermittently, making pig-like grunts whenever he rolled over in his sleep. Outside the rain pelted the barn.

The damp rain smell bothered Buckle and he tried to remember if he had seen any mold in the barn. Just thinking about it, caused his chest to tighten up a little and he laid flat on his back and tried to relax. He thought about other things, comforting things.

Rain storms on Methliana were among his fondest memories. Not storms such as the one that hit the night Roduct left but gentle rains. They were called farmer's rains and they fell lightly and evenly. They gave the soil a chance to soak up the moisture. When he was a kid, he and the other youths would run naked through the rain. Buckle smiled, thinking of the fun he'd had, running and sliding through the mud or scooping up handfuls of rain and mud and pouring it on a friend's head which always started a grand water fight. Sora would be furious with them, and Buckle often caught miserable summer colds because of it, but the next time it rained, he'd be back out there.

Later of course, it was enough to sit on the porch and watch the rain. The sight of a huge lumbering thunderhead rolling across a dark threatening sky evoked a thrill of excitement. The thrill was abetted by that pre-storm smell which triggered a tingling that started in his fingers and ran up and down his back and shoulders. And when the storm hit and sheets of rain poured from the sky, Buckle would stand by the porch rail, close enough to get just the lightest sprinkling of rain and to feel the coolness of it.

A footstep. Buckle lifted his head and looked at the guard. Urgallo leaned over his lackey, holding a torch. He grabbed the man's shoulder and shook him. When there was no response, he shook him harder and hissed at him to wake up. The bandit remained asleep, his head flopping back and forth like a cloth doll.

Urgallo gave up trying to wake the man. He lifted the torch over his head to cast the light into the dark corners of the barn. Buckle and the rest had only just in time put their heads down and pretended to be asleep, as the light washed over them, hesitated for a few seconds, and then vanished. Buckle risked turning his head to look at Zabeth. She shook her head slightly.

Urgallo pushed the bandit off his seat on the urn and knelt next to it. His arms started their strange motions and he mumbled his incantations.

Outside the patter of rain began to fade. Buckle breathed carefully so as not to be heard. Whatever Krinseth was planning, she had better do it now.

With a sudden bang, the loft doors, just above the barn doors, flew open. Rain poured in and lightning lit up the sky, silhouetting the figure of Krinseth as she stood above the kneeling figure of Urgallo. The bandit chief stopped his mumbling and looked up at her.

"Urgallo, you are meddling with forces you don't understand," cried Krinseth over the rain and thunder.

Urgallo stood and shouted for his men.

Zabeth shot out of the stall, followed by Bindle. She dropped Urgallo with a flying kick and landed on the other side of him. Picking him up by his collar, she proceeded to pummel his face and shoulders. Bindle took on the other bandit who had been awakened by the ruckus. Urgallo's torch lay on the floor, lighting the scene in guttering yellow. But already Buckle detected a white glow showing around the edges of the fighters.

"The urn," cried Krinseth. "The urn."

Buckle rushed to the urn, motioning Yazzle to follow. Pushing it, Buckle strained his back muscles, surprised at how heavy it was.

Finally, both he and Yazzle managed to tip it over. The urn thudded to the ground and rocked back and forth. But the cap was sealed with wax and didn't come off. Buckle kicked it, hit it, tried to roll it into the wall to break it but nothing worked. The air glowed white around him and his fingers were numb with cold. The torch sputtered out.

"Back," cried Krinseth and the rain slanted through the loft door, dowsing Buckle and Yazzle. Buckle was still cold but he saw that the white glow had retreated to the back of the barn.

"The urn, Buckle," she cried. "Smash the urn."

Buckle crouched before the urn and grabbed both ends, straining to lift it. He couldn't get it off the ground. Yazzle shoved him out of the way and took both ends in his huge hands and then with cords of muscle popping out of his arms and neck, the giant lifted the urn first to his chest and then over his head. The wet porcelain slipped and threatened to slide out of his grip but Yazzle held on and held the urn above his head.

The moment hung suspended in time. Buckle lay to the side and watched as the painted surface of the urn, beaded with rain, rose and fell with Yazzle's breathing. Zabeth straddled Urgallo, paused in the act of strangling him, to watch Yazzle. Urgallo himself watched with horror, his mouth trying to form words. Bindle and his foe stood gasping for breath. On the other side of the barn, the white glow stood at bay. In its midst was the frost covered figure of the bandit Buckle had injured, his arm in a sling.

Above it all stood Krinseth, calm and terrible in the rippling white light. Her eyebrows were arched far above her eyes and her nose flared like a bull about to charge.

"Smash it," she said.

Muscles corded and the urn lifted up.

"No," pleaded Urgallo.

The urn came down with all the force Yazzle could muster. It hit the floor and shattered into thousands of fragments. Buckle turned and covered his eyes. When he looked again the shards were everywhere, glowing like sparks in the white light. A foul liquid, slightly reddish, with the consistency of runny glue, splattered the walls and floor as well as Buckle and Yazzle. Glowing coals, which had been in a compartment in the bottom of the urn, lay in the middle of the goo and the fragments.

Krinseth shouted some mystical words and gestured toward the mess. Obediently lightning flashed, thunder roared, and a torrent of rain poured through the loft door onto the coals, extinguishing them in a cloud of steam. Krinseth stood in the loft door, soaking from the rain.

"My power," cried Urgallo, throwing Zabeth off him and running to the remains of the urn. He picked up fragments and tried to scoop the stuff into a puddle at his knees, but it was hardening and wouldn't move easily.

Krinseth regarded him for a moment and then said. "My friends, clear the way. I cannot hold it much longer."

Buckle pulled Yazzle back into the stall where they had been tied up. Zabeth and Bindle, along with the man Bindle was fighting, scampered to the side of the barn. Urgallo was oblivious, preoccupied with the ruins of his nefarious dreams.

Krinseth lifted her head to face the white glow.

"Come," she said.

Urgallo looked up and then back at his former pet as it slowly came forward.

"No," he breathed. He stood up, trying to ward the apparition off with his forearm. "In Dalmar's name, call it off. Call it off."

"I do not control the wooliman," replied Krinseth.

Urgallo backed into the door, spun around and lifted the bar. He pushed the doors open and bolted out into the rain. The white glow followed in a flash, leaving little flakes of snow in its wake. Everyone left in the barn crowded around the entrance, watching the glow as it raced through the wood and then paused.

There was a scream, a horrible sound, cut short before it reached its crescendo. Then a moaning reached their ears, a low regretful lament. The rain stopped, suddenly it seemed to Buckle, and the air felt cool, maybe even cold. The glow grew in intensity and the moaning died. Then the glow flickered out and a blood boiling scream, fraught with hatred and terrible vengeance cut through the night.

It was over.

12

They let the two remaining bandits bury their fellows in the morning. It didn't take very long for them to dig the shallow graves since the ground was so wet from the storm. The hardest had been the one man who had been frozen to death by the apparition. It was the man Buckle had injured. By morning he was still frozen stiff in a sitting position and had to be buried that way in a slightly deeper grave. He was also too cold to touch with bare hands, so his surviving companions carried him to his grave behind the barn using strips of cloth to protect their hands. Bindle, who guarded them, even though they were too dispirited and frightened to try anything, told Buckle they had dropped the frozen corpse twice before they got it to the hole.

After that they filled in the graves without ceremony. Buckle gave the two men a couple days' worth of food and sent them westward on foot. Zabeth was all for making two more graves and filling them. If the Sarondakis caught them, she argued, they would tell them about the group. The last thing they needed was a raiding party chasing them. But Buckle maintained that they had seen no evidence of Sarondakis west of where they stood and it therefore should be safe to let them go. The bandits would travel west to Delamer, or until some army, headed for the war, pressed them into its ranks. Besides Buckle had seen enough death in the last few hours.

They had searched for Urgallo but couldn't find him. Buckle was, in a small way, relieved to hear that.

The cart had been badly burned, though most of the provisions were intact. Yazzle peered under it and said he thought the axle had been charred clear through. The spare he had used the night before as a weapon wouldn't fit. When Buckle had tested the sides of the cart they broke off in his hand. So the cart was abandoned and the provisions were loaded onto the two draft horses. Zabeth and Bindle, as guard and scout remained on horseback, while the rest walked. The wood was ending and they were entering the foothills of the Barriers. They would have had to abandon the cart soon anyway.

By mid-morning of their first full day on foot, Buckle's feet hurt. They had only been hiking for about two hours, following the mounted figures of Bindle and Zabeth who took turns riding ahead to scout out the winding goat path Bindle called a road. They had decided not to split up the group after their adventure with the bandits, so neither of them went more than a few hundred yards ahead.

Buckle pulled his pack up around his shoulders, realizing in the process that his back hurt too. He glanced at his two walking companions who led the pack horses. Neither displayed any outward signs of fatigue. Yazzle, young and strong, seemed not to feel fatigue as he marched forward, his eyes scanning the horizon. And Krinseth walked along the side of the road, not even breaking a sweat in the summer sun. Buckle put his head down and walked with renewed determination. In another hour he could respectably ask if anyone was ready for lunch. Inside his boots though, his corns were throbbing.

The rolling hills through which they traveled grew higher as the company made its way eastward until they eventually became the Barrier Mountains. The hills were covered with a kind of scraggly grass with little purple flowers dotting it. For farming, the soil was poor. The topsoil seemed to go down only a few inches. Here and there rocks poked through. This land seemed only good for grazing, and indeed they had seen several abandoned herds of goats and sheep mulling about the landscape, grazing idly and looking up at them as they passed. Later in the day Bindle had said he would slaughter a couple of them and dry the meat to add to their provisions. There were no inns anymore. They passed an estate house and every so often they found a herder's shack, but both had been looted, everything edible or of value was gone and everything else broken. Buckle again re-shouldered his pack. Heavy as it was, it felt disconcertingly light.

He quickened his pace a little and came up beside Krinseth, figuring the time would pass more quickly in conversation.

"When's the next storm?" he asked, looking up at the cloudy sky.

Krinseth looked up also but shook her head. "Two days. It will be a strong one, though not strong enough."

Buckle nodded. "I wanted to ask you something."

"I told you all trace of Roduct is gone from the tunic. I don't know where he is."

"That's not it," said Buckle. "I wanted to ask you about that thing in the barn."

"Ah, the wooliman." Krinseth frowned. "There are things even wise ones shy away from. Perhaps they do so because they are wise. The foolish never hesitate."

"What was that thing?"

"I had heard rumors that someone was roaming the eastern forest with a wooliman. Urgallo fit the description and he had the smell of fire magic about him."

"That was why you picked a fight with him?"

Krinseth glanced at Buckle, a slight smile playing on her lips. "Yes. If you had not interfered, I would have dealt with Urgallo and his pet in my own way."

"Why should it bother you if some bandit has a wooliman?"

She shrugged. "It's part of what I do."

Buckle could tell he wasn't going to get any more out of her on that subject.

"What exactly is a wooliman," he asked.

"No one knows for certain but I suspect that woolimen are the wretched souls of Sarondakis who have died under soowooli."

"Great Dalmar," said Buckle.

"That was certainly a Soowooli urn Yazzle destroyed. The coldness you felt was the wooliman eating the fire of your life. Soowooli is a fire magic."

"How long had he been dead?"

Krinseth shrugged. "No way to tell. It could have been a couple months or a couple of centuries. My guess is that this one was left over from Skrike's age, over three hundred years ago."

Buckle gave a low whistle. "No wonder it was angry."

"Angry and uncooperative," said Krinseth. "Urgallo's men blamed the wooliman's imprecision on his inexperience in handling it. But the spirit was growing in power and was just about ready to free itself. Soowooli works on the principle of heating blood but in a spirit the blood ties are weaker. Given time and enough life fire to devour ... it is a good thing we dispersed the wooliman's blood."

Buckle walked in silence for a while, pondering this new information. The world outside of Delamer was indeed a strange and terrible place. He looked at Yazzle, who walked beside them, listening but not commenting. What thoughts were going through that yellow head? Was Yazzle as homesick as Buckle? Buckle wanted nothing more right now, than to turn around and head for home. He had a feeling that his feet would hurt less if they were pointed the other way.

Zabeth rode down the path quickly, bringing up her horse on two legs to halt it.

"We found a well," she gasped.

"Where," asked Buckle.

"By a shack just over this hill. Bindle's there, guarding it."

"Guarding it? Why?"

"We found a recently abandoned camp there, a day or two old at most. Bindle thinks it may have been Sarondaki."

Buckle and Krinseth exchanged a glance.

"We've got to chance it. Lead us to the well."

Krinseth confirmed that the camp was indeed Sarondaki. She sensed their traces all over the litter that was strewn throughout the shack and around it. Standing in the middle of the yard, which was fenced in by a rickety wooden fence, Krinseth said she thought the Sarondakis had gone north toward the East Road. Bindle visibly relaxed although there was something about Zabeth's manner that was almost disappointed. She turned away, mumbling something about scouting out the immediate area.

"Bindle start bringing water out of the well and filling our water sacks," said Buckle. "Yazzle if you could fix lunch? Just some cold meat for now. I don't want to stay here long." Even though Krinseth was sure the Sarondakis weren't coming back, Buckle disliked this camp. It was almost as if he could sense the Sarondaki presence as well as Krinseth.

The well was little more than a hole in the ground with a bucket beside it, tied to a rope. Buckle doubted very much that he could have gotten his expanded middle through the opening. Two months ago, when the journey started, he definitely couldn't have. Buckle patted his stomach and reflected on the rigors of a traveling life. He then sat down, took his boots off and massaged his corns.

Bindle hauled up the first bucketful of water and was about to pour some of it into his water sack.

"Stop," said Krinseth, and she grabbed the bucket. Bindle cast Buckle a perplexed look which was answered with a shrug.

Krinseth stuck her hand into the water and closed her eyes. After a second, she said, "Poison, I thought I sensed it."

Buckle stood up and went over to inspect the bucket in his stocking feet. "How did you know?"

"Water is the source of my power," she said as if that explained it.

"All right," said Buckle. "Pour it out. We'll have lunch and move on. Maybe there's a stream around here that we..."

"No need for that," said Krinseth, and she handed the bucket to Bindle, motioning for him to hold it out away from his body, just at the height where she could comfortably get both hands into it. Buckle stepped forward and watched. Krinseth's brow furrowed in concentration and her hands shook with effort, causing the surface of the water to ripple but not splash.

The water became oily and was turning a greenish yellow. Little bubbles of ooze rose to the surface and exploded, spreading across the top instead of sinking to the bottom. When this activity had ceased, Krinseth said. "Get a spoon and scrape the poison off the surface. The water should be fine afterwards."

Yazzle rummaged through his pack until he found a spoon. Then he dipped it into the bucket. The ooze lying on top of the water had a fetid smell and Yazzle took pains not to touch it as he scooped spoonfuls of the loathsome stuff out of the bucket. When they were sure they had got all of the slime out of the bucket they filled the first water sack and then repeated the process until they had filled all five.

On the ground lay a foul puddle of stinking poison. They ate their lunch as far away from it as they could. Only Krinseth drank any water.

That night they camped within sight of the Barrier Mountains. After supper Buckle walked to the top of a hill, just west of their camp and got his first good view of the infamous range. They stood hazy and purple in the westering sun, a jagged horizon in the east. Between them and Buckle lay about another week's travel over rolling hills and sparse tree cover. The mountains themselves were covered at their bases by dark green skirts of evergreens.

Too far from home, thought Buckle. If he had known, back when this quest had started, that he'd be standing here right now, he'd have thought harder about coming. And we're still going on, he thought, we're not headed back. But Buckle knew Roduct was probably in those mountains. He may be dead or captured, or even a murderous traitor, Buckle no longer knew what to think, but he knew he had to find out. He would travel twice as far, endure many more hardships for a chance of restoring his life to the way it was.

"So is this view worth all the trouble you've gone to?" Buckle turned around to see Krinseth walking up the path behind him. The sun shone through her hair which was drawn tightly into a bun on the back of her head except for a few uncooperative strands that stood out like the occasional stand of trees on the hilly terrain around them. She wore that half smile, which like everything about her, hinted at knowledge only she knew.

"I would have liked to have come this way under different circumstances," replied Buckle. "I don't mind travel, as long as it's comfortable and I know when the journey will end."

"You're not adventurous," she said, standing beside him and taking in the view.

"Not in the least," said Buckle, turning back to the mountains.

Krinseth waved her hand at them. "Beyond those mountains the Ratog stretches for hundreds of miles. And on the other side of it are other kingdoms, lands where they call the Sarondakis westerners. They look different from you and your friends and do things in strange ways. Doesn't that intrigue you?" She looked at him.

"If somebody wanted to go there and write a book about it, I'd read it, or if these people wanted to buy my corn and could assure me safe passage, I'd sell it to them. Otherwise, I say let them live their lives and I'll live mine."

Krinseth chuckled. "A typical Delamerian attitude."

"You don't approve?"

"It's not my place to approve or disapprove. I even understand."

"Really?"

"I felt that way for a long time. I thought I could just stay at home and let the world continue without me."

"What happened?" Buckle turned to look at her.

"The same thing that happened to you. The world came to me and interfered in my life."

"Where were you born, Krinseth?" Buckle stared at her. Her high cheekbones shone orange and red in the setting sun. Her blue eyes reflected the light and seemed to turn inward.

"No one remembers," she replied. "But I consider my home to be on the shores of Lake Zalphlyn, many weeks march to the south."

"The lake in the story? Where Dalmar met Methlyn and her sister, Zalphlyn?"

"Yes," whispered Krinseth, her features becoming sad suddenly. "That is where my power is the greatest."

"Don't you ever dream of going back?"

"Someday perhaps," she said and she smiled sadly. "Anyway, there are things I have to do first." And with that she turned to view the mountains again, ending the conversation. Lightly, before he knew what she intended, she slipped her hand into his.

"The Sarondakis are coming." The words, spoken calmly but with conviction by Krinseth brought everyone awake instantly.

"How can you tell?" asked Bincle from the edge of the camp where he stood guard.

"From where?" hissed Zabeth.

"The north."

"How far?"

"Close. We have only a few minutes."

Zabeth pulled out of her sleeping roll and kicked dirt into the embers of the fire. The light of the moon shone silvery and bright.

"Everybody hurry. Grab only what you need and get going."

They scrambled in the moonlight, grabbing packages and pulling straps over shoulders. Buckle's stuff was more widespread than usual. Earlier in the evening he had been showing Krinseth his last two doses of jimsonweed to see if she could tell if they were still good. He hadn't needed it since they had met Krinseth. Whenever he had an attack, she'd take him aside and clear his chest, just as on that first night. The remaining supply seemed stale to Buckle but Krinseth had assured him it was all right.

He felt the ground around his sleeping roll, trying to find it. His fingers only encountered sparse grass and dusty ground. He stood up, panic almost causing an attack right then and there. He tore around the camp, picking up the same bundles he had searched five minutes ago and throwing them down in disgust. Sleep still numbed his mind, confusing him.

"What is it, Master Buckle?" Yazzle knelt beside him.

"My jimsonweed. I can't find it."

"Come on Master Buckle, we have to go," whispered Zabeth. She and the others stood at the edge of the camp.

"I need my jimsonweed. You go on. I'll catch up."

Zabeth hovered at the edge of the stand of trees they had camped next to, uncertain. They heard voices coming from the north.

"Go," said Krinseth to Zabeth. "You can't reason with him like this. He won't leave without the jimsonweed." Zabeth and Bindle shot into the trees. Krinseth ran up to Buckle and grabbed his shoulder.

"Buckle, give me your amulet."

"What," said Buckle, his hand going to his amulet. "Why?"

"So I can find you." Yazzle was rolling up Buckle's sleeping roll and packing his other things. "Hurry."

Buckle pulled the amulet off his neck and handed it to her. She disappeared. "Hurry Buckle, find it quickly and follow us. I care about you." The disembodied words came to his ears, as he frantically continued his search.

Finally his hand fell on the small package of herbs. He opened it and sniffed it to make sure and then he stuffed it in his belt and stood. He shouldered his pack and called to Yazzle who was still searching the other end of the camp.

"Let's go Yazzle. I found it."

Yazzle picked up his load and they started to run. But their eyes were blinded when two torches appeared. They were held by giant sized men. Two more giants holding spears came forward out of the light and motioned to them to drop their loads. Letting his pack fall to the ground Buckle looked over at Yazzle and tried to silently communicate how sorry he was.

So these were Sarondakis, thought Buckle. The first thing he noticed was how much they resembled Roduct.

13

Krinseth sat on the ground, watching the sun as it clawed its way up the Barriers in a light show of orange and red. For once, the spectacle failed to move her. In her hand she turned Buckle's amulet over and over. Her brow furrowed as she concentrated on the traces left behind on the amulet by its owner.

He had been captured. That much she knew, and by Sarondaki. His image was almost completely obscured by fire magic. She got the vague idea they were heading east but she could have guessed that. And Yazzle was probably with him.

She looked at the amulet again. Its black triangle absorbed the sunlight. The insignia, cast in relief, was a rampant scorpion, its tail poised to strike over a field dotted with wheat bundles on the right and a field of five pointed stars on the left. Krinseth had seen many like it in her time. The scorpion was a common motif in the east on both sides of the Barriers where the nasty pests were so common.

Somewhere in the distance she could hear Bindle and Zabeth bickering. The fools, she thought, arguing when there still may be Sarondakis about. Krinseth briefly considered rejoining them but then decided against it. She hadn't the patience, or indeed, the knack Buckle had for keeping peace between the two. Krinseth suspected she would have dismissed them both by this time if she had been Buckle.

She had nothing against Zabeth. The girl was quite capable actually, intelligent, skilled with a sword and she had that mental toughness warriors need to live a life of violence and blood. She won't be green for long, thought Krinseth. If anything Zabeth was a little too strident, no doubt the result of being a woman in a man's profession. She tended to make the road more difficult than it needed to be.

Bindle on the other hand was the type of male Zabeth would be facing all her life. He was arrogant, conceited and sure of his superiority. And he wasn't even as bad as most. He was secure in his imagined dominance over her. One day, and soon, thought Krinseth, with a smile, he was in for a shock. Zabeth was far more capable than he.

Buckle puzzled her in some ways. Humble to a fault, he claimed no talents or ambitions. Yet he was undeniably the leader of his group without being the strongest, most skilled or even the most intelligent. He saw those qualities in others and used them to every one's advantage. Personalities which seemed to be stronger, Zabeth's, Bindle's, and Krinseth had to admit it, even her own, bowed before his for no other reason than he made sense. It was a kind of leadership that Krinseth had never seen before, and she'd been around many leaders in her time. Buckle for instance, was completely different from Dalmar, who led by daring and sheer physical bravery, the qualities that were his eventual downfall. Of that difference Krinseth was infinitely glad. She had never liked Dalmar even before the end, and had no wish to see Buckle share the same fate. Although, she thought guiltily, Buckle was probably going to the place where Dalmar had met his end. Still Dalmar had probably died in some desperate ploy to escape or kill Skrike. Buckle would do what he had to do and no more.

The more she thought about it the more sure she was that Buckle was the key to stopping Skrike. He had a weak-seeming outside that would disarm his enemies and a nugget of strength within that would come out just at the right time. In a way his being captured by the Sarondakis was fortunate, for now they would take him deep into the heart of their land, far deeper and faster than he could have gone himself. And time was becoming a factor.

She sighed and stood up, still holding the amulet. She did not envy him the trip.

"This is your fault."

"How is it my fault," cried Bindle, hands on his chest and leaning forward. Bindle was close to death, thought Zabeth. Oh, he stood and breathed and his blood ran through his veins well enough. But he was about one arrogant comment away from having an arm's length of steel through his gut. Zabeth's hand itched for the touch of her sword's pommel.

"You were on watch. You should have seen them."

He threw his hands up in the air, making inarticulate sounds from the back of his throat. "How could I have seen them? Even Krinseth didn't sense them with her magic."

"The witch betrayed us," said Zabeth. The comment sprang out automatically, born of Zabeth's dislike of the witch and her need to blame Bindle for Buckle's capture. Even in her excited state of mind, Zabeth could see there was no evidence in the claim.

"Now you're talking like a crazy woman." Bindle backed away with his palms held out when Zabeth took a step toward him. "It's more like she saved us."

"She didn't save Buckle." Zabeth clenched her teeth, biting back the emotion that almost cracked her voice.

"No she didn't and believe me I'm sorry. I liked Buckle. But," he looked around the small hollow they stood in. "She hasn't joined up with us so maybe they got her too. You think of that?"

"What's your point?"

"My point is that she's capable of protecting herself and Buckle if need be. She proved that against those bandits." Zabeth wanted to scream. She wanted to turn on her heels and run after the Sarondakis, yelling Buckle's name at the top of her lungs.

"So," continued Bindle, unaware of the earthquake building in front of him, "We should head west and find a company of the army to join..."

"You can do what you want. I'm going to rescue Buckle."

"You can't."

"I took an oath."

"Look," explained Bindle, "the Sarondakis have got him."

"I know that," shouted Zabeth.

"Will you be quiet? They still may be around." He paused for a second, listening. "I know this is hard for you but you have to understand. There are only two of us against a party that could be as many as twenty. That's twenty men who are bigger than us and stronger than us."

"You're afraid."

"I'm not afraid. I just don't want to throw away my life uselessly," he said, a slight rise of emotion cracking his veneer of calm.

"Our best plan of action is to head west and join the army, and hope Krinseth can rescue him."

Zabeth stared balefully at Bindle for what seemed like hours, before she leaned over and grabbed her gear. "You do what you want Bindle. I'm going east after Buckle." She stalked toward her horse which was tied with Bindle's to a scraggly tree a little way down the hollow.

"Now you listen here young miss," shouted Bindle, his voice going down in pitch in an attempt to sound authoritative. "We are going west until we find an army and that is that. I have made my decision."

Zabeth stopped in her tracks. Her gear slipped out of her fingers and clattered to the ground. Suddenly she felt a calm, the calm that comes before action. Aware of every movement her body made, she turned. "What?"

"You heard me. Buckle's gone, so I'm the leader, and I decide where the expedition goes."

"You, the leader?" Zabeth's voice was flat and cold.

"Of course, I'm the man."

Zabeth drew her sword and advanced on Bindle who backed away, holding his hands out.

"Now there's no need for that. Put your sword away. There's a good girl."

"Draw," said Zabeth, feinting a thrust at Bindle's midsection.

"I'm not going to fight you, Zabeth," he said, retreating up the hollow. "It wouldn't be fair. I'm a man."

"I killed two men in the barn. Draw."

"Yes, but you see, you had the advantage of surprise there, and they were simple, untrained highwaymen. I'm a highly trained warrior."

He tripped over a rock and sprawled backwards. Getting up, he dusted himself off.

"You're a coward," intoned Zabeth, thrusting again, this time at his head.

"I am not. Nobody wants to fight more than I do. It's just that you have to pick your spots and..."

"Your sword, you yellow dog," roared Zabeth.

"All right," said Bindle, halting his retreat and reaching for his sword. "I'll teach you a lesson or two. But when this is over just remember, you asked for it."

At the instant his blade cleared the scabbard, Zabeth was on him with a combination thrust and cut, which to her surprise, he parried. Then she showered him with a blistering onslaught of cuts, thrusts and two handed swipes, driving him to the top of the hollow. His parries were slow, and he got nicked a few times, but Zabeth realized that Bindle was a first class swordsman. Not as good as Grazzle, of course, but in the same class.

When her attack was played out, he was bent almost double, looking up at her with wide eyes. "You're pretty good, if only all flash," he said between gasps. "But now I'll show you how it's done."

He charged her, feigning a thrust to her left and turning it to the right at the last moment. A good move, but Zabeth saw it coming and knocked it aside effortlessly. His next few combinations were, thought Zabeth, imaginative and the execution was crisp and sharp. But there was nothing there that old Grazzle hadn't drilled her in a thousand times. He was good. Good enough to live, decided Zabeth. When a suitable opening came, she smacked him across his brow with the pommel of her sword.

He toppled backwards with a cry, dropping his sword and bringing his hands to the wound over his eye. It was beginning to bleed. He sat on the grass, cursing as Zabeth strode past him. She sheathed her sword and said, "Maybe I'll see you again sometime, Bindle."

"Wait," he said, getting up and scrambling for his sword, "I'm going with you."

"I thought you didn't want to throw your life away uselessly," said Zabeth, picking up her gear and walking toward her horse.

"I can't leave a woman out in the wilderness alone," explained Bindle, catching up to her. "I'm a warrior. I have a code."

They were well on their way before Zabeth could stop laughing.

14

Buckle stumbled, and before Yazzle could catch him, he flopped to the ground like a sack of corn. Too tired to even lift his arms, his face smacked the ground with full force. Weakly, he spit dirt out of his teeth. Yazzle lifted Buckle's head slightly to ease his breathing. He then tore a strip of cloth from his shirt and wiped the mud off Buckle's face. Around them, the other prisoners in the caravan lowered themselves to the ground. Most looked drawn and exhausted. Yazzle could see blood staining the backs of an unlucky few who didn't move fast enough to suit the whip bearing Sarondakis. All the prisoners moved slowly and painfully.

The Sarondakis had been driving them mercilessly for two weeks, and the pace was killing Buckle. He had used his last dose of jimsonweed on the third night when the guards had threatened to kill him if he didn't stop coughing. In the nights since, Yazzle had seen Buckle fingering the dwale. Once he had taken a pinch of it and brought it up to his mouth. He wasn't even going to bother smoking it. Fortunately he stopped before Yazzle could interfere. Yazzle wished he could get the stuff away from him.

The troop of ten Sarondakis that had captured them, had marched them up to the East Road where they joined a prisoner caravan of a hundred or so men. Most of them were soldiers. They were marched under lash and other terrible inducements to wherever they were now. Yazzle guessed they must be on the eastern side of the Barriers. They had traveled the East Road with only a small detour around Unity which Yazzle gathered had not yet fallen somehow.

The Sarondakis would not let the prisoners slow them down. When a prisoner died along the way, little time was wasted, as the guards made sure he was dead by shoving a spear into his side. This effectively discouraged anybody from trying to feign death. Then the body was tossed over to the side of the road, which, when they were in the mountains meant a considerable drop.

Yazzle had, at first urged Buckle to keep pace, and then carried him as his attacks grew worse and exhaustion came over him. Yazzle had about worn himself out with the effort but was proud and relieved that Buckle had yet to taste the lash.

Yazzle could feel the painful scars on his own back whenever he stretched. Compared to these devils, the overseer on his old estate was a baby whipping a string. Sarondaki whips were tough leather, soaked in water and then dried in the sun to make them hard. Barbs were braided into the tails to bite into flesh and rip it. He had heard the Sarondaki guards refer to them as 'Raganorth surplus." Yazzle didn't know much about Raganorth except that his mother used to tell him she'd send him there if he was bad. He'd also heard it called "Skrike's Hell." Yazzle wondered if that was where they were going.

Buckle groaned and shifted onto his back, Yazzle rushed to make him comfortable. Bunching their packs into a pillow, he placed them under Buckle's head. Buckle lay on the ground, trying to slow his breathing. A couple of times in his fitful sleep he had called out for Krinseth.

"We're stopped for the night, I think," whispered Yazzle. They had stopped in some kind of village. The huts stood in a circle around the road. They were made of some kind of gray wattle, and for the most part their outward appearance gave no clue as to their function, although Yazzle did recognize a stable when they entered the village. Everybody Yazzle could see, except for the prisoners, was Sarondaki.

Surrounding the village, as far as the eye could see, were mountains, giant blocks of earth and stone, taller than Yazzle thought things could be. Delamer was as flat as a newly laid wooden floor compared to them. When they first entered the mountains, Yazzle had almost panicked, thinking the behemoths would topple over on him at any second. But after a while, when they didn't, Yazzle decided he rather liked them, even if it was a little more tiring always climbing up and down. But if he dawdled to stare, a lash would kiss his back, and he'd hurry on, remembering the circumstances that brought him here.

123

Another prisoner caravan was being marched into the village and it was halted across from Yazzle and Buckle's group. Yazzle looked over at them. They looked much the same as his own group, a collection of exhausted men and some women lying on the ground, trying to get comfortable. They wore rags and their backs were scarred. Most were soldiers but some had obviously been civilians, people who didn't start west in time, Yazzle guessed.

The aroma of the Sarondaki cooking fires came to Yazzle's nose. He strained his neck to see where the cooks had set up. At the other end of the square, two Sarondaki women, in their sand colored robes, were pouring the unspeakable slop they called food into a cauldron of boiling water. The fire was uncomfortably far away, thought Yazzle. By the time they got to him and Buckle, they'd be making the portions smaller to make the food last. The prisoners at the end would be served the dregs at the bottom of the cauldron and their portions would be cold. The stuff, which resembled a liquefied form the goop the Sarondakis used to make their huts, was barely palatable hot. Cold it lay on the tongue like a slimy dead reptile and then churned in the stomach like an indigestible octopus. More than once he had seen the cooks toss bugs and various weeds into the mess. They spat into it too.

But Yazzle ate every bite of it and forced Buckle to do the same. When he could, Yazzle slipped to the side of the road to gather what sparse grasses and berries he could to supplement their awful diet. He wasn't familiar with most of the plant life in the area so he mainly took what he saw the Sarondaki guards and the other prisoners eat. For the most part the guards let them forage, as long as they didn't leave the road or hold up the caravan. If you wandered too far or took too long you got a lash and were forced to drop your food.

Most of their guards were beasts, merciless bastards who were easy with a shove or the lash. They delighted in playing cruel tricks on the prisoners such as offering a portion of their own rations, which to Yazzle's mind were only slightly less disgusting than the prisoners' and then just when the unfortunate victim was about to eat, taking it away and giving him a whipping for his impertinence.

A few of the guards were less cruel. They did what they had to do, of course, but no more. The prisoners quickly learned which were which, and the "good" guards were constantly petitioned with requests for indulgence such as extra time to make a rest stop or a little extra food if they were sick. But even among the less lash-happy guards such favors were rarely granted.

When it finally came, Yazzle's meal was every bit as indigestible as he'd thought it'd be. After he had scraped his bowl clean with his fingers he fed Buckle, who after one taste tried to refuse to eat but Yazzle made him. He would scoop the glop up in his fingers and if necessary open Buckle's mouth and put it in. Sometimes he would have to force Buckle to chew and even swallow. It was just like feeding a child, and Yazzle wanted to cry at the necessity of it. But Buckle was delirious now. He rarely spoke and made no sense when he did. When not marching or being carried, he lay on the ground wheezing.

The bowls were collected before Yazzle was finished feeding Buckle. Yazzle had to scoop the remaining food out of the bowl and finish feeding it to Buckle out of his hand. Usually at this time the prisoners were allowed to sleep. Today, however, after the bowls were stowed, the prisoners were rousted and forced to stand up. The few moans of protest were stifled by shoves and the cracks of whips.

When Yazzle saw what was happening, he grabbed Buckle by the shoulders and picked him up. His knees quivered and gave out but Yazzle supported him with a strong arm across his shoulder.

"You must stand, Master Buckle," he whispered. "They're using their whips."

Buckle looked up at Yazzle, his eyes lined with mucus. Yazzle feared he wouldn't comprehend, but finally, understanding sparked in those eyes and the knees held.

The guards were forcing the prisoners into a line. The ragged unfortunates stumbled and slouched. Most were weaving on their feet. When they were all standing, the guards stood at attention themselves. Yazzle saw them cast an occasional glance toward the far end of the square. On the other side of the square, a similar scene was being played out with the other prisoner caravan.

Finally an important looking Sarondaki with a retinue of aides and guards strode into the square. He was older than most Sarondakis, Yazzle had seen and better dressed. His cloak, sand colored like the rest, was trimmed in black and had an abstract pattern woven into it. Underneath he wore leather breeches and chain mail. At his side was a long broadsword. His aides were similarly attired if not as grandly.

The resplendent group was approached by the leaders of the two prisoner caravans and some words were exchanged which Yazzle couldn't hear and wouldn't have been able to understand if he had.

Then the group moved forward. They walked slowly along the line of prisoners Yazzle was in, the caravan leaders commenting on various things to the important looking Sarondaki who nodded almost mechanically at the comments, every once in a while asking a question.

We're being reviewed, thought Yazzle. This man is some kind of important leader and he is deciding our fate. Maybe this was even Skrike himself. Yazzle's own knees trembled at the thought. He looked over at Buckle but there was no sign he had even noticed the figure, whoever it was. When he looked back the group was almost to his position in line.

The guards nearest to them growled threats and their hands went meaningfully to their whips. The prisoners, in response, straightened out the line. Yazzle gently pulled Buckle back a half step, thinking to keep him inconspicuous. If this important person noticed a sick prisoner, he may have him killed to save food. Yazzle had seen worse things happen in the last two weeks.

The important Sarondaki and his entourage came up to Yazzle's place in line. The caravan leaders were explaining away, when suddenly the figure stopped. Yazzle held his breath as the important Sarondaki looked right at him and then walked up to him, the leader of Yazzle's prisoner caravan at his heels. The important Sarondaki looked down at Yazzle which made him uncomfortable since not many people could. He looked first at Yazzle's face, then at his forearms and legs, assessing him in the same way he'd seen Buckle assess cattle back on Methliana.

The Sarondaki spoke in the harsh guttural tones of his native language. Yazzle's blood froze. He looked around in a panic at the guards. The leader of the prisoner caravan leaned over and said something to the figure who nodded.

"So you are not Sarondaki, eh?" said the important looking figure, now speaking Dernian. "You're big enough to be a warrior, and more than one Sarondaki has sought to escape us by disguise. Still..." He squinted as he examined Yazzle's face. "I can see that your cheekbones are not as pronounced as ours and no warrior would have such fat flabby skin." He pinched Yazzle's biceps and made a face of disgust.

"Are you Skrike, sir," croaked Yazzle. The caravan leaders and other members of the Sarondaki's entourage seemed somehow frightened at the question. They cast nervous looks at each other. One

126

of the guards with the prisoner caravan drew his whip and started for Yazzle.

"Westerner scum, you'll speak only when the Warlord tells you."

But the Warlord waved him off. He smiled and then broke into an ugly laugh. When he did this the others around him laughed too. "No, I am not Skrike," he said, "I am merely Marduct, Chieftain of the Eastern tribes and Warlord for this glorious re-conquest of the west. Who are you?"

It felt like Yazzle's heart would beat so hard it would tear a hole in his chest and leap out. "I am Yazzle, a Delamerian."

Marduct thought about this for a moment and then said, "You are a long way from home, Delamerian. I wonder what has brought you this far?"

"We could find out Warlord," offered the caravan leader, eyeing Yazzle belligerently.

"No need," said Marduct, holding up a restraining hand. "In a few months, our troops will be marching into his homeland and whatever reason he has for being here will be irrelevant." The others around him nodded.

"Yazzle of Delamer, since our chat has been so pleasant, I'll let you know your fate. You are to be taken to the Castle Skrike, where incidentally you may well get a chance to meet Skrike if you're lucky or perhaps the better word is 'unlucky.'" The Sarondakis in the entourage and with the prisoner caravans laughed. "Once there, you and your fellow prisoners will be forced to mine coal for the war. This coal will be used to make steel for our unbreakable swords. You are fortunate. We have worse places to send you and worse things you could be doing."

"Thank you sir."

Marduct laughed until he was well out of earshot.

When he got through inspecting Yazzle's line of prisoners, Marduct worked his way up the other line across the square. Only one other time did he stop to closely inspect a single prisoner. It was a tall figure, almost directly across from them. He wore a hood that covered his features. Marduct walked up to him and the tall man tried to turn away. But the Sarondaki Warlord grabbed him by the shoulder and spun him forward. Then Marduct yanked the hood off the man's head.

Yazzle gasped. It was Roduct. The face was thinner than Yazzle remembered and caked with grime but the features were undeniable. This was Yazzle's lord and master, a mere prisoner like himself. Roduct, now that he had been recognized, stood up straight and looked the Sarondaki Warlord in the eye. Guards came up behind him and whipped him but he didn't flinch. They kicked him and hit him, but he remained standing. The only expression on Roduct's face throughout this was one of steady defiance, even when Marduct joined in the activity by spitting on him and slapping him.

Yazzle's throat tightened and he swallowed. For that one moment, it all seemed bearable, the endless marching, the sickening food, the lash. Yazzle had always been grateful to Roduct and respectful, holding him in the awe peasants properly showed to royalty. But until that moment, it was all form and duty. None of it came from his heart. But watching his lord face a terrible enemy and show no trace of fear, even though the fate awaiting him was much worse than the one Yazzle was looking forward to, brought that duty to life. For the first time Yazzle felt love for Roduct, like he had felt for Buckle from the start, and fierce loyalty.

But the new contents of his heart made it brittle, and it shattered when the guards seized Roduct and dragged him into the space between the two caravans. Yazzle looked at the guards, standing in a line in front of the prisoners. They were armed with sword, bow and whip. Roduct was beyond Yazzle's help. He squeezed his eyes shut to hold in the tears.

"Lord Roduct." It was a breathy whisper from a clogged throat. Yazzle opened his eyes and looked down to see that Buckle had recognized the Lord. "Lord Roduct," he repeated. Yazzle laid a restraining hand on his master's arm. But Buckle yanked his arm away and started waving. Fortunately his voice was too weak to carry very far. There was no telling Marduct would have done.

But the nearest guards heard and saw. Buckle showed every indication of walking right up to Roduct and ending his quest. Yazzle almost panicked as the whips came out. He grabbed Buckle by the shoulders and forced him back in line.

"Let go...fool," Buckle said, struggling against Yazzle's grasp. "Can't you...see? That's...Lord Roduct." He gasped for breath every few words.

"Master, you must stay in line." Yazzle held tighter as a guard broke rank and approached.

"They're going to use their whips," pleaded Yazzle.

The guard strode up to Buckle. Fortunately, he was one of the good guards who warned before he struck.

"Back in line, prisoner."

Buckle stood confused for a second, looking at the guard, as if for the first time. The guard held up his whip menacingly.

"Master Buckle, please."

Buckle wavered for a second, his eyes going from the guard to Roduct and back again. Finally he seemed to grasp the situation and stepped back in line, watching Roduct intently. The guard went back to his place in line.

The quest was over. Now all they had to do was survive.

Meanwhile in the middle of the square, Roduct was being forced to his knees by two burly warriors. Marduct stood before him, a resplendent contrast to Roduct's raggedness. The Sarondaki warlord spoke loudly in the desert tongue, a harsh guttural sound which Yazzle couldn't begin to understand, although he did pick out Roduct's name several times. Roduct strained against his captors. Yazzle could see the veins popping out of his neck. Marduct laughed and casually walked over to Roduct and smacked him with the back of his hand.

Down at the end of the line another entourage had arrived. This group was headed by a strangely clad Sarondaki. He was smaller than most and wore a costume. It sat on his back like a hooded cape and resembled a scorpion. The legs stuck out the front of the cape. They were made of some kind of stiff material. Hanging by the sides, were the pincers. The head with its many eyes was pulled over the man's head. Yazzle could see the opening that allowed the man to see. Behind him, stretching back six feet was the tail. It looked convincing; the segments were hard and covered with bristles. And at the end was a gleaming black sting, a foot long and barbed. Behind this figure came four young looking warriors carrying an urn like the one Yazzle had destroyed in the barn.

The costumed man, who Yazzle took to be some kind of priest, stopped in front of Roduct. The Delamerian Lord looked up at him with defiance. Standing perfectly still, the priest regarded the prisoner.

With a motion, Marduct stepped aside and the guards holding Roduct grabbed his left arm and forced it out in front of him, palm up. The priest also made a motion and one of his aides reverently removed the sting from the tail. Never taking his eyes from Roduct, the priest accepted the sting and lightly curled his fingers around its hilt. Yazzle could see Roduct fighting, straining against the guards who held him.

Two more rushed in to help when Roduct almost broke their hold. The four could barely contain him and still force his left arm out.

The priest started moaning, a strange low chanting that grew in pitch and intensity. His feet shuffled from side to side until the energy of the chant seemed to force him into the air, the sting held above his head, and the tail of the costume swinging behind him. After a series of spectacular leaps, the priest dropped to his hands and knees and scooted back and forth across the ground. The tail was rigged with some kind of string or wire which caused it to curl upwards over the man's torso. He looked very much like a man-sized scorpion, jittering and dancing before Roduct.

Finally the chant stopped and the priest stood up again, still holding the sting. He lifted it up and circled it over his head three times. After the last revolution it came down and bit into the palm of Roduct's hand. He inhaled sharply at the puncture and then gasped as the barbed point came out again.

Immediately the warriors, carrying the urn, opened it and brought it under Roduct's dripping hand. The blood fell into the urn as Roduct struggled to pull his hand away. The four guards held him until the priest intoned a few words and Roduct's form went slack. Then the guards let go and Roduct dropped to the ground.

Marduct stepped forward and commanded Roduct, who stood up on shaky knees. The blood still dripped from his hand. The urn was sealed and taken away. Marduct again barked out a few words and slowly Roduct turned and walked away with the guards who had been holding him. They went in the direction that Marduct and the priest had come from earlier.

Yazzle looked over at Buckle. He saw that tears had made trails through the grime caking his face.

15

Zabeth hated to admit it but Bindle was actually proving useful. He nosed his horse along the path ahead of her. Around them the mountains rose, their crests poking through the clouds. The path was narrowing again and soon, she knew, Bindle would tell her they'd have to dismount and lead the horses. He knew the mountains, Zabeth thought. A couple of times she had almost made a misstep or some other kind of mistake that would have landed her at the bottom of some ravine or under a ton of boulders and he had stopped her.

But he was so insufferable about it. He didn't say anything, but every time he stopped her from erring, he put that silly half smirk on his face. One of these times she'd have to make sure that he noticed that there were a lot of perils she had avoided, things that Grazzle had told her about. She'd also bring to his attention the fact that she never made the same mistake twice. In a few more days, she was confident that she'd be able to move as quickly and efficiently as he did. More so, she thought.

Bindle stopped and looked further down the trail. "We'll have to get off here and lead the horses."

"Are you sure this trail parallels the road?"

"Of course, we used it many times on patrols. It takes you right into the eastern foothills about a half day's march south of the East Road. I remember once..."

"I don't care to hear it," snapped Zabeth. She had grown tired of his endless stories. Bindle was maybe five years older than her, and yet he had this wealth of experience. She hadn't seen or done anything before this trip. Those men in the barn had been the first persons

131

she'd ever killed. It had been quick, and when it came down to it, easy. She hadn't had time to think about it. The first man had pulled up the tarp and the next instant he was dead. The instant after that the second man was dead too. At that point the little doubt in the back of her mind, she hadn't even known it was there, vanished. She was good at what she wanted to be. She could kill. Not that she reveled in carnage. In fact, she hadn't liked having living blood on her blade and had cleaned it off at the first opportunity. And when it was all over and nobody was looking, she had inspected the bodies, examining their faces. She wanted to remember them. The taking of life, old Grazzle used to say shouldn't be done lightly. Zabeth knew they had been in a dangerous predicament, and killing had been the price of getting out of it. She didn't feel bad about killing the two men. They'd have done the same to her. But the loss of the two lives took a certain edge off her moment of victory, the moment when she first became a warrior. She made sure that she'd always remember those two faces.

"You might want to get off there," said Bindle. "There's more room." He slipped out of his saddle, deftly twisting his body so that he landed in front of his horse, there being no room to the side.

"I can get off a horse anywhere you can," said Zabeth nudging her mount just behind his and dismounting in the same fashion. It wasn't a good thing to do, and immediately she could hear Grazzle's voice in her head saying not to take stupid chances. It was a speech she'd heard more than once from him. Bindle shrugged his shoulders and clicked his teeth at his horse, guiding it along the trail.

"It goes on like this for a couple hours. Then there's a ledge where we can camp," said Bindle.

"If it's suitable," mumbled Zabeth. This was a strange way of communicating. She couldn't see Bindle unless the trail bent to the left. Most of the time all she could see was the rump of his horse with his voice apparently coming out of it. The effect amused her.

"What do you mean if it's suitable? It's a camp. We used it all the time."

"Did it occur to you that someone else may be using it?"

"Well I'm sure the Sarondakis don't know about it, so whoever would be using it would be friendly."

"I don't want to run into anybody."

"For Dalmar's sake, why not?"

"Because I don't want anybody getting in the way of my rescuing Buckle."

"And you won't accept any help?"

"Why should a company of Barrier Scouts help me rescue him?"

There was a pause while Bindle considered this. "They won't follow you into the desert, only I'm stupid enough to do that. But they may give you some provisions, a few directions, and tell you where the Sarondakis are and where they're not."

"Or they may just throw me over a cliff because they think I'm a spy."

"I'm pretty well known in these parts," said Bindle. "If it's a big group there will probably be somebody in it that knows me. You'll be safe."

Zabeth rolled her eyes toward the sky. It was her own fault, she supposed. She'd had an opportunity to kill him after all.

For the next hour they kept up an uneasy silence. The path narrowed and all their concentration had to be focused on laboriously picking their way along the ledge. Both of them had staffs made from tree limbs found among the sparse stands in the western foothills. With these, they would gently test the ground in front of them, proceeding only when they were sure it would hold them and their horses. Bindle constantly stopped, and Zabeth could hear him tapping the ground with his staff. Every so often, he would point out a spot toward the edge of the cliff and tell her to avoid it. In this, at least she heeded his every word. Her pride was important, but not worth dying for, at least not here.

Her eyes would wander to the vast expanse that yawned to their left. Purple mountains rose like mighty warriors, their shoulders draped in clouds. Below was a drop whose depth Zabeth didn't care to think about. The bottom was covered with jagged boulders and some snow. The thin air made her gasp, the more so because it chilled her lungs when she breathed it. She had a winter cloak from the supplies they'd brought from Delamer. It was a forest green garment made from wool, but the constant wind cut right through it. Bindle, she noted, seemed quite comfortable in the fleecy hide he wore as a cloak. He had told her that it was the skin of one of the nimble mountain rams they had seen. Chilled to the bone, Zabeth had been tempted to shoot one for its hide. But there obviously wasn't time to skin an animal and then cure the hide. They were almost out of the mountains now anyway. The fact that she had gotten through with only a thin cloak was more proof of her physical superiority over Bindle.

Bindle stopped. They stood on a part of the trail that curved to the left so Zabeth could see him as he kneeled and examined the ground. His breath came out in puffs of white smoke and his brow furrowed as he puzzled over what he saw. His tightly curled hair had grown long after months on the road. He did shave regularly for which Zabeth was grateful. She hated beards. Zabeth had kept her hair cropped close to her skull ever since the night she had tried to run away. She had so many disadvantages when it came to wrestling, she didn't see the need to add one more by having long hair that someone could grab.

"What is it?" she asked.

"A boot print," he replied, looking ahead. "And fresh. Someone's ahead of us."

"I told you."

He rolled his eyes and ground his teeth at that. "Yes you told me. But they don't look like Sarondaki boots so we're probably safe."

Zabeth looked up at the sheer rock face that stretched above them. It came down to the trail which jutted outward from the cliff and then continued down for a stomach churning distance. "Is there any way we can sneak past them?"

"On this trail? I don't think so," said Bindle. "When it widens out it's only six feet wide. No chance."

"Well," said Zabeth, pinching her lip. "What about using the rope and crawling along the cliff below them?"

"We have no mountaineering equipment, and even if we did, they'd hear us hammering in the pitons. And besides what would we do with the horses? What a stupid suggestion."

"Well why'd you bring us on such a stupid path?" She balled up her fists and wished she could get past Bindle's horse to throttle him.

"Maybe you would have preferred sharing the East Road with the Sarondaki army?"

"Well if we did meet them, at least we'd have been able to hide or sneak around them."

"You don't know anything about it," Bindle said, his voice petulant. "Have you ever been on that part of the road? Do you know what it's like?"

"No," said Zabeth sullenly. She hadn't been anywhere and he knew it.

"Then just leave those decisions to me." Zabeth looked at her boots, her mouth drawn in an obstinate frown. She drew in a breath and then reached around her horse's head for her gear. "What are you doing?" asked Bindle.

"We'll camp here tonight and then just follow them until we reach a place where we can pass them unnoticed. It'll take longer but it's the only way out of this mess you've gotten us into."

"What are you so frightened of? I've already told you they aren't Sarondaki."

"You don't have to be born in the desert to have the heart of a Sarondaki." That made twice she had used the old saying on this trip. It proved to be very true the first time.

Bindle stared at her with an open mouth. "Look it's about time we talked about this..."

"I hope you're not going to pull that 'I'm the man' crap again. Because if you are I'm coming over there and I'm going to throw you off the cliff."

"That's not what I was going to say," he said. "I'm just asking you what are you going to do when you get to the Ratog?"

"Rescue Buckle."

"Yes but how?"

"I'll figure it out when I get there."

Bindle let out a strangled groan and lightly banged his head against the cliff.

"How can I make a plan before I get there and see the situation?"

"He could be guarded by a whole army."

"Or he could be with hundreds of other prisoners guarded only by a couple of warriors. That makes more sense. They are planning an invasion."

"But don't you think you should have some more people at your back in case you find the army?"

Zabeth bowed her head a little and pursed her lips. He had a point. But the problem was how could she trust strangers to want to rescue Buckle. He wouldn't be much help in fighting or strategy making. He'd just eat provisions, and at best stay out of the way. No serious company of warriors would carry such extra weight, and Zabeth doubted that Buckle could find his way home even with Yazzle's assistance. She wished she knew where Krinseth was.

"I can handle it," said Zabeth.

Bindle sighed. Not the exaggerated sigh of exasperation he usually expressed, but this was a tentative sigh, a sigh someone makes before imparting hard truths. "Look you are a very impressive woman. I didn't want to believe it but now I have to admit that you are a warrior. You're very good with a sword."

"Better than you."

Bindle's jaw tightened but he got the words out. "Better than me."

"So what's your point?"

"My point is that a good warrior knows his limitations."

"You haven't seen mine yet."

Bindle looked straight at her. "I think I'm seeing one now. You're too confident, too proud. You're talking about taking on the whole Sarondaki army. Believe me I've seen this before. It's the people like you, who think they can do anything, who always go down first in a battle."

Zabeth looked away. The words hit home. They were too much like many of Grazzle's lectures. She didn't like it, especially from Bindle.

"I have no choice, Bindle," she said to her horse's forelock.

"You're right there young miss," said a voice from behind Bindle. They both turned to look and saw a blond haired man standing at the point where the path bent to the right. He was big with muscled arms that poked out of his fleecy vest which went down to his ankles. He had a beard that was almost as red as it was blond. In his left hand he held a bow with an arrow crossing it. Zabeth got the feeling that the arrow could be nocked in a split second.

"Kebble, you old dog," cried Bindle.

"Bindle? It is you. I thought I recognized your voice. Aren't you with Renwick these days?"

"Long story." Their reunion was so spirited Zabeth thought they would topple themselves off the ledge. She watched as the two old friends slapped each other on the back and punched each other's arms in a comradely fashion. She wondered if she would ever make friends like that.

When she got tired of watching the display, she spoke up. "So what did you mean I had no choice?"

"What?" said Kebble, looking up at her, appreciation forming in his eyes, not the vulgar leer of most men she met but a simple acknowledgment that she was pleasant to look at. No matter, thought Zabeth, her interests were not in that direction. "Who is this?" he asked Bindle.

"This is Zabeth."

"I'm a warrior," stated Zabeth.

"I was going to tell him."

"Didn't look like you were in any hurry."

"No matter," said Kebble, raising his hand to stop the argument, "I could tell you were a warrior when I saw you. You wear your sword with confidence."

Zabeth cursed inwardly as she felt her face grow hot. She'd heard praise for her looks before, even from people she respected. But she barely knew this man, so why did he have such an effect on her? Zabeth looked at his rough and callused hands, and found herself thinking about them touching her. She shook her head and forced her voice to be calm and terse.

"Why do you say I have no choice?"

Kebble smiled and Zabeth's heart beat a little faster. "I like a woman who gets to the point. Well Zabeth, it's like this. Me and my men are heading toward the desert. I'll tell you why as soon as I'm sure I can trust you. If I meet strangers along the way, my orders are to do one of three things. Kill them if they are spies, recruit them if they're soldiers and send them west if they're civilians. Nowhere does it say, let them on through to the desert to accomplish their own goals."

"I'm going to rescue my master."

Kebble held up his placating hand again and said, "I can see that. Let's make a compromise. Tell me the situation, and I give you my word that if I can rescue your master and accomplish my mission too, I'll do it. Fair enough?"

Zabeth looked at him for signs of deceit but couldn't find any. Bindle was looking from one to the other, hoping she would agree to Kebble's terms.

"Fair enough," she said, adding, "for now."

Kebble laughed, "I suppose that's all I can ask for. C'mon let's get to my camp."

They turned the corner and saw Kebble's camp which was located on the widening in the trail Bindle had mentioned. He cast an embarrassed look back at Zabeth. The camp was about one hundred feet down the trail from where they had stopped, much closer than he had told her. Kebble explained they had heard arguing and he'd gone to investigate.

Bindle took the ribbing pretty well and after a while asked, "So what's going on with the war?"

137

"Haven't you heard?" asked Kebble.

"No, we've been on the backroads for the last few weeks."

"I guess that would be right," he said, stroking his chin. "Well Delamer has entered the war."

"What," said Zabeth and Bindle together.

"That's right. A lord named Fazzle is massing a force in Tarion right now. Armies are coming up from Massillay and down from the northern coast. It's somewhat of a surprise, considering the rough spring they've had, one storm after another pounding the coast and marching inland."

Bindle nodded his head. "We've been in several of them, the latest as far east as the foothills."

"Well I guess it's freed up a bunch of harvesters to become soldiers but for the life of me, I don't know how they're going to feed them."

"I hear they have plenty of food," said Keruct, one of Kebble's men. He was a big man with bushy black hair and a beard to match. Tied into his beard were many small bones. He wore a fleecy vest like Kebble's only shorter. "From what I understand the storms have all followed more or less the same path. Only in that corridor is there much destruction. The rest of the land is fine."

Zabeth wondered at that and then thought of Krinseth who always seemed to know when the storms would hit.

"Well no matter," said Kebble leaning back against the cliff face and lighting a long stemmed clay pipe. "They are joining what's left of our army in Tarion and marching east in a few months. Some little village between the foothills and Tarion is about to become famous. It'll have a battle named after it and then a thousand songs."

"I wish I could be there," said Bindle.

Kebble looked at him. "So do I, Bindle. It'll be much safer than what we have to do."

Bindle swiveled his head around to regard his old friend. Kebble nodded his head toward Zabeth. "I'll vouch for her," said Bindle. Zabeth bristled but she was too interested in knowing Kebble's mission to complain.

"All right," he said, laying down his pipe and leaning forward. "My orders are to slip into the desert and cause trouble. Attack supply lines, reinforcements and any other strategic targets, anything to get them to pull divisions away from their main force and attack us."

Bindle looked around and said, "You have fifty men here, at most."

"That's all I wanted. Just my regular company. We can move fast and without being noticed. Any more and we'd be prime targets."

"I take it they're not saving your place in next year's archery contest," said Bindle.

Kebble laughed, "Yes my friend, it will be a struggle to survive. But if anyone can do it, it's you and me. We've been through a lot of tough scrapes together." Then they started in on hitting each other again while the men looked on and laughed. But Zabeth could see that beneath the smile Bindle wore, there was a trace of worry.

For her part Zabeth was excited at the prospect of being a partisan. In all her daydreams about battle and glory, it had never occurred to her that she could travel east and join such a company as this. Yet here she was, in the Barriers, with a sword and a chance to prove herself. She glowed with confidence that in the next few weeks she'd stand out and begin to make a name for herself. Yet in the back of her mind, she thought about Buckle, and she knew that before she could feel right about doing the job ahead she'd have to rescue him and get him to safety. Honor was the most important thing, Grazzle's voice said in her mind.

She thought of these things as she huddled against the cliff wall, later that night. She'd taken the midnight watch because she couldn't sleep. The sky had cleared after the sun went down, and millions of stars burned above her. An almost full moon shone silver on the snow crested peaks around her. A gentle wind glided over the sides of the mountains. It whistled softly in her ears, mixing with the sound of horses nickering and muted conversations from the camp. Once again Zabeth cursed the flimsiness of her coat. She shivered and clutched the cold stone cliff as the wind sprang up anew.

"Cold?" asked a voice.

Not again, she thought. Three times tonight, she'd been bothered with offers to keep her warm. All of them involved intimate physical contact of the most repulsive kind. All three offers were refused, one quite violently, although the person hadn't been thrown off the ledge, a favor for which he seemed most ungrateful.

Zabeth sighed and looked up at the speaker, and was surprised to see it was Kebble. In his hand he held one of the fleecy vests they all wore. "I thought we had some spare vests and I was right." He held it out to her.

139

"And what do you want me to do for it?" asked Zabeth, not reaching for the vest.

"Nothing," said Kebble, throwing it on the ground in front of her. "I just want you to wear it and be warm."

Zabeth reached out a tentative hand and touched the fleece. It was soft and warm. Obviously it had just been near the fire. She rubbed the wool between her fingers but then stopped and withdrew her hand.

"I can manage," she said, looking back over the mountains.

"I'm sure you can, but why be cold if you don't have to?" When she didn't answer he sat down next to her. She squirmed away. "Don't worry," he said, pulling out his pipe and his flint and steel. "I won't try anything. I doubt if I could, even if I wanted to. I saw that shiner you gave Neruct."

"Why can't you men accept me for what I am?"

"As a warrior?"

"Yes."

"Well," said Kebble, lighting his pipe. "Men don't even accept other men as warriors until they've seen them fight."

"You don't understand."

"Maybe not. I understand one thing though. You may be a warrior, as Grazzle says, but what you are also, is a woman, no matter how much you want to deny it."

"What are you suggesting?" Zabeth turned three quarters to face him. Her blood seemed colder than the air around her.

"Nothing," he said, his hand up again to keep the peace. "In fact, I wish you wouldn't. That kind of thing only causes trouble on a campaign." Zabeth settled down.

"It's just that these men have been on the march for about three months. We didn't get any leave after our last patrol. And they haven't seen a woman in that time."

"Are you warning me about them?"

"No, judging from Neruct's eye I think I should warn them about you. No Zabeth, I want you to understand them and be patient with them. With a close knit outfit like this, it always takes time to build up acceptance. But if you're as good as Bindle says you are, they'll take you in...as a warrior."

Zabeth leaned back and said nothing. He made sense. He was repeating something Grazzle had told her a hundred times. But there was something about this that even Grazzle hadn't understood. It was something about being a woman in a man's job. She had to be flawless because, as a woman, she only got one chance where a man would get a couple. Weakness or incompetence would land her back in a kitchen or in front of a loom, or worse in some harem. Kebble spoke the truth as he understood it, but Zabeth knew that he would never see it from her view.

Kebble sucked on the pipe, causing the embers to flare up a bright orange that washed over his features. He tilted his head and looked at her.

"For my part," he said, "When I read those letters of introduction I was impressed."

Zabeth cast an irritated sidewise glance at him, wishing he'd go away or at least put out the odious pipe. The wind picked up again, and Zabeth shivered in spite of herself. Weakness.

"My father rode with Grazzle," continued Kebble, pretending not to notice. "For a period of about two years, he was away more often than not, riding patrols. He got a Sarondaki arrow through his eye on Grazzle's last patrol. I remember the great man himself came by the farm and told us the news. He brought us Father's gear and his horse, as well as his pension. He was great with Mother. He just held her until she stopped crying. Then he bounced me on his knee. I was only five at the time. He told me that I had to take care of the family and the farm now. From that moment on, I wanted to be just like him, like him and Father."

"Grazzle was like that," said Zabeth, staring out at the mountains, awash in her own memories, 'ruthless in war and training for war, but kind in everything else."

Kebble looked at her with that smile of his, maddening and yet endearing, and then he put away his pipe. "I guess the point is, Zabeth," he said, standing up, "I'm proud to have you with us." He walked away, disappearing behind the bend in the trail.

Zabeth's eye returned to the vest lying before her. She shivered in the wind, her teeth clattering like pebbles in an avalanche. The fleece looked warm and soft. She tried to think of Buckle, somewhere, maybe in these mountains, colder than she, but just then a gust howled, cutting through her cloak like it was nothing.

She grabbed the vest and hurriedly put it on.

Krinseth was glad she had made Buckle give her his amulet. His traces on it were strong. She could trace him even though he was partially shielded by the fire magic of the Sarondakis around him. The desert made things worse. Her magic was weak and grew weaker as the air became drier. She sat on the sand and watched the moonlit road as it cut straight across the scrub of the western desert. Hundreds of miles to the east she knew the road was no road at all. The constantly shifting sands and the terrible wind storms that sprang up like angered demons had buried any road that might have existed there long ago. A traveler just kept going east and hoped to pick the road up again at the desert's edge.

But Buckle would never see those lands east of the Ratog that they had once talked about. The prisoner caravan had turned north which meant its destination was Castle Skrike and forced labor in the mines under it. Buckle would be in the vicinity of her enemy. Right under him, as a matter of fact. Inwardly, she squirmed at the thought of using him this way, but she crushed the guilt. Her task towered above everything in its importance. She couldn't let her personal affection for one human jeopardize the achievement of her goal.

Still, she thought, standing up, I'll save him if I can, even if it means the end of my story. She walked down the road, keeping her ears and eyes open as well as the senses only she had.

16

Buckle decided the thing he hated most about the desert was walking. The sand ran into his worn boots with every step and made his feet feel as heavy as millstones when he tried to pull them out. The shifting sand beneath his unsteady feet, made it feel like for every step forward he took, he slid back two. Several times he had slipped and almost fallen. Fortunately, Yazzle had caught him and placed him on his feet before the guards arrived.

In spite of all that Buckle felt better than he had in the month, or so Yazzle had told him, since they had been captured. The dryness of the desert climate had cleared up his nose and chest. It felt good to breath, even if it was the stiflingly hot air of the Ratog desert. But Buckle still felt weak. His movements were dull and mechanical and he cursed his brain for its ponderous and agonizing slowness. Only gradually did he come back to his senses and become aware of his surroundings.

He remembered seeing Roduct's fate though. Buckle squeezed his eyes shut to avoid losing moisture. How was he going to get home now, he wondered? Roduct was now, if Buckle understood the bizarre ceremony correctly, a Sarondaki slave, subject to the will of Skrike. Probably at this moment, he was marching into Goswick or Joswell with the rest of the huge Sarondaki force that had attacked the west. Buckle winced, thinking that if Erklin ever found out on whose side Roduct marched in this war, they'd never see Methliana again. Erklin would make no distinctions as fine as Roduct's magical enslavement being the reason for his treason.

Buckle shook his head and almost laughed. Here he was being driven through the middle of the Ratog desert, the most notorious place on the map of his world, and he was worrying about the prejudices and petty jealousies of a provincial Delamerian sheriff. Erklin was a problem he'd love to be dealing with right now.

The prisoner caravan stretched before and behind him almost as far as he could see. The Sarondaki guards marched up and down the line, screaming and threatening and occasionally beating prisoners who had fallen or stopped. More than once, Buckle and Yazzle had passed a broken, beaten corpse or worse, an injured man who was only near death, his blood pouring into the thirsty sand. The live ones would look up with glossy eyes, not even hoping. They wouldn't even fight when other prisoners would steal their boots or clothes. The injured man would simply lie in the sun and die.

"We should be stopping soon," said Buckle. "They have to give us water soon." He stumbled over a ridge and Yazzle caught him. Buckle's mouth was as dry as the sand in his boots and he could feel it beginning to swell and blister.

"I'm sure we'll stop soon, sir," said Yazzle. He hadn't said anything about the weeks when Buckle was delirious but Buckle was sure he owed Yazzle his life. Men whom Buckle was sure started out stronger than he, now lay by the roadside, the sand and sun bleaching their bones. Buckle thought of his own untouched back when he saw the liberal use of the whip in the line and especially when he saw the bloody stains on the back of Yazzle's shirt every morning. The lad had been covering for him, perhaps even carrying him at points. And it showed. Yazzle had a scraggly beard, stained with blood. His hair was plastered to his head with grease and he had grown considerably thinner. Like everyone else in the caravan he swallowed compulsively. But there was still a spark in those eyes, still an intelligence, a will to survive. If it was within Yazzle's power, they'd get through.

Buckle wondered how he looked. His own beard itched terribly in the desert heat and his hair, usually curly and kept short, hung around his shoulders. The curl was almost gone, the weight of all the grease and sweat straightening it out. His clothes hung in tatters. His tunic provided little protection from the sun and the breeches were shredded almost up to his belt.

They marched on for a few more hours until the sun began to set. In the relative coolness of twilight, Buckle sat on the small pack he had been allowed to keep. The pack seemed heavy in his condition but there was actually very little inside it. His blanket was the most important thing. It had probably kept him alive during the cold nights in the mountains and even in the desert. A blanket was a rare item in the caravan and threadbare as it was, it was much coveted by the other prisoners. Yazzle had stared down many a would-be thief or extortionist.

Also in the pack, was the bundle of dwale Buckle had bought from the innkeeper in Wyckham Wood. He didn't know why he had kept the stuff after Krinseth had told him it could be deadly to him. He guessed that somewhere in the back of his mind was the hope that she was wrong. Up to now though, he had been afraid to try it, and since they reached the desert he hadn't needed it. The Sarondakis didn't seem to know what it was. At their last camp in the western foothills one of the guards had asked him, and he had almost said medicine but stopped himself. If they had thought he was too weak to make the journey they might have killed him then and there. So he told them it was tea. They had laughed and ridiculed him but they hadn't confiscated it.

Yazzle sat beside Buckle on the sand and they watched as the Sarondakis set up camp for the night. Like every night, several fires were built around the caravan, enclosing it in a ring of fire. When some of the more lively prisoners near Buckle had asked why, the guards replied that it was "to keep out the larger scorpions." No prisoner ever mentioned it again.

"I wonder if it's far," said Buckle, scanning the horizon to the north.

Yazzle drew in a ragged breath and said, "Don't know, sir. We've been walking...it seems like forever, and then all the traveling we did before that. I never dreamed the world was so big."

Buckle snorted and said, "You know something? Neither did I."

The first cool breeze of the night blew in from the west. Buckle pulled on the collar of his tunic, and let the wind carry away the heat built up on his chest. Then he opened his eyes and sniffed. For a second he thought he had felt just a hint of humidity. But the feeling didn't return. Buckle shrugged his shoulders. The breeze kicked up a little and sand devils, about three feet tall swirled through the camp. Tent flaps fluttered and a few stray articles of trash blew out onto the desert.

"Another cold night," remarked Buckle.

"Yes sir," said Yazzle. He glanced at the setting sun. "Master Buckle, what will happen now?"

"What do you mean?"

"I mean with Lord Roduct taken over like that, how can we get back to Methliana?"

Buckle looked at the lad and sighed. "I have to say it doesn't look very likely that we'll get back. With Lord Roduct or without him."

"Surely Zabeth will rescue us?"

"If she's alive, she might try," said Buckle. "But Yazzle, we're in the Ratog desert now, the heart of Sarondaki territory. I held out some hope in the first few days, before I got sick, but this far into Sarondaki territory, we may be beyond rescue."

"What about Krinseth? She could do it."

Buckle had to agree, if anyone could, it was Krinseth. But would she? "I don't know Yazzle. All we can do is stay alive and hope the west wins the war." Buckle bowed his head. The words didn't sound very encouraging but they were all he could offer.

"Then I've been doing it right so far?"

Buckle leaned over and grasped Yazzle's broad shoulder. "My friend, you've been doing it more than right. I'll probably never know how many times you saved my life over the last weeks, but I do know I'll never be able to repay you."

Yazzle looked down at his hands, his face blushing through the grime. "I'm just paying you back."

"Great Dalmar, what for?"

"Hiring me, so I could get away from that other estate."

"It was that bad there?"

"Better than here in some ways, but worse in others."

"They used the lash?"

Yazzle nodded his head, "A lot. They didn't use the kind with metal barbs, but they'd hand out more strokes. Sometimes one hundred, two hundred lashes at a time, especially to the seasonal workers." That was illegal. The limit was twenty-five in Delamer. Buckle was horrified. Not only was it inhuman but it was also senseless. What good was a field hand after he'd had a couple of hundred lashes? The man would be a cripple.

"The sheriff up there was like Erklin, he tended to look the other way on things like that, especially if the lord was a friend of his."

"I understand," said Buckle, coldly.

"I had a friend who got caught with one of the lord's daughters...you know, up in the hay loft."

"What happened to him?"

"She was the oldest girl and they couldn't marry her off. All her sisters were long gone. My friend offered to marry her, after he got caught but that just enraged the lord. He said he wouldn't have his daughter marrying a common field hand. He gave my friend..." Yazzle looked away for a second, his jaw tight. "He gave him four hundred lashes. I maybe could have survived something like that, but Zach was just a little guy, and skinny. I think he died around the two hundredth lash." Yazzle paused and swallowed. His eyes were watery.

"But they just kept whipping him, even after he stopped feeling it, after he was dead. They gave him four hundred lashes. His body looked like ground up beef, only raw with blood and the bones left in.

"I and a few others had to bury him. His grave is unmarked and hidden. After that I left. I didn't feel safe no more. I walked for weeks. South. Out of that county and the next. I wanted to get as far away as possible, out of fear of what they'd do to me, since I saw the whole thing."

Just then, some fellow prisoners came by with the evening's drink of water. A guard followed, watching them closely. Buckle and Yazzle gulped down the tepid and stale water. In the air was the smell of the evening meal cooking. The wind gusted again and Buckle had to cover his eyes with his arm. He wondered if they were in for a storm. The desert, he had heard, was prone to sudden violent storms which proved deadly to those caught in them. He looked at the guards, but they didn't seem concerned, so Buckle assumed there was nothing to worry about.

If Yazzle had told that story to Roduct and Buckle three years ago, when he had come to Methliana, they would surely have brought charges against that lord in the council. Such things were hard to prove, however, especially against a lord. And with county sheriffs being the corrupt and tight bunch they were, Buckle doubted that Yazzle would have been safe, even on Methliana. Buckle railed at the unfairness of it. Even the Sarondakis wouldn't give a man four hundred lashes.

Commotion broke out at the other end of the camp. The guards were pointing and shouting at a group of Sarondakis who entered the camp dragging some kind of animal. Whatever it was, it put up a fight, kicking up dust and sand. Harsh cries in Sarondaki filled the air as the guards, not immediately engaged in some task, rushed to lend a hand.

"What's going on? What have they got there?" asked Buckle.

"I can't see, Master Buckle," said Yazzle. He stood up and tried to pierce the billowing sand.

"Sit down, slave," growled a guard, approaching with his whip. Yazzle dropped to the ground.

"What's going on, sir?" asked Buckle.

The guard looked at Buckle sidewise and grinned. "That's our sport tonight."

Buckle looked over at the group again and saw that they had a large scorpion, about the size of a man, trussed up like a pig about to be butchered. There was strong rope holding its pincers closed, and another rope around its tail with a large warrior lagging behind, keeping the rope and the tail taut. Another rope was tied around the base of the tail, and this they tied to a stake and pounded it into the ground. That done, three warriors approached the beast, one each on the two pincers and one on the tail. Each held a knife in his hand. Looking at each other, they counted to three and then rushed in and cut all the ropes except the one tied to the base of the beast's tail. They scurried away as the scorpion spun and struck with its tail. Pincers clacked in the air and the scorpion's legs scrambled in enraged fury as the beast struggled against the rope that held it in place. The warriors around it laughed at its antics. Buckle, on the other hand cringed, even though he was a good fifty yards away. The creature was threatening, all armor, pincers and stinger. It stopped thrashing and stood with its pincers open and its tail hoisted high into the air as far as the restraining rope tied around it would allow. As guards walked past it the beast would slowly rotate to keep facing whoever was closest and moving.

"They don't see very well," said the Sarondaki guard. "But they do have an ear on their bellies that hears anything walking on the desert for miles around."

"It's so big," whispered Buckle.

"This is a small one. They can grow as big as one of your houses in the west."

Buckle hoped he meant an ordinary farm house, which would be bad enough, and not a house like Roduct's manor house. Actually this one was quite a bit larger than Buckle felt comfortable with.

"How common are these big ones?"

"They're everywhere. So if you're thinking to escape, that's what's waiting for you." He pointed to the scorpion and then walked away. Buckle hoped that his face was so dirty and bearded now, that the guard couldn't see it go white.

Night came swiftly after the meal. The guards moved the prisoners into a circle with the scorpion in the center. Whatever entertainment they had planned, Buckle and Yazzle and all the prisoners were going to get a good view. The guards forced prisoners to walk in front of the scorpion, just out of range so that it would rotate its body to face them, keeping its pincers open and tail upraised. To Buckle it looked as if they were trying to tire it out. Eventually its pincers wavered and the tail slouched a little.

Then the Sarondakis seemed satisfied. A group of them which included the leader of the caravan pointed at the beast and seemed to be coming to a consensus. In their midst stood a Sarondaki youth, wearing only a loincloth and armed with a spear, its metal point reflecting the torch light. He looked anxious but confidant. His gaze kept returning to the scorpion. Buckle felt a queasiness in his stomach as he guessed what was about to happen. Suddenly the leader stepped forward and spoke in Dernian.

"We have a surprise for you tonight, and I think it is indeed good and proper for you, the slaves of the Sarondaki Empire, to witness this ceremony. This is our rite of manhood, the thing that makes us strong. Arduct here," he motioned to the youth, "is sixteen years old. It is his time to become a man. Watch well, slaves, and see why your masters are superior to you. We live longer. We are bigger and stronger in our bodies. And in the desert we have developed that toughness of mind that will sweep us to victory. Lord Skrike will rule to the sea again, and no longer shall you inferior humans block us from the best farmlands and the easiest trade routes." Then he shouted something in Sarondaki and waved to Arduct who advanced on the scorpion.

The beast rose up on unsteady legs, sensing its moment had come. The youth circled around the beast just out of range. More softening up, thought Buckle. A strange scene unfolded before him. A circle of ragged prisoners, guarded by fifty or so stern Sarondaki guards, watching a youth battling a primeval desert nightmare. The scorpion skittered in its well-worn circle, its tail arched over its head, waiting to strike, its pincers open and deadly.

Charles Ebert

Arduct feinted to his left, drawing a lightning strike from the tail which hit only sand. Jamming his spear in and out of the beast's torso, Arduct leaped over the claw which swept at him from his right. He rolled out of range just in time to avoid another strike of the tail.

The Sarondakis cheered and Arduct quickly raised his spear and then lowered it. The fight wasn't over yet. The scorpion raged, yanking at its restraining rope so hard Buckle wondered if it would hold. A translucent white ooze bubbled out of the beast's wound and it listed toward the damaged side. The pincers clacked open and shut in fury.

Arduct circled again in the direction of the scorpion's lame side. Now the beast faced the young warrior not head on but at an angle, as if it were leading with its right pincer. The tail twisted toward the right, always facing Arduct. The youth tried another feint to the left but the beast either didn't see it or didn't fall for it. Then Arduct stopped circling and stood very still. The scorpion faced him for a few moments and then seemed to grow restless. It swiveled back and forth a few times, as if trying to find its adversary. Arduct carefully, not making any sudden motions put the end of his spear into his right hand and then, using all the length of his arm he reached over and tapped the sand to his right. The scorpion instantly turned that way, leaving its flank open. Arduct leapt, driving the spear into the beast's carapace, just behind the right pincer. He had time to jab and twist the spear a couple of times before the beast whirled about and struck with its tail. But by then, Arduct had withdrawn the spear and had cartwheeled out of range. The scorpion stung itself.

More cheers from the guards. This time Arduct took longer to acknowledge them. He smiled but it seemed kind of forced to Buckle, who also noticed the youth breathing hard, and when the inevitable circling started, Arduct definitely limped. He must have hurt himself, getting away after his last sortie.

The scorpion, however, was worse off. Its right pincer dragged uselessly on the ground. The other one dropped almost to the sand and the tail wavered visibly, like a tree branch in a strong wind. The beast still rotated to follow Arduct, but it was quite a bit slower now. Arduct almost succeeded in getting behind it.

Then the standing still began again. Arduct stood with his back to Buckle and Yazzle. He held his spear in front of him and very slowly he unwrapped the thongs that held the point onto the shaft. When he had them separated, he drew the shaft back and threw it in a

150

high arc over the beast's head. The scorpion turned when the shaft landed on the other side of it, leaving its back exposed. Arduct took the spear point and leapt onto the back of the monster. He grabbed the tail and straddled it like he was climbing a tree. Using the spear point like a knife, he started hacking away at the last segment of the tail which held the sting. The scorpion tried to flex its tail, but Arduct was too heavy. It rotated as fast as it could first one way then the other. But Arduct hung on, wedging the blade into the space between the last segment and the second to last. He pushed on the end, trying to pry the sting segment off while the white ooze poured out of the wound.

The tail slumped to the ground, kicking up sand and dust. Arduct struggled with the spearpoint, first pushing then pulling it. Finally he braced his legs on the beast's body and pushed with all his strength. The blade snapped and Arduct shot into the sand behind the scorpion. It wheeled about, and the tail went up and down, landing the sting into the stunned youth's chest five times before the guards drove it back with long spears and dragged Arduct out of range. The youth didn't move, and blood spurted out of the wounds in his chest.

A stunned silence settled over the camp. The guards stared in open surprise at Arduct's mutilated body. And the prisoners watched the guards. Only the sound of the sputtering torches broke the silence. Until one prisoner on the other side of the ring from Buckle, stood up and cheered. It caught on and soon all the prisoners were cheering, throwing their possessions into the air and stamping their feet which caused the scorpion to spin around like a weathervane in a tornado. This made the prisoners cheer louder, thinking the beast was acknowledging them.

The guards surveyed the scene with dangerous looks on their faces. The leader shouted and cursed as he ran around the inside of the circle, motioning for silence. He finally signaled to the guards who started in with the whips until the cheering stopped.

"Arduct was weak," shouted the leader. "He did not know his enemy or his weapon. This is how we cull the inferior warriors from our race. Arduct's death makes us stronger."

"Why don't you kill it then," came a voice from somewhere in the ring. The comment drew a chorus of "Yes, you kill it," and other comments from the prisoners. The guards grabbed their whips and looked into the crowd for the culprit.

"When I was of age, I killed a scorpion half again as large as that one...with my first attack,"

"Well then maybe you should tie one arm behind your back when you kill it." The prisoners roared with laughter. The leader stood watching them silently, while the guards scanned the crowd for the loudmouth and waited for the signal to shut them up.

The leader smiled instead and said, "Well, since all the rest of us have proven ourselves men, and since you slaves don't seem to have gotten enough sport, I think we'll depart from tradition and put one of you in with it." The laughter stopped.

"What's the matter? You aren't afraid are you? Look at the pathetic thing." He motioned to the scorpion which now rotated mechanically, its one pincer dragging. The rope holding it to the stake was twisted and tangled, reducing the beast's range. "A baby could kill it."

The guards chuckled. The leader started pacing along the inside of the circle, scanning the faces of the prisoners.

"Come on, surely somebody in this group is ready to become a man. Any volunteers?"

He stopped in front of Buckle and Yazzle. "You, the big one," he said, pointing at Yazzle. "Bring him forward."

The guards grabbed Yazzle by the arms and dragged him into the circle. Yazzle tried to resist but the Sarondakis were too strong.

"How about it, Friend of Marduct?" The leader sneered. "Do you wish to prove yourself?"

"I don't know how to fight."

The guards erupted in laughter. The leader smiled and said, "Well you better learn. Give him a spear." He motioned to a guard who threw a spear to Yazzle. It bounced off Yazzle's chest and hit the ground. The guards laughed again.

"Pick it up slave," said the leader.

"But...but..." The leader motioned to one of the guards who loosened his whip. Yazzle bent down and picked up the spear. He turned around to look at Buckle.

"Be careful Yazzle," said Buckle, wishing he had better advice to offer. Yazzle nodded and turned to the scorpion. The guards gave him a shove which almost deposited him face down inside the scorpion's range. Buckle pushed his way to the front of the crowd and watched in helpless terror.

Yazzle tentatively approached the beast which rotated to face him. It didn't look very formidable in its injured and dying condition but Buckle knew that was probably a deceptive perception. That tail could still strike faster than a man in Yazzle's condition could get away.

"Circle it Yazzle," shouted Buckle. Yazzle looked over at him, and Buckle nodded. The lad started shuffling to his right in a great circle. His spear shakily pointed inward. The scorpion followed. "Keep circling." Buckle hoped the scorpion was nearly dead, and if Yazzle circled it enough, it would collapse. Already its legs were shaking as it scrambled to keep up.

Unfortunately the Sarondakis wanted to make a point. At a signal from the leader one of the guards advanced and poked Yazzle with a spear, forcing him forward. The scorpion lurched forward and struck, missing Yazzle only by a few inches. Its good pincer swung viciously at Yazzle's legs. The lad stumbled back, almost dropping the spear. Buckle could see the confusion and terror in his face.

A guard stepped in front of Yazzle and loosed his whip. The lad stared at the guard with more hatred than Buckle would have thought was in him. "Get in there slave," growled the guard. For an instant, Buckle thought Yazzle would use the spear on the Sarondaki. He fingered it lightly and looked down at it. But that way lay certain death. At least with the scorpion he had a chance, however small. Yazzle screamed and whirled around, charging the beast.

He leapt over the disabled right pincer and jammed the spear into the scorpion's body. The point transfixed the beast and stuck in the ground. When Yazzle's momentum carried him, past the beast, the spear broke off in his hand leaving the rest of it sticking out of the scorpion's body. The beast twisted as far as it could until the rope stopped it. Then the scorpion started stinging itself. The tail went up and down, piercing the beast's armor and kicking up the white ooze.

The prisoners and guards watched the spectacle with horror. Yazzle lay on the ground with the remaining part of the spear in his hand. He threw that away and stood up on unsteady legs. He wobbled over to the far side of the ring where there was a big rock. With an effort he picked it up and carried it over to the scorpion. He raised the stone high above his head. The scorpion lay twitching on the sand, its tail curled up at the end of its body. Still it sensed Yazzle's presence and the tail came up slowly and with a ponderous waving motion. Yazzle strained and threw the rock downward, crushing the beast beneath it. Its twitching stopped.

The cheers went up, louder than before. Prisoners charged into the middle of the circle to swarm Yazzle. Some danced with energy renewed by the victory and some used the opportunity to try and escape. One prisoner grabbed a torch and swung it around like a club, reenacting the fight in pantomime. Buckle saw another smearing his body with the ooze and entrails of the scorpion.

Buckle tried to keep his head while he plowed into the circle, searching for Yazzle. The press of humanity was too thick to allow easy passage. Jubilant prisoners stumbled into him as he called out for Yazzle and tried to poke his head above the press to find him. How, he wondered were the Sarondakis going to take this?

In answer to his question, the cries of the riot were punctuated by the cracking of whips, and changed to cries of anguish and defiance. Buckle caught a few glimpses of the guards wielding their whips in cruel circles above their heads, the lash coming down to lacerate flesh. Bits of spongy red flesh flew in the air and blood spurted onto the sand. At least one Sarondaki fell though. Buckle saw it clearly, as about five prisoners leapt on him from behind, biting and scratching. The warrior fell under their weight, clawing uselessly at his sword as they pulled it away from him and cut his throat.

Then Buckle heard a whistling sound and a man beside him fell with an arrow in his eye. Turning Buckle saw a line of about ten guards nocking arrows into their bows and shooting into the melee'. He doubled over and tried to make for the far side of the ring, hoping Yazzle would do the same. Men started dropping around him with arrow and sword wounds. The sand was soaked under his feet.

When Buckle broke through to the other side he found himself facing a big Sarondaki warrior with a whip in his hand. Blood dripped off the lashes making a spotted pattern in the sand. The guard grabbed Buckle and threw him forward out of the riot. He landed face down, getting a mouthful of sand. There was a crack and then excruciating pain as the lash clawed at his back, tearing through tunic and skin. Buckle screamed and writhed in pain. But the lash came down again. And again.

"Master Buckle," cried Yazzle. And Buckle felt a great weight land on top of him. In his ear he heard Yazzle's voice. "I'm sorry Master Buckle. This never should have happened." There was a crack and Yazzle convulsed, his mouth let out an involuntary cry. It happened a few more times but all Buckle could feel was the weight on top of him and the tears that fell onto his neck and mingled with blood and scorpion ooze. Then came blackness.

For the next few days, it was Yazzle who needed help. Buckle supported him as they stumbled across the desert with the whipped and beaten caravan. For the rest of the journey, Buckle could look back and see scavenger birds circling the site of the riot where there lay the bodies of over twenty prisoners and two Sarondakis. Buckle felt the pain of his own wounds, but gritted his teeth and bore it when he saw the welts scarring Yazzle's back.

The Sarondakis drove them harder, doubling their pace and traveling longer hours. All of them were in a sour mood. Whips cracked liberally. Every so often, a guard would rejoin the train after having been sent out to round up the escaped prisoners. He would be carrying the head of the quarry or in some instances the whole or part of the body if there were some good scorpion stings on it. The prisoners were shown all these things and then given a harsh lecture on the futility of escape.

The Sarondakis now forbade talking among the prisoners. Stragglers were flogged, or killed if they persisted in slowing down the train, or could not go on. Which was why Buckle made Yazzle lean on his shoulders. It was a good thing that Yazzle could walk with only a little help because Buckle could never have carried him. Yazzle complained and begged to be left behind but Buckle ignored him.

By the time the caravan reached Castle Skrike a week later, Yazzle was walking unaided. But he was strangely silent, answering only direct questions and then with as few words as possible. He kept looking at the stripes down Buckle's back. A couple of times Buckle had tried to console him but the lad insisted on blaming himself.

The sight of their destination filled Buckle with a mixture of emotions. Foremost, strangely enough, there was hope. They would survive the ordeal, the cold of the mountains, the heat and savagery of the desert which had taken so many of their fellow prisoners. And for Buckle there was the private anguish of seeing his lord broken and enslaved. That hurt more than his split and bleeding feet, more than the welts on his back. But he and Yazzle had survived. And when the west won the war, they'd be freed. It occurred to Buckle that it might happen too late to save Methliana but with things the way they were, that seemed unlikely anyway. And in the end, he guessed, life was more important.

Doubt grew, however, the closer they came to the castle. Dark walls with needle-like towers loomed ahead like some kind of obsidian

155

spider, sitting atop a mountain. For the castle was actually built into a mountain with jagged natural ramparts disguising the spiraling path up to the entrance.

In the accumulating gloom of twilight, they dragged up the road to the castle. Now they encountered traffic coming the other way. Messengers on fast horses or important official parties galloped by, hardly sparing them a glance. Each prisoner had to look away, under pain of flogging, when a Sarondaki rode past.

Buckle's breathing became labored, not with an attack but with trepidation. The other prisoners showed signs of fear too. Heads swiveled around, as if some last minute escape route would open up in this hellish place. The caravan moved slower until the guards started in with the whips. Buckle wished harder than ever he'd never left the estate.

They stopped before a huge black gate set into the side of the mountain facing west. There they stood in a widening of the mountain road, which continued on up to the castle's main gate, or so Buckle guessed. He could see the rim of the sun disappearing behind the mountains. A guard banged on the gate with his spear and another Sarondaki poked his head out of a barred window to the side. After a short conversation in Sarondaki, a grinding metal sound was heard and the gate lifted upwards, slowly revealing the black abyss behind it.

"Take a good look at the sun, slaves," shouted the leader over the din of the gate opening. "It's the last you'll ever see of it."

"No," cried a prisoner, and the man clawed his way out of the crowd and scrambled up the cliff face that served as a parapet. In front of him lay the road with the prisoners and guards. Behind was a drop of several hundred feet.

"I'm not going in there," he cried, pointing at the now open doorway.

"Come down from there, slave," shouted the leader.

"We killed the scorpion. We deserve to go free."

"You killed nothing. That man," he pointed to Yazzle who hunkered down a little, "killed a pathetic and dying creature. Accept your fate and come down now. I have no time for this."

"No," screamed the prisoner and he picked up a rock and threw it at the leader. It went wide and hit the cliff wall. The leader motioned to the guard beside him who nocked an arrow and let loose. The arrow landed squarely in the prisoner's chest and he fell backwards over the cliff, screaming.

That was one way to escape, thought Buckle as he filed into the dark gateway behind Yazzle. One I might consider, if all hope is lost. He thought of the dwale in his pack. But not quite yet.

They trudged down a long dark hallway which was illuminated every fifty feet or so by a torch. The air stank of smoke and human closeness, and Buckle could feel his chest tightening. Around him, the prisoners walked, fear showing on their torch-lit faces. Somebody behind Buckle wept dry tears, muttering, "No, no, I want to go home."

The hallway widened into a huge room which the prisoners were herded into. At one end were several Sarondakis in cloth tunics, not the leather armor and breeches of the desert warriors. Four large ones stood at strategic points around the room. They had short swords at their belts and the inevitable whips in their hands. Standing behind a podium at the far end of the room was a group of important looking Sarondakis. Their tunics were bedecked in insignias and strange designs. One Sarondaki in particular, standing in the center of the group, looked to be in charge.

The caravan leader went up to him, bowed and spoke a few words. The regal figure surveyed the group of prisoners with a look of obvious distaste. He motioned the leader away. He and the guards who had driven them so hard across the mountains and the desert left through a side entrance. Buckle never saw them again.

The Sarondaki in charge picked up a stylus and made a few marks on a paper. This he handed to another Sarondaki, who scurried away with it. Then he motioned to the four guards who sprang to life. They shouted and cracked their whips, driving the caravan into the tunnel.

They went down a great spiral staircase. Then they marched through black tunnels lit only by smoky torches, always going down. The lower they went, the colder and wetter it got, and Buckle felt like he couldn't breathe. His vision filled with multicolored stars and comets but he dared not slow down.

After what seemed like hours of this, Buckle was thoroughly exhausted and confused. He'd never find the way back even if he could escape his guards. Somewhere inside him, a little more hope died. When they finally stopped, he squatted in a long hallway, gasping for breath, and thought of the prisoner outside, lying broken on the ground with an arrow through his chest.

The hallway was lined with iron doors, black and heavy, each with a small barred window set at eye level for a Sarondaki. The four guards were grabbing several prisoners at a time and shoving them into various cells. When they got near, Yazzle bent over and picked up Buckle, so the guards couldn't separate them. With a shove one of the guards pushed up the bar that secured the door of the nearest cell. It swung open to reveal a small cell maybe fifteen feet deep by ten wide. The floor was covered with greasy looking straw, upon which sat about fifteen prisoners. They looked up at Buckle and Yazzle, most with indifference, but a couple with open hostility. The scene was lit by a stubby candle set on a rickety stool in the center.

"What the hell is this," said a large prisoner, standing up. He confronted the guard. "We've got too many in this cell already. You said we wouldn't get any more until some of these bastards died." He jerked a thumb at his fellow cell mates.

"Shut up Bruct," snarled the guard, lifting his whip. Bruct backed away, but resentment still smoldered in him after the guards left.

The door creaked shut and the bar fell home with a clang that echoed through the hallways. Buckle looked around at the faces that stared back at him. He wondered why he ever thought this place would be safer than the desert.

Bruct, most of all, scared him. The look on the man's face was more frightening than the scorpion had been. He turned on the pair and eyed them harshly. Buckle and Yazzle stood in the middle of the circle. Bruct was walking around them.

"You shouldn't be here," he said. "I had guarantees from the guards that there'd be no more prisoners assigned to this cell."

"So much for Sarondaki guarantees," said Buckle, trying to smile.

Bruct rounded on Buckle and shouted into his face. "Shut up. You only talk when I tell you."

He looked down at Buckle's pack. "What have we here?" He grabbed the pack. "If it's anything useful, I may let you live."

He rummaged through the pack, pulling out the blanket. "This is nice," he said, holding it up. "A little worn but serviceable. Arvindle, you need a blanket don't you?"

A scrawny-looking man stood up and scampered to Bruct's side, pawing the blanket. "Yes, Bruct I do."

"It's yours," said Bruct, tossing the blanket over the man's head.

"Hey," protested Yazzle, but Buckle stopped him by placing a hand on his arm.

"Thank you Bruct," said the toad. "I owe you. I'll pay. Arvindle pays his debts." He sat down, covering himself with the blanket as if he were a king and it his robe.

"What's this?" said Bruct, pulling out the packet of dwale.

"Tea," said Buckle.

"Tea? What the hell are you bringing tea in here for? Oh well, the pack is good." He surveyed them with distaste. "Your clothes are worthless and shoes worse so you can keep those and keep the tea too." He threw the packet at Buckle who caught it.

"You sleep over there by the privy." He motioned to the back wall of the cell, where there was a small hole in the stone wall.

Buckle and Yazzle stepped over the reclining bodies to make it to their assigned space. They sat down amongst the hard stares of their new neighbors. That is, some of the stares were hard. Others, Buckle didn't want to guess what they meant. He looked away when one man winked at him. Underneath the straw, the floor felt slimy. Buckle brushed some of the straw away and examined the floor. It had a finger's width coat of mold covering it.

Krinseth squeezed her tongue with her dusty fingers, trying to work up some spit. She lay in a crevasse she had found on a hillock by the side of Skrike's Road. It was perfect for her purposes, being completely hidden from the road and open to the sky only by a small hole at the top. This, she had partially blocked up with boulders until it spanned only a few inches. Now Krinseth lay in a sarcophagus not much larger than herself. It provided a reasonably safe place to hide and wait.

She dug her fingers deeper into her mouth and pressed on the saliva glands. Finally a few drops of spit squirted out. Krinseth immediately grabbed Buckle's amulet and rubbed the moisture on its iron surface. The object was very important to him. His trace was still strong, and that was the only reason she found him, for her powers were weak in this desiccated landscape.

Faint images superimposed themselves on her thoughts. Men sitting on dirty straw staring at her with hostile looks. Smearing their faces was a black substance. Coal dust? It had to be. Buckle had made it to Castle Skrike. Her plan was still viable.

Somehow that seemed less important though. Buckle was strong mentally but not physically. He was suffering much, and to her surprise, Krinseth found that distressed her. Even more upsetting was the fact that he would have to find out about her role in this. How would he feel about her then?

Krinseth laughed and put the amulet back into her pack. Here she was, she knew not how many centuries old, and yet she worried about how a man might feel about her. Did Methlyn feel this way about Dalmar, she wondered. Most of the men in Krinseth's life had been assigned to her, which was the way of her race. An elder points to you and says 'reproduce with this man,' and you do it. None of this human fuss surrounded it.

Methlyn, of course, went against all that. She devoted herself exclusively to a human male. And, thought Krinseth sadly, paid the price. She must remember that.

Krinseth felt not sleep but inaction coming upon her. The rains were coming but they were still a few weeks away. In that time, she had to conserve her strength. She wished she could sleep but that was not the way of the Tenar. She would be awake and alert for every second until her damnfool son managed to complete his task.

17

"We should be attacking prisoner caravans," said Zabeth. She paced up and down the length of Kebble's tent, her boots kicking up sand. Kebble himself sat back on a chair with his feet up on the collapsible map table. His pipe calmly disgorged puffs of blue smoke. He wore his desert garb now, a light tan tunic with leather armor and a cloth hanging from the rim of his helmet to keep the sun off the back of his neck. The armor and the tunic were unfastened from the top almost down to his belt. Zabeth tried not to look at his muscular chest.

"Can't do it, Zabeth," he said.

"Why not?"

"They carry about a hundred prisoners in each caravan. What are we going to do with them once we've liberated them?"

"They can join your force. We can build an army," cried Zabeth waving her arms in frustration.

"After being force-marched over the mountains and across half the desert, I doubt any of them would be fit enough to fight. Besides, what do I feed them with? Better to let the Sarondakis take care of them until the war is over."

"The Sarondakis will torture and kill them."

"They'll die pretty quickly in the desert without any food or shelter."

"Well if you're too cowardly to rescue Buckle, I'll go do it myself." She stalked toward the entrance.

"You know I can't let you do that," said Kebble, peacefully contemplating the bowl of his pipe. Zabeth stopped just before the door with her back to him.

"Assuming you could stop me, why?"

"If you're caught you'll give away our position, strength, supply points and other important things."

"I wouldn't crack under torture."

"Well, nobody knows that until they've experienced it. And besides they don't use ordinary torture. They use magic which no one can resist."

Zabeth spun around and glared at Kebble. "Then what am I supposed to do?"

"Help me win this war," said Kebble and he looked straight at her. "Then, if we're still alive, march with me into Castle Skrike or Raganorth or wherever he's being kept and free him."

Zabeth bent her head and examined the ground beneath her feet. Her anger smoldered in her midsection and she struggled to damp it out.

"What if he dies?"

"Then he'll be like thousands of other people in this war including possibly...no probably you and me and Bindle."

"I took an oath to protect him."

"And you did a good job. Is there anything you'd have done differently?"

Zabeth resumed her angry pacing. "I'd have forced him to come with us that night."

Kebble emitted a low whistle. "You must have had a lot of influence over him if you can order your master around like that. In my experience masterss do what they want, no matter if it's the right thing or the smart thing to do."

"Buckle's not like that."

"Maybe not usually, but when the situation is urgent sometimes the strangest things can seem important."

"It shouldn't have happened," said Zabeth, finally sitting down.

"Whole damn war shouldn't have happened," remarked Kebble. He lifted his feet off the table and yawned. "Ought to be about time to eat."

"Kebble," said a voice from outside. It was Bindle's.

"Enter Bindle," said Kebble, putting his pipe away.

Bindle strode into the tent and paused, looking first at Kebble with his loose tunic and then at Zabeth, her clothes loosened also. He frowned and his eyebrows knit together.

"What is it Bindle?" asked Kebble after a moment.

"What is it? Oh yeah, the scout's back. Says he has something."

"What?"

"Some kind of caravan, not far to the north."

"Great," exclaimed Kebble. "Let's move out. I'll talk to the scout as I'm saddling up. Tell the men to each get a couple of hunks of salt beef. We'll eat as we ride." He tightened his tunic and armor and strapped on the helmet and his sword. Zabeth fetched his bow and quiver from the corner and tossed them to him. The next instant he was out of the tent, leaving Bindle and Zabeth alone. He stared at her as she adjusted her armor.

"What?" she snapped, noticing him staring.

"Is there anything going on here?"

She looked at him strangely.

"I mean between you and Kebble." His arms flailed.

"Hell of a time to be worrying about that," she said, striding toward the entrance. "Get on your horse." She was out of the tent.

Minutes later, Zabeth felt the powerful muscles of her horse under her as the company sped along a small trail through the rocky desert. Dust and sand, kicked up by the other riders clouded her vision and coated her teeth. Behind her, she could sense Bindle struggling to come up beside her. She just urged her horse faster.

What was he thinking about? Something between her and Kebble? Impossible. Kebble, was to be sure, a good looking man with his blond hair and muscular body. But he was also infuriating. He never became angry. No matter how much she yelled at him, Kebble always remained calm, almost serene. He explained his position in his low voice, completely unstressed and natural, smoking that damn pipe. And the worst thing was he was usually right.

However, most of the time, he was good company, and Zabeth liked talking to him. Perhaps he could be a friend if such a thing were possible. Most men in her experience couldn't consider women as friends.

She shook her head to clear her thoughts. Now, as she had told Bindle was not the time to think about these things. Ahead, Kebble raised his hand to signal a stop. The partisans crowded around him. They were on a hill. Before them was a gently sloping cliff. On the other side of a dirt road at the bottom were steep dunes which combined with the cliff to make a canyon.

"There will be a caravan along this stretch of road in about half an hour," he said, motioning to his right. "My group sets up here. Gredle take your boys and set up across from us. Watch for scouts. They have no reason to suspect an ambush but the Sarondakis can be very thorough and conservative if they want to be. Get going."

Zabeth was in Gredle's group, about twenty men and her, so she sped off down the canyon, leaving Kebble with a single backward glance. Now, ironically, he was motion personified. He darted from one group to another, helping set up a temporary hitching line to tether the horses and placing his men in strategic positions atop the wall of the canyon. It was as if he kept his energy in a bottle or a jug that he was able to cork when he didn't need it.

Zabeth cursed when she caught herself thinking about him again. She was about to enter her first battle and she couldn't concentrate. Silently, she ran through her preparation litany, checking over a mental list of everything she'd need in the next few hours. Sword strapped to her waist. Bow over her shoulder. She removed it and slipped it into its holder on the horse's saddle. She had a full quiver of arrows, about thirty, strapped securely to her back. She had two knives; one on her belt, opposite the sword, and one in her boot for surprises. She leaned over and touched the silver pommel of her boot knife. Grazzle had never liked the idea, but then he'd never had to worry about being overpowered in hand to hand fighting. The boot knife had come in handy more than once.

When they got to a point where they could cross the road, they pulled up and Gredle sent a rider ahead to scout. Gredle was a short but stocky man with hard muscles and a black beard, which he kept well-trimmed. His black hair flowed past his shoulders. He never said much and Zabeth had never seen him be unfair. In her mind she had been putting Kebble's men into one of two categories: pigs and acceptable. Gredle, at this point fit solidly into the acceptable slot.

The scout gave the all clear signal and they raced across the road and doubled back on the other side of the canyon. On this side there was sand which piled up in dunes as far as Zabeth could see to her right. The horses kicked up a lot of the sand and progress was tough. Gredle pushed even harder. Soon they were caked with sand and Zabeth spit several times to get the taste of it out of her mouth.

One of the men, Zimmelwick, yelled and pointed to their right and just ahead. Zabeth looked up and saw a lone mounted Sarondaki on the crest of a dune. He was watching them, and when he saw he'd been noticed he began to gallop away.

The whole band pulled up when Gredle stopped. Zabeth grabbed her bow and pulled an arrow out of her quiver.

"Zimmelwick, you've got the fastest horse, after him."

"Shoot him," said a trooper but Gredle shook his head.

He's just within range and moving. It'd be a waste of an arrow."

But Zabeth's arrow was already in the air. It sailed in an arc over the sand and thudded home in the Sarondaki's neck. The warrior slumped forward and to the side of the horse's neck. The horse stopped when its reigns went slack, and it now stood, looking confused. Eventually, it started pushing the sand around with its nose in a vain attempt to find some grass.

Zimmelwick pulled up when the arrow hit and turned around. The entire group, in fact, was now staring at Zabeth, their mouths open.

"I knew I had to hit him in the neck. At that distance the arrow wouldn't have had enough power to get through his armor." She kicked the sides of her horse and galloped away, smiling at the look on their faces.

When they reached their station on the opposite side of Kebble's men, Gredle started placing them. Zabeth had no argument with his placement other than the fact that she was put well back, away from any hand to hand action. She could hardly fault him for that though. All he had ever seen her do was shoot an arrow. Gredle had to place his people according to their skills as he knew them.

Zabeth lay face down on the crest of the dune, her bow lying just ahead of her with an arrow crossing it. She examined the road to the east carefully, squinting into the glare. Dust rose from the surface, marking the passage of whatever they were attacking. Bitterly, Zabeth reminded herself it was probably a supply caravan. Troops were too dangerous, and Kebble had made himself clear about attacking prisoner caravans.

As the dust cloud grew closer, Zabeth made out details. She often recognized features at the same time as Rissle, who had the best eyes in the troop and was stationed nearest to the front of the pass.

He'd tell the next person in line what he'd observed and that person would pass it on.

"It's a supply train," said Tondle, the last link before Zabeth who was at the end of the pass. "About a hundred feet long...with fifty odd camels and...twenty mules. A hundred warriors, half on horse."

It matched what Zabeth saw. They would be outnumbered. She hoped the scout she killed was the only one. The dust cloud grew nearer. Soon the hot desert breeze brought the sound of camels and mules braying, bells tinkling and drivers shouting. The plan seemed to be working. They looked as if they didn't suspect anything.

When the supply caravan halted just before entering the canyon, Zabeth held her breath. She could see clearly and had already begun to pick out targets. They were just within range but of course they had to wait until the whole train was in the canyon. Zabeth slowly eased forward to get a better look.

Two riders broke from the caravan and rode into the canyon. They searched the escarpment to their right and the dunes to their left presumably for any sign of an ambush. One even rode part way up the dune and peered into the desert beyond. Any further and he'd have seen their horses. Satisfied, the riders gave a signal, and the whole train started to move. Zabeth shook her head. They had no reason to expect an ambush this time. It would never be this easy again.

The next few minutes crawled past as the first riders in the supply train rode nearer and nearer to the end of the canyon. Zabeth's fingers itched, longing to feel the twang of the bowstring. She could see the arrow piercing the chest of the lead rider on her side. She imagined blood flowing into the dry sand.

When the lead riders were just below her, Zabeth heard a cry from the other side of the canyon and arrows began to fly. She nocked her arrow and let go all in one motion. It sang as it flew and then pierced the Sarondaki's chest, just as she'd imagined it.

Arrows crisscrossed the sky, killing dozens of Sarondakis and their animals as they scrambled about first to find cover and then to fire back. A few tried to charge out of Zabeth's end of the canyon, but she and the other men near her and on the other side, perforated anyone who got close. Cries of Sarondaki dying rose up like a chorus and to Zabeth's ears sounded sweet.

The bodies mounted and provided cover for the Sarondakis who dived behind the carcasses and fired back. From across the road came the cry to charge, and Kebble's men poured down the sides of the canyon, shouting and waving their swords. Zabeth, with a few other superior archers hung back, pinning the Sarondakis behind their ramparts so they couldn't fire into the onslaught. Zabeth shot arrows until the partisans got to within a few feet of the enemy. Then she was about to cast off her bow, when she saw a group of about fifteen Sarondakis, five mounted, escape at the far end of the canyon.

She shouldered the bow and ran down the dune to where the battle raged on the floor of the canyon. The nearest partisan to her was Keruct. Keruct sported a huge belly, but boasted it was all muscle. He may be right, thought Zabeth, as she watched him wield his broadsword like an epee.

"Keruct," she shouted, "we're being flanked. Come on."

"I'm a little busy right now," he replied, bellying up to a Sarondaki warrior and shoving him into the dirt.

"Oh, for Dalmar's sake," Zabeth grunted and stepped in front of Keruct. The warrior, an agile youth did a backward roll and came up on the balls of his feet in fighting position. Zabeth feinted to the head and when the Sarondaki's sword went up to parry, she pistoned back, quick as lightning and went in under his guard, driving the blade halfway up his gut.

Pulling out, she heard another warrior come up from her left, even as Keruct shouted to warn her. In an instant her dagger was out of its sheath and holding the Sarondaki's broadsword at bay. With a quick flip of the wrist, her blade slipped out of the first warrior's gut, just a bloody arc and then up the second's. He started falling before the first one hit the ground.

She turned to an amazed Keruct. "Get about four men and meet me by the horses." She wiped her blade on her tunic and ran up the dune. She had untied and mounted her horse, when Keruct and two others came over the crest of the dune. They were Vorkle, a Goswickian, who was fatter than Keruct and about half a head taller, and Tiacin, a reedy Ternian with thin arms covered with ropy muscles. Zabeth shook her head disapprovingly; four on fifteen would be tough. But she pointed in the direction they had to go and rode off, leaving them to scramble onto their mounts and follow.

After riding for a minute she spied the Sarondakis. They were circling the side of the dune, giving it a wide margin. Zabeth stopped her horse and watched them pick their way through the sand. The others rode up beside her.

"You all got your bows?"

They nodded.

"Shoot five arrows and then charge. Remember to disperse. I want about twenty feet between each rider. On my word."

"Keruct," said Tiacin, "you didn't tell me it was her."

"Nor I, Keruct," rumbled Vorkle.

"There's no time for this," shouted Zabeth.

"Silence, Wench," said Tiacin, without looking at her. Zabeth drew her sword but Keruct stopped her reaction with a look.

"I saw her fight back in the canyon, Tiacin. Even you don't want to get her mad. Grazzle taught her well."

The two partisans looked at her suspiciously. After a few seconds passed and no decision seemed to be forthcoming, Zabeth said, "Look, we've got fifteen Sarondakis about to flank us. Shall we do something about it or continue this discussion in Hell."

All three looked at each other and then at her. They nodded their heads.

"Good. On my word."

She held up her hand. At that moment the Sarondakis saw her and scrambled to get out their own bows, Zabeth brought her hand down and shouted, "Now."

Four arrows shot into the air followed by four more and two Sarondakis dropped while the rest scurried for cover. But in the sand there was little of that, so five more fell before Zabeth shouted for a charge.

They rode forward, kicking up sand like a storm in the desert. Zabeth had her sword out and to the side. Arrows whistled above her head. She rode low, peeking at her destination from around the horse's neck. She found herself in the lead, the other falling back on her flanks, forming an arrowhead formation.

When the arrow hit home, Zabeth wielded her sword in a terrible arc over her head. The blade came down on someone's shoulder. She sliced downward through muscle and tendon and then yanked the sword up and drew it across the warrior's neck, killing his cries of agony. She spun her steed around and chopped indiscriminately at the enemy. The others hit seconds after her and in a few moments the Sarondakis were in full retreat across the desert. Twelve bodies lay on the sand in the middle of a growing circle of red. Mostly they were old men and green adolescents, not fit for frontline duty but perfectly able to guard supply caravans behind their own lines. Or so the Sarondakis had thought.

Keruct rode back from chasing the runaways a small distance to make sure they didn't double back. Zabeth and the others rode among the bodies, making sure. She looked up at him.

"They all gone?"

He nodded his head, "And they won't be back. It'll be a miracle if they even survive to tell anyone."

"Good. Let's finish up here and get back to the battle."

"Hey Zabeth," said Keruct.

"What?"

He smiled. "I'm glad you're on our side."

"Me too," said Tiacin. "If all the women in Delamer fight like you, tell them to forget about sending the men."

"Fair lady," said Vorkle, making a little bow from his saddle, "You are the most illustrious woman to don armor and ride into battle since Methlyn herself."

"Are we done with this?" asked Zabeth, impatiently.

"But you have the temperament of her sister Zalphlyn."

Keruct threw his head back and laughed loudly as did the others. Zabeth looked at each one of them in turn and saw something there she hadn't seen before. When she first joined the company, she had, at first glance, put every one of these three into the pig category. They had done nothing, until now, to change her mind. Now, after a single, rather easy bit of soldiering, they were laughing and carrying on with her like they did among themselves. She decided that it felt good.

She didn't hear it in time. A scrape of sand, an exhaled breath all should have warned her but she was distracted. A brown hand reached up and grabbed her leg, pulling her off the horse. She tumbled to the sand and grabbed the wrist of the Sarondaki who tried to plunge a dagger into her chest. His weight bore on her and she labored to breathe. More importantly, he was stronger and the knife point came down slowly but inexorably.

She pulled her right leg out from under him and curled it up to where she could reach her boot knife. With prying fingers she pulled it out by the pommel, shifted her grip and plunged it into the man's back. He jerked and spat blood into Zabeth's face every time her dagger bit into his flesh. By the time Keruct and the others had removed the Sarondaki from on top of her, he was dead, his back and side bloodied from over a dozen wounds.

Zabeth staggered to her feet, spitting blood out of her mouth and wiping it out of her eyes. She still gripped her dagger which dripped blood and her armor and tunic were soaked. She walked away from the group for a moment, trying to contain her anger and, she tilted her head sidewise, looking internally, fear? If the Sarondaki had struck with his dagger first, instead of pulling her from the horse, these men would be burying her right now.

"You all right Zabeth?" asked Keruct from behind her.

"I'm...trying to get this stuff off me. Anybody have a clean rag?" Zabeth looked around at them. Keruct turned to look at the other two men, both of whom were as unkempt as he.

"Try scrubbing your face with a handful of sand. Just keep it away from your eyes."

Zabeth knelt down and did as Keruct suggested. She would have still preferred a rag, or even better, a bath but the sand removed most of the gore from her face. She looked down at her dripping armor.

"Nothing can be done about this I suppose."

Vorkle spoke up. "Armor stained with the blood of your enemy is a badge of honor." The others murmured assent.

Zabeth looked at them for a moment. "Very well then. Let it stain. Let's get back to the battle and see if I can't stain it some more."

The men cheered and they mounted up and rode off back toward the battle. When they got there, though, the fighting was mostly finished. A few men were mopping up around the fringes, but mostly they were trying to extricate loads of supplies from the tangle of dead bodies. A couple of partisans chased after runaway camels and mules, bringing them back to the valley. In the middle of the valley on the road a stood a group of prisoners being guarded by two partisans.

"Where have you been," asked Bindle. He rode up the slope of the dune toward Zabeth and her companions. His armor was torn and he bled from several wounds on his arms and legs. "You abandoned your post."

Zabeth stopped just above Bindle and glared at him. "We were being flanked. I took some men and dealt with it."

"Flanked," yelped Bindle, making a face. "Where?"

Zabeth pointed to the dark blotch on the horizon where the bodies of the Sarondakis lay and then motioned to their horses tethered together and trailing Keruct. The three warriors crossed their arms and smiled at Bindle's dismay.

"Oh, I see. Well, good job I guess." He looked around nervously. "But you still shouldn't have gone. If you saw something you should have alerted someone else and remained at your post while someone more qualified handled it."

"More qualified," bristled Zabeth, advancing on Bindle, "if you want to see how qualified I am, ride out there and take a look or better yet search your memory."

"Luck," he said. "I let you win that fight."

"You want to try it again," said Zabeth her hand reaching for her sword hilt.

"No time," said Bindle, a little quickly, "Kebble wants everybody to pitch in with the supplies. That includes you."

"Who are you? His messenger boy?"

"Well at least I'm not his..." Anger flashed in Zabeth's mind, and she could see Bindle back down. He turned his horse and rode down the dune.

"Idiot," yelled Zabeth.

No reply came.

"Hey Zabeth," said Keruct, riding up beside her. "You want us to find him later tonight and teach him some manners?" The other two nodded willingness.

Zabeth turned her head sharply. "Would you have made the same offer if I were a man?"

"Well...I don't know...I..."

"I can fight my own battles." She glared at them as they cleared their throats and looked everywhere but at her.

"Ah, sure, let us know if you need some help," said Keruct. They quickly rode off and Zabeth stared after them as they dismounted and started pulling a load of provisions off a dead camel's back. Maybe Kebble had been right about the company accepting her.

18

Buckle wondered, as he stared into the darkness of the cell, if Death's footsteps would echo through the hall when he came. Or would Death be ethereal, like a wooliman, and have no body to go clanking around in. A long cough wracked his body, starting from his stomach and rippling up his chest until it weakly emerged from his mouth. Stinging pain tortured his throat which was raw from coughing. His mouth was dry and blistered and he had trouble working up enough saliva to eat. The floor on which he laid was killing him. Yazzle had tried to scrape away the mold but it kept coming back.

And mold wasn't the worst of it. Every night when the candle went out the cell became full of the sound of strange gropings and scuffles. More than once, Yazzle had left his usual place by Buckle's side and struggled unseen in the darkness. There would follow the sounds of grunts, groans and the smacks of landed punches. When he'd return Buckle would ask Yazzle what had happened. "You don't want to know, Master Buckle," was the inevitable reply. And it was true, he didn't. Thoughts of home consoled him for a while but lately they seemed distant and painful. Now he spent most of his time laying on his back and listening for footsteps.

A metal door clanged somewhere and then came footsteps, but not the kind Buckle listened for. This was the morning routine. The guards were going around to all the cells lighting candles and waking the prisoners. Inside his cell, Buckle could hear some stirring, groans and muttered complaints as the din outside woke everybody up. By the time they opened Buckle's cell to light the candle, everyone was up.

This cell had the luxury of having a hole in the wall big enough to use as a privy. Every morning the inhabitants of the cell would line up in front of this hole, first Bruct's favorites who took a conspicuously long time, and then the rest had only a few minutes before breakfast.

Bruct ruled the cell by sheer physical force. The other prisoners had to do what he told them or face injury or even death. Only Yazzle could stand up to the petty tyrant but he would only do it when Bruct directly threatened Buckle or the few other prisoners that had weaseled their way under his protection. The small band had only semi-independence from Bruct.

Breakfast was the same disgusting mash they had served on the trek across the desert. The prisoners got one bowl of it and one cup of tepid oily water from an old Sarondaki woman. The meal was eaten sitting on the floor in the hall. Buckle ate slowly, having to choke it down but Yazzle made him eat every bite and would even have given him half of his own had not Buckle absolutely refused.

Yazzle didn't look too well. Apart from his scraggly beard and hair and the coal dust ground permanently into his hands and face, he now shambled more than he walked and his eyes had a vacant expression most of the time. A cough was starting to develop, not as bad as Buckle's, but Buckle knew that Yazzle was bringing up blood. And yet Yazzle still went into the mine every day and extracted his quota of coal and two thirds of Buckle's. Buckle had tried to get him to only do his own but Yazzle wouldn't budge. Those who didn't make their quotas were executed.

As bad as Yazzle was, Buckle knew he would die first, perhaps soon. He could barely make the increasingly longer walk to the working face, the point where they had left off mining the day before, much less do his share of work. His pick went into the black rock but only loosened a few stones. Then he'd have to rest. The mine was damp and cold. Guards came by every few minutes to keep the prisoners working or just to whip them for no reason. And just when it seemed conditions couldn't get worse there'd be a cave in somewhere or the tunnel would flood and Buckle would spend the night freezing in his wet rags. He didn't exactly want to die but he now expected to and figured that if he had to, he'd rather do it soon.

After breakfast it was off to the mines. These were, as far as Buckle could judge, two to three hundred feet under the prison cells and may have even been under ground level. They were lowered into

173

the pit by a wooden contraption supported by giant rusty chains. Prisoners stood at the top of the shaft and lowered or raised the platform by winding or unwinding the chains onto large barrels. It was a frightening descent, full of starts and stops, long delays and an occasional moment of terror when the platform dropped a little ways, seemingly out of control.

The platform jerked to a stop, leaving a two foot step, pretty good, considering some days the step could be six feet high. The prisoners climbed off the platform and into the shaft. In the dim torch light they picked up their picks and shovels from where they had left them on the floor of the tunnel the day before. It was swift and sure death to try and take one of these implements onto the platform.

The platform shot up after the last prisoner departed and the guard who ran it, small by Sarondaki standards had pulled the signal rope. Buckle retrieved a pick and shovel, noting that the only ones left after Bruct's group picked over them were dull implements whose shafts had been mended many times. In the surrounding desert wood was far more scarce than the iron of the pick itself. Buckle followed Yazzle's broad shoulders down to one of the working faces. Behind them came the guards, fingering their short whips, ideal for use in the enclosed confines of the mine.

The rest of the morning was spent swinging the pick and embedding its point in the rock and then pulling out as much of the black substance as possible. Then when a respectable heap had accumulated at Buckle's feet he would shovel it to a larger heap that represented his day's production. Every night at quitting time a guard would come along, holding a stick. If the pile were as tall, or taller than the stick, Buckle would live another day. For Buckle, the process consisted of several feeble attempts to swing the pick. Most of the time, it would only go in little ways and bring out a few flakes of coal. A lot of the time the point bounced off. Since each swing wore Buckle out to the point where he needed a five minute rest, such failures were devastating.

Yazzle though, worked steadily, chopping away at the rock face for fifteen minutes and then shoveling the coal into his and Buckle's pile. Every so often he switched sides with Buckle so he wouldn't get too far ahead. Watching this, Buckle was almost reduced to tears of frustration at not being able to help himself and his inability to get Yazzle to stop killing himself.

Toward the end of day they got another bowl of mush. Yazzle helped Buckle limp to the serving wagon and then they sat on the floor in front of the platform and ate with their grimy fingers. The mush tasted of coal. Buckle felt too tired to eat but once again Yazzle made him. Around them sat the other members of Yazzle's group.

Nergle, a short squirrelly kind of man, brought in after Buckle and Yazzle arrived, broke the accustomed silence. "I was talking to a guy from another cell yesterday. He said that some of these tunnels lead out of here."

He looked around at the group. Yazzle bent over his bowl, forcing his fingers to dip into the mush and bring the vile stuff up to his mouth. The rest of the group was doing much the same. No one paid any attention to Nergle.

"He says that Dalmar and Methlyn found the way out through the tunnels under the mine."

Shacknel snorted, the folds of skin on the old-timer's face flapping like a bulldog's.

"What?" said Nergle. "Don't you believe me?"

Buckle looked up and took a labored breath. "We've all heard that one Nergle." Gasp. "They tell it to all the newcomers."

"Also that story about Dalmar is a lie if you think about it," said Shacknel.

"It could be true," protested Nergle.

"If they got out, it'd be in the songs."

"Maybe they kept their escape a secret."

"Bah," barked Shacknel with a swipe of his wrinkled hand. "What possible reason could they have had for that? Look, I'm not saying they might not have slipped past the guards and wondered around in the tunnels down there. People have done that, even in my time. But they didn't get out. Nobody ever does."

Yazzle got up suddenly. Everybody looked up at him. He avoided their eyes as he took Buckle's bowl, and with his own, he walked over to the pile of dirty bowls and placed them on top.

"How can you live like that," hissed Nergle. "Without hope?"

"Hope's what kills you down here. Best to give it up and live as best you can until Death takes pity on you."

Yazzle returned and the conversation died. But Buckle thought about the exchange between the two prisoners. Was Shacknel right? Were they better off without hope? Buckle could feel the hope in his own chest dying a little every day. He no longer dreaded death. Would someday he actually come to long for it? He looked at Shacknel. The old man sourly chewed his gray mush. If he was out of hope, waiting for death, why didn't he hasten its coming? Deep down Buckle knew why he himself didn't. Hope died very hard and when as far as you know you only have one life, giving up on it would take more than just a few months in this hell. Shacknel, though, might be at the breaking point, he might be ready to throw himself down the shaft or pick a fight with Bruct or the most efficient method: refuse to work.

Bruct came by and snapped, "Back to work, slaves before the guards come and give you the beatings you deserve." He spat at them and laughed. Then, with his closest lieutenants at his side, he marched down the tunnel leading toward the working face. With multiple groans, Yazzle's group rose and straggled afterward, Yazzle holding on to Buckle's arm to support him.

That night as Buckle lay, shivering from cold and his nightly struggle to breathe, he watched the swirling lights that danced in his vision. It felt like the inside of his skull was tingling and he could almost feel his faculties fading. Like every night, he wanted to scream and beg for someone to help him, help him take just one clear breath. It had been so long since he'd had one. The back of his throat tickled so much, it actually hurt; he would swallow and then try to relax until the tingling returned. Eventually, he knew he would start the painful coughing again.

Greens, blues and yellows streaked slowly across the blackness. In the middle of all this, he noticed one dot of light, pure white in the center of his vision. It grew, shining brighter, actually casting light into the room unlike the other sparks. Then it dropped down to just above his head. Buckle felt his chest relax, a total relaxation that he had never been able to achieve on his own. The mucus in his chest disappeared. His eyes drifted shut and he felt himself sinking in a warm pool of sleep.

"Are you death," he asked the light in a horse whisper. The act of talking broke open the scabs on his chapped lips and he felt a warm trickle of blood, a salty taste in his mouth. The light didn't answer but somehow before the pool of sleep engulfed him he knew the light was not death but perhaps the opposite.

The next day Buckle's chest was clear and he was stronger. He could walk, slowly but unaided. Eating was still difficult because his throat was still dry and swollen but he didn't have to stop so often to breathe, and best of all, he made most of his quota of coal. Yazzle only had to supply a little.

The light appeared again the next night late, after all the vile activity that occurred after their candle was blown out had finished. Buckle awoke from a rare deep sleep and saw the glimmering white light shining on the wall. He rolled over and watched the shining sphere hovering over the hole in the wall. It bounced in the air a couple of times and then dived half way into the hole. Pausing in the gap, Buckle got the distinct feeling it wanted him to follow. But beyond the hole was a drop of maybe hundreds of feet and a horrendous smell. Buckle turned his back to the sphere and after a while the shimmering light blinked out.

The next day after they had been brought up from the mines, Buckle sat on the floor, throwing pinches of dwale around his sleeping area. They had discovered that the herb was good for killing rats which served the double purpose of cutting down on the vermin and adding a meat supplement to their diet. So far, they had kept the herb's usefulness a secret from Bruct.

Yazzle lay on the straw next to Buckle, his arm over his eyes, trying to get some sleep. But Buckle could tell that sleep wasn't coming to him. The lad had too much on his mind. Because of his size he had suddenly found himself in a position of leadership, responsible for the protection of the four people who made up his gang. And every day Bruct pushed him a little bit further. At first Buckle tried to advise Yazzle between rasping gasps of breath. But as the days wore on, Yazzle grew more despondent and unresponsive. He still acted when Bruct threatened one of them, especially Buckle but very little else drew much response.

Hopefully things will get better now, thought Buckle as he folded up the package of dwale and put it under the few things he had accumulated down here. Buckle had made his quota today unaided. He even threw a few stones on Nergle's pile which looked a little short. Yazzle had made his by the afternoon feeding, and when he saw Buckle was going to make it, he crept into a crevice and took a nap. A few more days like that and maybe he'd be back to his old self.

Shacknel walked into the cell, his expression sour. "How is he?" He pointed to Yazzle.

"I think he'll be fine," said Buckle, "as long as Bruct doesn't stir up any trouble."

Shacknel snorted. "Maybe I should get Nergle in here. Keep him out of Bruct's way."

"It's all right. Bruct seems to be more interested in talking up the guards today than causing us problems."

"Yes."

Buckle watched as Shacknel sat next to him.

"How long do you figure you been in here, Shacknel?"

"I don't know," said the old man, his flabby features tightened in thought. "Maybe twenty years."

Buckle emitted a low whistle. "I'll never last that long."

"No, you won't." Buckle looked at him sharply but Shacknel was concentrating on rearranging some of the straw. He didn't mean anything by his comment. He was simply stating the truth as he saw it. Politeness didn't have a place down here.

"How'd you get here?" asked Buckle.

Shacknel cast Buckle an irritated look. "I used to be a scholar," he said. "I made a living tutoring on an estate in eastern Joswell. They mostly had cattle and horses. For most of the year I taught the lord's children and those of the staff. But when spring came around and most of the kids were needed to help round up the stock, I was left on my own. I would go off into the mountains by myself to a few places I knew where the Sarondakis had once built outposts. Some of them dated back to before Skrike's first invasion."

"How could you tell?"

"By the pottery they left behind, mostly. Styles change. For instance, there are no Soowooli urns before Skrike. The practice of Soowooli is apparently Tenaryan and Skrike brought it to the tribes. But the point is that it's possible to trace Sarondaki history by the shapes and patterns on their ceramics."

"And you could do this?"

Shacknel pulled himself up a little. "I was one of the foremost scholars on the subject in the west."

"So what happened?"

"One spring, I wondered a little too far east and the Sarondakis captured me." He shrugged and lay down on the straw.

"And you've been here ever since?"

"They don't give you sabbaticals down here."

"I bet you've heard a lot of rumors about escape routes?"

"I've heard 'em all," he said, not looking up.

Buckle leaned over toward him and said quietly, "Have you ever heard of anyone seeing strange spheres of light?"

"You seeing lights?" He looked up at Buckle.

Buckle nodded.

"You won't last as long as I thought, if you're seeing things already." He shook his head and went back to pushing the straw around on the floor in front of him. After a moment he looked up and said, "What do the lights do?"

"There's only one," answered Buckle and then he described its actions of the night before.

"Hmm," said Shacknel, scratching his chin in thought. "There're some old stories, very old, about people seeing lights. They would appear at the ends of tunnels and guide men into the bowels of the earth, supposedly to freedom. You say this thing wanted you to follow it?"

"That's the feeling I got. No real communication, just sort of an urge to go."

"And nobody's mentioned people seeing lights to you before?"

"No," said Buckle, watching the old prisoner.

Shacknel bowed his head and pursed his lips, an action that almost made his mouth disappear. "Probably nonsense," he pronounced and turned over on his side.

"Has anybody looked in that hole?"

"Why should anyone want to look into a privy?" said Shacknel, turning back and making a face.

Buckle looked over at the hole and then at the open cell door. Bruct was no doubt down the hallway at the little table the guards sat behind when not patrolling the hallways. The big prisoner was almost always seen in the company of guards and he got himself and his gang a lot of special favors because of it.

"I'm looking in that hole," said Buckle, rising and grabbing the candle. He kneeled before the opening which was just wide enough to get his shoulders through,. He held the candle in front of him. The stench was overpowering, almost causing Buckle to drop his light. But he held on and was able to look around.

Opposite him, at a distance short enough to step across, was a solid stone wall, painted black. The outlines of the stones were just visible in the flickering candlelight. A ledge, wide enough to walk on, was carved into the wall. Its edges crumbling, it looked unsafe. Below lay an abyss of darkness and stench. Buckle tried to ignore it.

Off to the right though was a darker patch of black just out of the range of the candlelight. Buckle strained his eyes but couldn't make out any details in the blackness. The tunnel into which he had stuck his head seemed to go on infinitely to both sides of him. Vaguely, he wondered what it was originally built for.

"What do you see," asked Shacknel from behind him. Buckle pulled his head out of the hole and described the scene. Shacknel bit his lip and stroked his chin.

Finally, he said, "Tear a strip of cloth off your shirt. I'll look for some dry straw."

He rummaged around the cell for some clean straw while Buckle tore a strip of cloth from his sleeve. Shacknel finally found some suitable straw over on Bruct's side of the cell. He grasped a handful of it and then tied it into a clump with the strip of cloth.

"Get ready," he said and Buckle positioned himself in front of the hole. Hands shaking with age, Shacknel put one end of his straw clump into the candle flame and handed it to Buckle. Buckle held the burning clump of straw before him as he stuck his head into the hole again. Then with a careful flip of his wrist he tossed it into the area of blackness, illuminating it.

It was a tunnel, or rather a cave. The side Buckle could see in the spitting light of the burning straw was stony and irregular not man made like the wall in front of him. He of course, couldn't see how far it went back.

"What's going on here?" Bruct's voice startled Buckle so much he banged his head on the inside edge of the hole, trying to get back into the cell. He knelt on the floor, rubbing the back of his head while Shacknel looked up at the bully, too old to be intimidated.

"We were looking in the hole," he said.

"That's disgusting, why?"

Shacknel and Buckle exchanged glances. Did they dare try to make up a convincing lie? Buckle thought better of it.

"We thought there might be an escape route there." An unconvincing lie would make Bruct suspicious whereas a half-truth might just satisfy him.

Bruct broke into laughter. "Ho, ho I can just see you two swimming to freedom in a river of piss." Buckle thought for a moment the bully would lie down and roll in the straw, he was laughing so hard. "I wonder," he gasped, "if the guards would find this funny." He sneered at them, thinking he had the upper hand with his attempt at blackmail.

"I think it's more likely they'll just close the hole," said Buckle, his heart in his throat.

"That's right," said Bruct, sobering up. "Not a word of this gets out. If they take away our hole you guys will be sleeping in the new toilet.

"Nothing back there anyway," said Buckle, hanging his head.

"Well if I catch any of you looking in that hole again you're going in it. Understand?" Bruct picked Buckle up by the front of his shirt. His dark features knitted together in an unpleasant expression. Buckle returned the gaze steadily. Shacknel watched from a corner.

Only Yazzle reacted. He jumped up from the floor and grabbed Bruct's shoulder, spinning him around. "You don't have your friends here to help you Bruct, so leave Master Buckle alone and get out of the cell."

The bully looked at Yazzle and then back at Buckle. His face displayed a range of emotions from fear to disgust, until he gained control over it and it donned its customary sneer. He broke Yazzle's grip with a jerk of his shoulder. Then he backed toward the door.

"You don't scare me Westerner," said. "I've killed a desert scorpion."

"So have I."

Bruct laughed. "I've heard that story. Mine was uninjured before I fought it."

Yazzle took a step forward and Bruct slipped out the door. Buckle watched the lad stare at the door for a moment and then turn away, rubbing his eyes. He stumbled back to their section of the floor and sat down. That's it, thought Buckle, making up his mind. Yazzle had once thanked him for delivering him from an estate that treated its workers like slaves. Buckle had felt good about that. But here they both were prisoners, slaves in fact, treated far worse than Buckle would have imagined possible a few months ago. They would escape or die trying. He owed it to the lad.

"Master Buckle," asked Yazzle, softly. Buckle knelt by him. "I heard you and Shacknel talking." His lips were bleeding. "This light, is it real?"

"I believe it is Yazzle."

Yazzle nodded his head. "What's in the hole?"

Shacknel scooted up on the other side of Yazzle. "We think it's a tunnel," he said.

"To the outside?"

"We don't know," said Buckle. "But here's what I believe. If we use the tunnel, the light will guide us to freedom."

Yazzle leaned his head back. "Then we must go."

"It could also lead to death," said Shacknel.

"Death is freedom," said Yazzle and Buckle couldn't disagree with him.

19

Zabeth kicked the sides of her horse and pulled its nose toward camp. Beside her, visible in the silver blue moonlight, Keruct did the same. They edged their steeds off the ridge where they had stopped to get one last look at the Sarondaki campfires. When they reached the desert floor they broke into a full gallop, the loose sand muffling the sound of their hoof beats. Or so Zabeth hoped. She looked up at the moon, its light making her uncomfortable. The two riders skirted dunes and hunched down on their horses' backs.

The camp suddenly opened out before them. Sand colored tarps provided effective camouflage. Under them some forty partisans hunkered down, their armor strapped on, swords drawn and ready for the order to move. Zabeth could imagine every one of them, grim-faced and determined, each going through his own private ritual before entering battle. She knew them now. Her list of pigs had gotten smaller and the list of men she could trust had grown.

She pulled up and then dismounted, handing her reins to Keruct who galloped off to tie up the horses while Zabeth made her report. Cautiously she approached the sentry who challenged her and when she offered the correct response let her by. A stray desert breeze cut through her light tunic but she resisted the urge to pull her cloak around her shoulders. Some of these men went shirtless at night. She was glad of the chain mail covering most of her torso.

Dug into the side of a dune, Kebble's tent was the only one with a torch lighting it. But it was a small torch and necessary to plan strategy. Zabeth entered and found Kebble and Bindle in conversation. The blond leader was, as usual seated comfortably. He fingered the stem of his pipe absently and spoke in a calm voice. Bindle was hunched over, his hands chopping the air. He broke off his statement to look up when Zabeth walked in.

"You've got the scouting report," challenged Bindle.

"Of course I've got it. You think I've been out to the oasis for a midnight swim?"

"Before we get to the shouting, why don't you tell me what you saw?" Kebble whacked the bowl of his pipe against his palm and looked up at her with his sky blue eyes twinkling in the torch light. The lines around them crinkled up as he gave her a wry smile. For a second Zabeth could only look at him. He was better than Buckle when it came to diffusing her temper. When he looked at her something in her insides fluttered like a leaf in the wind.

"Well," demanded Bindle.

Her thoughts snapped and she came back to business. "There's about two hundred and fifty of them camped in a tubular formation like so." She squatted down and drew a thick line in the sand. "They have guards posted at even intervals around the edge of the camp and two scouts roaming the immediate area. Keruct and I took care of them."

"Are you sure there were only two?" asked Bindle.

"Yes, I'm sure," snapped Zabeth.

"When are the scouts due back?" asked Kebble.

"No way of knowing but we got them just as then were leaving the camp. Knife to the throat stuff. No noise."

"Good, that probably gives us a few hours." He leaned over in the chair. "We'll wait till their campfires start going out. Zabeth," he said, pointing his pipe stem at her, "step one will be you. Take your men and eliminate the guards. Don't raise any alarms."

"Yes."

"Bindle."

"Yes."

"Your troop will form south of the camp, mine north. You attack the east side. I'll attack the west. That's the right."

"I know."

"Now tell your men this is just a ride by and shoot. We attack, raise some hell and then run away. I don't want to get into a pitched battle with a force this size. Hopefully, we'll get them to chase us a little ways."

"They'll understand."

"Good. Get your men ready. After the raid we'll meet at our rendezvous point."

"We'll be there." He stood up and stepped toward the exit but Zabeth blocked his way. Their eyes met and for a moment Zabeth thought she saw something other than the customary belligerence in them. His gaze dropped in confused embarrassment and when Zabeth stepped out of his way he hurried out of the tent.

"Any more orders for me, Kebble?" Zabeth faced him. He leaned back in his chair and yawned, stretching his muscles to their fullest extent.

"No, I think we've about covered it."

"Good. I'll round up my men." She turned to leave.

"Zabeth."

"Yes."

Kebble looked up at her from his chair. "I just wanted to say that you're doing well here." He twirled the pipe and looked at a spot somewhere to her left. "You've been outstanding in battle and have gained the respect of the men. And...if we survive this campaign I look forward to...serving with you again."

"That would be nice. I'd like to stay in the east, hopefully in the Barrier Scouts. That is..."

"That is what?" Kebble stopped playing with his pipe and met her eyes.

"I don't know if the Scouts would ever take a woman."

"You're here aren't you?"

"This is different. There's a war on and I sort of stumbled into it. What happens when Skrike's defeated?"

"You mean if," sighed Kebble. "Actually constables in the Scouts can ride with whoever they want. As long as I have a company, Zabeth, you'll be welcome."

"What if I want a company of my own some day?"

Kebble puffed on his pipe and contemplated the blue smoke. "I honestly don't know, Zabeth."

She looked at the sand, disappointed. She didn't know what answer she could have been expecting, however. "It won't matter, anyway, if I can't rescue Buckle." She knew Kebble didn't agree; it was in his eyes but he didn't say anything. She knew, however, that she would never be able to happily embark on a career if she didn't do everything she could to fulfill her oath.

Charles Ebert

Kebble looked down at Zabeth's diagram drawn in the sand. "I'll do what I can, Zabeth but you have to know my mission comes first."

Zabeth sighed and walked up to him. "I know Kebble, and I understand that he's probably better off where he is than out here. So I'll wait and I'll survive. But when we march into Castle Skrike, I'll tear the place apart until I find him."

Kebble shifted in his seat and said. "Nobody knows what it's like in those dungeons but it's bound to be horrible. He could be dead, Zabeth."

She sighed and looked at Kebble. "I know he's with Yazzle and possibly Krinseth. They'll protect him. What is this about Kebble?"

"I just don't want you to be disappointed."

"I can handle disappointment. You know something."

"Unconfirmed reports. It could be nothing." Kebble waved his hand in the air, trying to dismiss the importance of his information.

"What?"

He sighed and said, "The courier who caught up with us the other day...He's been with us before and heard you asking questions about Buckle so he made some inquiries. Apparently a couple of months ago in Zaron a tall blond westerner in a prisoner caravan was interviewed personally by Marduct. One of our spies witnessed it."

"Yazzle," said Zabeth, her hope rising. "Was Buckle with him?"

"Don't know. But if he didn't do or say anything significant the spy may not have noticed him. The prisoner caravan was bound for Castle Skrike."

"So if Buckle's anywhere, he's there."

"Assuming it was Yazzle."

"It was," said Zabeth, her blood pounding. "I feel it as sure as I've ever felt anything. And Buckle is still alive. I know it."

"Now Zabeth..."

Direngoss stuck his head into the tent. "Campfire's are going out, Kebble."

"Let's go," said Kebble, leaping to his feet and shoving the torch into the sand. Zabeth shot out of the tent behind Kebble and scrambled for her horse. Waiting by the horses were Keruct, Vorkle and Tiacin, her men. She explained their orders and they mounted.

186

They rode part-way and then dismounted, tying their horses together and then leaving some food so they wouldn't wander off. Zabeth's part went smoothly. Blue steel flashing in the moonlight, digging into throats and chests. In a few minutes the camp was unguarded and the four rendezvoused and counted up the dead. When they were sure all eight guards were taken care of, Keruct gave the signal to attack which was a passable imitation of the mating call of a desert wolf.

"Tiacin, get the horses," whispered Zabeth as she took her bow from her shoulder. They could hear the distant thunder of hoof beats, and in the Sarondaki camp the warriors were stirring.

Zabeth and her men weren't fifty yards from where the Sarondakis had their horses tied up. She nocked an arrow and sent it speeding into the heart of the first warrior to approach his steed. Keruct and Vorkle followed her example. The Sarondakis returned fire but they were in light while Zabeth and her men hid in darkness. By the time the horses were eclipsed by Bindle's men by shooting arrows and chopping down the sleepy Sarondakis like wheat, Tiacin came up with their horses.

"Mount up," cried Zabeth, as she continued arcing arrows over Bindle's head into the Sarondaki camp. The others climbed onto their horses. They stood, waiting for her as she launched one arrow after another.

"We gotta go Zabeth," shouted Keruct.

"Just a second."

"Come on, Zabeth," boomed Vorkle from his saddle.

"One more."

"Wait. I saw a warrior escape the camp," said Tiacin. "He's heading this way."

"Get on your horse, Zabeth."

Zabeth peered into the darkness between them and the camp, searching for the oncoming Sarondaki. Bindle's men were setting fire to their tents and the blaze shone bright but flickered with the movement of the battle, making it difficult to pick out a target.

"Are you sure? I can't see him," she said.

"Come on Zabeth. We should be out of here," said Keruct.

"All right." She grabbed her horse's reins and was about to swing into the saddle when she saw a flash of steel. She ducked and rolled to her right, pulling off her bow and quiver. She unsheathed just in time for a blind parry over her head. The Sarondaki sword forced her blade down to within a few inches of her head. Slowly it lowered. Zabeth kicked upward and caught the warrior in the abdomen. He backed off, giving her time to roll to her feet.

But the attack was on again, almost immediately, right, left, head. Combinations Zabeth had only seen herself and Grazzle do, performed at lightning speed. She could barely follow them. Her opponent manipulated her position, keeping her between him and her men, who were frantically trying to join the fight.

The Sarondaki feinted left, made a sort of scooping motion toward her head that made Zabeth duck and then he cut a backhanded swipe like an executioner. Zabeth saw it, but not in time. She leapt back, causing the blade to miss her head but it bit into her leg just above the knee as the swordsman adjusted the arc of the blade downward in mid-swing. She screamed in agony and dropped to the sand, sword up in a last effort to block his killing blow.

Horses rode past her on both sides and the blow never came. When her vision cleared of the shooting stars caused by the pain she saw Keruct and Tiacin harrying the Sarondaki from their horses. The warrior ran between his two new adversaries, beating one back before charging the other. His strategy obviously was to take up time until help arrived and it seemed to be working. Neither Tiacin, whose strong point was the sword, nor Keruct could penetrate the Sarondaki's guard.

Zabeth limped to her horse where Vorkle still held it and climbed into the saddle. Red shooting lights blurred her vision and her lower left leg was soaked with warm flowing blood. Tiacin looked at her, his face scrunched up in concern. She waved him off.

"Keruct, Tiacin, I'm ready. Let's go before he gets help."

The two rode back away from the Sarondaki warrior who stood feet apart and sword in hand. Zabeth's blood dripped off the tip. He pointed it at her just as she was about to turn. "Your name warrior," he demanded.

"Zabeth of Delamer."

"A woman?" His voice sounded amazed.

"Yours."

"Deruct of the Eastern Tribes. We shall meet again, warrior."

"I'll be ready." She kicked her horse's flank with the heel of her good leg and rode off with her men.

The three companions hung back a little, Zabeth noticed. And besides questions about her leg, they spoke little but looked at her strangely. Zabeth was content with that. The sound of the raid died out as they rode further away from it. Every jolt the horse made introduced her to new worlds of pain.

Finally they reached the rendezvous point. A few warriors were already there. They stayed on their horses, ready to go when the rest of the group got there. Zabeth gratefully stopped and leaned forward to rest her forehead against the horse's neck.

"How's the leg," asked Keruct.

"I'm going to need a bandage," said Zabeth. She sat up and tore a strip of cloth off the bottom of her tunic. Laying that across the other thigh, she pulled apart the slice in the knee of her breeches, exposing the wound.

"Great Dalmar," cried Keruct, who started to dismount.

"Stay on your horse. I can manage," said Zabeth. She pulled her water skin and pulled the cork out with her teeth and rinsed out the wound, grimacing at the sharp pain caused by the action. Then with excruciating effort she lifted the leg and slipped the strip of cloth under her knee and tied it tightly. Stars exploded in front of her eyes and she felt dizzy and nauseous. She wanted nothing more than to fall off her horse and go to sleep in the sand. But with her men watching and the certainty of having to flee at any moment, rest was impossible.

"That warrior was good," observed Zabeth.

"He was Deruct," said Tiacin. "If I had known that, I'd have never attacked him."

"I'd have grabbed you and put you on your horse," said Keruct.

"You'd have tried. So the warrior has a reputation?"

"A deadly one." Vorkle's voice rumbled out of his deep barrel chest. "You have made a powerful enemy Zabeth."

"You shouldn't have told him your name. Now he'll come looking for you," said Tiacin.

"He'll die before he stops chasing you," said Vorkle and he leaned forward in his saddle. "You see, he has your name."

"Well lads," said Zabeth, trying to sound brave but her voice quivered with the pain in her leg. "Kebble's always saying none of us are going to survive this war. If I have to die, it may as well be by the hand of the best they've got."

Her three men shifted uncomfortably.

"They say he's killed scorpions," said Keruct, "and not just in his manhood rite, but wild ones, unchained."

"I've seen the scorpions out here," said Zabeth, waving the thought away.

"You've seen babies," said Keruct. "Out on the high desert there's scorps the size of houses and bigger."

"Fish stories."

"I've seen them," said Keruct. "Thankfully from afar."

Zabeth looked at him and as far as she could see in the moonlight there was no lie in the man. She shrugged her shoulders. Tomorrow wouldn't be any business of hers until tomorrow.

"Here they come," yelled the sentry, and the small group, as one, rode out of the temporary camp. Zabeth cast a backward look at Bindle's men. They were riding hard across the sand with Kebble's about fifty feet behind. Behind them the Sarondaki camp burned in confusion. Even from this far away, Zabeth could hear their harsh voices calling for arms and horses. She wondered where Deruct was in all that confusion.

She shook her head and kicked the side of her horse wincing at the pain that shot through her injured leg. In a second, she was galloping across the desert, watching the silver blue night kaleidoscope across her vision. Pain and nausea filled her body and she bit her lip until it bled and she swallowed her vomit.

She rode like that all night, sometimes holding the reins for dear life. But she kept up their pace. Every once in a while Kebble would send back a scout to see if the Sarondakis still pursued them. He seemed especially anxious about it and was always pleased to find they were. Zabeth knew it had always been his plan to draw off large forces from the Sarondaki army and lead them south to waste energy, food and men before they eventually gave up the chase and staggered back to the main road. They had done it several times in the last few months.

They reached an oasis at dawn.

The rising sun tinted the small pool blood red which matched the sand around it. The partisans lined up, hollow-eyed and exhausted. They stretched their spines and began to brush down their horses. Some broke out hard tack or jerky for breakfast. The pool only allowed one person to comfortably drink at a time. Most men would immerse their heads, drink a few gulping mouthfuls and fill their water skins. Then he'd water his horse and let the next man in line have his turn.

Zabeth angled away from the oasis, waving off Keruct and Vorkle. "I'll be all right. Get in line." She guided the horse behind a dune and then let it stop.

Gingerly, she lifted her right leg and swung it backwards over the horse's rump to dismount. But when she put her weight on the injured leg it gave way and she tumbled backward with a weak cry. She lay on her back for a few seconds riding out the waves of pain. Then she turned over and discharged the contents of her stomach. Through the spasms, she felt her horse nudge her in the small of her back.

"Go on," she said, gently swatting at the horse's muzzle behind her. "Get some water. I'll be along eventually." Her stomach pulled itself inside out again and through her retching, she thought she heard the horse walk away. She could feel the sand caking her sweat soaked body as she jammed her forehead into the ground, marshaling the strength to move.

"Zabeth, here you are," said the familiar yet aggravating voice of Bindle. "This is no time to sleep." She could hear his footsteps as he marched toward her. "Get in line and fill your water skin. And take care of that horse. You won't find another one for..."

Zabeth found the strength all of a sudden and turned over. Even the wave of pain caused by jarring her wound, was squelched by her fury.

"You bastard, I'll..."

"Great Dalmar, your leg!"

"Damn right my leg. I'll use it to kick your teeth in if you come a step closer."

"Kebble, come here," he shouted, "Zabeth's been hurt." Then he knelt beside her and unstrapped his water skin.

"Get away from me, Bindle or I'll..."

"Just hold still and let me..." He held the water skin above the wound.

"Don't you touch me."

He pressed his hand on her leg above the wound, well above Zabeth thought, and poured water on it. Zabeth strangled a scream through clenched teeth. Her spine contracted, forcing her chest up into the air and her head back.

"You did that on purpose," she gasped when she could talk again.

Bindle shrugged, still looking at the wound as his hands unwound the bandage.

"What's the problem...Great Dalmar." Kebble dropped into view beside her, his face, caked with dust and sand seemed a little haggard.

"Kebble, kill this man." She pointed to Bindle. "No wait, don't kill him. Save him for me. I'll kill him as soon as this heals. I'll drink your blood Bindle."

"I think she's going to be all right," said Bindle, glancing across at Kebble, who took over unwrapping the bandage and smiled.

"The same can't be said for you," she growled, grabbing for his arm.

"Whoa, Zabeth," said Kebble, grasping her shoulders and pressing her to the ground. "Just relax. Here have some water." He squeezed some of Bindle's water skin into her mouth. It was tepid and had a sour taste of sulfur and calfshide but Zabeth gulped it eagerly until Kebble pulled it away. He handed the skin back to Bindle and finished unwrapping her leg. He wadded up the cracked and bloody bandage and tossed it aside. Zabeth watched his face as he surveyed the wound. It's usually serene look had been replaced. The brow crinkled and he bit his lower lip.

"How is it," she asked.

"Not too bad. You'll need stitches. Does it hurt?"

"Yes, but I can bear it until we get to a safe place."

Kebble shook his head. "No I'm too worried it'll go bad. I'll stitch it now."

"There's no time," Zabeth protested.

"Bindle, hold her down."

"He doesn't touch me." Bindle stopped in mid-action, looking at Kebble.

"Zabeth, the Sarondakis are about an hour and a half behind us..."

"So put me on my horse and let's go."

"It'll take me fifteen minutes to sew this up if you cooperate." Kebble rummaged through his pack, which Zabeth knew contained medical supplies. "Here, drink some of this." He pulled the cork out of a metal flask and held it to her lips. The liquid burned its way down her throat and Zabeth coughed, almost dry heaving again.

"What the hell is that," she gasped. He was laying out everything he needed for the operation.

"It's made in Kareez. I get it from a trader of the Eastern Tribes. He once told me they make it by fermenting potatoes." He swabbed her leg with a clean cloth and then held up a needle and thread. "Hold her down Bindle."

"I said..." But with his other hand, Bindle upended the flask into her mouth, leaving her spitting and sputtering. Her anger burned so bright she barely noticed the sharp pricks in her knee. Bindle sat above her head, his muscular arms pinning her shoulders to the sand. She tried to spit some of the stinging alcohol into his eyes but it kept missing, falling into her own. Her only consolation was that he was probably sitting in the place she had vomited.

"So how did this happen," asked Kebble, when she had settled down. The alcohol had produced a warm and calming haze which covered her whole body.

Zabeth described the fight in detail, remembering to mention the roles of Keruct and Vorkle. When she got to the part about exchanging names he looked at her.

"His name was Deruct?"

"That's what he said. The men explained to me who he is."

Kebble smiled, causing Zabeth's heart to pick up a beat. "Zabeth, you have done well."

"Well!" said Bindle. "He'll chase us into hell if he has to."

"Precisely," said Kebble. "And he's an important young chieftain, probably in charge of that whole force and maybe more if he split his forces. Now they'll be tied up chasing us and not fighting in the west."

"What do we do when they catch us?"

"Let's look on the bright side of things. Our duty is not to get caught for as long as possible. This is better than I could have hoped for." He chewed off the thread at about her knee and in his enthusiasm swung upwards and planted a quick kiss full on Zabeth's lips. It tasted of blood and salt and sand and was gone before she could really savor it. Then they hoisted her to her feet.

"Ah, your horse," said Kebble. Keruct stood holding the horse's reins. He looked at the newly bandaged wound on Zabeth's rubbery legs. "She'll be fine. We may have to tie her to her horse but she'll be fine."

"I watered her horse and filled her water skin," said Keruct, holding out his hand to give her a boost up.

"Good man," said Kebble, giving a hand by pushing her up from behind.

"Hey," protested Zabeth.

"Sorry."

Zabeth watched the sand underneath the feet of her horse and tried to keep her eyes open and follow the conversation.

"By the way," said Kebble to Keruct, "thanks for...well you know."

"Skrike's Hell, Kebble, we've stood by and just watched her fight so many times. It never seems like she's in any danger you know? But I think Deruct surprised her and it was dark and..."

"And it was Deruct."

"Yeah." Keruct paused and Zabeth could hear him nervously kicking the sand. "I better get on my horse. I'll take her reins for a while so she can rest."

"Kebble we've got a dust cloud." A sentry shouted down at them from the top of the dune. Kebble scrambled off.

"Zabeth," said Bindle softly.

"Ugh," muttered Zabeth, trying to get Bindle into focus and deciding it wasn't worth the effort.

"How does it feel?"

"Ugh, like a vacation in Raganorth. How do you think it feels?"

"Look, I just wanted to say I'm sorry for how I've been treating you. It was unfair and it won't happen again." He stared at her waiting for a response but Zabeth had closed her eyes and was concentrating on controlling the waves of pain and nausea.

Bindle licked his lips. "When I think of it! Deruct! Great Dalmar, you could have been killed. I don't know what I would have done."

"Bindle, you know what Kebble told me before the battle?"

"What?" He glanced at her sharply.

"Buckle's alive and he's in Castle Skrike."

Bindle cast his gaze downward. "That's great, Zabeth."

"Yeah, when we turn north again, I'm going to split off for a few days and get him out. You can come along if you like."

"Uh sure, I'll consider it."

"It'll be great having Buckle back again." She pushed her nose into the horse's mane. "And Yazzle too. Though I could do without that Krinseth."

"Bindle," yelled Kebble from on top of the dune. "Get on your horse. They're closer than we thought. Let's move gentlemen. That's Deruct who's chasing us. Southward." His horse reared up and then shot off in the indicated direction.

"Bindle," said Zabeth but he was gone. Instead, there was Keruct on his horse, holding the reins for hers and trotting them south.

20

The storm raged unabated into its second straight day. Or at least Nittle thought it was near dawn as he pulled his feet out of the sticky mud while following his escort to the tent that served as the royal headquarters. He wasn't real clear on which way was east. Darkness, rain and fatigue conspired to befuddle his senses. Gray soaking rain pelted him, pounding his shoulders like sledgehammers. It was the kind of night where it was best if you forgot about ever being dry again.

They arrived at the tent. Nittle's escort transferred him to the soldier guarding the entrance who pushed the flap in slightly and motioned Nittle inside.

The two kings and one lord were, of course, dry. King Nodwick of Goswick, King Tetwell of Joswell, and Lord Fazzle, the highest ranking Duke in Delamer since the mysterious disappearance of Roduct, all sat in canvas chairs before a table with maps strewn all over it. Cups of steaming ale sat on the maps making circular patterns on the paper. Nittle eyed them enviously.

Nodwick looked up. Nittle knew him from way back. He had been the second brother in the royal family and therefore had been allowed to join the Barrier Scouts. Only partly because of whom he was, he had worked his way up to Constable, and was a good one. When his brother died of a fever, he had been called back to assume the duties of the heir. He had gone reluctantly. Nittle had served under him for a number of years.

"Sir Nittle," said Nodwick. The old king stood and his hand massaged his lower back. Nittle noticed the lined face and the way the skin hung on his head pulling his bald scalp taut. "Glad you're in one piece."

"Thank you, Your Majesty. Just a little bruised but I'm here."

"We lose any old friends?"

"Kugle and Natwell, I believe you knew, Your Majesty. The rest were probably after your time. I lost about a hundred in all."

"Ah." He shook his head. "Kugle, he was the fat one who always had the funniest stories, right?"

"Yes, Your Majesty."

"Good man with an ax too." He ran his fingers across his bald pate. "He was with me for four years in the northern Barriers."

"He went down the third time they tried to take the hill, Your Majesty."

Fazzle, a fat man with chipmunk jowls, a receding hairline and a slip of a mustache cleared his throat meaningfully. "This is all very touching but we must get to the business at hand." The two kings cast him long-suffering looks but refrained from protest.

"Very well," said Nodwick. "I suppose Lord Fazzle is right. Give us your report Sir Nittle." All three looked up at him with expectant eyes. Fazzle motioned to an aid-de-camp in the corner who took up paper and quill and began to write when Nittle talked.

"Well Your Majesties and Lord, the plan was working almost perfectly up until the time we crossed the Navium. The storm hit when we were on the north side of the river. After a couple hours of forced marching we reached the ford and found it too deep to cross on foot."

"What did you do then?" Nodwick's chair creaked as he leaned back and regarded Nittle.

"I went to a nearby stretch that I knew, where the river is narrow but deep. There I had my strongest archer, Trindle, a capable man, Your Majesty, shoot an arrow across the river with a rope tied to it. Then I took volunteers to cross, using the canoes we brought for this kind of emergency." Nittle looked down at his muddy boots. This was the tough bit. "I lost five men. Their names were..."

Tetwell held up a restraining hand. "This is an informal briefing. Give the names to our clerk later. They will be honored and their families will get pensions. You were quite right to call for volunteers there." Nodwick nodded his assent. Fazzle continued staring at him.

"Thank you, Your Majesty. The sixth attempt was successful and we used the rope to pull the rafts across the river much like a ferry. I lost two rafts, a total of forty men."

"Go on," said Nodwick.

"Yes, Your Majesty. Once we were securely on the south bank, I sent out scouts who confirmed that the Sarondakis had no idea we were on their flank. Then we moved into position. By an hour after dawn we were set."

"What about your horses?" snapped Fazzle.

"Lord?"

"Horses man, horses. You had a company of cavalry with you. What did you do with the horses?"

"Lord, we had to leave them on the north side of the river."

"You mean you forced over fifty knights to dismount and fight on foot?"

"No, Lord," said Nittle, a little too quickly. "When I said 'them,' I meant the entire company was left behind."

"So you divided your forces?"

"I didn't see any alternative, Lord. The cavalry would never have made it across the river."

"And what about yourself?"

"Lord?" said Nittle, his discomfort growing.

"You are a knight. I sat in this very tent and watched King Nodwick make you one. Knights are mounted cavalry, always. What did you do with your horse?" Fazzle leaned forward in his chair, his eyes glittering.

"Lord, I sent him back to camp with the cavalry."

"You dismounted and continued on as if you were infantry?"

A flash of anger shot through Nittle when he heard the disparaging tone of Fazzle's voice when he said "infantry." Nittle suppressed the hot feelings. "Lord, I had to lead the mission."

"Still..."

"This is preposterous," said Nodwick. "The man wins the most important battle of the war almost single-handedly and you're berating him for getting off his horse?"

"The ancient tradition of Dern..."

"Oh blather, you don't know any more about 'the ancient tradition of Dern' than the rest of us..."

"Gentlemen," said Tetwell, barely raising his voice. The two others looked at him. Tetwell was not a large man but there was something in his manner that was impressive, even intimidating. For one thing he had a vast store of knowledge at his command. In these briefings, Nittle had seen him quote astounding facts seemingly out of the air. The Joswellian King seemed to know the population of every village and the height of every hill in the three western kingdoms. He also knew how to handle the temperamental Delamerian duke.

"Lord Fazzle, you must take into account that, until recently, Sir Nittle was an infantryman. We've lost so many knights in the past year, we've had to make new ones at an unprecedented rate. Sir Nittle has never been to court. He knows nothing of the traditions of which you speak. He's a pragmatic man, who saw what needed to be done and did it. I think in this case we can overlook a breach of military etiquette."

"Well," said the Delamerian lord, looking from one king to the other. "If you put it that way...I suppose I can let this go. But those were Delamerian knights in that company, fresh ones, that were looking to you, Sir Nittle, as an example of how to comport themselves, and you did not provide a very good one. Please be more careful in the future."

Actually, reflected Nittle, they were a bunch of loutish, arrogant and corrupt dunderheads, hastily raised from the constabularies of local Delamerian districts. If Nittle had had to take them into the battle, he judged that there was a very good chance things wouldn't have worked out so well.

"Yes, Lord," he said.

"Very decent of you Lord Fazzle," said Tetwell. "Please continue, Sir Nittle."

"Thank you, Your Majesty. We waited until King Nodwick began the main assault. When his attack drove the Sarondakis toward the river, they took the path between the two hills on which I had positioned my men. When they were close enough, I gave the order for the archers to start firing. I don't know how many Sarondakis died there."

"Not enough apparently," said Tetwell. Nittle sighed and looked down at his hands.

"No, Your Majesty. The rain affected the archers. And with the dark and the trees I couldn't see the Sarondakis until they were almost next to us. We didn't have time to kill as many as the plan called for."

"So what happened?"

Charles Ebert

"They got behind us," said Nittle. "I could hear them thrashing about below. They were heading toward the river. The plan was in jeopardy."

"It should never have been attempted," declared Fazzle. "Once the storm hit you should have turned back."

"Be fair to the man Lord Fazzle," said Nodwick. "The storm hit when he was on the north side of the river. He was already committed."

"Besides," rumbled Tetwell. "We were certain that Marduct was going to attack today. Something had to be done and Sir Nittle's plan was the best alternative."

"First of all," retorted Fazzle, "I am not entirely convinced the Sarondakis would have attacked today. And secondly, I think we would have been able to hold them off."

"We hadn't won so much as a skirmish all summer," said Nodwick. "What makes you think we'd have had a hope of winning a major battle without some kind of special strategy?"

Fazzle waved his stubby fingers in the air as if to say the answer was obvious. "We are close to Tarion. It would have surely fallen had we lost. Naturally the soldiers would have fought harder given the consequences of losing."

Nodwick slammed the table with his palm. He said with some heat, "May I remind the esteemed lord from Delamer that both Goswick and Joswell have been overrun in the past months. Our men have been fighting hard...for their homelands. Marduct has outnumbered us and been better equipped."

"Who's fault is that?" Fazzle tossed out the question like he would cast aside an apple core or a peach pit.

Nodwick stood, his face red and hands balled into fists. "Why you..."

"Enough," snapped Tetwell. He remained seated and looking down at the map, but the authority in his voice was enough to deflate Nodwick's anger. The king sat down again. Fazzle puffed in indignation.

"I think you're missing the point, Lord Fazzle," Tetwell went on, "we did win the battle."

"At a high cost of men and materials," said Fazzle.

Nittle who had sat quietly while the nobles bickered, chewed his lip in anxiety. Fazzle was right about that one point. Nittle had lost over a quarter of the men under his command, far too many.

Tetwell turned his head to Fazzle. "Do you wish to press this point, Lord Fazzle?"

The Delamerian looked at both of the kings and shrugged his shoulders, irritably. "I didn't mean to imply that Sir Nittle did a bad job, merely that he could have done better."

Nodwick, his face carefully neutral but obviously seething, looked at Nittle and asked, "What did you do when you realized Marduct was passing your position?"

"I attacked, Your Majesty, or rather I feigned an attack."

"Explain."

"Well, Your Majesty, I told my archers to cease fire and then sent twenty or so men down the river side of the hill where about a third of Marduct's force had already passed us. Then I sent one of our fastest messengers to the other hill to tell the men there the plan."

"And the plan was?"

"I had the attack horn sounded. The men shouted and shook tree branches to make it sound as if they were attacking. This slowed down the Sarondakis enough that your Majesty's forces caught up with them. Then we charged their flank and they counterattacked. We occupied them for two hour hours like that."

"Giving my knights time to rout the bastards," said Nodwick with a triumphant look at Fazzle.

"For your information, Nittle," said Tetwell, "the Sarondakis are retreating eastward along the Navium. They are disorganized and dispirited and I intend to keep them that way."

"You're pursuing them?" asked Nittle.

"Only to the Barriers," replied Fazzle. The two kings looked at him.

"And possibly beyond," said Tetwell diplomatically.

"I see your Majesty."

"Yes, well if there are no other objections," said Tetwell, eyeing Fazzle who sat motionless, "I think this business is over for now. Get some sleep Nittle."

"Sir Nittle," said Nodwick, a note of officialness in his tone. The old king rose on unsteady legs. He drew his sword. "Please kneel."

"I must protest..." sputtered Fazzle.

"This is an internal Goswickian matter, Lord Fazzle."

"But we'll have to give him more men."

Charles Ebert

"He is a capable commander, Lord Fazzle," said Tetwell. "I have no objection. Proceed Nodwick."

"Thank you Tetwell. Sir Nittle..."

Reluctantly Nittle knelt on the soggy ground cloth of the tent. With his right hand, he grasped the ring secured on the pommel of the king's sword. After he had repeated the ancient oath of vassalage, Nittle stood up, aware that while his status in life was going up, so was the number of his responsibilities and problems.

"When the war is over, I'll find a suitable estate for you," said Nodwick. "Any preferences?"

"Something near the mountains, Your Majesty," he said, knowing that after the war, he'd never be able to roam them again with his comrades in the Scouts.

"I think that can be arranged. You may go Lord Nittle." Nittle winced at the title.

"Thank you Lord Fazzle, Your Majesties," he said and then turned and walked out into the rain, wishing for the good old days when he was just a soldier.

Buckle's eyes snapped open when the silver light penetrated his closed eyelids, forcing him awake. The sphere floated about six inches above his nose and bounced up and down slowly. When it was sure he was awake, it glided toward the hole, stopping in front of it to wait. The rest of the prisoners in the cell lay in deep sleep. Buckle could see them clearly in the light. Bruct laid in the driest and cleanest corner his arm around one of the young new prisoners. Buckle couldn't remember his name but he had blond hair, now sullied by grime, and a fresh face. He was so young, the weeks of imprisonment had barely produced fuzz on his chin. Buckle shuddered, remembering the boy's screams and sobs the first few nights after the candle went out.

Beside Buckle was Yazzle, sleeping fitfully and Shacknel, snoring softly next to Nergle who was curled up into a tight ball. Morale among the four had improved greatly in the last few weeks especially Yazzle's. All of them were making their quotas early in the day so they had plenty of time to make plans down in their shaft. They had stolen a pick from the mines, fabricating a replacement from a good sized hunk of coal. The project had occupied a week. They finally smuggled the pick to the cell in Yazzle's breeches. That was the largest risk they'd taken so far. If he'd been caught, Yazzle would have been killed on the spot, but he was the only one of them strong enough to walk normally while encumbered with the heavy pick. They had also managed to steal a few torches and some rations.

The sphere bounced impatiently, catching Buckle's attention. "All right, all right," he mumbled. "But I'm not leaving tonight. Not without my friends." They hadn't set a time yet but all agreed it had to be soon. Yazzle was the most eager to leave, Shacknel the most reluctant. Buckle knew it depended on the sphere of light.

Buckle crawled through the hole, stepping across the gap onto the ledge or the other side. He held his breath against the stench as he sidled over to the cave opening where the sphere waited. He ducked inside, noting that their supplies were undisturbed. They had used almost all the dwale, sprinkling it on and around the sack of food to keep the rats away. Buckle had held a little back to execute a plan of his.

The sphere led him deep into the cave until it dead-ended at a pit. The grayish rock shone dully in the silver light of the sphere. Buckle could see the bottom of the pit in the glow also. He wiped his hands on his breeches and tentatively stuck his foot into the pit, turning around to face the way he'd come. After a few seconds of groping, he found the first foothold and then the second, third and in a few minutes he stood on the lower level. He turned around again and before him stretched another tunnel, narrower than the first one and barely tall enough for him to stand in.

The sphere hung before him, waiting for him to continue. The walls down here were black. He was in a coal vein, probably mined out years ago. He could see the braces holding up the ceiling. The tunnel yawned before him forebodingly black but inviting at the same time, considering what lay behind him.

He ducked his head and followed the sphere into the blackness.

The tunnel went straight for a good while then it twisted, going downward. The walls alternated between the black and the gray. Every so often, the tunnel would divide. Buckle tried to keep track of which tunnels the sphere led him down at these forks but lost count after a while. He hoped the sphere would be there when they made their escape.

Finally it stopped, hovering above another pit, waiting for Buckle to step up to the edge. He couldn't see the bottom in the sphere's glow only the sides going down and meeting somewhere in the blackness. Circling the left edge of the pit was a ledge about six inches in width. The pit itself couldn't have been more than about twelve feet wide.

Buckle started toward the ledge but the sphere stopped him, moving into his path.

"That's as far as we go tonight, huh?" The sphere floated back to the center of the pit. Then it descended, spiraling downward into the depths. Buckle watched in fascination as the sphere grew smaller and fainter. The darkness around him grew. After a minute the sphere began to grow again, slowly at first, then with gathering momentum. Its light seemed somehow filtered, like a sunbeam shining through dust motes. And gradually he heard a high pitched squealing sound emanating from the hole. Buckle went to one knee and leaned over the edge of the pit to get a better look. Silhouetted against the silvery light, Buckle thought he saw leathery wings connected to furry bodies. He leaned further out when a stone gave way beneath his knee and he tottered for a second, fighting a battle with gravity he knew he would lose.

Something pushed him back; an icy hand on his shoulder or a chilly wind gusting in his face. He was never sure what, but it sent him sprawling on the cave floor well away from the pit as the sphere cleared the edge and the air exploded with bats.

Buckle curled up on the floor and covered his head. The squealing of the beasts was deafening and Buckle could feel the leathery touch of their wings against his back and neck. He wanted to scream but it stuck in his throat.

Then through his eyelids he noticed a silver brightening. He opened his eyes and saw the sphere in front of his face. It floated toward one of the tunnel openings on the other side of the pit, the bats following. Gradually through the shock and the noise, Buckle's mind began to work. What was the sphere trying to tell him? He inched away from the edge and then he realized. The bats were flying toward the exit. They wouldn't be here if there wasn't some way to get out. And it had to be close. Even Shacknel would be encouraged at this news.

The racket died out, leaving Buckle in silence and darkness. He sat on the floor feeling his blood pounding in his temples. He didn't dare get up for fear of falling into the pit. But as the minutes passed and the sphere didn't return, he began to panic. What if it had deserted him, leaving him in the middle of a maze with no hope of finding his way back? Buckle fought down the panic and began to think. He knew his back was to the tunnel down which he'd come. Slowly, he began to inch his way backward, expecting at any moment to go tumbling into a bottomless abyss.

Instead he backed into a wall. He'd obviously been thrown back at an angle so the tunnel was either to his right or his left. Buckle had no idea which. He had started feeling the wall on either side when the sphere appeared down the opposite tunnel. It grew and gradually the light returned. Buckle drew in a shaky breath when he discovered the pit about two feet away from him in the direction he had decided to go.

The sphere entered the cave and floated above the pit. Somewhere deep in his mind, a thought appeared. There was nothing unusual in that except that Buckle was sure that the thought was not his own. And the thought did not manifest itself in words or even an image. It was an impression, a feeling. Buckle's heart rate increased with what he recognized as anticipation.

"Soon." The word escaped his lips and then realization came over him. "The escape will be soon. The next opportunity. Yes, we're ready. Just tell me when."

The sphere floated above him.

"You're right, I'll know." Buckle's breathing became uneven, he was so excited. Soon this nightmare would be over. Soon he'd be on his way. Another feeling welled up, a comfortable warm feeling, like sitting on a porch during a summer evening with a pipe and a cup of ale. Buckle sat back against the wall. He hadn't thought about home since the early days of his imprisonment. His eyes watered and tears made tracks down his grimy face.

The next morning, as they trudged down the dark smoky tunnel to their working face, Buckle told Yazzle, Shacknel and Nergle about his expedition into the caves. Shacknel listened impassively. Even the news about the bats didn't get a reaction. Yazzle and Nergle listened with more enthusiasm.

"When can we go?" asked Nergle, running ahead of them slightly and looking back at Buckle with wide eyes.

"Will you pipe down," hissed Shacknel, "Bruct's spies could be anywhere."

The youth cast a rebellious look at Shacknel but repeated in a soft whisper, "When?"

"We'll know," said Buckle. "Or rather I'll know. Don't ask me how."

"This is starting to get too metaphysical for me," mumbled Shacknel. He re-shouldered his pick.

"What do you mean by that," asked Nergle.

"Well I mean strange unidentified feelings, balls of light only Buckle can see. We're not basing this on much."

"Oh, you've just been here too long," admonished Nergle.

"That's true," said Shacknel softly.

"I'll follow you anywhere as long as it's away from this place, Buckle." Nergle waved his hands at the black walls of the tunnel. Buckle nodded at him.

"Do you doubt my master's word?" said Yazzle, looking down at the floor.

"Oh you don't have to worry about me," said Shacknel. They arrived at their working face. Buckle shoved their torch into a niche in the wall. Oily smoke came off the flame. Buckle watched his companions from over his shoulder.

"I'll follow Buckle as far or farther than you two simply because I'm tired of living here, or maybe I'm just tired of living. But make no mistake, I fully expect to die in those tunnels." He turned to the wall and picked out a place to strike the day's first blow, scraping off some loose dust with his thumb.

Buckle put his hand on the older man's shoulder. "Can't you allow yourself a little bit of hope?"

The gray head shook, a barely perceptible motion. He reared back and drove his pick into the coal. The others got to work.

As usual, Yazzle had half his quota by mid-morning. He took a break and sat by Buckle, watching him swing the pick and pull it out with a few lumps of coal. Buckle had gotten pretty good at it. His stamina had improved and he'd developed an eye for finding just the right point to strike to get the maximum amount of coal to fall out of the wall. He knew how to wiggle the pick once it had penetrated to widen cracks between lumps to get even more. It wasn't all strength that was involved although it was still back breaking work. The big strong bullies like Bruct got their flunkies to do their quota which gave them the energy to terrorize the other prisoners.

"Master Buckle," said Yazzle from behind.

"Yes Yazzle," replied Buckle, pulling the pick out of the wall and stepping back so the shower of coal wouldn't fall on him.

"How soon do you think the escape will be?"

"Soon, maybe today."

"I hate this place," said Yazzle. Buckle turned around and saw the blond giant staring at the ground. "It's worse than the first estate I worked."

Buckle leaned his pick against the wall and squatted down in front of Yazzle.

"I think about home all the time," said the field hand. His eyes threatened to overflow. "I mean Methliana. I thought the harvests were hard work but this..." He waved his hand feebly at the wall of coal Buckle had been working on. "We may not even have an estate to go back to. How long have we been here?" He leaned forward, his brow wrinkling in anxiety, bordering on panic.

"Yazzle, Yazzle," soothed Buckle, putting a hand on the big man's knee. "We'll deal with that later. Right now we need to get out of here and we're ready. Soon we'll be on our way home."

Yazzle looked up at him. "What about Lord Roduct?"

Buckle shrugged. "I think we both witnessed Lord Roduct's fate. The best course for us is to go back to Delamer and tell Erklin that Lord Roduct is dead. In a way it's not even a lie."

"I hope we're not too late."

"So do I." Buckle stood up and grabbed his pick. "I'd better get back to work."

After the midday meal the group worked at the wall of coal diligently. Hope of making the escape that day dwindled as the hours passed by. But every so often, Buckle would stop working, and try to feel something. The others would pause too, watching and hoping.

When Buckle got to within a few inches of his quota, he figured the time wouldn't come that day. After all the sphere hadn't specifically told him it would be today. It hadn't told him anything. Perhaps, thought Buckle as he pulled his pick out of the wall, he was insane and the sphere a hallucination. But if it was it was a hallucination with a damn good sense of direction. Buckle shrugged to himself as he carried the lumps of coal over to his pile. If he was insane he was insane. The thing that mattered was that soon he'd be out of this dungeon.

Shacknel flung a last lump onto his pile, putting it just over the quota and sat down with a thud. He held his pick across his knees. Buckle stood across the tunnel floor, one hand against the rough wall, wiping the sweat from his eyes with the other. Yazzle and Nergle still worked, trying to meet Nergle's quota. Nergle at the end of the day was near useless. His spindly arms could barely hold up his pick. He'd swing weakly at the coal and the tip would only go in a fraction of an inch, not enough to hold. Yazzle took mighty swings that would bite into the rock with a chunk and pull out lumps as big as a man's hand.

A rumble shook their tunnel and little falls of dust sprinkled them like black snow. Everybody stopped in mid action, eyes on the ceiling to see if it was going to fall. Cave-ins were almost a weekly occurrence. They were usually fatal.

"Cave-in," shouted someone down the tunnel. "It's trapped some of the guards."

Buckle looked at the others in the flickering torch light. The whites of their eyes made brighter by their black grimy faces asked the question that he was himself searching the depths of his mind for.

The answer came.

"This is it." Yazzle tossed his pick on the floor where it clattered. He pulled Shacknel to his feet and then all three were standing before Buckle.

"What do we do?" asked Yazzle.

"We've got to get back up to the cell."

"How?"

Buckle bowed his head, slapping his pate with his palm a few times to jar the answer loose. Suddenly a wave of urgency flooded him.

"The shaft," he cried. "We've got to hurry they're about to pull the transport car up."

They broke into a run, stopping only at the place where their side tunnel intersected with the main tunnel. Yazzle poked his head out and scouted the situation.

"There're lots of people, including guards but they're all busy, rushing to the cave-in."

"Let's go," said Nergle.

"I agree," said Buckle.

"Unwise," said Shacknel. "But I bow to the majority."

Yazzle nodded, took a breath and rushed into the main shaft. Panic ruled. Prisoners ran frantically. Some trying to organize a rescue effort, others were waving their picks over their heads, screaming for a revolt. The guards were trying to push through the throng, unmercifully using their whips and swords. Most were heading in the direction Buckle presumed the cave-in was. Others tried to make their way to the agitators, murder in their eyes.

The four held hands to make a chain and snaked through the mob, avoiding the more violent sections of it. In the ruckus they couldn't hear each other. Yazzle bulled his way through, pulling the others after him. Several times Buckle almost lost his feet.

As they approached the shaft, the transport car came down and out ran ten or so Sarondaki guards. Yazzle pressed the group flat against the walls as the grim-faced guards pulled their swords and rushed into the riot. Buckle looked back at the transport and shouted as it started to rise.

The four made a dash, diving onto the car's platform. Nergle missed, hitting the front edge. Yazzle caught him before he bounced off and fell down the shaft. With a mighty pull, Yazzle yanked the skinny youth up on to the platform just before his legs were shorn off by the wall.

They laid on the platform, gasping for breath. Buckle watched as the walls of the shaft passed by them and the dot of light that was the top of the shaft grew larger. The platform made halting progress up the shaft, stopping every so often or falling back with an alarming jerk that left their hearts in their throats. The sound of the riot slowly died as the platform climbed higher.

"There's bound to be more guards at the top of this shaft," said Shacknel, looking upward with a scowl.

"He's right," said Nergle. "What do we do?"

Buckle looked around. On the corner of the platform was a heap of burlap tarpaulins used to line the walls of old tunnels to keep the dust down. "Quick, under those."

They scrambled under the tarpaulins. Buckle's vision was cut off by the burlap, and the ride seemed even more interminable than usual. The coal dust which caked the tarpaulins threatened to make him sneeze. He held back the sneeze as its pressure grew and strained the linings of his nose.

The platform stopped. It shook with the footsteps of Sarondaki guard rushing onto it. Buckle could hear their grunts and orders spoken in Sarondaki. He peeked out from under the edge of the tarpaulin and saw about fifteen of them or the back of their knees anyway.

"Let's go," he whispered and the four escapees shed their cover and dashed off the platform just as it started going down again. The

209

guards tried to grab them but they were too quick and they had surprised the Sarondakis. In an instant they stood in the deserted hallway of the dungeon.

Buckle peered down the hallway where their cell was. A lone guard sat at the other end, sipping a cup of the foul smelling hot liquid that the Sarondakis were fond of. Over the edge of his cup his eyes darted in several different directions, looking down first one hall and then another. Buckle turned back to the group.

"I think he's suspicious. So we'll have to be careful." He grabbed Shacknel's arm. "We'll distract him and you two slip into the cell."

They nodded. Buckle looked at Shacknel and counted to three silently. They started yelling and ran around the corner. The guard slammed down his cup and pulled his sword. Buckle and Shacknel ran up to him, waving their arms. The guard looked at them, his suspicious sword following them.

"There's a cave-in," shouted Buckle .

"They need you down in the mines," cried Shacknel.

"Why...here," said the guard. He was on the few who didn't speak Dernian well.

"Cave-in," said Shacknel, holding up his hands palms out. "They sent us to get you."

"Kracrun kree nutt." The guard motioned at them with his sword.

"No, no," said Shacknel. "We," he motioned to Buckle and himself. "Sent by guards. You go to mine. Cave-in."

"Know cave-in. Told stay here. Why here?." He pointed at them again.

"We need him looking down the other hall," whispered Buckle. Shacknel nodded. He approached the guard slowly, his hands up. The guard turned as Shacknel put himself in the line of sight of the other hallway. Buckle followed behind. In his belt, he found the remaining dwale which he slipped between his fingers. Shacknel kept trying to explain to the guard why they were there.

"Guards in mine sent me." He pointed to himself. "Tell you...go to mine."

"Kracrum kell nani. Why here?" Buckle reached over the table and slipped the dwale into the guard's cup. He hoped the stuff was still fresh enough to work.

"I told you," Shacknel sighed. "Let me see if I can remember. Truguct na...tructorum trinwi."

"Tre...Tre," said the guard, making a perfunctory chopping motion with his hand. "Told stay here. Get in cell." He motioned with his sword toward the nearest open doorway.

"No, sent to..."

"Get in cell." The guard took a step toward Shacknel.

This wasn't working. The guard would lock them up in any cell. He didn't care and the closest was the most convenient. Buckle knew he had to get the Sarondaki to drink the dwale. Screwing up his courage he reached out and grabbed the cup.

"Trost, trost," he said, holding the cup in his two hands and putting it to his lips.

"Bah," shouted the guard and grabbed the cup from Buckle. "Mine." He smacked Buckle with the back of his hand, sending him reeling against the wall. Eyes unfocused, Buckle watched as the guard gulped down the rest of the stuff and slammed the cup down on his table.

"Get in cell," the guard repeated.

"Run," shouted Shacknel, grabbing Buckle.

Buckle stumbled down the hallway, Shacknel pulling him by the shoulder. The guard kept shouting, "Back...here," and running after them, sword raised.

"You shouldn't have let him hit you," complained Shacknel, yanking Buckle down the hall.

"I wasn't aware I had a say in the matter," said Buckle, shaking his head.

"You couldn't have ducked?"

"I'm a farmer, not a warrior." Buckle tripped and fell sprawling on the hard stone floor with the guard bearing down on them. Shacknel went down in a heap beside him.

"Yazzle, help," cried Shacknel.

The guard ran up to them, sword arm raised. Suddenly his eyes went unfocused. He staggered backward a step. The sword slipped from his loose fingers and clattered to the ground. The guard soon followed his head hitting the stone with a crack. The dwale finally worked.

Yazzle skidded out of the cell and surveyed the scene. He dived to Buckle's side when he saw the blood coming out of a cut over his eye. "Master Buckle, what happened?"

"No time to explain but I'm all right." Yazzle helped him up and he stood for a moment. His head was clear again and vision focused. "I'm all right. Where's Nergle?"

"In the cell, waiting," said Yazzle.

"Get this guard into an empty cell, and let's get out of here before others come."

"They're bound to start bringing prisoners up here as soon as they can," said Shacknel.

Yazzle grabbed the sleeping guard by the armpits and dragged him into a cell across the hall from theirs. When he emerged from the cell he was carrying the guard's sword. Yazzle closed the cell door with a clang and drove home the bar.

Inside their cell, Nergle waited anxiously, looking inside the hole. "I can't see the light."

"Nobody can except Buckle."

"Can you see it Buckle?"

"No, not yet, but we're not in the tunnel. I know the first part of the way pretty well. Maybe it'll appear after that. Light the candle Shacknel."

The old man stooped over and retrieved the cell's candle and then stepped into the hall to hold the wick to the nearest torch. When he returned, the room filled with its weak flickering light.

Nergle ducked into the hole and retrieved two torches from where they were hidden on the ledge and soon all three were lit, making the cell brighter than Buckle had ever seen it. Yazzle put down the guard's sword to take a torch.

In the corner a rat squealed in protest at the sudden increase in light. It was a big fellow with matted hair and wicked teeth. After it had had its say it squeezed through a crack in the wall Buckle wouldn't have thought it could get through.

The cell was gray and black, littered with stale straw and the few meager possessions people managed to hold onto. Bugs and lizards crawled among the cracks in the ceiling and walls as well as on the floor. The worst thing was the gloom, the darkness that hung like smoke in the corners and on the ceiling that not even three torches could penetrate.

"Not a very pleasant place to live is it?" commented Buckle.

"It's my home," said Shacknel, looking around. "I shan't be sorry to leave it though."

"We're wasting time," said Yazzle. "Nergle, take a torch and get into the cave."

He turned to Buckle. "Is it time?"

"It's time," said Buckle, slapping him on the back. "Let's leave this place."

Shacknel climbed into the hole and Buckle handed him a torch and then climbed through himself, accepting in turn a torch from Yazzle. Yazzle stuck his head in the hole and looked around.

"Phew it stinks," he said, wrinkling his nose.

"Never mind that. Come on."

The lad nodded and pushed himself into the hole but stopped with a grunt.

"What's the matter?" asked Buckle.

"I can't fit," said Yazzle, straining to get his shoulders through the hole. "My shoulders are too big."

"Try feet first." The head and shoulders disappeared and were replaced by a pair of legs, the feet wrapped in rags. They went in up to the torso and then stopped.

"It's no use, Master Buckle," said Yazzle's muted voice from inside the cell. "I won't fit. You go on." The legs disappeared.

"I'm not leaving you here without you, Yazzle," said Buckle. "Shacknel, hand me the pick." Buckle looked at Yazzle. "I'll get you the pick and you can knock out a little more of the wall."

"I don't know, Master Buckle..."

"It'll be just like mining the coal. Take a big swing and enlarge the hole." Shacknel held out the pick and Buckle grabbed it.

"What's happening?" Shacknel's wrinkled features shone red and yellow in the flickering light of the torch.

"Yazzle can't fit through the hole."

"Oh great Dalmar. Didn't he ever think to check before this?"

Buckle just shrugged and leaned over, placing his hand against the opposite wall for support. He pushed the pick into the hole.

"What's going on here," said a familiar sneering voice. Buckle pulled the pick back into the tunnel. Standing in the cell's doorway was Bruct and the blond youth.

"What's that?" asked Shacknel.

"Bruct's in the cell."

"How in Skrike's Hell did he get there?"

Buckle leaned into the hole. "We're escaping Bruct. We've found a way out. Want to come along?"

"What are you doing," hissed Shacknel.

"Do you think he'll let us out of here without a fight or telling the guards?" Buckle stuck his head out of the hole. He held the pick in his hand out of sight but ready.

Inside Yazzle stood in the middle of the cell, watching Bruct who stood in the doorway, holding the guard's sword.

"Well, well," said Bruct, with an evil smile. "Buckle's in the shit hole. How appropriate."

"How about it Bruct?" said Buckle. "Escape, I've seen the way out. This is a sure road to freedom." Bruct looked at him uncertainly almost said something and then stopped. "Wouldn't you like to see the sun again, Bruct? To walk outside without a guard in sight and feel fresh air blowing against your face."

"You're lying."

"It's no lie. I've seen it."

Bruct stepped back and looked down the hall in both directions. Then he looked at Yazzle and then Buckle. His huge frame blocked the doorway. The sword in his hand reflected the candlelight.

"Guard," he shouted.

"He won't answer," said Yazzle. "We took care of him."

"You what," growled Bruct.

"He's in a locked cell," said Buckle. "Unconscious."

"You'll never escape. There's nothing but death out there. And if you go you'll ruin things for us who stay behind."

"You're wrong." Buckle didn't like the look on Bruct's face.

"Get out of there." He pointed the sword at Buckle.

"No Bruct, I'm going to escape."

"I'll kill Yazzle." Bruct turned the sword on the big lad who backed up involuntarily.

"Master Buckle," said Yazzle uneasily, "You go on, I'll catch up later if I can."

Buckle brought the pick up so that it was just out of sight but could easily be shoved into the cell.

"I'm staying right here, until you can come with us," said Buckle, edging the pick forward. Bruct's attention was split between Buckle and Yazzle. "Just walk over here and crawl through the hole."

"But Master Buckle..."

"Just do it."

"Don't move," growled Bruct, brandishing the sword.

"Come on Yazzle, he won't hurt you," coaxed Buckle.

"The hell I won't." Bruct lunged forward, sword up in the air.

"Yazzle," shouted Buckle and he pushed the pick into the cell. Yazzle stumbled moving sideways but kept his feet and grabbed the pick. He brought it up just in time to block an overhead cut by Bruct. Yazzle backed away, circling to his right.

"I've waited for this a long time, Yazzle," said Bruct, his sword point shaking just a little.

"Seems to me you've spent most of your time avoiding it," said Buckle.

"Silence. I'll deal with you later." Bruct turned to shout at Buckle. Yazzle rushed him and pushed the head of the pick into Bruct's stomach. He doubled over with a whuff but managed to hold on to the sword while he backed away. Yazzle watched him, holding the pick in his sweaty hands.

"Yazzle," said Buckle, "This is your chance, kill him."

"But Master Buckle..."

"We don't have time. Do it and let's go."

Yazzle took a deep breath and shifted his hands on the handle of the pick. He charged, making great arcing sweeps with the pick. Bruct retreated across the room in the face of the wild onslaught. He gasped for breath, Yazzle's blow having knocked it out of him. Bruct stumbled to the door, grabbing the frame for support. He still held the sword.

Yazzle stood before the bully, pick in hand but not comfortably. He constantly shifted his grip. He backed up a step.

"Yazzle, I know this is hard," said Buckle. "But you're going to have it do it. Do you want to escape?"

"Yes."

"One more swing and we're free."

The head of the pick raised into the air where it stayed for a few seconds and then came down.

"Look at that," said Bruct, straightening up. "He's scared. He's not going to kill me. He hasn't the stomach for it. If I had known that, I'd have crushed you all long ago." He brought the sword up and its edge flashed in the candlelight.

"What's going on," hissed Shacknel, his head poking out from the cave. Nergle's too was there. Buckle waved them to silence.

"I won't hesitate," said Bruct, advancing on Yazzle.

"Yazzle," cried Buckle. The sword went up. But then Buckle saw a flash of blond hair behind Bruct. A stone went up into the air

215

with the sword and came down on Bruct's skull. When the bully crumbled to the floor the blond youth stood behind him, the stone still clenched in his hand. A little blood dripped off it. On the boy's face was a look Buckle hoped never to see again.

"Bastard," he cried in a rage choked voice. He clutched the stone so hard, Buckle thought it would break into pebbles.

Yazzle knelt beside Bruct and put his head to the bully's chest. "He's still alive, Master Buckle."

The boy moved quickly, dropping the stone and snatching the pick from Yazzle's hand.

"Yazzle, look out." Yazzle got his head out of the way just in time. The boy plunged the pick again and again into Bruct's chest. Blood and gore spewed all over the cell. With each downward swing a hysterical high pitched grunt would emanate from the youth's throat.

Buckle bolted out of the hole and grabbed the kid's arms, kneeling over Bruct's body and facing the blood soaked face of the boy.

"It's all right, son," said Buckle as calmly as he could. He could feel the boy's hysterical strength as he fought Buckle's grip on his wrists but Buckle held on and gradually the energy drained out of the boy's form. The pick fell with a clatter behind them.

"Yazzle, the pick," said Buckle. The lad gingerly picked up the bloody tool and shook it a few times to get the worst of the gore off of it. Then he went to work on the hole.

"What's your name, son?"

"Lathel," squeaked the boy.

"All right Lathel, you know if they find you here with Bruct, they'll kill you."

Lathel didn't speak but Buckle thought he detected a slight nod.

"We're going to escape, Lathel. Do you understand that?" Again a slight nod. Do you want to come with us?"

Lathel looked down at Bruct's face. "I...I killed him."

"Yes you did," said Buckle.

"He'll never do that to me again." The boy shook his head but his eyes searched Buckle's face for confirmation.

"Nobody will," soothed Buckle.

A chunk of the wall fell back into the tunnel and Yazzle stopped working.

"Master Buckle, we're ready to go," said Yazzle.

Buckle nodded. "We have to go now Lathel. Can you move?" Another nod and Buckle stood up, pulling Lathel up by the arms. Carefully he guided the youth's foot over the bloody ruin of Bruct's body and then stepped out of the expanding pool of blood on the cell floor.

"How is he?" asked Yazzle.

"He'll be all right," said Buckle. He put the boy's head down and shepherded him into the enlarged hole. "Let's go."

When they got into the cave, Shacknel said, "Who's this?"

"Lathel," said Nergle, looking at the youth who couldn't have been much older than himself.

"That's one of Bruct's favorites," said Shacknel, accusingly.

"Bruct's dead," announced Buckle, shouldering the sack of food and handing the water skin to Yazzle. "Nergle can you help him along for a while?"

"Yes, sir," said Nergle and he grasped Lathel tightly by the shoulder. "Come on Lathel, we're escaping. Can you believe it?"

They grabbed the rest of the gear and walked into the cave.

21

Sand.   All around them was sand.   It glared so brightly, Zabeth had to tie two rags over her eyes, looking out of the gap between them, a trick Keruct had taught her.   The rags were soaked with sweat which stung her eyes but it was better than going blind. She fought the urge to remove the bandanna tied on her head.   Keruct had told her that the direct sunlight would bake her brains and drive her crazy.   She wore a long flowing tan colored robe that Kebble had given her.   It resembled the robes the Sarondaki wore and provided camouflage and protection from the sun.   All the partisans wore them.

She squatted on top of a dune, scanning the horizon to the west and listening to Kebble and Bindle.   All around her the sand rustled.   It got in her eyes, in her mouth, and her clothing was caked with it.   Her feet were rubbed raw by the sand in her boots.   The wind from the west blew tiny waves of sand over her feet as if she were in a shallow creek or on a beach with her toes in the water.

Water.   She licked her chapped lips and tasted blood.   Must not think about it.   The water skin at her side held only a few drops but it hung heavy and Zabeth frequently found her thoughts returning to it.

"See it," said Bindle, pointing to the west.   He had tied a cloth over his head, securing it with some rope.   His mouth and nose were covered by another cloth.   A few strands of black curly hair peaked out the front.

"Yes," said Kebble, who was dressed practically the same, except he had a strip of wood covering his eyes with a small slit in the middle to see out of.   Zabeth had seen similar devices on the Sarondakis they had been skirmishing with all the way south.

"He's cut us off again," said Kebble.   Zateth pushed up the rags covering her eyes and after they had adjusted to the glare, she finally spotted the dust cloud signifying movement.   Deruct.

"He must be riding day and night," said Bindle, hotly.

"He doesn't have to worry about us knowing where he is."

"There isn't another depot within ten days ride."   Bindle paced to the crest of the dune.

Kebble strolled to Zabeth and squatted beside her.   Even under his mask she could tell he had that gently amused smile. "Deruct has to make a move soon.   He's been chasing us for over a month.   Marduct must be livid at having one of his chieftains take a whole army south, chasing a dwindling band of partisans."   He nudged Zabeth with his elbow.   "Thank Dalmar for Sarondaki honor."

"Kebble," said Zabeth, "it's me he wants.   Why don't I just go to him and accept his challenge?"

"If this were one of your Delamerian fireside tales that would be the solution.   But I'm afraid that at this point Deruct doesn't dare return with anything less than a massacre.   And my head on a spear."

"We've only got two days of water left and you can't ration anymore," said Bindle, turning to face them.   "I say we turn west and fight our way through."

"That's suicide," said Zabeth.

"That's the idea, isn't it?"   He looked at Kebble.

"Its war, Bindle," said Kebble "We're not out here for plunder or glory.   We're fighting for something bigger.   And there isn't one warrior here who isn't ready to make the sacrifice if need be.   And I know I can count you among them."

Bindle stood still, looking at the ground.   "I for one," said Kebble, "do not intend to die without taking as many of those bastards with me as possible.   Zabeth, take Keruct and find me some place that's defensible.   I know," he said, holding up his hand, "there are only dunes out there but do the best you can.   You have until nightfall."

Zabeth stood up and looked at the sun, shading her eyes.   She only had a few hours.   "East of here?" she asked.

"Yes."

"All right."

She found Keruct brushing down his horse.   All the horses looked like they could have used it.   She could count their ribs and their eyes were gummy and unfocused.   They bowed their heads almost to the ground and hung their tongues out.   A few of the sicker ones lay on the sand.

And there were half as many as had started the ride south. The camels looked little better.

"I thought you'd be asleep," said Zabeth, untying her horse's tether.   The rest of her troop was huddled under lean-tos, sleeping in the shade.

"Who can sleep in this heat?" complained Keruct.   He had taken his sun and sand protection off and worked in the shade of his horse.   His greasy hair and beard were streaked with sand.

"Interested in a mission?"

Keruct thought for a second and nodded.   "Sure, it'll beat laying around here thinking about how thirsty I am."

"Then mount up."

As they rode eastward, Zabeth explained to Keruct what Kebble had instructed them to do.   He gave a resigned shrug and pulled on the bones entwined in his beard.

"So he told us to find a good place to die?"

Zabeth rode alongside silently, feeling her horse's weakness through her thighs.   "I don't intend to die, Keruct."

Keruct spouted a short ironic laugh.   "Then you better be moving along lady, cuz if you stay here, dying is exactly what you'll be doing."

"We've gotten out of these scrapes before."

"That was up north where there's more water."   He shook his head, rattling his bones.   "No, we're almost out of road and Kebble knows it."

"You think he planned it this way?"

"He's always said it might…would probably come to this.   I don't like it but I will say he's done his best to avoid it.   He's kept us alive far longer than we had any right to expect."   Keruct looked down at the sand.   "I guess I can't complain.   Most constables don't want men like me with them.   Tiacin, Vorkle and I aren't like the others. We ride for a while, plunder a few villages or supply caravans and ride off when we've got enough.   Most would call that desertion."   He glanced over at Zabeth.   "But Kebble don't care.   We're good fighters and he appreciates that."

"So why are you still here?"

"I don't know," said Keruct. "Got stupid somewhere along the way, I guess."

Zabeth smiled under her mask. She knew Keruct long enough to see how insolent and cynical he was to everyone but her. Even Kebble had felt the sting of his bitter alienation. But he had always followed her orders with little question. Zabeth wondered if that was because of her leadership or because he lusted after her. The latter was a fact he did little to conceal. Zabeth noticed his longing hungry looks at her but since her first days with the company when everybody had tried, he had not made any advances.

They searched the rest of the afternoon for a likely spot for a last stand. But the landscape was crenelated only by low dunes that were visibly moving like waves. Nothing even remotely defensible. When the sun was an hour above the horizon Zabeth stopped and heaved a disgusted sigh.

"We'd better head back. Any number of these dune formations we've seen will do for cover."

"Barely better than no cover," commented Keruct. Zabeth just shrugged. What could she do?

A sudden gust of wind brought sand swirling past them and they covered their faces. The sand flowed into the gap between Zabeth's arm and her face. It got in her eyes and she tried to blink it out, resisting the temptation to rub.

When the wind died down and her eyes cleared, Zabeth looked around one last time. On a dune about fifty yards away she saw an outline, a right angle looking very peculiar coming out of the curved surface of a dune. It was the same color as the dune but obviously not a part of it.

"It's some kind of building," said Keruct, after they had ridden to it. He got off his horse and squatted by the stone structure. Cupping his hands together, he started shoveling out the sand. "If I could just find a door. Wait." Biting his lip, he wedged his fingers around something buried in the sand. With a yank, he pulled it out into the blinding sunlight. It was a shovel.

"This is it Keruct," said Zabeth. "You'd better go and get the others. I'll dig out the door and get things ready."

Keruct nodded and handed her the shovel. "I won't be back before nightfall. So you might want to build a fire. I don't think I can find this place in the dark."

"Right. Before you go, scout a little ways south. Maybe there's an oasis connected with the building."

He nodded and turned his horse south. Zabeth set to with the shovel. It was tough going for a while. For every shovel full she removed it seemed two would slither back. The tunic and breeches she wore under her cloak were soaked by the time she uncovered the top of a door frame. It was made of good solid hardwood. Obviously this building was maintained somehow. The doors and windows were kept shut to keep out the drifting sand. Whoever the building belonged to probably knew where to look for it, even if it was buried. The shovel was kept in a convenient place to ease digging out the front door.

"Hey, Zabeth come here," Keruct shouted. She stopped digging and looked up to where Keruct stood. He was on top of a dune about fifty yards south of her. He waved at her to join him. She scrambled to where he stood. He pointed eastward to where the desert sank to form some kind of basin. In the middle of the basin was an oddly arranged series of dunes.

"You think this is more defensible?" asked Zabeth, dubiously.

"Skrike's hell, no," said Keruct. "But we don't have to worry about our backs."

"Why not?"

"That's a scorpion down there, a big one." Zabeth gave him an unbelieving look. "You can tell by the pattern of the dunes. See there's the tail." He pointed to a line of dunes pointing southeast. Zabeth's expression didn't change. "You don't believe me." He smiled almost giggling. "Here, hold my horse. I'll show you."

He put the reins into her hands and slid down the dune into the basin. Then he jumped up and down several times. Zabeth was about to ask him what the meaning of this strange behavior was when a movement caught her eye. The dunes in the basin were moving. As she watched in shocked horror, a massive scorpion tail rose into the air, sand pouring off of it. Then came the pincers and legs and the torso, until standing in front of her was the largest living creature Zabeth had ever seen. She could feel the blood draining out of her face.

"Well?" said Keruct as he climbed back up the dune to join her.

"It's as big as the manor house on Methliana." The words were spoken in simple awe. Zabeth couldn't help but stare in terrible fascination.

"It's as big as any I ever seen," said Keruct, a little awed in spite of himself.

Zabeth looked at him, suddenly alarmed. "Shouldn't we be running or something?"

"Running's the worst thing you can do. It can't see too well and it can't hear or smell good either. But you see that flap of skin under its belly?"

Zabeth noted a pinkish protrusion underneath the monster's torso. It looked like the fin of some kind of fish. She nodded.

"It senses vibrations coming through the ground. If you ran anywhere near that thing it'd sting you and gobble you right up."

"Why isn't it chasing us?"

"Cuz we're too small and too far away to bother with. The bigger they get the more sluggish they are. This boy probably exists mostly on magic."

"On magic?" said Zabeth, looking the scorpion again.

"Sure, you think something this size could live in the middle of a desert with no food or water anywhere nearby? The scorpions are attracted to places that have a lot of earth magic. That's how they get so big. Otherwise, the largest would only be about the size of your hand."

Zabeth shook her head. The scorpion, not sensing any further threat, began the complicated process of folding its legs and lying back down.

"I agree," she said, "our back is covered. You'd better get going." She looked at the sun which was starting to turn red.

"Right." Keruct mounted his horse and trotted it down the western face of the dune and started back toward the partisans. Zabeth gave the now reclining scorpion a last shuddering look and returned to her digging.

After two hours, she had the door completely exposed and with some effort she pushed up the latch and the door swung open. The interior was pitch black, giving Zabeth no indication as to the building's size. A dry musty smell wafted from the interior. Zabeth saw sand flowing across the threshold and felt a twang of guilt for letting in the elements somebody had so carefully kept out.

Once her eyes were better able to pierce the gloom she spied a table beside the door with flint and steel and a pile of torches on it. She lit a torch and gingerly stepped further inside. The building was not large, only a dozen or so feet across its single room. Really no more than a shack, Zabeth thought as she inspected the stone walls. They were thick, about twice as thick as a man. Built to withstand mountains of sand she figured. The ceiling was lined with strong wooden beams, solid oak, probably from Joswell. Zabeth held the torch up to the doorjamb and inspected the finish which was functional but crude. Still she figured the house carpenter on Methliana would have appreciated the workmanship.

In the middle of the room, lay a table with six stools round it. They had a dull brown look to them and some of the supports for the stool legs were broken. The table was bare and the floor looked swept except around the door where the sand continued to rustle over the threshold. In the far corner two boxes were stacked. Zabeth stuck the torch in a holder and crossed the room to inspect them.

The first was filled with some kind of jerked meat. Zabeth took one of the dark slabs and sniffed it. Satisfied she then nibbled a little off the end of the slab. She held the morsel against her tongue and considered the flavor. Camel, she decided, and put the slab back. There was enough in the box to add another week to their food supply with severe rationing. But that was irrelevant since they only had two days' worth of water. She turned her attention to the second box.

In it was a hackbut. Grazzle had told her about these weapons which some Sarondakis affected, although they were made in a kingdom somewhere to the east of the desert. A deposit of gunpowder was placed in the barrel followed by a small round ball made of iron. This was secured by a bit of wadding. A fuse was put into a small hole in the back of the tube. When the fuse was lit it burned down and ignited the gunpowder which exploded, sending the ball out of the tube at a lethal velocity. Grazzle disdained the weapon, saying it was unreliable and that it took too long to load. A bow was much faster. Besides it smacked of fire magic. But Zabeth was curious so she stuffed the hackbut into the back of her belt and gathered up the leather bags which contained the gunpowder and the wads and balls. She stuffed them into her pack.

Getting back to inspecting the building she crossed to the opposite corner which held a stubby metal cylinder. It was brown with rust and sat on a wooden palette. A lid covered it and on top of the lid were two big stones. With a heave Zabeth moved the stones to the floor and then removed the lid. She could see nothing but shadows in the apparently empty barrel so she retrieved her torch and peered inside.

She almost dropped the torch. In the bottom of the barrel was six inches of water. Hurriedly she put the torch back and dipped her cupped hands into the water. She leaned over the barrel as she brought her hands up, making sure every drop spilling between her fingers went back into the cistern. The water was stale and tasted of metal and the dust on her fingers but was by far the best she had ever tasted. She licked it off her fingers and from around her mouth. She gathered the drops that ran onto her throat and chest and licked her fingers again. Then she looked down into the cistern and noticed a beaten metal ladle sitting at the bottom. Grabbing this, she took another drink that was pure heaven.

She was about to have a third when she stopped, considering. Best not to waste it, she decided, and put the ladle back. That cistern represented a couple more days of life for the partisans. She filled her water skin and closed the cistern.

Then she got to work. First she set up a line of torches extending three hundred feet south and north with one torch every hundred feet. That would improve Keruct's chances of finding the depot in the dark. After that she tried to dig some trenches but gave up. The wind was drifting the sand too much. It was all she could do to keep the door clear. She dug out the one window in front of the depot and was in the process of digging out the roof when Kebble and the rest rode.

"This is excellent," he called out. The torch light brought out the traces of red in his blond beard and hair. "Better than I could have hoped for. Zabeth?"

"I'm here," she said, sliding down the dune. She walked up to Kebble's horse and looked up at him, shovel still in her hand. "There's a little water and some food inside, not much but some. This must be a depot you didn't know about, maybe for the southern tribes."

Kebble nodded his head. "I thought there had to be one around here. But I didn't dare hope you'd find it."

"Almost didn't. It was blind luck."

"Only a little water and food you say?"

Zabeth nodded, suddenly weary. He swung off his horse and called, "An extra half ration for supper tonight men, and for breakfast. We'll need something in our bellies for the fighting tomorrow."

"Last meal," someone grumbled. Zabeth thought it sounded like Keruct. Kebble ignored it.

Charles Ebert

"You look exhausted," he said.

"I'll be fine. Look, the building itself is a little low for a good defense but I figure if you put people on the roof and on the dunes surrounding it, we could probably retreat to the depot."

"My thoughts exactly, Zabeth," said Kebble, putting his hand on her shoulder and guiding her to the door. "Why don't you eat your rations and get a couple of hours sleep?"

"I already ate."

"Good, then find some place where you'll be out of the way and lie down." He took the shovel out of her hand. She had forgotten she was holding it and her fingers released it without a struggle. Her eyelids kept closing and she kept leaning from side to side.

"I guess you're right."

"Of course I am," he said. He set her down against the depot began digging out a hole by the side of the building. Bindle was in front quietly giving orders as the partisans dismounted and prepared for the coming battle. Bindle caught eye and smiled at her. She made a face and turned away.

"Kebble," said Zabeth.

"Yes." He didn't stop digging.

"Did Keruct tell you about…" She jerked her thumb in the direction of the scorpion.

"Yeah, we'll be careful."

"I've got an idea."

Kebble stopped digging and looked at her. "Not a chance, Zabeth."

"Why not?"

"It's dangerous."

"We'll die for sure if we don't do something."

"We'll die for sure if we do what you're thinking."

Tiacin came up. "Here's your pack Zabeth. Vorkle's moving your horse over by ours."

"Thanks Tiacin," she said, taking the pack and pulling out her tent. Tiacin walked away. "I'd rather go down fighting."

"You will, I promise," he said, grabbing the ground cloth and putting it in the hole he'd dug. She set up the poles and together they draped the canvas over them and tied it down.

"I'd rather have a chance to win," she said, climbing into the tent.

226

"I don't see where this is a chance to win."

"You won't have to ask for a volunteer," said Zabeth, facing him. "I'll do it."

Kebble sighed and looked at the ground. "I know. That's why I don't want to consider it."

Zabeth looked at him until he stopped fidgeting with the tent rope and returned her gaze. After a moment, she made her point and he sighed in exasperation.

"All right but only as a last resort and I'll go."

"You're too important."

"That's crap."

"Nevertheless, it's true," said Zabeth.

Kebble paused, looking at her as if he wanted to say something couldn't. "We'll see what happens tomorrow."

Zabeth nodded and pulled the tent flap closed and tied it. The sound of the men preparing for battle lulled her to sleep.

When she awoke, dawn was just breaking. She poked her nose out of her tent and surveyed the still scene of the camp cast in the red from the emerging sun's light. About five tents stood in front of the depot. Little dunes of sand had built up beside them in the night. At least one sentry with a pike squatted in the sand about a hundred feet to the west. Zabeth could only see a black dot with a line sticking up like a musical note. Sand had built up along the walls again. They'd have to dig out the door one more time. The morning air was chill but already warming up. In an hour it'd be unbearable.

Zabeth climbed out of her tent and sat in the threshold to eat breakfast. She took a mouthful of water and then ate a strip and a half of jerked meat, washing it down with another swig. By now the others were climbing out of their tents. No one spoke. They just ate in silence. Someone had a persistent cough.

Zabeth broke down her tent and stowed it in her pack and then went looking for a private place in which to relieve herself. She wound up on the other side of the dune, looking at the scorpion. It had had a restless night and in spite of the drifting sand much of it remained uncovered.

There was something hypnotic about the monster. Zabeth had noticed it when Keruct had first shown it to her. Nothing could be more terrifying than a scorpion many times larger than you with its tail up, waving in the air like an angry fist. No weak spots in its armor are visible. You want to run but you don't dare turn your back on the thing.

Zabeth shuddered and stepped lightly as she finished her business and kicked sand over it. She scanned the rim of the basin, looking for the lowest part. There seemed to be a gap about two hundred feet to the south around the circular rim. She could do it, she thought, if only Kebble would let her.

She walked back to camp. Bindle was in front of the depot giving orders and lending a hand where he could. Zabeth stood at the crest of the dune and watched him. She had to admit, he was in his element. During the long chase south, he'd come up with more than a few good ideas that had gotten them out of tight spots. He was a good swordsman, a fair archer and according to Kebble, an excellent companion, a man you'd want with you in a crisis. He may complain but he'll be there.

Even now, facing death he played out the end game. He and Kebble had had many arguments and Bindle had lost every one. Kebble had duty and his orders on his side. Bindle didn't like dying here and said so frequently. But he'd do it. A good comrade in arms, Zabeth guessed. Too bad he was so damn annoying, especially since he started being so nice to her.

She tried to walk past him.

"Zabeth," he said, "Kebble wants everyone's gear stowed inside."

Zabeth sighed and truned to get her pack. "What about the horses?"

"They stay outside until near the end."

Zabeth nodded and pushed past him.

"Zabeth I…" She stopped and stared at him. "I…ah just wanted to say…"

"What?"

"Nothing." He turned away and Zabeth shook her head and retrieved her pack. Then she carried it into the depot. She kept her quiver and her bow as well as her sword and knives. She also took a small pack of personal items.

She went outside and found Keruct, Vorkle and Tiacin beside the depot. Keruct and Tiacin were engaged in a gambling game which seemed to depend on the outcome of throwing seven chicken bones onto the ground. Vorkle sat with his back against the wall of the depot, scribbling on a scrap of parchment.   His lips moved as he wrote.

Keruct shook the bones in his hands and rolled them.   Tiacin idly watched the outcome as he reclined against a sand dune.   They all looked up when Zabeth sat down, silently acknowledging her presence.

"Ha, Tiacin," said Keruct, "you owe me five hundred gold coins."

"I'll pay you tomorrow," said the Ternian with a crooked smile. It faded after a second though.   His fingers twisted his earring slowly. He looked out at the expanse of sand.   "I always thought I'd die at sea, not in a stinking desert."

"Too hot to move, much less die," observed Keruct, gathering up the bones for another throw.

"My philosophy," rumbled Vorkle, not looking up from his writing, "is the hotter, the better."   They all looked at him and he inclined his head slightly.

"When that Sarondaki blade pierces my vitals in a few hours, it'll be so hot in this damn place, Hell will seem like an ice house."

"I wish we could have gotten to a village somehow," said Keruct.   "I'd have loved one last tumble, even with a Sarondaki girl." He shook his head and cast a winsome look at Zabeth.

"Well, I for one, will not die unfulfilled," announced Vorkle. He waved his parchment in front of them.   "It's finished."

Keruct rolled his eyes and Tiacin resignedly shook his head.

"What is?" asked Zabeth.

"The Lay of Dalmar and Methlyn by Vorkle last of the great Joswellian warrior poets."

"You're not going to read it to us are you?" said Keruct. "Because it doesn't seem fair to have to die and listen to one of your poems all on the same day."

"Just the last verse, of which I am particularly proud."   He cleared his throat and read aloud in a booming voice.

> Dalmar looked to the west
> And no one was there
> Methlyn's hand, he did hold
> On Skrike's castle walls
> They knew despair
> And what happened next can't be told

The large warrior reverently folded the parchment and placed it in his pack. "If any of you should survive me, please take the work to a publisher in Tarion."

They all nodded and exchanged embarrassed looks, even Zabeth who knew nothing about poetry.

Keruct looked at her.

"How about you Zabeth? Is it a good day to die?"

"As good as any, I suppose. But if I have to go, I'll take Deruct with me."

A voice cried out from the west. Zabeth looked and saw the sentry waving his arms and shouting. His image was already shimmering in the heat. She stood up and without a word scrambled up the dune to the roof of the depot. Kebble, Bindle and Rissle were already there, scanning the western horizon.

"I see a dust cloud," said Rissle, "about an hour away."

"They could be closer, Kebble," said Bindle. "They've fooled us before."

Kebble nodded. "Everybody get in position," he shouted.

"Where do you want me?" asked Zabeth.

"By me in case they want to parley. In the back with the archers, once the fighting starts. Which side do you want?" He looked at her significantly.

"South," said Zabeth.

"Take your horse." Zabeth nodded. He was going to let her do it.

"Rissle, stay here and keep an eye on the horizon. Bindle, go down and make sure everything's going well."

"Sure," said Bindle. He turned to go and then stopped, looking at the two of them. After a second he went on.

Kebble leaned over and pulled up a wooden door on the roof. "One of the men found this last night," he said.

He climbed down a rope ladder into the depot and Zabeth followed. Already, there was a large temperature difference between the inside and the outside. Zabeth shivered a little in the darkness. As her eyes adjusted she could see the stack on which everyone had placed their packs. It reached almost to the roof. The cistern was covered and the table and stools were gone, taken outside to be used as battlements.

"Here," said Kebble, motioning toward her water skin and removing the lid of the cistern. "I want you to give your horse a little extra."

"She'll need it," said Zabeth. She watched as he tilted the cistern to get the last remaining drops.

"Lucky you found this water. We can put up a good fight now."

"You don't think we can win, do you?"

Kebble shook his head, not meeting her eyes. "It's pretty obvious. Shame really, in your case. You could have had a great career if you hadn't fallen in with us."

Zabeth looked at her feet and then back up at Kebble.

His eyes caught hers. "Are you scared?"

"A little," she admitted. "But I just don't feel like I'm going to die today."

Kebble smiled. "Every great warrior I've ever met has told me about that feeling. Your confidence in your abilities outweighs the facts before you."

"You've never felt that way?"

Kebble chuckled. "No, I fully expect my head to be stuck on a pike and headed north by sundown."

"I hope not," said Zabeth. She became aware that her heart was beating faster and she became hot even in the cool interior of the depot. Her knees threatened to buckle.

"Zabeth, I..." Before she knew it, she was in his arms. His mouth covered hers in a passionate kiss, her first of that kind. His beard brushed against her cheek and chin, stimulating her further. After a second she thought she should push him away but was surprised to find she didn't want to. His arms pinned hers to her sides anyway and his hands ran up and down her spine. Her resistance was being eaten up with passion. Even the smell of his unwashed body added to the rising tide that eroded her will.

Kebble finally broke off the embrace and stepped back a few paces. He looked at her, at once contrite and appraising her reaction.

"I'm sorry," he said, "but it occurred to me right then that if I had lived my life without ever having kissed you I would have died in vain." He looked down. "It won't happen again."

They left the depot without another word.

The rest of the morning went slowly. Zabeth, after having watered her horse and getting her into position, sat in a corner of the roof, silently cutting her hair with a small knife. Kebble and she studiously ignored each other. He sat on the edge of the roof, scanning the horizon. Bindle lay on the roof, trying to rest but actually looking from one to the other of them. How much he guessed of what went on down there Zabeth didn't know.

If we survive, thought Zabeth, maybe I could go with him. She could be in his company, roaming over the mountains and the desert, fighting Sarondaki raiders and the bandits west of the mountains. But she knew it could never be like that. Men, being like they were, the jealousies and petty arguments that would arise over only one man having female companionship would tear apart even the most closely knit outfit. Even this one, thought Zabeth, looking at Bindle.

Besides what if she got pregnant? She couldn't imagine riding into battle, or crawling through the sand to an ambush with her child bloated stomach. She'd have to stay home, possibly for years, because somebody would have to take care of the child or children. She doubted that it would even occur to Kebble to volunteer.

No, it wouldn't work, decided Zabeth. She cast a longing look at Kebble. If he was right, they'd all be dead by tonight anyway. She wondered if she should take him by the hand and lead him down the rope ladder to finish what he had started earlier. She watched his buttocks as he stood to scan the horizon and imagined them bare. His blond hair, short and soft would cover the cheeks like a lamb's fleece. In her mind, he turned around.

She stopped the fantasy right there by looking down at her boots. Fortunately the grime on her face covered her blushing. She hastily put away her grooming knife and put the small pack back into its place in the back of her belt.

"They're coming," said Rissle. Zabeth pulled herself up and walked across the roof to stand beside Kebble. He glanced at her, his expression unreadable behind the device covering his eyes.

Out on the horizon, Zabeth could see a column of dark figures, marching toward them. Most were on horseback with a few on camels. They kicked up a great deal of sand as they progressed. It flew into the sky in a yellowish cloud, trailing above and behind them. The figures were still a couple hundred feet away when they stopped and formed in loose ranks, bristling with pikes and swords. A single figure detached itself from the group.

"White flag, Kebble," said Rissle.

"Here it comes," said Kebble under his breath.

A lone Sarondaki rode atop the dune that marked their forward bulwark. He was challenged by two partisans with pikes.

"Let him pass," shouted Kebble.

The warrior topped the dune and sidled down. A white piece of linen tied to a pike fluttered above his head. Over his eyes, he wore a similar device to the one Kebble wore and the usual Sarondaki robes.

As he approached the depot, Kebble said, "That's far enough."

Keeping his hands visible at all times, the rider dismounted and stood beside his horse.

"I have a message from Deruct to Kebble."

"I am Kebble," said Kebble quietly. Zabeth stared closely at the warrior. Something about the voice was familiar. Perhaps it was one of the few warriors she had encountered in sword or hand to hand combat.

"Your men do not have to die. If you surrender yourself and the woman Zabeth, we will pull back and let your men march away."

Kebble barked a short sarcastic laugh. "I can cite a least a half dozen instances in the past ten years where Sarondakis have made the same offer and massacred the whole army anyway. Tell Deruct I find him without honor. Only a rogue would try to undermine the loyalty of a man's troops. Are you with me boys?"

Every member of the tight knit band of partisans cheered. Kebble waved a defiant fist in the air. Only Zabeth saw him breathe an inaudible sigh of relief. He looked around at his men with gratitude.

The Sarondaki did not seem at all surprised. There was something familiar about his gestures though, and Zabeth's sense of recognition grew. Who was he? He was big like most Sarondakis with wide shoulders and tanned skin. His hair, where it peeked out from under his desert hood was jet black and unkempt.

The messenger spoke again. "I also have a message for the woman Zabeth."

"Go on," said Kebble, crossing his arms.

"Deruct will not let this day pass without meeting you on the battlefield and finishing what he has started."

Zabeth stepped forward, her blood cold and calm. She bored two holes into the Sarondaki's skull with her eyes.

"If Deruct wants to die this day, you tell him to come see me."

233

The men cheered again. But Zabeth watched the Sarondaki as his head jerked towards her upon hearing her voice. His dust covered hand pushed up the device covering his eyes.

"Zabeth, it is you," he said, "I had hoped it was another."

"Roduct," she shouted, her blood igniting. "You are a traitor." In a second she had an arrow nocked and was ready to let fly. But Kebble grabbed her arm.

"White flag," he said simply.

"That's Lord Roduct?" said Bindle, "the man you were looking for?" Murmurs of confusion rose from the ranks.

Zabeth met Kebble's eyes and found the strength to abate her rage there. Slowly the tension on the bowstring eased and her arms came down. She fought to control the shaking which threatened to consume her.

"Damn his soul to Skrike's Hell," she whispered. "He's the reason Buckle's in a dungeon and I'm unable to help him. Because of his treachery."

"It may not be that simple, Zabeth," said Kebble, just as softly.

"Zabeth," said Roduct, "why are you here?" He removed the rags draped over his mouth and nose to reveal the face of Zabeth's former lord.

"Buckle's in a dungeon under Castle Skrike," spat Zabeth.

The words struck Roduct like a blow. His mouth dropped open and his eyes grew larger. "How?" he stuttered.

Zabeth, in short unfriendly syllables, described their adventures from the discovery of the murdered Sarondaki in Delamer to where Buckle was captured by the raiding party in the foothills.

"We must get Buckle out," he said. "First of all things."

"You seem to forget," said Zabeth dryly, "you're about to massacre us."

Roduct looked up at her and took a deep breath. "I don't know if I'll be able to tell you this.' He paused, looked at the ground and clenched his teeth. When he looked up again his face contorted into a grimace and his voice sounded strangled. "This tribe has…a Keeper of Blood."

"Where?" Kebble stepped forward beside Zabeth.

"With the baggage…scorpion motif…on his robe."

"The urn?"

Roduct staggered back a step, hands going to his head as if to stop it from flying apart.

"What's the matter with him?" asked Zabeth.

"Soowooli," said Bindle.

"I've never seen anybody fight it so well," whispered Kebble. "The urn would be near the Keeper, yes?" he prompted the struggling Roduct.

"Yes…on a camel…never leaves its side."

"How many are under Soowooli?" asked Kebble.

"I swear," Roduct's tortured voice rose in pitch, "half this army will turn." He staggered to his knees. "Free me." Then his shoulders relaxed and he stood, brushing the sand from his knees. He retrieved his pike and replaced all his protective headgear.

"Since you will not accept Deruct's generous offer of mercy you will all die. I withdraw to deliver to him your answers. Prepare yourselves for the afterlife." He swung up on his horse and edged it up the dune.

"I understand that Roduct is under their control," said Zabeth. She slipped the arrow back into the quiver and shouldered the bow. "But how was he able to betray them?"

"Rissle, watch them," said Kebble, pointing to the western horizon. The sharp-eyed Goswickian nodded. Kebble turned to Zabeth. "From what you said about his history, Roduct broke Soowooli once before during the last war. It's not surprising that he could do it again. And hearing the news about Buckle, for whom he obviously feels a great deal of loyalty and affection, probably gave his mind the leverage to lift the effects of Soowooli, at least temporarily."

"What I can't understand is why half that army is under Soowooli," said Bindle.

"Deruct's a young chieftain, ambitious, proud, not very good at keeping his opinions to himself. There's a lot of jealously in the Sarondaki upper circles. So they stuck him with a second rate command, one that's vulnerable. It's ironic. You'd think that an army over which you had complete control would be an advantage. But when all the opposing army has to do is kill one warrior and break an urn it turns into a serious disadvantage. I've always thought Soowooli was overrated."

"They're going to protect the Keeper though," said Bindle.

Kebble smiled. "That's the beauty of this situation. All we have to do is have Zabeth here stroll right up and kill the man."

"What?" said Zabeth.

Charles Ebert

"Deruct has your name, Zabeth," explained Kebble. "That means he has to kill you himself. I guarantee that army is under orders not to harm you."

"That won't stop them from killing her if they see she's after their Keeper," said Bindle.

"No," said Kebble, "but she can get closer than any of us."

"They're coming," said Rissle.

"Look alive men. They're on their way," shouted Kebble. Below in the trenches was a flurry of activity. Arrows were nocked, swords drawn; pikes were thrust into the sand where they'd be handy. The men accomplished all this with the efficiency and fatalism of professional soldiers. Forgotten was the emptiness of their bellies and the dryness of their throats. Only the job at hand mattered now. They waited in their trenches, breathing the hot dusty air.

Zabeth turned to take her position on the dunes just south of the depot when Kebble grabbed her arm.

"I'll signal you when to make your move."

Zabeth cast a questioning glance toward the dune to the east.

"I don't think we'll need to but..."

"Right." Zabeth turned and jumped off the roof, sliding down the dune that half covered the building. Then she scampered up another dune to take her place beside Roundel and the other archers. Behind them at the bottom of the dune stood her horse, tied to a stake, its nose poking through the sand. At her feet were a couple of extra quivers, full of arrows. At this point most of them were Sarondaki arrows recovered hastily from battlefields and then sharpened. The shortage of arrows had been a problem plaguing them for months.

"Archers," Kebble's voice sounded thin and reedy in the heated air. "Let fly on my signal."

To the west it looked as if one of those swift but devastating desert wind storms were closing in on them. A cloud of dust and sand rose as the tiny figures approached. Kebble had guessed that the attrition of their month long running battle had whittled Deruct's army away until only about half of it, five hundred men remained. Kebble's force which had been fifty when he crossed the Barriers was now reduced to thirty-five, most of the casualties coming in the last month. Giving an extra edge to the Sarondakis, was the fact that they were well fed and watered, all the oases being to the west.

"Ready," shouted Kebble. He held his sword high in the air.

She looked at the approaching horsemen. They were close enough now, that they were resolving into distinct figures. Zabeth with her sharp eyes picked out a preliminary target. Already they could hear the thunder of their approaching hooves and their wild war cries.

She pulled back the string of her bow, giving her target what she judged was the right amount of lead with one eye and watching Kebble with the other. Details about the enemy became apparent. They looked strong. Zaebeth thought of the wrinkled brown and red faces of her companions and her own dry, dust covered tongue and reflected that the Sarondakis had to have water with them. Then she dismissed the thought from her mind. The worst thing she could do in this situation was to start thinking about water.

"Now," shouted Kebble and the sword came down in a glittering arc.

Zabeth released her arrow and her target jerked back and fell, tumbling over the rump of his horse into the path of the charging warriors behind him. The horses veered off, causing the charge to part around the warrior's body.

One Sarondaki, seeing the effect, started shouting and waving his arms for the charge to disperse. Zabeth put an arrow through his neck. But the horsemen dispersed anyway.

When the first wave hit their forward pikemen, the partisans' line almost broke. Zabeth saw Dennidar eviscerate a horse that reared up before him. The beast fell sideways pinning its rider who was quickly dispatched by Malruct. Then a horseman came and clove Dennidar from his shoulder to his sternum with a battle-ax. Zabeth loosed an arrow that sailed straight into the Sarondaki's eye even before he had removed his axe from the bloody ruin that had been Dennidar.

She had shot maybe five or six arrows since Kebble's signal, three finding their targets. Now with the enemy closely engaged with her companions she had to pick her targets carefully. If they broke over the last dune she'd have to charge forward and fight with her sword. If that happened the battle was lost.

She spied Vorkle, swinging his great mace, keeping two horsemen at bay. They danced around him, their questing blades looking for the slightest opening in the huge man's defense. Zabeth shot an arrow that transfixed the neck one of his tormentors. The Sarondaki screamed and went down. Then Vorkle uppercut the snout of the other assailant's horse, causing it to rear up, tumbling the rider. The warrior no sooner hit the sand then Vorkle's mace turned his head into red gooey jelly. Vorkle ran off, screaming some horrible Joswellian war cry, gore hanging from the sharp studs in the mace's head.

Just in time, Zabeth saw two enemy archers loose arrows in her direction. She dived, lying flat on the sand as the arrows whistled over her head. Roundel, also on the ground, smiled at her.

"All yours," he said.

Zabeth sprang to one knee and shot an arrow straight across the space between her and the Sarondaki archers. It pierced the one on the left in the groin and he went down in an agonized heap. She fired another arrow at the one to the right of her first victim. It missed but forced him and the rest to back out of range.

Zabeth scanned the battle for more targets. With the horses and men kicking up so much dust and sand it was difficult to see. She caught only glimpses of the action, the flash of a sword here, a thrusting pike there. And all around war cries and the agonized screams of the wounded and dying assaulted her ears. It was maddening. She desperately wanted to throw away her bow and charge into the melee, sword swinging, biting into flesh and bone. But Kebble's orders were clear. Archers were to keep their positions until he gave the word or the line broke. Standing there, seething with blood lust, Zabeth heard old Grazzle's voice in her ear, "Discipline wins battles." Also if she were in the middle of the battle, if would be more difficult to get away and execute her plan.

She looked around and noticed a party of about fifteen horsemen riding to the rim of the scorpion's valley. Zabeth whacked Roundel on the arm and pointed at them.

"I'm going after them," she shouted. "Keep an eye on the battle"

Roundel nodded.

Zabeth scampered across the intervening dunes like a sand spider. She kept her head up watching the Sarondakis ahead of her. Two were off their horses, looking into the valley. One was pointing and the other, shaking his head. They, more than anybody else know what lay there.

Zabeth slid down the side of one dune and scampered up the next. She judged that she was just within bow range and wanted to keep as far away as possible from them. They might try to capture her if she got too close.   From here she felt confident she could get back to the depot on foot before they could catch her.

She nocked an arrow and then let it fly.

When the shaft appeared suddenly in the sand at their feet the Sarondakis looked up and saw Zabeth.   Several bows went up to retaliate but one of the warriors on foot held up a forestalling hand. He recognized her.   Zabeth advanced, nocking another arrow.   The Sarondakis retreated, keeping just out of range.   The two on foot quickly mounted and the party was motioned back.

Zabeth tossed a handful of sand at their retreating backsides. "Cowards, dogs.   Come back and get me," she screamed but they showed no sign of having heard.   They rode to Deructs's baggage, just visible as a blur toward the western horizon.

She headed back to the battle at a trot.   Topping the last dune, she stood beside Roundel.   At first glance very little had changed. The red-headed Goswickian smiled and reported that actually the partisans' line had firmed up well and was holding off the charging Sarondikis.

Even as she watched, the warriors sounded a withdrawl and started galloping back to a point just out of bow range to regroup. Zabeth took a few shots at the retreating enemy but couldn't hit any of them.   The dust settled, revealing the carnage they had wrought. Dead bodies, most of them Sarondaki lay strewn across the sand in front of the depot.   Red stains emerged and grew on the dunes, collecting into one hideous crimson blot.   The surviving partisans milled about, dragging their own wounded and dead back to the depot and making sure of the enemy's casualties.   Zabeth saw Keruct plunge a knife into the chest of the archer she had wounded across the way. Out on the dunes to the west, three riderless horses wondered aimlessly through the sand.   Zabeth looked up and saw the inevitable vultures overhead.

Zabeth and Roundel remained at their stations.   There was no telling how long the Sarondakis would take before they renewed the attack.   Kebble, dust covered and bloody, emerged from the depot and stretched his back.   He looked up at Zabeth and trotted up the dune toward her.

"You hurt?" he asked and nodded to Roundel.

"No, you?"

"A scratch here and there but nothing serious."

"We held off the first charge," said Zabeth. Kebble looked down and caught her eye with the corner of his.

After a pause, he said, "At a price."

"How many?"

"Two dead. Dennidar and Lerano."

"I saw Dennidar go. Got the warrior who did it."

Kebble nodded grim approval. "Three injured. Kredlneck lost an arm. I don't expect him to live. Bertuct took and arrow in the shoulder. I don't know if he'll pull through or not. And Tiacin…"

"Tiacin," said Zabeth. Kebble held up his hand in a familiar gesture.

"He'll be all right. Nasty sword cut on his leg. I'll sew it up if I have time and put him up here. You'll switch to being a swordsman, Roundel."

"No problem, Kebble."

Zabeth breathed a sigh of relief. Tiacin could not have been badly hurt if Kebble, protective mother hen that he was, was considering letting him fight again this day.

"How many of them did we get?" asked Zabeth.

"Bindle says he counted ten dead around the depot. They carried away maybe half that number in wounded."

"Pretty good ratio," said Zabeth.

Kebble shook his head. "Not good enough. We can't hold off another charge." He held her eyes for a second and a silent communication passed between them. Zabeth nodded imperceptibly. She glanced over at Roundel who had wondered over to the crest of the dune to watch the regrouping Sarondaki force.

"Zabeth," said Kebble, "I, ah…"

"Kebble, she started, "about what happened in the depot…"

"Don't," he said, holding up his hand. "I've made a decision. If we survive this, we'll be heading north again and you'll want to rescue Buckle. I don't intend to stand in your way."

Zabeth's heart leaped in her chest. "Really?"

Kebble nodded a little sadly. "I have a feeling that events in the west may already have broken one way or the other and our strategy will have to change."

She nodded, agreeing with him. The news they had been getting from the west had been very optimistic.

"You better get going. The armies should be separated when you do it."

Zabeth looked around at her waiting horse and nodded. Her mare stood in the unrelenting sun, her head drooping as she dozed. When Zabeth turned back to say goodbye, Kebble was gone. She scanned the camp for him but was unable to spot him. She sighed in frustration and disappointment. She had wanted to tell him...what? Half an hour ago she had decided in was impossible. And yet she had these feelings.

She shook her head and slid down the dune to where her horse was tied. Untying the rope from the stake, she patted the horse's shoulder. It nuzzled her affectionately.

"Good old girl," said Zabeth, "We've come a long way together. All the way from Delamer."

She swung up onto the horse's back and turned around to face south. While eyeing the circle of the ridge, Zabeth became aware of a coolness in her bones. She recognized it as the feeling she got when she knew her abilities were about to be tested. Deep inside she was confident she would not be found wanting. She kicked the horse's flanks and trotted south.

The Sarondakis, no doubt, would see her. They may even send a few warriors out to stop her from whatever they thought she was doing. Deruct himself may ride out to keep their appointment. But Zabeth smiled grimly, as she thought they would never in a million years guess what she was actually doing.

When she got to the gap on the south edge of the valley her horse shied, instinctively afraid of what lay there. But Zabeth laid a calming hand on the horse's neck, feeling the cartilage and her racing pulse.

"It's all right old girl," soothed Zabeth as she slipped her bow from her shoulder and drew an arrow out of the quiver. "Just do what I say and we'll come out of it." Horse and rider seemed to leave all doubt behind as Zabeth kicked the horse's sides again and they galloped into the valley, Zabeth screaming like a mad woman.

She galloped half way to the end of the beast's enormous length when it finally started moving. First the chitinous tail rose into the air and towered above her. Sand slid off the surface and from the cracks between the segments of the tail. Fortunately the wind blew most of it away from her or Zabeth would have been blinded. The sound of the falling sand was loud down on the valley floor. The legs quickly poked out of the sand and lifted the torso and abdomen. The giant claws lifted into a fighting attitude and clacked aggressively. It rotated to face her even as she moved across the valley floor. Its movements were quick and jerky. Grimly, Zabeth wondered how fast the horrid thing could run. She pictured the tiny scorpions of the western desert which scurried around fairly quickly.

Between her legs, she could feel the horse's panic. It took almost all her energy to keep control. She spared a glance back at the scorpion. It still rotated to keep facing her but it wasn't advancing.

"Skrike's Hell," she spat and jerked the reins back. The horse reared into the air several times and tried to keep going. Zabeth had to pull so hard the horse's muzzle bent forward against its neck before she finally stopped. When Zabeth slipped off her back, the horse tried to charge but she held the reins. Tying them loosely around her thigh, Zabeth kneeled in the sand and brought her bow up and shot an arrow into the monster's eye, or what she guessed was an eye. She got ready to run back to the horse but the arrow seemed to have no effect on the beast.

She shot another one and still it didn't respond. The horse shrieked and pulled on the rope almost pulling Zabeth over in the process. This was no good, she thought, trying to get her brain to work. It had to follow her.

Then she remembered Keruct telling her about the special flap of skin underneath the torso that allowed the beast to sense vibrations. She peered closely beneath the torso and saw it, a dusty appendage, sweeping the ground like a broom. Biting her lip she judged the shot. It would be difficult. There could be no arc on the arrow's flight at all. She was facing the flap head on so there wasn't much surface area to aim at. Plus with her horse almost jerking her leg out from under her every few seconds it was hard to steady herself.

Zabeth held her breath and brought the bow up. She pulled the arrow back until the arrowhead almost touched her knuckles. The rope around her thigh jerked tight. The horse kept up the pressure, its head bowed, trying to dislodge the rope or drag her across the valley floor.

Zabeth let go and the arrow zinged away. With a split second of the observation, she could tell the arrow would strike true. She pulled the reins from around her leg and bolted toward the horse which stumbled backwards. That was the only reason Zabeth was able to leap upon her back before she shot toward the nearest wall of the valley. Behind her, Zabeth could hear the slip-sliding of displaced sand.   She could feel the tingling on her back and her neck as she expected, at any moment, the giant sting to strike her.

She managed to guide the horse toward the lowest part of the ridge lining the valley.   It was still a steep incline and the horse sunk up to its forelocks in the sand.   Frantically, it pumped its legs up and down, sand spraying everywhere.   The sound of pursuit grew louder. She could hear the clack clack of pincers.   Zabeth reached back and slapped the horse on the rump.   It jumped and in a spray of sand was over the ridge.   A concussion shook the ground and a shower of sand fell on her as she rode away.   Zabeth looked back and saw a gap in the ridge where she had just crossed it.   The tail was rising again.

The scorpion scrambled out of its valley and set off in pursuit of Zabeth as she veered the horse around to the west and pointed its nose toward where the Sarondakis were still regrouping.   Behind her the monster scrambled, its tail in the air, ready to strike.   Its back was arched so much it seemed to have been only using its front two pairs of legs to move.   The claws were held up and clacked incessantly.   With panic rising in her throat, Zabeth realized it was gaining.   She kicked the sides of her horse.

Ahead she could see the Sarondakis gathering themselves for another charge.   They mounted their horses and hefted their weapons. The archers shouldered their bows and replenished their quivers.

Zabeth let out one of the terrifying ululating war cries she had heard the Sarondakis use.   She stiffened her back and waved her bow over her head.   Her hood dropped away and she peeled off the rags that were meant to cover her eyes but had slipped down to her neck.

The Sarondakis, almost as one, looked toward her.   An arrow was shot before the leader of the assault, realizing who it was that was bearing down on them could restrain them.   Then they saw the thing behind her.   Warriors and horses panicked, shooting off in all directions in spite of the leader's efforts to keep them in formation. The scene was a flurry of dust, sand and confusion.

Zabeth smacked her horse's rump once more and cut into the rioting Sarondakis like a knife into one of Sora's puddings.   She drew her sword and hacked at any figure that came near her.   A shrieking figure somehow grabbed onto her cloak, forcing her to drag him along until she grabbed the knife out of her boot and stabbed the man's hands.   He let go and was flung into the maelstrom around her.   She made the motion of putting the knife into her boot, fully expecting it to fall from her hands and be lost.   But somehow it stuck securely.

She emerged from the Sarondakis and headed west toward their encampment. Riding with her were several Sarondakis, some of whom took a few cuts at her with their swords, orders be damned.

Zabeth fended off the blows and retaliated. The warriors rode on, more interested in running than fighting and Zabeth couldn't catch up no matter how hard she kicked her horse's flanks.

The next thing she knew she was tumbling forward; the world became an alternating view of yellow and blue, sand and sky. Instantly, she made herself into a ball and rolled as she hit the sand. When her momentum stopped she was on her back, she sword hilt jutting painfully into her spine. Her body hurt in a thousand ways but she found she could move. Sitting up, she shielded her eyes from the sun and saw the black mass of her horse's body where it had collapsed.

She was about to rush to the horse when she saw that the scorpion, which had been venting its wrath on the few unlucky Sarondikis who couldn't get away, was now skittering after the nearest source of vibration. Kebble, forewarned, knew to keep all the partisans around the depot still. But the Sarondakis, who were on the verge of victory and then were plunged into defeat and panic, were trying to get away, forgetting long lifetimes of experience with the monsters.

The scorpion was headed right toward the Sarondaki baggage. Zabeth put her face to the ground and pulled her hood over her head while the awful beast skittered past.

Now Zabeth could feel the scorpion's vibrations as its trunk-like legs dragged across the sand so fast the scraping was like a shriek. She dared a peek out of the side of her hood and saw the horrible beast passing not fifty feet from her, sand spouting into the air with every step. Zabeth felt a chilling terror creep down her spine, paralyzing her until long after the scorpion had passed.

A wheezing sound brought her out of her paralysis. Remembering, she scrambled over to the dying mare. The poor animal's nose lay half-immersed in a pool of blood and foam. Zabeth sat beside the head and gently lifted it and cradled it in her lap, stroking the scrawny neck. The horse's black eye regarded her with a panicked and betrayed look. Zabeth painfully remembered promising that they'd be all right. Its chest heaved with the effort of breathing and its legs pawed uselessly at the air and the sand as if it were still trying to run, still trying to obey, to be all right.

Choking back the tightness in her throat, Zabeth pulled out her knife and slit the horse's throat, ending its suffering. As the black blood flowed freely onto her robe she avoided looking at that eye. Old Grazzle came to mind. He appreciated good horses but would have scorned her now. "Don't start thinking a horse is your friend. A good horse will serve your enemy just as well and as faithfully as you, assuming he treats it well." That was why she had never named the horse. Grazzle wouldn't have approved.

Shaking her head, she pushed the horse's head out of her lap and stood up. Her body protested but she ignored the pain and gathered up her spilled things. Her bow, incredibly had survived although the string had broken. She bent the wood experimentally, expecting some hairline fracture to make itself apparent but it was sound. It only took a moment to get a spare string out of her pack and re-string the bow. Her quiver lay under the inert body of the horse all of the arrows smashed into splinters. It took a moment of sifting through the sand to find two intact arrows. Zabeth shouldered her bow and held the arrows in her hand.

Across the sand she could see that the Sarondakis had organized some kind of resistance to the scorpion. Archers were firing arrows with ropes tied to them over the body of the beast to encumber its legs. They lit torches the sizes of pikes and topped with huge wads of fabric making large fireballs, bright even in the harsh desert sunlight. These they stuck in the ground in front of the monster in an arc. They obviously intended to encircle it in a ring of torches. The beast seemed to be afraid of the flames. It wouldn't cross the line of fire. All around it, making sure that it didn't escape before the circle could be closed, were jumping and shouting Sarondakis. The beast spun around and around in confusion, trying to face its enemy and getting tangled up further in the ropes.

With a grim smile Zabeth guessed there was enough confusion in the Sarondaki baggage for her to sneak into it. Her only fear was that the Keeper would be the center of activity. Still that was what arrows were for. She grasped the two she had recovered and started to circle her way toward the camp.

She came up on it from the south. Ducking between the rows of staked camels and mules she quickly approached the riotous encampment. So far she had seen no sign of any Sarondaki that answered Roduct's description of the Keeper. He must have been on the north side of the struggling scorpion.

245

Zabeth stepped forward and then saw a young warrior spot her. He was a sentry, obviously paying more attention to the fight with the scorpion than to his duties. Sword in hand, Zabeth ran toward him. No use in going on the defensive now. He had seen who she was and had run away, shouting for Deruct.

"Oh, Skrike's Hell," she muttered and pulled out her knife. Taking careful aim, she threw it. The hilt hit the youth in the back of his neck. He fell more from the surprise than anything. Zabeth quickly ran up to him as he tried to get up and slid her sword between his ribs. She never could throw a knife.

She circled the perimeter of the camp, scanning the interior for a sight of the Keeper. Finally she saw him, a resplendent figure in a long robe with a black scorpion embroidered across the back. He hung well back from the activity but still shouted orders to the laboring warriors. Beside him stood a heavily laden camel with two guards, one holding the reins, the other was obviously supposed to be watching for any threat. In reality he was staring with a gaping mouth at the scorpion.

They were just within bowshot, but Zabeth wanted to be sure so she scrambled forward, covering her telltale blond hair with her hood. The two arrows rubbed against each other in her sweaty hand. When she got to within twenty feet of the Keeper, she stopped, went to one knee and began lining up her shot. Suddenly her view was blocked. She focused on the eclipsing figure and saw it was Deruct, his head exposed to the sun and a smile on his dark features.

"A pleasure to see you again, Zabeth of Delamer. How very gracious of you to keep your appointment with me."

Zabeth brought up her bow which had sunk at the sight of her enemy. She drew the string back.

"You won't kill me. You have too much honor," he said, squaring his shoulders to give her the broadest possible target.

"For someone who has only met me once, you're assuming a lot."

Deruct laughed, a grating sound. "No protégé of Grazzle of the Foothills could be without honor. You won't kill me. Nor can I allow you to kill my Keeper of Blood."

He turned and shouted to the ornately robed Sarondaki.

Zabeth saw her opening and took it. She shot the arrow. It whistled over Deruct's head and planted itself in the Keeper's chest just as he turned around.   Zabeth dashed forward, rushing past Deruct before he had a chance to respond.

The guard holding the camel knelt beside the Keeper.   The other drew his sword and waited for Zabeth.   She slid to almost a complete stop and fired the last arrow into the second guard's chest. He fell back, his sword flung to the side.

Zabeth cast away her bow and ran as fast as her sore feet would carry her and leaped onto the camel's back.   The load the camel had been carrying was in fact an ingenious disguise.   It consisted of a wooden framework with rags and dummy packs glued to the outside. On the top was a hole with a wooden grate over it.   Inside it was hollow except for an ornately painted urn sitting in a special harness.

Zabeth clung to the outside of the fake load, peering into the shadows covered by the grate.   She could see a faint red glow where the coals burned to heat the blood in the urn.   It was a little larger than the one Urgallo had had so long ago.

She took out her boot knife and cut the strap holding the arrangement on the camel's back.   Unfortunately her knife also bit into the camel's side, drawing blood.   The creature hooted and lifted its front legs into the air, causing Zabeth and the load on its back to slide off.   Then the beast ran off, shucking the burden off its back completely

Zabeth hit the sand with a thud, followed quickly by a crash as the ersatz load landed beside her and split open to reveal the red and white urn, still apparently intact.   Zabeth grabbed a plank and whacked the surface of the urn.   A hairline crack appeared across the pattern.

"Stop her," cried Deruct, as Zabeth took another whack which caused a chip to fly off.   Red viscous fluid started heading around the edges of the crack.   She reared back and gave it one last smack that shattered the urn.   The red goop crept out onto the sand.   Then Zabeth knelt and scooped handfuls of sand into the broiler at the bottom of the urn, extinguishing the flame.

Arms closed around her and flung her to the side.   She rolled on the abrasive sand and finally stopped, her mouth full and her body aching even more.   She felt like she could lay there forever.

"Get up," screamed Deruct.   Zabeth shifted her head with her sore neck and eyed him.   He was a defeated Sarondaki.   His eyes were wide with fury.   His nostrils flared and a string of saliva hung from his mouth.

"Get up," he screeched again. "You are without honor, just as this Kebble is without honor."

Zabeth spat sand out of her mouth and forced her sore arms to push her body into a sitting position. She glared at the raving warrior.

"If this is how Grazzle taught you war then he was without honor too."

Zabeth was up, blood spurting through her veins like liquid fire.

A voice rang out across the sand. It might have been Roduct's. "Free Sarondakis, come to me. To me."

"You," barked Deruct. He stammered, trying to find strong enough words to carry his hatred.

"Yes, me," said Zabeth. Then she attacked.

She opened with a lightning head stroke, followed by a vicious cut aimed at his groin. The surprised chieftain parried both but was caught completely off guard when Zabeth used her momentum to bowl into him, knocking him to the ground. Zabeth recovered and caromed off to her left. She stopped, pivoted and was on him again in a second. She rained blows as he scooted back crab-wise, sword over his head to parry.

Zabeth shifted her grip on the hilt at the top of her swing and brought the sword down in an eviscerating arc which just missed when Deruct rolled. He kicked sand into Zabeth's face. She coughed and then felt a kick in her midriff that sent her sailing backward. She released the sword.

She rolled backward, instinct telling her to keep in motion. A second later she was on her feet and had her bearings. Deruct charged, swinging his sword in reckless arcs which he never would have done had she been armed. Zabeth ducked and backpedaled, trying to work her way around him to get at her sword but he kept cutting her off. His eyes were wide and his mouth set in a terrifying grimace. Zabeth could hear his grunts with every swing of his sword and she could feel the wind its passage over her head, hot with the desert air.

She waited until he finished a mighty swing and then charged, butting into his stomach with her head. She saw stars as her skull collided with his buckler. But off balance from the swing, Deruct toppled over. Zabeth landed on top of him, grabbing a handful of sand with the intention of jamming it into his eyes. But Deruct, either out of anticipation of her strategy or just pure instinct, covered them with his arm and Zabeth couldn't pry it away.

So she stuffed the sand down his throat. He coughed, the sand exploding out of his mouth. Zabeth rolled off and ran for her weapon. She could hear his dry grating cough as she sped across the sand and grabbed her sword.

When she looked up Deruct was nowhere in sight but he had been replaced by ten Sarondakis, standing in front of her, swords out. Zabeth gulped and started to back away. They followed her step for step. They held their swords with the points downward, not threatening but since there were so many of them, they wouldn't need to threaten her. Zabeth considered her alternatives. Surrender would probably mean the resumption of the duel with Deruct at a later time, when perhaps he would have a more level head. Flight then? She felt the weariness in her bones and knew she couldn't outrun the warriors. Her only choice was to fight. Presumably, they were still under orders not to kill her so if she could kill and injure enough of them she might get away.

Zabeth lifted her sword to strike when one of the nearer Sarondakis knelt before her and held out his sword in a yielding position. Zabeth blinked in surprise when the rest of them did the same, the sand rustling around their bended knees. They must have been Sarondakis under Soowooli just freed by her actions.

"Who speaks Dernian," she said.

A couple of them raised their hands. She pointed to the first to do so.

"Take the rest and find..." She hesitated. She was going to order them to find Kebble but they wouldn't know what he looked like and there wasn't time to describe him. "Roduct or any other westerner. "Go."

"Yes, M'Lady," he said.

She turned and saw a chaotic battle raging. Sarondaki fought Sarondaki as the former slaves took their grim revenge on their masters. Zabeth saw them continue to hack at bodies long after life had fled. The living ones were being flayed and mutilated. It was a battlefield devoid of mercy.

In the midst of the chaos, Zabeth caught a glimpse of Keruct, leading a band of Sarondakis and partisans. Kebble must have charged out of the depot when the Sarondakis started fighting themselves. She looked but couldn't see any other members of the partisans.

Over all of it was the scorpion. Still struggling with ropes entangling its legs, it was being driven back by Sarondakis wielding the torches. Zabeth hoped they were on her side. The scorpion looked confused. Its tail pumped up and down in indecision. Two of its back legs were tied together. It came close to toppling over a few times as it scooted back before the advancing warriors, who were herding back into its valley.

There was no sign of Deruct.

She searched among the clumps of fighting, sometime lending a hand if she could figure out which side was which. She avoided the more grisly scenes. Once she spotted Vorkle about twenty feet away clubbing an unfortunate warrior to death. He saw her and swung his weapon over his head, yelling his terrible battle cry. Zabeth waved her sword in exultation and then continued her search. She paused once in a while to stand on tiptoe and look for Deruct.

Finally at the edge of the fighting, she spied a group of Sarondakis with their horses and camels, making for the west. At the head she recognized Deruct. He was retreating with what little force he had, that had remained loyal and had kept alive.

Zabeth ran after them, screaming until one stopped and shot an arrow at her which landed at her feet. She skidded to a halt as another arrow was nocked. She looked back for a large number of men to command to follow but the mopping up was well under way and nobody saw her.

She wanted to throw her sword to the ground and kick sand in frustration. Instead she turned and yelled, "Deruct."

The figure at the head of the retreat stopped and turned. He shimmered in the heat. "I have your name." He looked at her for a moment and then turned back and continued retreating.

22

"Another fork," lamented Nergle as they came upon the two passageways, one extending to the right, the other to the left. Both looked equally foreboding to Buckle as he stared down each of them in turn.

"Do you see anything Master Buckle?" asked Yazzle.

Buckle gasped for breath and shook his head. Slowly he sat down and leaned his back against the wall. His attacks were back and his chest was clenched so tight he could barely breathe. It felt good to sit even against a wall with rocks jutting into his back.

Buckle looked up at the disappointed faces around him in the flickering light of their torch. Yazzle, bearded and filthy, leaned against the wall. Even his great reserves of strength were near their end. He let fall from his fingers the bag of rancid mush that was their supply of food. It was distressingly small after five days of wandering. Shacknel sat also. He propped his arms on his knees and stared downward at the floor. The wrinkles in his face were deeply etched grooves at this point and large purple sacks hung under his eyes.

Only Nergle and Lathel had any energy. Lathel stood back a ways in the tunnel they had just come through. He wore his usual preoccupied frown, his blue eyes focused inward. Nergle stood at the opening of the left hand tunnel, peering into the blackness, perhaps expecting to see the apparition that up until now only Buckle had been able to see.

It irritated Buckle that none of the others could see the glowing sphere, almost more than the fact that he could only see it at certain times, himself. When they came to situations like this one, where they had to choose which tunnel to take, the sphere eventually would appear. But there was no telling when. It could be minutes. It could be hours. And Buckle could see on the faces of Shacknel and Nergle a growing doubt as to the existence of the light at all.

"We'd better save the torch," said Yazzle. He nodded to Nergle who reluctantly extinguished the light, plunging them into total darkness.

"I think it's the left hand tunnel," said Nergle.

"What makes you say that?" said Shacknel. His voice dragged the words out of his mouth.

"I can feel a draft coming out of it."

There was a pause. "Well best to be sure, I guess." Was there a hint of impatience in his tone? Buckle shrugged inwardly and then concentrated on relaxing his shoulders. There was a scuffling sound as everybody sat down to wait and then silence broken by Buckle's wheezing.

One fortunate thing was that when the sphere did reappear Buckle's attacks would go away. This was reassuring in two ways. The first was the obvious relief from suffering. The second was that it provided tangible evidence for the sphere's existence. At least to Buckle's mind. The rest remained skeptical. All Buckle knew was that in the presence of the sphere he could breathe freely and he desperately wanted to breathe freely. It was like when Krinseth would clear his chest.

He was surprised to find that his mind wandered to the subject of Krinseth. He hadn't thought about her in months. All during the tortuous trek through the desert he had half expected her to try and rescue him. Every night as he rolled over to sleep he had imagined being shaken awake by her. She'd put a finger to her lips to shush him. Then under a spell of invisibility, she'd lead them out of the camp.

Those fantasies died of course when he entered the dungeon. While toiling in Skrike's mines and suffering the degradation of Skrike's imprisonment, Buckle had deliberately kept his thoughts from the things he had lost, Krinseth and her growing interest in him, his home, Methliana, and most especially Roduct. Even now, months after he thought he'd cried his last midnight tear, Buckle could feel a trickle of wetness on his cheek. Of all those things, Roduct was the one Buckle knew he had lost for certain. Roduct was now a creature of Skrike's.

Buckle looked around him and saw that he and his companions were bathed in a silvery light. Almost as an afterthought he noticed he could breathe freely. The sphere hung just inside the right hand tunnel. It bounced slightly as if being disturbed by some cosmic wind. Buckle sighed, relief welling up in him as he looked at the sphere.

"Thank you, Matron," he whispered. He had no proof whatsoever, that the sphere was female. It was something he just felt. Its presence seemed somehow feminine.

He looked around at his friends and said, "It's the right hand tunnel."

Nergle looked up in surprise. There was no reaction from Lathel who had wondered a little ways down the tunnel. Yazzle stood up with a groan and prepared to move on. Shacknel looked sharply in Buckle's direction, obviously not believing.

"Are you sure?" asked Nergle. He stood before the left hand tunnel, the palms of his hand out to feel the slight draft he'd reported.

"Yes, I'm sure," snapped Buckle.

"No need to bark at the boy," said Shacknel. "I must admit, I'm a little skeptical myself. It would make more sense if our escape route went down the tunnel with the draft."

"I don't know why but the sphere is pointing down the right hand tunnel," insisted Buckle. He forced himself to stand up.

"Is it here now?" asked Nergle.

"Yes," said Buckle, struggling for balance on his sore and sleeping feet. Multi-colored stars danced across his vision and he had to stand still for a moment, his hand against the wall until his vision cleared.

"Well, let's go." Buckle reached into his pack for the flint and steel they used to light the torch. When he had it going, he looked up and saw Nergle staring at him defiantly. Shacknel, who hadn't moved, looked as if he wanted to cause trouble too.

"I say we go down the left hand tunnel," stated Nergle.

"That isn't where the sphere is pointing," reasoned Buckle.

"What sphere?" shouted Nergle. "I've been wondering around down here for days and I haven't seen any sphere."

"We've already been through this. We agreed that following my sphere was the only plan that even remotely gave us the possibility of escape. Have you come up with something else?"

"You know what I think?" said Nergle. "I think that this sphere you keep talking about is a hallucination. I think you've gone insane and now, because of it, you're going to lead us to our deaths." Yazzle stirred at that and loomed beside the youth.

Charles Ebert

"Hold it Yazzle," said Buckle. He turned to look at Shacknel. "What do you think?"

Shacknel scratched his head and looked at them. "I don't think you're insane, Buckle. But the boy has a point. Maybe we've been doing things your way long enough. If we have an indication that the way out is somewhere other than where this thing leads us, maybe we should take it."

"Yazzle?"

"I go with you Master Buckle. If you say you see a light, I believe it." The lad crossed his arms, refusing to even consider any other possibilities. Buckle walked over to Lathel and put his hands on the youth's shoulders. This brought forth a momentary reaction of panic which subsided when Lathel's blue eyes focused on Buckle.

"Lathel," said Buckle, looking in the boy's eyes for further response.

"Are we out yet?" asked the boy.

"You won't get anything out of him," said Shacknel.

"Not yet, Lathel," said Buckle. "We need your opinion. Which tunnel should we take?"

He led the boy to the tunnels. When Lathel peered into the right hand tunnel the sphere retreated, flying down the tunnel about ten yards.

"That's odd," said Buckle and he described the sphere's actions.

Nergle wasn't interested. "Well if he's going to scare the sphere away, we may as well go down my tunnel."

"He didn't scare it away. It's still there. It just keeps its distance from him."

Shacknel walked up to Lathel and waved his hands. "Do you see the sphere, Lathel?"

The boy looked at him with a quizzical expression.

"You know, Buckle's magic?"

He shook his head. "Can't see magic. It don't work around me."

"What?" said Buckle.

"Magicians...witch stuff, never works if I'm close."

"Why not?"

"Dunno."

"This isn't getting us anywhere," protested Nergle.

"Now wait," said Buckle. "He had wandered down the tunnel just before the sphere appeared, or at least he was down that way when

254

I could see. I wonder if he's the reason it sometimes takes the sphere a while to show up."

"You mean it can't appear to you when he's close?" asked Yazzle.

"Yes."

"Never mind all that," said Nergle. "Which way is he voting?"

Buckle tried several times but he couldn't get the boy to understand the situation. After a while Buckle decided Shacknel was right. They'd never get a decision out of the boy. He turned to the others. They were looking at him.

"I say we split the food and go our separate ways," said Nergle.

"Oh, shut up, boy," snapped Shacknel. "We won't split up."

"But..."

"Silence," Shacknel looked up at Buckle. "Since we're deadlocked, let me suggest a compromise."

Buckle nodded.

"Nergle and I will go down our tunnel for a ways, maybe a couple hundred feet and if that draft increases we'll all take the left-hand tunnel. If not we'll go your way."

Buckle stroked his chin in thought. "I don't know."

"What can we lose?" asked Shacknel, "except a little time?"

Buckle looked over at Yazzle and then said, "All right."

"Good," said Shacknel, struggling to his feet. "May as well get started now."

He limped past Buckle who stood staring at the floor. Taking the torch from Yazzle, he entered the tunnel. Footsteps echoed through the tunnels as the orange light from the torch faded, leaving only the hard silver light of the sphere.

Behind him Buckle could hear Yazzle sitting down again. Lathel lay on the floor and curled into a ball. Buckle watched the wretched boy with pity. He wished Krinseth were here so he could ask her about this magic thing.

Assuming his previous sitting position, Buckle watched as the sphere floated impatiently in the right hand tunnel. It wanted them to hurry.

"Not without my friends," he whispered.

For the past couple of days, he had been growing more and more convinced that the sphere was for him. The fact that only he could see it was the most overwhelming clue but there were others. When they negotiated areas of the tunnel where the footing was treacherous, the sphere would be right above Buckle, showing him exactly where to put his feet. A few times he had slipped or overbalanced and something it felt like a hand, but not one made of flesh, had pulled him back. The others slipped and fell all the time, causing delays while they were rescued or treated. For some reason he was being watched over, and as this realization came to him Buckle began to wonder why. Did this tunnel really lead to freedom or was the sphere using him or leading him toward something worse than what he was running from?

Buckle looked up at the apparition and tried to feel what it was thinking as sometimes happened. But the sphere, upon seeing that he was regarding it, renewed its frantic efforts to get him to follow it. He could sense no ill will in it and so far it had done him no harm and much good. Buckle turned away. The others must follow him, if only for their own safety.

"I'm going after them Yazzle," said Buckle, standing up.

"Won't that be breaking our agreement, Master Buckle?" asked Yazzle.

"They have to be made to understand..."

He was interrupted by an earthshaking crash and a yell pierced the air and echoed down the tunnel walls. Buckle hobbled down the left hand tunnel.

Instantly, the sphere was in front of him, the light blinding him, trying to drive him back. Buckle swatted at it, as he would a swarm of flies and he kept moving down the tunnel as fast as his sore feet and tired legs could carry him.

"I've got to save them. They're my friends," cried Buckle. "Please!"

The sphere relented and led the way. Along the tunnel the floor was cracked and broken. Huge chunks of stone were simply gone, leaving gaping black holes, big enough to fall through. Buckle watched the floor carefully as the sphere lit the way for him. Once or twice the floor seemed to move. It was no wonder the sphere didn't want him to come this way.

Buckle came upon Shacknel hanging by his fingertips on the edge of a hole. Already the edge where his white knuckles were grasping was crumbling. Shacknel's face came alert when he heard the sound of Buckle's approach.

"Shacknel," yelled Buckle.

"Buckle?" growled the old man. "Have a care. There's a big hole here."

"I know. I can see it. Just hold on. I'll get you out of there."

"You can...see it?" gasped Shacknel. Buckle ignored him and grabbed his bony wrists. With all his might Buckle heaved, pulling Shacknel out of the hole. When the old man's legs came even with the edge, he scrambled out of danger. They sat for a moment to catch his breath.

The sphere was urgently pointing the way back.

"Nergle," shouted Buckle down the hole. "Nergle."

"It's no use, Buckle," moaned Shacknel, "the boy was caught completely by surprise. He must have fallen several hundred feet. He screamed all the way down."

Buckle peered down the hole, trying to pierce the shadows to catch a glimpse of the youth. All he saw were shadows.

A grinding sound rent the air and the floor seemed to drop. Buckle had a bad moment when it seemed as though the motion would tumble him in after Nergle. But once again an invisible hand braced him just before he fell and set him on his feet.

"We'd better get out of here."

Shacknel lay on the floor and waved his hand weakly. "All kinds of holes and ruts. In the dark we'd have to go slow and this floor's ready..."

"Come on, I can see," snapped Buckle. He grabbed Shacknel by the shoulder and half pushed, half carried him along the tunnel, guiding his feet around obstacles.

Behind them Buckle heard the floor give way with a rending of rotten timbers and a crash of breaking rock. The floor moved now every time Buckle put his weight on it. It swayed like the deck of a ship and Buckle definitely had the feeling it was being held up by something other than the rotted wooden beams below the stone.

"Stay by me and you'll be all right," shouted Buckle.

They approached the end of the tunnel. Yazzle stood in the entrance, trying to see through the darkness. The sphere, unseen by him hovered over his head, illuminating a gap in the floor that wasn't there when Buckle had first raced down the tunnel. Yazzle was about to step into the gap.

"Yazzle, don't move," shouted Buckle.

"Master Buckle?"

"It's all right. Step back."

The lad took a step backward, clearing the far side of the gap. Three feet of blackness yawned before them. Buckle brought Shacknel to a halt and let the old man rest for a moment before preparing him for the next task. The sphere vibrated in panicky agitation.

"You're going to have to jump, Shacknel," said Buckle.

"Jump? But I can't see."

"It's only a short way but we need to hurry."

The old man wavered in fear, holding back. "I can't," he stammered. "Go on without me." Buckle was sympathetic to his predicament. Shacknel was in total darkness. He couldn't see that the jump was really only a long step. Buckle doubted that he would have been able to do it.

"We're not going to leave you behind, Shacknel. It's only a small gap. Just a little effort and you'll be across."

The floor wavered, dropping a short distance and then magically floating up. It still swayed sickeningly and the sphere performed complex acrobatics to get Buckle's attention. Obviously whatever power was holding up the floor couldn't do it for much longer.

"We've got to go now, Shacknel," shouted Buckle. But Shacknel didn't need more urging. He leaped across the gap, tumbling on the other side and bowling Yazzle over. They both landed on the floor, tangled up with each other.

Buckle jumped across, and the floor behind him gave way with a rending crash. He looked back and saw only shadows stretching down the passageway. A cloud of black dust came wafting out of the tunnel, causing them to cough.

"Is everyone all right?"

"Yes," replied Yazzle and Shacknel together.

"Where's the sphere now?" asked Shacknel.

Buckle looked up at the apparition. "In the right hand tunnel again."

"Let me rest a few minutes and we'll go on. I'll never question you again my friend."

Buckle put a hand on the old man's shoulder as he sat gasping for breath against the wall. He could feel the shoulder bone heaving under his skin. It felt frail, like a dry twig.

They resumed their march. After three hours of trudging through tunnels with only the light of their last torch to guide them, the four escapees were stumbling from exhaustion. Buckle's chest was beginning to tighten up again and he walked slowly, trying to relax his shoulders. The sphere had abandoned them even though they made sure that Lathel walked well behind them. Buckle assumed that meant there were no forks in the tunnel or any dangerous obstacles in their path, at least for the moment. Idly, Buckle wondered what the sphere did when it was away.

Next to himself Buckle figured that Shacknel was in the worst shape. The old man limped along, his ancient joints hampered with stiffness. He gritted his teeth against the pain and never said a word or even uttered a groan. Beside him Yazzle limped too and looked little better. Under his eyes just above the ragged line of his beard, huge sacks hung, all purple and lumpy. His hair, formerly blond, was slicked down and almost black with grease and coal dust. Every few minutes now he had to shift the torch to another hand as his arms became exhausted. Buckle thought he should offer to carry it for a while but knew Yazzle wouldn't have allowed it, and Buckle was too weary and short of breath to insist.

Lathel even showed signs of fatigue. The youth stumbled across his own feet every so often. His eyelids drooped almost to the point of closing. The peach fuzz on his face had grown into a patchy beard.

Buckle tried to lift his hand to feel his own beard but found he couldn't. The strength just wasn't there. Definitely time to stop, he thought, but then the idea suddenly seemed painful. He remembered his feet, long since numb from walking but once they stopped, and Buckle had experienced this several times, the blood would flow back into them and it would feel like a thousand tiny needles being stuck into his ankles and heels and especially his arches. He could feel the sharp stabbing pain now, just below the numbness. To Buckle it seemed much less trouble to keep walking until he looked down and saw bloody stumps at the end of his ankles.

Another look at his companions, however, convinced him that they had better stop. He was about to say so when they emerged into a cavern. The walls on either side fell away and the ceiling rose to about twenty feet, just visible in the torch light. The air suddenly felt damp and they could hear the sound of lapping water.

"Water," whispered Shacknel, licking his cracked lips with a dry tongue. The lapping sounds came from both sides and in the light of the torch Buckle began to see that they were on a causeway in the middle of an underground lake whose dimensions he couldn't make

259

out, the outer edges extending beyond the range of their feeble torch. To either side the stone causeway descended to the inky black surface of the water.

"Yazzle," said Buckle, "I'll take the torch. You go down there and see if the water's any good."

Yazzle nodded and handed the torch to Buckle who had to hold it up with two hands. The lad sidled down the embankment.

"What do you mean 'see if it's any good?' We're about out of water. I say we take our chances," said Shacknel.

"This could be a lake or it could be a sewer," replied Buckle, watching Yazzle as he neared the water and dipped a finger in and brought it to his mouth.

"If it were a sewer, we'd smell it," stated the old man.

Buckle looked at him. "Are you sure? I can't smell much beyond my own stench at this point."

"The water's drinkable, Master Buckle," announced Yazzle. Buckle considered for a moment. Yazzle could very easily be mistaken. They were all so tired and thirsty that any water, no matter how foul, might seem like pure water from a well in Delamer. And there was the possibility of poison to consider. This was Castle Skrike after all. And yet Sarondakis had to drink water too didn't they? Who was to say this wasn't the castle's water supply? Or perhaps even the area's? This could be the entire water supply of the northern Ratog, hoarded by Skrike in this giant cistern as a reserve in case of siege.

"Fill the water sack Yazzle," said Buckle. "We'll rest here a few hours. Everybody drink as much as you can."

After an orgy of drinking and bathing, the group rested, all of them sleeping soundly on the stone causeway. Morale improved considerably after they'd had their fill of water and their ration of food. They looked better too. Yazzle's hair approached its original blond. His skin seemed a little lighter except in the places where the coal dust had been rubbed in permanently. They all had that, Shacknel, most of all. He was almost entirely blackened after years in the mine.

Even Lathel drank and bathed. He spoke more too but not much of what he said made sense. It seemed to Buckle that the boy was more aware. His blue eyes focused on things more. Perhaps the boy was pulling out of his shock. Buckle hoped so.

Only Buckle himself had problems. His chest tightened up like a vise. For most of their rest period, Buckle lay flat on his back, trying to relax, to open his airways. He imagined Sora bending over him, her fingers poking into his abdomen, pushing on the exhales, letting up on the inhales. She'd berate him in a gentle voice about pushing himself or helping out with the harvest in fall when all the goldenrod would be out. Buckle couldn't help but smile, but at the same time he realized he'd probably never see Sora again.

And then there was Krinseth, who could stop his attacks with a small spell and a hand on his back. Buckle wondered where she was, if she thought of him. The witch had taken his amulet, saying she'd use it to find him. But surely she couldn't reach into the heart of Castle Skrike? Her powers would be diminished in the desert. And yet here he was surrounded by water. Surely that would help. Perhaps he could contact her if he concentrated.

Instead he coughed, bringing up a little mucus which he spat out to the side. He lay in total darkness, the only sounds were lapping water and Shacknel's snoring.

Later, they moved on. Buckle walked slowly like an old man with a bad heart. The tips of his fingers tingled and stars shot across his vision. The back of his throat tickled so much it was an effort not to cough. He staggered along, lagging behind even Lathel. He could see Yazzle and Shacknel exchanging worried glances in the torch light twenty feet ahead.

And then suddenly, he could breathe. Buckle almost fell to his knees with the shock of it, even though he had experienced it several times in the last few days. His head swam and his vision danced giddily before him. But once it settled down, Buckle could see everything, the causeway, his friends, the underground lake bathed in silvery light, and above it all shone the sphere.

"Thank you," he mumbled.

"Master Buckle," cried Yazzle, rushing back to him. "What's the matter? Are you all right?"

"Yes, I'm fine Yazzle," said Buckle. He stood up straight and stretched his back. "The sphere is back."

"Can you tell why?" asked Yazzle. Lathel had stopped also and was staring blankly at the torch Shacknel held.

Buckle looked around. For the first time he could see the entire cavern. Or most of it anyway. Ahead of them, even the sphere's silvery light couldn't penetrate the gloom which obscured that part of the cavern. But the walls were clearly visible in the other three directions although hundreds of feet distant. The causeway was a black ribbon of stone extending into the gloom ahead of them, its end unseen.

Just ahead of them, it was cluttered with debris. Several large rocks bristling with planks of rotten wood and beams of rusty metal lay strewn across the causeway, spilling into the shallow edges of the lake, looking like spiny sea monsters. Overhead, there was a hole in the ceiling, revealing a large room above.

Buckle described the scene, once he and Yazzle caught up with the others. The sphere hovered over the wreckage, well away from Lathel.

"The sphere must have appeared to get us, or you rather, over that clutter," said Shacknel.

Yazzle walked over to the pile of debris and cast the yellow light of the torch over it. He craned his neck and stood on tiptoe, trying to find an easy path through the clutter.

"It doesn't look too bad, Master Buckle," he said. "I wouldn't want to try it in darkness though."

Buckle and Shacknel walked up to where Yazzle stood, and examined the wreckage for themselves. Buckle of course, could see much further. The debris only extended thirty feet or so and nowhere was there a major obstacle as long as one had light.

Then Buckle looked up, trying to peer into the room above.

"What do you see up there?" asked Shacknel who was doing the same. Yazzle too craned his neck, trying to pierce the gloom above.

"There are shelves. The whole room must be full of them and..." In spite of the sphere's light he couldn't see much detail. On the shelves were little white cylinders that as much as anything reminded him of insect larvae, such as he'd seen sometimes in open wounds in animal carcasses, when on Methliana, they came upon some unfortunate cow or sheep that had died a few days before. They also looked like grains of rice. Of course that was only from a distance. Up close they would be larger...

"Urns," said Buckle.

"What?" Shacknel cast a glance at him.

"Those are urns, like the one Urgallo had. Remember Yazzle?"

The lad nodded his head, staring at the hole in the ceiling. His face looked distinctly uncomfortable at the memory and at the thought of uncounted numbers of the urns overhead.

Shacknel bent over and picked something up. It was a white shard of porcelain with an ornate crimson pattern painted on the convex side of it and dark splotches staining the other side.

"Soowooli urns," said Shacknel. "We must be under a storeroom full of them. I imagine it's been unused for years or maybe centuries or they would have noticed the floor had fallen in."

"Don't the urns need to be heated?" asked Buckle.

"All these warriors are probably dead," said Shacknel, turning the shard over in his hand. "Yes this pattern was used over six hundred years ago." His knurled finger pointed to the red swirls on the shard. "This warrior probably fought in the first Sarondaki war."

"When Skrike conquered to the sea."

The old man squatted and started feeling around in the rubble. He found a few more tiny splinters. He held one up to the torch light. It seemed spectacularly white when held in the old man's black fingertips.

"In my younger days I would have longed for this more than a mountain full of gold." He looked up to the storeroom. "I wish I could get up there."

"Even if you could, we wouldn't have the time to spare," said Buckle.

"I know, I know," said Shacknel, getting up. "But a couple of days to myself up there would almost make up for forty years of slavery. Almost."

"Perhaps if things go our way you can return."

The old man nodded, understanding.

They pressed on. The going was tedious, even hazardous at times and the toughest part was getting Lathel to make the necessary steps and grasps to get him over the pile of debris. The youth took only a dull sort of interest as Yazzle and Buckle patiently guided him over the obstacles. It was especially difficult because the sphere wouldn't go near him.

Buckle thought back to when the boy had just arrived in the dungeon, part of a new group of prisoners led into the depths below Castle Skrike in much the same way Buckle and Yazzle had been. Bruct had taken an immediate and unwelcome liking to the youth and pulled strings to get him into the cell. Lathel at first was scared and avoided everyone. Bruct befriended him and protected him from the other gangs in their part of the dungeon. This brought the youth round and he seemed to open up.

That was until the night Bruct made his move. Buckle remembered it with a chill. Minutes after the candle went out, there was scuffling and then Lathel's voice protesting and Bruct's soothing. Buckle had huddled in his area of the floor while Lathel screamed and begged for help. It had ended in weeping and sobbing.

The boy didn't say much after that. He clung to the shadows and tried to stay out of the way. But when he had talked, he'd made sense. There had been reason behind those eyes. Buckle wondered just exactly when the boy's wits left him, after the murder or just before? Did he have to become insane to commit the act or did the act itself drive him insane? It was a question that something deep inside Buckle wanted answered.

Up until now he hadn't really taken a life. Back in the barn with Urgallo and the wooliman, he'd been protecting his own life and those of his companions. It had been difficult but he was ready to do it. And Buckle could say with a reasonable amount of confidence that he hadn't killed the bandit. The wooliman had.

When Buckle looked inside himself, though, he didn't see the capacity to just sneak up on someone and put a pick through the back of his skull, no matter how much he hated that person. He looked at Lathel and wondered how that capacity could dwell in one so young.

Yazzle and Buckle lifted Lathel off the last stone block and set his feet firmly on the stone of the causeway. Buckle stretched his back and looked up at the hole in the ceiling one last time. This view offered nothing significantly different from the opposing view on the other side of the pile. Shacknel stepped up beside him and looked up.

"I wish I could see what's up there."

"Just what I described to you."

"You're not a scholar. You don't know what you're seeing. If only we could get some light up there. Just a glimpse could maybe tell me volumes."

"Maybe you can," said Buckle and he told them a plan that had just occurred to him.

"I don't know Master Buckle," said Yazzle, "this is the last of our food."

"It's really not important, anyway," said Shacknel. "Not enough to throw away the food."

Buckle looked at the causeway which stretched ahead of them, disappearing into blackness. Then he looked up at the sphere which floated in the hole, its luminous bulk silhouetting the hole's ragged edges.

"Something tells me that it is important," replied Buckle looking at the sphere. "I think we're near the end,"

The others cast questioning glances at him. "I don't think we're going to need any more food. I don't know how I know this but..." His hands flailed in the air while his mouth tried to form words he had yet to think of.

"I don't think this is my idea."

"The sphere?" asked Shacknel.

Buckle nodded and looked to Yazzle's uncomprehending face. The lad looked frightened but still ready to do what Buckle asked him.

"I say do it then," said Shacknel. "The sphere hasn't let us down yet."

"All right, first let's get a handful each to eat." He opened the sack and stuck his hand into the oily mess. "On second thought, let's just do it."

Buckle held out the torch and Yazzle held the sack over it. The bag ignited and yellow flames spurted out of it. Yazzle began swinging it in a great arc at his side. Then he tossed it underhand into the air where it sailed into the hole. Buckle had a close moment when it passed through the sphere but their luminous guide didn't seem to notice. Then the burning food sack disappeared, landing with a thump in the room above. They waited a few seconds.

"Nothing," said Shacknel, who had been watching keenly. "I can't see a thing."

"I wonder why the sphere had us do it then?" said Buckle.

Shacknel shrugged his shoulders and turned to walk down the causeway. "I expect we'll find out," he said. The rest followed but it was a long time before Buckle could get the incident out of his head.

After a few hours of walking along the smooth straight causeway the sphere still remained with them. Buckle was sure now that something was going to happen. He constantly scanned their surroundings, expecting danger-some kind of monster living in the underground lake or the ceiling falling in. But nothing of the sort happened. The entrance to the great cavern faded in darkness as they moved away from it while the other side remained in shadow. The sound of falling water, faint at first, but growing louder with each step, came to their ears.

Buckle was so busy looking around that Yazzle and Shacknel were the first to see it in spite of their being handicapped by not seeing in the light of the sphere. Ahead of the group the causeway ended. The stone surface dipped down to where it slid under the surface of the water. Beyond lay a span of some fifty feet of fast moving water. Beached on the edge of the causeway were the ruins of a rowboat. The broken keel and the staves, separated and sticking out, made the boat look like some kind of bleached ribcage one would find in the desert.

The splashing water was now so loud, they had to raise their voices to be heard.

"That's as far as we can go, I guess," said Buckle, his voice cracking.

Shacknel sat down with a groan. "Can we swim it?" He stared across the gap.

"The water's going too fast," said Yazzle who sat down also. Lathel remained standing.

The torch sputtered and threw out a few sparks and then burned a little less brightly.

"Only a few minutes of light left," said Buckle. He sank to the ground at the end of the causeway, stretching out his feet to immerse them in the water. "I'm sorry I got you fellows into this."

"I'm better off than I was before," said Shacknel from behind them.

"Especially you, Yazzle. You had the good life you had fought so hard for and I forced you to give it up."

"I volunteered, Master Buckle. I have no regrets unless you have found my service lacking."

"Not at all my friend."

Yazzle didn't answer but after a few seconds Buckle thought he heard a stifled sob, though it was hard to tell with all the noise. He didn't turn around to see. He closed his eyes tightly against his own tears.

When he opened them again the light was doing flip-flops. The shadows cast by his knees grew and shrunk in a perplexing rhythm. Buckle sat up and saw the sphere across the gap in the causeway performing all kinds of gymnastics to get his attention.

"What in Skrike's Hell..."

"What is it Buckle?" asked Shacknel.

"The sphere, it's..." Buckle studied the apparition, trying to find the words in his mind to describe its actions. It danced in the air, bouncing and dashing around in circles and figure eights. Then when it seemed to be confident it had Buckle's attention it descended halfway into the water at Buckle's feet and floated toward the other side of the gap.

"I think it wants us to wade," said Buckle. A sensation of confirmation came into his head.

"To wade?" asked Shacknel. The old man climbed to his feet and limped over to the edge to stand beside Buckle. "I wonder how deep it is."

"I can go in partway to find out, Master Buckle." Yazzle came up behind them.

"No, I'll do it," said Buckle. He put up his hand to quell any argument. "I can see better than you and the sphere isn't going to let me get into any danger."

Yazzle obviously didn't like it but he bowed to Buckle's logic and stubbornness.

Buckle stood up and waded into the water. It was cold and its swift motion cut like an icy wind. In the dank coolness of the cavern the chill water drew all the warmth out of him and he shivered as each step down the steep slope immersed him in deeper and deeper water. When he was about twenty feet from the end of the causeway the water was up to his chest and the stone under his feet had leveled off. He turned around and said, "I think this is as deep as it gets."

Shacknel cast a look at Yazzle and then shrugged his shoulders and went in. Buckle watched as the black water encircled the old man's spindly legs. Yazzle followed, guiding Lathel with one hand and holding up the torch with the other. After a minute, Shacknel stood beside Buckle.

"Well let's hurry," said the old teacher. "This water's cold."

As Buckle waded, the resistance of the flowing water made his movements slow but the reassuring light of the sphere drew him on. The silvery cast of the light made the water look thick and luxurious like a piece of black velvet.

Only the biting cold of the current belied the illusion. Buckle shivered, trying to force air deep into his chest which was contracted with the cold and the pressure of the water.

Suddenly his lead foot didn't touch bottom. He flailed it around for a moment but failed to find a surface. Then he tried to lean backwards but the current ran too strong and swiftly pulled his unanchored body up off the bottom. Buckle twisted around and reached back for help but his companions were likewise engaged in trying to keep their footing. Yazzle dropped the torch and the flame sizzled out. Then Buckle's head dipped under the surface.

The next thing he knew he was being swept along by the current. He tumbled and spun until he had no idea which way he was headed. But no matter how violent his motions he was always brought to the surface for air before it was too late. The sphere led the way. Even under water Buckle could see it, bubbles boiling around it. Not for the first time, he wished the light had some heat to it.

Buckle broke the surface and tried to tread the water and get his bearings. The light of the sphere helped and soon he could see in which direction he was going.

And immediately wished he hadn't. Ahead of him, lay a waterfall, the source of the now deafening noise. It was a U-shaped cataract, not as tall as some Buckle had heard about but it was by far the largest he'd ever seen. Just beyond it, Buckle could see solid rock. He felt like he was in a runaway cart nearing the top of hill in those few moments just before plunging down the other side.

He screamed and almost got a lungful of water as the current dragged him down and spun him around like a ball on the end of a string. His arms flailed helplessly and he shut his eyes to avoid seeing the sphere which followed him down.

Buckle surfaced again and was near the edge. He made a few feeble attempts at swimming away from it but the current carried him over. He shot downwards and after a long fall splashed into another body of water. There were a few moments of relative peace as his momentum dragged him to the bottom. In the silvery light he floated, too numb to be cold. He reached out and with blue fingers touched the bottom. Then the current dragged him away and upward.

When he broke the surface a strangled yell spewed out of his chest. Painfully he forced air into his lungs and spat out ice water. When the stars stopped swirling in front of his eyes he saw that he was in some kind of underground river. The water around him bubbled and foamed into rapids and consequently was a little warmer.

It was only then that Buckle realized that the air above the river channel was suffused with an ambient light for which the sphere was not responsible. This light, though dim, shone yellowish. Hope, unlooked for and perhaps unwelcome welled up in Buckle's chest. Did the river lead to the outside? Was that why the sphere led him into the current?

As he neared a bend in the river, the channel suddenly narrowed and the water boiled over his head. It churned and tossed him like a twig. He slammed painfully against a rocky shelf but somehow managed to hold on. His searching foot found purchase and he climbed up to find himself on top of the shelf, knee deep in water that was warm, even hot. The tingling this caused in his limbs was almost unbearable and he staggered under the shock.

The warm water flowed from a cave just ahead of Buckle and flowing from it also was a shaft of golden sunlight. The floor of the cave angled upward at a gentle gradient that Buckle thought, even in his weakened condition, he could climb.

He had risen to his feet and taken a step toward the cave when another figure caught up on the shelf and clung like a barnacle on a ship's hull. With relief and delight, Buckle saw the blond locks of Yazzle. He helped his friend on to the shelf and watched as the warm water revitalized the lad.

Next came Lathel who must have clung to the shelf purely out of instinct. He still wore that vacant look. Yazzle pulled the youth onto the shelf and out of the water while Buckle scanned the river for Shacknel.

The rapids showed no sign of disgorging the old man. Panic began to well up in Buckle's gut as the minutes went by. He stood in the stream with his feet uncomfortably hot and shivering in the cool unearthly air that blew off the surface of the underground river. His clothes hung in sopping rags about him.

"Shacknel," he cried, his voice cracking. Yazzle appeared beside him.

"Shacknel," Yazzle shouted.

"Come on, old man," muttered Buckle.

Then a figure slammed into the shelf at their feet. Yazzle dived for it and Buckle had to scramble to hold onto Yazzle's knees to keep both of them from being pulled back into the stream. With much splashing and great effort they hauled Shacknel up onto the shelf.

As the old teacher was carried into the warm water a cloud of blackish red bloomed by his head. Buckle turned the head to examine the left side and saw a horrible gash. He'd obviously banged it somewhere in the stream. The old man's lips and fingers were dark purple and even in the streaming water from the cave he felt cold.

Charles Ebert

Buckle propped the silver head on his knees and gently nudged the old man into consciousness. Yazzle stood by and watched, a mournful expression on his soggy features.

Those yellow eyes opened and recognized Buckle. He tried to speak but fell instead into a wracking coughing fit. He almost passed out again but Buckle could see him struggle against the oncoming unconsciousness.

"I can see," he said in a barely audible voice.

"Yes." Buckle tilted Shacknel's head up so he could see the cave and the sunlight streaming out of it.

"Take me over there."

Buckle nodded and waved Yazzle over. Together they carried the old man to the entrance of the cave and laid him down in the golden glow of the sunlight. He looked up at the golden orb which seemed to be right at the other end of the cave. Buckle and Yazzle looked at it too, marveling at its brilliance.

And then Buckle thought of Shacknel. How many spring days had the old man missed in forty years of being locked away in a damp dungeon. How many picnics in grassy meadows or walks along rivers with the sun shining through the trees. Forty springs, forty summers lost, now forever. Buckle could feel pressure building up behind his eyes. He looked down, hoping to be able to express some of his feelings to Shacknel. But the old man was dead. His eyes were open and unfocused.

Without conversation, they carried him up into the shaft, somehow feeling that it was proper that his grave should be in the sunlight.

23

He had been deep in meditation when the storm hit his island. With a start his eyes snapped back into focus and he ran to the entrance of his cave to watch the rain and wind. Off on the horizon lightning struck and then a few seconds later thunder. It had nothing to do with him.

He examined the storm with a critical eye. It was small compared to his latest efforts but respectable. Like most natural storms, the winds blew in generally the same direction but gusts would veer off on tangents. Inefficient. The rain could only be described as intermittent, not the steady downpour of his latest accomplishments.

Still, he thought, rubbing his hands together, it was a good base to work from. He cast an eye toward the larder he had made out of some stone slabs he had hauled up from the island's small stream. Perhaps a small repast first to build up his energy? Some men from a neighboring island had come earlier that day, bringing him a whole wild boar already salted and cut up. Then they had politely asked him to stop making storms. It was disrupting their fishing. He had assured them he was almost done. And indeed, he was coming up against his mother's deadline. Hopefully they got back before this storm broke.

He eyed the larder longingly but then decided against it. This natural storm was a tremendous piece of luck and there was no telling how long it would last. And even he needed conditions to be right before he could cook up a storm from scratch. And it might take days for conditions to be right again. So with a sigh he darted out into the weather and picked up the path toward his storm summit.

Once he stood on his pinnacle, he surveyed the waves with an artist's eye. As it was, the storm wasn't much. It would probably crash into the coast and die if he didn't intervene.

With a big arm swing he smoothed out the wind, gathering all the stray gusts and puffs and set them into a spiral. Then, turning his attention to the sea, he arranged the wave fronts in neat orderly fashion, sending them racing one by one toward the mainland. With everything in line, he was able to boost the power. Hurricane force winds screamed past him, threatening to sweep him away. He marshaled the storm's forces, holding them until the power built up to just the right level, and then he sent the whole thing ripping eastward.

For two hours he danced atop his summit, summoning stronger winds and pulling deeper waves out of the ocean, until he was sure his creation was powerful enough to serve his mother's purpose.

Then wet, spent and above all hungry, he dragged back to his cave, visions of cooked salt pork floating in his mind. There was also a certain satisfaction in a well performed task. Mother would be pleased and, he decided, there was no need to tell her he'd had a little help from nature.

Even though she had done it for the last two days, Zabeth was still surprised when she woke up in a bed. It was only a straw mattress on a rickety frame but such a thing seemed unimaginably luxurious after...how long had it been? Zabeth swung her legs out of bed and sat up trying to remember. Six, seven months since they had left Delamer. She shook her head. It seemed longer.

A muffled groaning attracted her attention and she looked back at the hulking form of Kebble as he turned over in his sleep. That was as strange as sleeping in a bed: Sharing that bed with a man. She had had trouble getting to sleep at first. Not that Kebble snored or thrashed around too much. It was just his warm breathing presence. Even if she rolled over with her back to him she could feel him. By the second night, she was able to sleep a little more but she could tell this sharing a bed was going to take some getting used to.

Kebble had been only a little less surprised than Zabeth when she suggested they spend their time off together. The long trek north had been arduous though thankfully peaceful. With Deruct's army smashed, many of the southern tribes had offered them aid and had even joined Kebble's growing ranks. Kebble had given everybody four days when they had arrived in this village which was one of the southernmost and had no love for Skrike. After he had told the partisans of his decision and they had gone their separate ways, screaming and carrying on, Zabeth had marched up to him and made the suggestion almost as if she were asking for further orders. He stammered a bit but finally assented, not asking any of the questions Zabeth could see flashing across his face. She had been glad. She wasn't sure she could answer them.

She pushed the blanket off of herself and examined her body. Kebble had said nothing about her small chest or the scars that marked her as a warrior. Of course he had more than a few himself. But somehow, Zabeth thought, they looked better on men. He didn't care about all that. He had made love to her passionately and unhesitatingly. The experience had been painful at first. When he entered her, breaking the barrier, Zabeth's reaction had been to fight back and instinct had almost taken over. But after that it got better, much better. And Zabeth decided that she liked it more than she thought she would. When it was over, he had held her in his arms, radiating contentment. Oddly enough, she had liked that part too.

She stood up and put on her clothes.

After fighting the spiders and scorpions for room on the toilet seat, she went down into the common room and had some rancid bacon and corn meal for breakfast. She sat at a table which wobbled and was so scarred and rutted she wouldn't have wanted to write on it.

The door banged open and Zabeth turned around to see Roduct standing in the room, looking around. He wore his desert robes, dusty from travel. His visor was placed up on his forehead. He spotted her and walked over to where she was seated.

"Is Kebble up?" he asked.

"No, but he was stirring a few minutes ago. Should be down soon. What's going on?"

Roduct looked at her, as if sizing her up. They hadn't said much to each other since the battle in the south. Roduct was by nature a taciturn man who kept to himself. How he had inspired so much loyalty in a man as giving and outgoing as Buckle was a thing Zabeth could never understand. On the estate almost everyone felt more loyalty to Buckle than to Roduct who was never seen. Also she couldn't get over the fact that here was one of the elite, one of the landed gentry who governed the land of her birth.

As they had staggered north after the battle though, her respect for Roduct grew every day. Kebble and Bindle had explained to her what a difficult feat he had performed in breaking Soowooli. And what's more his desert craft and long memory for the locations of ancient depots and obscure oases had saved them countless times.

What Roduct thought of Zabeth she could only guess.

"A rider came to the drop-off point where we were camped. He had some news."

"What is it?" said Kebble. He padded up to the table and sat down. His hand lightly brushed Zabeth's neck and shoulders.

"Kebble," said Roduct, apparently not noticing the contact. "Good, I won't have to say this twice. The western armies have crossed the Barriers."

"I take it Unity's been retaken."

"About two weeks ago. The courier told me that the Sarondakis hadn't found all the secret entrances yet." Roduct smiled grimly.

Kebble rubbed his chin.

"What's the matter?" asked Zabeth.

"I wonder what happens now."

"They'll drive Marduct back into the desert and destroy his forces. Skrike will be captured and killed. And with this army you've been accumulating, we're in perfect position to be the vanguard, that's obvious." Zabeth bit the end of a strip of bacon.

"Is it?" said Kebble, looking at her. "To us maybe. But to them? I don't know."

"What are you worried about, Kebble?" said Roduct.

"Whenever I get orders from King Tetwell and the others, I sense some indecision, maybe even division. I know Nodwick and Tetwell but this Fazzle?" He shrugged. "I wish you were still on the council Roduct."

The Sarondaki looked down for a moment and shrugged.

"I know Fazzle," he said, "a pompous ass, but he lives for details. The messenger told me that people are still marveling at the job he did mobilizing Delamer for war. A ten thousand man army in three months, they say, and I believe it. No doubt he has an efficient and brilliant mechanism for arming and supplying the army. But the desert's awfully hard on logistics. More than one army has starved out here. And Fazzle isn't a risk taker. Plus like most Delamerians he's an isolationist. Somebody probably had to move heaven and earth to get him to come as far as the mountains, much less cross them."

"Then there's a chance they won't come any further?" said Kebble.

"My guess is that right now Fazzle is threatening to pull his troops out of the alliance."

"That's monstrous," cried Zabeth. "That's...that's exactly..."

"What happened the last time," said Kebble. "There are many in Delamer who would call it justice."

"I call it an outrage that they'd even consider it." Zabeth's face flushed with indignation. Every fiber in her being vibrated with righteous anger.

"What are you going to do Kebble?"

The partisan leader rubbed at his blond beard. He glanced at each of his companions in turn. "Let me ask you. What would both of you do if I turned south again and made my way over the mountains through some secluded pass?"

"What?" cried Zabeth. Her insides burned with hurt and betrayal.

"My mission's done," said Kebble. "I've lost well over half my men. Surely they can't ask any more of me?"

"You promised..."

"I said I wouldn't stand in your way, Zabeth. And I won't. But I don't know if I can help you. I'm asking you what would you do if I couldn't?"

"I'd go to Castle Skrike and rescue Buckle." said Zabeth, looking Kebble straight in the eye. "Even if I had to go there alone." He broke off the gaze by looking down at the table.

"And she wouldn't have to go alone," added Roduct. "I'd take my warriors and attack the castle.

"How large is your force?"

"Counting the freed Soowoolis from Deruct's army and the warriors I've picked up on the way north, I've got about three thousand."

"And every village we pass through, we get offers of help from the Sarondakis," said Zabeth, feeling the excitement. "We could have a five thousand man army in two days' time."

Kebble leaned back and nodded. "Well Skrike and Marduct are now fighting a losing war. My guess is that Castle Skrike is under-defended. Every available warrior who can walk will be with Marduct.

Every report I've had verifies this." He looked up at them from under his eyebrows.

"I think we can take it. If we hurry."

"You mean..."

"I'll go with you."

More relief than Zabeth would have admitted to flooded through her.

"You'll be taking a risk," said Roduct.

Kebble shrugged. "With an army that size, we might be able to fight our way out if the western armies don't advance. Besides, I'm counting on them acting when they hear what I'm doing."

"But if they do, they may drive Marduct right into your flank."

"That's why speed is essential. Can I ask you to grab a quick breakfast and then ride back to your troops?"

Roduct stood up. "I'll eat in the saddle," he said.

"Get back tomorrow. I leave in two days."

The tall Sarondaki nodded and quickly exited the room.

Kebble pushed back from the table and stood up. "Where's Bindle?"

"What do you want him for?" Zabeth flashed an irritated look at Kebble and scooped up the last of the cold corn meal in her fingers.

"Because we're going to need his help in planning for this."

"Dalmar help us if we're so badly off we need his help."

"You're underestimating him."

"Not at all. He's one of the few people I've ever met that I'd want at my back in a fight but he's not the smartest man in the world."

"I don't have time to argue this with you again. Do you know where he is?"

"He moved into the other inn."

"Why did he do that? Never mind. I'll go get him."

"Wait." Zabeth stood up and crossed over to the rickety stairwell and took a few steps up until she could see down the second story hallway. The sun shone through the window at the end, casting the cracked adobe walls in a harsh yellow light.

"Keruct," she bellowed. There came the sound of someone fumbling in one of the rooms.

"What," yelled Keruct, sticking his head out of one of the doorways lining the hallway upstairs.

"Need you to go over and get Bindle."

He looked into his room and Zabeth thought she heard giggling. She noticed his bare chest.

"Now?" he asked.

"Afraid so."

He looked into the room again and said, "I'll do it." He slammed the door shut.

Kebble watched her from across the room. "What was that about?"

"They'll probably make you a count or even a duke, just for what you've done already. You're too important to run your own errands."

Kebble laughed. "They haven't made me a duke yet. I'm still a lowly constable."

"You're in charge of an army aren't you? That makes you at least a count."

"Five thousand men. Most of them Sarondaki adolescents, old men and women. Not much of an army."

"But all yours." Zabeth paused while Keruct thundered down the stairs, fully dressed, gave them a glance and then left. "Besides I wanted to talk to you."

"What about?"

Zabeth walked up to him. She bit her lip, trying to find the best words to say this. "Are you doing this because of me? Because of us?"

Kebble laughed and Zabeth felt like hitting him. He leaned against the table and said, "Partly. And partly because I do think it's my best strategy." He sat in the chair, the laughter gone. "But mostly it's because of history. Dalmar is the only person who's ever attacked that castle, and while I'm no Dalmar, I do see that I have an opportunity to finish his work." He looked up at her, completely serious now.

"And Zabeth, somebody has to do that. Skrike must be destroyed, not just beaten. Or else he'll rise again and again."

She nodded her head in approval. "I'll move my things down the hall."

"What...why do that?" Kebble looked up at her, a hurt expression on his face.

"Because we're on campaign again. You remember our agreement?"

"Yes but we're not marching for two days."

She looked at him. "Kebble if this is going to work, we have to stick to our ground rules. You said yourself, a woman in camp, sleeping with a man, causes morale problems."

"You're right," he said. He looked at the floor. "It's just that...I thought we'd have more time."

Zabeth cast a look toward the door and then around the room to make sure they were alone. Then she went to him and put her arms around his neck.

"When this is over and if we're both still alive and..." she looked down, seeing the blond hair peeking out the top of his tunic. "Anyway, we'll have a lifetime then."

He tilted her head up by the chin. "Is that what you want?"

"Yes," she said softly.

"Then I guess I can wait." He drew her close but she stopped him with a hand on his chest. She took a step back and saluted.

"Do you have any orders for me, sir?"

Kebble sighed. "Yes put your gear in the empty room and then report back to me. We'll probably be in conferences all day."

The door banged open and Zabeth saw Keruct and Bindle silhouetted in the frame. Keruct supported Bindle as they hobbled into the room. Bindle's head was soaked and it bobbed like a weathervane in a breeze.

"Is he hurt?" asked Zabeth.

"Oh, he's feelin' fine," laughed Keruct as he deposited Bindle none too gently onto a chair. "I found him lying on the floor of his room in a puddle of vomit, three empty wine bottles and a half empty rolling beside him."

Zabeth caught a whiff of the cheap alcohol and other odors emanating from Bindle. "Disgusting."

"I cleaned him up a little bit," continued Keruct with a sardonic smile. "Dunked his head in a water trough."

"Thanks for going to the trouble," said Kebble.

"Oh, I enjoyed it."

"Kebble," said Bindle, his head swiveling back and forth suddenly.

"I'm here old friend." Kebble moved into his line of sight.

"I'm going to whip you like a dog." He leaned forward, used the table for support and then stood up, swaying in a non-existent breeze. He brought his shaking fists up in front of him.

"And why are you going to do that, Bindle?" Kebble stood four feet away with his arms crossed.

"Because you're a son of a bitch woman stealing hound, that's why." He took a swipe, the momentum of which toppled him over. He managed to catch himself on another table. Leaning over the table a sob escaped his throat and a line of spittle fell out of his mouth.

"You bastard," he said in a choked voice. "I saw her first. I saw her first."

"Keruct, take him into the kitchen and see if there's anything that will sober him up in there."

The big man nodded his head and grabbed Bindle by the shoulder. "Come along Bindle, we'll get some food down your throat and you'll feel better."

"That's what you said about the water trough."

"Yes and I was lying then too. Let's go." The two limped past Zabeth on their way to the kitchen. Bindle cast a bleary eyed gaze at her as he went past. A tear rolled down his cheek. Then he was gone.

"What was that all about?"

Kebble looked at her, his eyes wide with surprise.

"You're kidding?"

"No. Why was he saying those things?"

"You really don't know do you?"

Zabeth wanted to screech in frustration. Kebble stood there with an incredulous smile on his face, genuinely amused that she couldn't see what was apparently right in front of her. And she couldn't.

"What?" she screamed.

"The man's in love with you."

The news shocked her. She stood blinking in the grungy sunlight that filtered into the room as every contact she ever had with Bindle passed for review under her mind's eye.

"You're the best warrior I've ever seen, Zabeth, but you know nothing about people."

"He hates me," protested Zabeth.

"He loves you."

"But he's always giving me a hard time, criticizing everything I do, everything I say."

Kebble laughed. "That's Bindle's rather perverse way of courting you. I have to say his logic is sound. You live for conflict. If he'd had a little more time..."

"Never."

Kebble put his hands on her shoulders and smiled. "As happy as I am to hear you say that, I think you're wrong."

Zabeth needed to pace. She turned and walked away from him. "Is this going to be a problem?"

Kebble sighed and walked over to the door, pushing it open a crack. "Once he sobers up, he'll be able to control himself. And once he meets another woman he'll get over you." He paused, seemingly rapt with the view outside. "Things may never be the same between him and me though."

"Does that bother you?"

"A little." He let the door close. "When you go up to move your stuff, bring the maps down out of our...my room. We can at least go over some plans today."

"Yes sir." Zabeth ran up the stairs, still wandering about the morning's revelations.

24

Not suddenly, but a little bit at a time, her powers returned. A trace of moisture in the air, the distant promise of rain, filled her drained reservoirs one drop at a time. Sustained entirely on this meager magic, for her stomach was empty and there was little blood in her veins, she opened her eyes and slowly crawled out of her tomb. It took her fifteen minutes to work up a drop of spit. This she put on the amulet. Dimly she saw where he was. The plan was working, at least for now. On wobbly legs she made her way across the sands.

"I wonder who they were?" said Yazzle. Buckle stood at the entrance to the cavern, watching Yazzle as he squatted next to the two skeletons they had found. Their bones had been bleached white by the desert sun even though it probably only shone on them a couple hours a day. This couple--even in their decayed state Buckle could see how they clung together--had probably been here for centuries. Shacknel would have known.

Buckle thought of the small pile of stones they had built in another cavern across the spring. At least he had seen the sun before he died. They had been able to do that much for the old man.

"I don't know Yazzle. Probably they were prisoners who escaped and managed to get this far." Actually Buckle had an idea who they were but didn't want to say. The two people had been richly dressed, the ruins of their fine but durable clothes hung on their frames like flags on a windless day. One, the male Buckle decided, since he

281

was bigger and held a sword in his hand, sat against a pillar, his head leaned back against the stone, watching the gap in the roof, hopeful to the last. He had his arm protectively draped around the woman's shoulders. She was turned slightly into him with her head on his chest.

Around them, and indeed in all the sunlit caverns he and Yazzle had explored on this side of the spring, grew an assortment of fruit bearing trees. Well shrubs really, none of them were taller than Buckle's knees and yet they bore oranges, figs, dates and several fruits Buckle had never seen before.

It had to have been magic, considering that they were growing in dry sand and had only a couple of hours of sunlight a day. Nothing should have grown much less strange plants with ostentatious fruit. At first Buckle had had doubts about eating them, fearing the taint of magic. But those thoughts soon passed. He'd rather be tainted than dead.

"The sword has a Delamerian seal on it," said Yazzle.

"It does?"

"Yes, Master Buckle. It's different from the seals I've seen before, more..." He squinted, trying to think of the word he wanted, "ornate."

"It's probably older," said Buckle. "It doesn't look rusted at all. Bring it along. We might need it."

Yazzle looked up at him, uncertainly. "Should I?"

Buckle grinned. "I don't think he'll mind."

The lad shrugged and grabbed the blade just above the crosspiece and tried to slide it out of the bony grip. It didn't move. Yazzle tried again and then a third time, grunting with the effort.

"It won't move Master Buckle."

"Maybe it's rusted to the rock."

"It must be. I can't get it to budge." He grabbed the hilt and then, placing a foot against the pillar pulled with all his might.

"Nothing," he said when it wouldn't give. "I'm sorry, Master Buckle."

"That's all right. If it's that rusted, it's probably no good anyway." He turned back into the large cavern, puzzled. The sword looked bright and shiny, not rusted at all.

He surveyed the large cavern one more time, contemplating spending the rest of his life here. To the right the hot spring bubbled out of the wall which was stained bright yellow and red. Most of the cavern was a pool, steaming with volcanic heat. The deepest parts of the pool only came up to Buckle's waist. It was surrounded by a system of caverns and drained through the shaft, now on Buckle's left, through which they had come up into the sunlight.

That had been two weeks ago and since then they had found everything they needed: food, water and shelter. Everything except a way out. It was so frustrating because the roofs of these caverns had fallen in long ago. They could see the sky, feel the sun and even an occasional breeze. But the walls were too steep to climb. Some of the stalactites that jutted out of the pool like trees were tall enough to climb to the level of the ground but weren't situated close enough to the side to jump over. They were better off than they had been but they weren't free.

Buckle had briefly considered having Yazzle shimmy up one of those stalactites and tie a shirt or something to the top to attract the attention of any passersby. But he discarded the plan when he realized that the only people passing by here were liable to be Sarondakis. He would hate to come this far only to be tossed back into the dungeon again.

He hadn't seen the sphere since it had led them up into the caverns.

Yazzle went past Buckle and splashed across the cavern. "I'm going to look in on Lathel, Master Buckle."

"Good." The youth had been showing signs of improvement lately. He was talking more but was still distracted. Most of his day was spent in a fitful sleep on the floor of one of the darker caverns on the other side of the spring. Mercifully, he would eat without prompting and was able to tend to most of his own needs.

Buckle sighed and turned around to get an orange from one of the caverns, not the one with the skeletons. He entered the cavern to the left of it. Bending over to pick the fruit he saw his shadow cast over the strange tree shrubs. Then something moved. A shadow crossed in front of him. He spun around, the oranges forgotten and stared at the ragged hole in the ceiling.

Nothing. Just the sky, tinged yellow by the sun.

Buckle shrugged and walked back into the large cavern, trying to get his stubby fingers to peel the orange. His fingernails, weak from months of bad food, had all been ripped down to the cuticles by earlier attempts to peel oranges.

Giving up, Buckle began looking on the ground for a flat stone with a sharp enough edge with which to slice open the fruit. Then he saw it again. A shadow cast on the ground in front of him. This time it stopped and wavered. Buckle looked up and saw a ragged figure tottering on the edge of the roof.

"Hey, be careful, you're right on the edge..." The figure toppled into the cavern.

Buckle was running even before the figure hit the surface of the water. He splashed toward it, shouting, "Yazzle, get out here."

When the water got up to his waist Buckle lunged toward the strangely silent figure. Dog paddling up to it was faster than trying to run.

Yazzle shot out of Lathel's cavern and stood for a second, assessing the situation. Then he dived into the pool and started swimming for the figure.

Buckle got there first and grabbed the figure by its shoulders and forced it to the surface. He turned it around to get a look at its face.

"Krinseth," he cried.

The old woman opened her eyes at the sound of his voice and then regained her feet. She looked thin, the flesh on her cheeks hung loosely about her face. Her arms felt alarmingly bony through her ragged tunic. Ripped down the front, Buckle could see her withered breasts and count her ribs.

Yazzle appeared beside them and Krinseth glanced over at him and then gently disengaged herself from Buckle's grasp and turned away. Placing a hand on her sternum, she convulsed and a great quantity of water poured out of her mouth and nose. She bent her knees and immersed herself again. When she surfaced, she was swallowing water and gasping for air. She repeated the process two more times. Each time she looked better, her face filled out, her breasts enlarged and Buckle could no longer see her ribs.

"Food," she gasped after surfacing for the last time. Buckle was about to send Yazzle to get some fruit when he saw the orange in his hand. He held it out to Yazzle.

"Can you peel this for her Yazzle?"

"Never mind." Krinseth grabbed the orange and with her finger she traced the circumference of the sphere. Then along the line where her finger touched, the skin peeled back until the two halves turned inside out and fell into the water.

The witch jammed the fruit into her mouth and gobbled it hungrily. The juice poured down her chin and onto her chest, mixing with the water. When the whole thing had been devoured she splashed water on her chin to wash away the juice and then looked up at Buckle. Except for her ragged clothes, she looked like the Krinseth Buckle remembered.

"I'll need more in a minute," she said. Then she hugged him. "Buckle, it's so good to see you alive after all you must have been through. And you, young man." She turned to Yazzle and hugged him. The lad's hands reluctantly closed on her. He stared at Buckle with an alarmed look on his face. Buckle smiled at him.

"I imagine you're more than a little responsible for keeping him alive," said Krinseth, pushing herself back to get a look at Yazzle.

"Yazzle has saved my life countless times," said Buckle, making eye contact with the lad.

"I knew he would."

His face turned red. "I just did what I had to do."

"We all did my friend," said Buckle quietly. "Anyway we have all the time in the world to tell you all about it. Unless you were traveling with someone?"

"Of course not, why?" She waded past him to the pool's edge.

"There's no way out of these caverns."

"Let me worry about that. We leave tomorrow."

"How did you find us?"

She stopped and pulled a rag out of her belt and opened it up to reveal Buckle's amulet. Wet sand dotted her hands and wrists. "You can have this back now." She gave it to him and watched as he put it on.

"I didn't think your kind of magic worked in the desert."

"Not very well. But if you're determined..." She turned and started wading again. "Besides I had a good idea where you'd be."

She climbed up onto the rocky edge of the pool and surveyed the caverns.

"Did you..." she said, her voice wavering. "Did you find a...or two..." Buckle instantly knew what she was asking.

"This way." He led her to the cavern with the skeletons.

When she saw them she stopped, staring at the tableau while Buckle cast concerned glances at Yazzle.

"Damn you," she whispered, her fists clenched. "You killed her." She approached the figures.

"You dragged her into this hell and she died because she loved living things and nothing could live in this desert." She sunk to the

285

ground and jammed her fists into her eyes. "My sister, you needed to be free to roam the forests and glens; to place your bare feet on rich fertile soil. I tried to tell you, but you wanted to be with him, his slave just as he was a slave to his own death wish. I'll never understand that. Oh, Methlyn..." She threw herself onto the ground, her shoulders rising and falling with her sobs. Faintly, at first but with growing intensity, the sphere appeared above her and lowered itself onto her heaving shoulders. Buckle turned and walked out, taking Yazzle with him.

"Start collecting fruit in the other caverns. I guess we're leaving tomorrow." They went about their task, working to the sound of weeping.

Later that afternoon, they had accumulated a sizable pile of provisions which lay at the edge of the pool. Beside it Buckle and Yazzle worked at making packs out of some strong and flexible vines they had found in one of the caverns. They weaved the vines together to make a sort of net that could be gathered up by the edges to make a sack which would be quite suitable for carrying food.

"Can she really get us out of here, Master Buckle?" Yazzle looked up from his net.

"I don't doubt it, Yazzle, not for a second." He bent over to tie a knot. "You've seen the things she's done."

The lad nodded. His yellow beard, quite huge now, flopped with the motion. Buckle felt the scraggly growth on his own chin.

"She can do a lot more than we originally thought," said Yazzle. "If you don't mind my saying so."

Buckle looked up at him, not actually surprised that Yazzle would notice such a thing but that he would say so aloud. What's more, the comment was made as a plain statement of fact. Yazzle attached no judgments to it at all. Well, the main lesson of all they had been through was that they had little control over events. Yazzle probably figured that if Krinseth had not been completely honest with them in the beginning that was fine as long as she helped them now. Buckle, however, wasn't so sure.

Krinseth slumped out of the skeletons' cavern and knelt by the side of the pool. She splashed water into her red rimmed eyes. As she rubbed her face, Buckle got up and walked over to her.

"Those people in there? They are..."

"Dalmar and Methlyn." She finished his thought. "Surely you'd guessed that?" Buckle nodded.

"And she's your sister?"

Krinseth stared at the rippling surface of the pool. A bead of water gathered under the tip of her nose. When it had sufficient weight, it dropped and began to form again.

"Yes," she said.

"Which makes you Zalphlyn of the Lakes, a full blooded Tenaryan, immortal with unlimited power."

"Not unlimited," she said, still staring at the pool. "And we can be killed."

She looked at him. "Does it bother you?"

Buckle settled back. "I don't care who or what you are. You've helped me and my friends and for that, I'll be eternally grateful. If the gratitude of mortals means anything."

"The gratitude of some mortals means a great deal to me."

"But there's something we have to do before this is over, isn't there?"

She gave him a wry smile. "You are very astute. Follow me." She got up and led him into the skeletons' cavern.

The sunlight shone orange through the top of the cavern. It slanted through the dusty air and lit the far corner of the cavern, leaving Dalmar and Methlyn in darkness.

Buckle was surprised to see that their remains were unmolested especially Dalmar's, considering the violence of Krinseth's emotions earlier. Perhaps she couldn't quite get up the nerve to disturb him but Buckle figured it was probably more out of respect for her sister. Either way both skeletons were untouched when Krinseth stood beside them and motioned to Buckle to approach. She pointed to the sword.

"That sword was forged from Tenaryan steel. Spells have been cast over it using all four of the magics. It is lethal to Skrike. It was given to Dalmar by the Tenaryans to kill Skrike. Take it."

"I can't. It's rusted to the rock. Yazzle tried to pry it loose but he couldn't budge it."

"Did you try?"

"Well no. If Yazzle couldn't do it, what's the point in my trying?"

"Try it."

Buckle shrugged and bent over to grasp the crosspiece of the sword in both hands. He braced his feet and took a breath. Krinseth gave him a reassuring nod and then he pulled the sword with all his strength. It came out of Dalmar's grip easily. Buckle stumbled over backwards with his momentum. The sword fell to the sand.

Buckle rolled over and looked up at Krinseth who stood next to Dalmar, her arms crossed.

"Dalmar has chosen you."

"For what?"

"To finish the task he could not."

Buckle looked at her, not comprehending.

"You must kill Skrike."

An hour later Buckle sat at the edge of the pool, dangling his feet in the warm water. Night had fallen and the desert air felt cool, prompting Yazzle to build a fire. It must be winter, thought Buckle. It was the slowest season on Methliana with nothing to do but feed the animals, plan for next year and hope the supply of food holds out. Most of the field hands would be down south, trying to find work harvesting winter wheat or fishing in the southern bays of Joswell. The few hands Roduct kept on all year would be huddled around fires in their cabins, trying to keep warm.

It was a hard time of the year and yet Buckle enjoyed it. He imagined his favorite of the many sitting rooms in the manor house. He would recline in a comfortable chair, reading, while a fire crackled in the grate and the whiteness of snow-reflected sunlight pressed against the windows. Outside the buildings would be covered with white garments of snow. Children would be sledding on the hill or throwing snowballs, getting under the feet of Sora and the other adults as they did their chores. And at the solstice the entire household would gather together and feast, mumbling the ritualized prayers to the forgotten Dernian gods to bring the sun back again before the food ran out.

A footstep behind him brought Buckle out of the tranquility of his daydream. His thoughts returned to the sword, resting under his palm, to the dry chill of the desert night and to Dalmar and the murder of a tyrant. Krinseth sat beside him.

She stared at the ripples in the surface of the pool that her feet made and the way the firelight reflected off them, waiting for him to speak first.

"Do I call you Zalphlyn or Krinseth?" he asked.

"Whatever you want. But I haven't gone by my true name since Methlyn died." She looked at the black wall of the cavern.

"I'll call you Krinseth, then." She shrugged, not looking at him. "I've heard many songs speculating on why you disappeared, not all of them very flattering."

"I've heard most of them," she said, smiling, "even wrote a couple, mostly for the benefit of Skrike's spies."

"Is that the real reason you disappeared? To hide from Skrike?"

"Mostly. Sarondakis make very good assassins. Skrike knows that I and a few others are still in the outer realms. If he knew where he'd surely kill us. Also," she leaned back on her hands, "after Methlyn died, I wanted anonymity. To be someone else for a while. It made the pain more bearable."

Buckle nodded and thought of Roduct. The anguish of watching his lord and master being subjugated was almost more than he could bear. But Krinseth's pain must have been worse. A sister, and one as close as her and Methlyn were reputed to be...three hundred years wasn't enough time to dull the pain.

"I just have one question," he said. "Why me?"

"Why not you?" Krinseth replied.

"I'm weak. I've never killed anybody. I've had precious little training with a sword."

"You handled yourself pretty well in that barn in Joswell as I recall."

"That was self-defense. I and my friends were threatened, and besides those brigands were no experts either. What you're talking about here is assassination. I don't know if I can kill someone like that."

She looked over at him, her face neutral. "Not even the tyrant who conquered your country and ruthlessly oppressed it for hundreds of years."

"That was a long time ago."

"He may very well do it again if he's not killed."

"I realize that." Buckle rubbed his eyes. "This is important. Why have they left it to me? Why can't you kill him?"

"I'm a Tenaryan. He would sense me coming if I came with that intent and be prepared."

"So it has to be a human. Well, why not Zabeth? She'd have no problems with this."

"Western women do not fare well at the hands of the Sarondakis and while Zabeth would undoubtedly have taken many warriors down with her, in the end she would have suffered an awful fate. No I couldn't have sent her into the enemy's bosom."

"Yazzle then?"

Krinseth shook her head. "You don't understand. Physical strength, skill with arms, or even magic isn't the key to success in this venture. Skrike is too powerful. We have to use our brains."

"And Dalmar's sword," mumbled Buckle.

"The fatal weapon must be magical for Tenaryans cannot be killed by ordinary weapons."

"What killed your sister then?"

Krinseth looked down at the rippling water. "Love," she said.

Suddenly screams erupted from the other side of the pond in the direction of Lathel's cavern. Buckle stood up in the shallow pool, trying to see through the gloom.

"Yazzle," he called, as he started wading across the pool. "Get some torches."

Vaguely he heard Krinseth splashing behind him. Yazzle rushed to meet him, carrying two lit torches, one of which he handed to Buckle.

When they entered Lathel's cavern, the youth was on his feet, spinning one way and then the next, as if trying to discover an attacker, sneaking up on him. He turned to the light of the torches and for an instant Buckle thought he was going to charge them. The boy's eyes were large and his chest heaved, taking in gulps of air.

"Where is he?" demanded Lathel, his young voice cracking.

"Who, Lathel?"

He stammered the name. "Bruct."

"Why did you run like that? Who are you talking to?" asked Krinseth. Buckle, concentrating on Lathel, barely heard her.

"Bruct is dead," said Buckle. He took a step forward but Lathel backed against the wall. Buckle stopped and held his hands palms out.

"I just heard him...in the dark he-he..."

"Oh my," muttered Krinseth.

"I know what he did, Lathel. But that was a long time ago and now he's dead."

The boy paced to the other side of the cavern. "My father will have him horse-whipped for what he did. I've seen him do it. A couple of stable boys cornered me in the barn once. I didn't understand what they wanted until...Father came just in time."

Lathel stopped in the middle of the floor and shouted, "Horse-whipped them. One of them died."

"Lathel," said Yazzle, coming forward and casting Buckle an apologetic look. "Bruct is gone. Join my group and I'll protect you from now on. You know me don't you?"

"You're Yazzle," he said, blinking up at the lad. "The one they say killed a scorpion. You lead a gang."

"That's right and I'm asking you to join."

"Really? I..." He shook his head. "I can't. I'm part of Bruct's gang."

"Listen. If I can kill a scorpion, I can handle Bruct."

The youth stopped fretting and looked up at Yazzle. "You're not going to touch me are you?"

"No, I don't do that. Ask Master Buckle or anybody in my gang. I'll protect you." The boy looked from side to side in indecision. "We've got a fire over here. Sleep next to it tonight. I'll be close but not too close." He motioned the boy through the entrance to the cavern with the torch. Buckle caught his eye and gave him an approving nod.

"I think I saw some berries in one of the caverns that will calm him down," said Krinseth.

"Can't you do some magic on him to clear up his thinking?" Buckle followed her out of the cave.

"No, magic will not work on him. He's magic blind."

"Magic blind?"

"Yes, it's rare but there are some people whom magic does not affect. That's why I didn't see him at first. This place is so wet and I'm so powerful that I was unconsciously using magic in place of my natural senses. It's something we Tenaryans are prone to."

"He did mention that magic didn't work around him and the sphere..."

"Precisely," she said. She paused just before stepping onto the other side of the pool. "This gives me an idea. Bring along the sword." She stepped up and then disappeared into one of the caverns. Buckle bent over and picked up the sword, wondering what she had in mind.

Krinseth emerged from the cavern, holding a fistful of dark berries. Motioning him to follow she approached Lathel and sat the berries down in front of him. The youth, his eyes now alert watched her hands.

"I'm going to ask you a few questions son. Would that be all right?"

"Sure." He looked around at each of them in turn. Yazzle was eyeing Krinseth closely.

"What is your name?"

"Lathel," he said.

"Where are you?"

The boy's face fell and Buckle thought he'd start to cry. "I'm in the dungeon of the Castle Skrike. I'll never see the sun again."

"Where are you from?"

"Goswick. My family owns a horse ranch near the foothills. We supply the Barrier Scouts," he said, his chest puffing out proudly.

"How did you get here?"

"I..." he began but then stopped. He looked around, confused. "I don't know."

"Try to remember."

"The alarm bell rang. I remember that. And all the hands, running around, grabbing weapons. I got a sword but father told me I was too young and frail and made me put it back and then...and then."

"Then what?"

"I can't remember." The boy shrugged. "Father always told me I didn't have the temperament to be a warrior. Said I wouldn't be able to kill people." The image came unbidden to Buckle's mind of Lathel standing over Bruct's mutilated body with a dripping pick in his hands.

"Lathel," said Krinseth. "Who is that?" She pointed to Yazzle.

"That's Yazzle, my new protector."

"And him?"

"Buckle, he's in the gang too."

"And who am I?"

The youth squinted into her face. "Shacknel?" Krinseth looked over at Buckle questioningly.

"Buried in one of the caverns," he whispered. She nodded.

"One last question Lathel and then you can eat a couple of these berries that'll help you sleep."

"I'd like to sleep," he said.

"In a minute. You see, we found this sword and we need to know if you can use it." At a motion from her, Buckle placed the sword in front of Lathel who eyed it warily. His hand reached for the hilt and his fingers closed around it. He lifted it easily. Buckle stared in disbelief as the silver blade sparkled in the firelight.

"It feels light," said Lathel. "I like it but I don't know anything about swords."

"That's all right, son. Give the sword to Buckle and he'll hide it from the guards."

"Oh yeah," he said, handing the sword to Buckle and cringing at the thought. "We wouldn't want that or for Bruct to find it either. Hide it well."

"I will," said Buckle.

"Now eat two of these berries and lay down," said Krinseth, proffering the dark spheres to him. When he had gobbled them up she and Buckle walked a ways from the campfire while Yazzle tended to Lathel.

"He could be useful," she said.

"You're not thinking of using him to kill Skrike are you?"

She shook her head. "He'd never be able to do it. No, I mean that while he's carrying the sword, it's cloaked from Skrike's scrutiny. I couldn't sense it when he held it. Of all of us, only he can sneak it into the castle. In fact, he could probably lay it right at Skrike's feet, making what you have to do as easy as possible. Skrike will never see him."

"I still don't know if I can do it."

"Can you doubt that it's right?"

"No I suppose not, still this doesn't sit well with me."

She smiled at him and grabbed his shoulder. "When the time comes you'll find the strength and the right reasons. Now get to sleep. We leave early tomorrow. There'll be a rainstorm before nightfall."

Buckle looked up at her as she walked away. "You're kidding, a rain storm in the desert?"

She ignored him.

25

Zabeth sat in the darkness, polishing Grazzle's sword. It had been awhile since she had had the time, so the blade was pretty nicked up. The half-moon and brilliant desert stars provided ample light for the task.

As she rubbed the blade vigorously with a cloth, her eyes strayed to the hulking shape of Castle Skrike, a black void with towers and parapets that dominated the northern horizon. They had arrived here at the foot of the castle's mountain just after darkness had fallen. The castle's defenders had to have known they were here from the dust cloud which was visible for miles. But the Sarondakis wouldn't know exactly where they were camped.

Kebble's army, made up of the remnants of the original company of partisans and a couple thousand rebellious Sarondakis would need every advantage it could get. Scouts had reported that the castle walls were manned, not fully but adequately. With Marduct's retreat barreling down the Main Road, they didn't have time for a siege. The castle had to be taken in a raid. And that looked difficult.

A footstep behind her interrupted her thoughts. Instantly, she was on her feet, her sword poised in her hand.

"Zabeth." Roduct stepped forward, his hands in the air.

"Oh, it's you," said Zabeth. She felt like she should say something more but nothing she could think of seemed appropriate. Roduct had already told her that she didn't need to address him by his old title but he still had that distant air about him that discouraged closeness. Zabeth and he hadn't had one conversation of any length during the entire trek northward.

Actually she was amazed that he remembered her at all. Roduct hadn't been one to mingle much with the staff, especially the drudges.

"I wished to speak with you," he said, motioning to Zabeth's still raised blade.

She lowered it. "Very well," she said, motioning him to sit down on one of the flat boulders near her tent.

When they were both seated, he said, "I feel I owe you an explanation."

"Me?" she said.

"It's probably more precise to say that I owe Buckle an explanation."

Zabeth nodded her head in agreement. Even in the light of the stars and the half-moon she could tell Roduct was nervous.

"I want you to know and to tell him in case I fall tomorrow."

Zabeth nodded her head. Tomorrow, she thought. She might be released from my oath tomorrow.

"I did kill the Sarondaki in front of Scarver's. He had my blood and was going to use it for Soowooli. There are laws in Delamer that make this self-defense. The shunt with my blood on it is in my saddlebags. I'm sure Bertam will know how to use it."

"Why did you run?"

"Skrike had decided to try to use me," he said. His voice was flat and emotionless as always. "Even though I had stopped the first attempt, I knew he'd send others and they wouldn't be so easy to spot. Sooner or later I knew he'd get me under his control."

"I see."

"Do you?" he said. "I was on the council and very powerful when I left. I was working on getting Delamer into the war early. Skrike could have forced me to reverse that position and used me to keep the country out of the war until it was too late."

Zabeth nodded slowly. "So you...'

"So I had to leave Delamer and make sure I couldn't ever come back. That's why I gave the estate to Buckle."

"But why didn't you run west instead of east? Hide on some island where Skrike couldn't find you?"

Zabeth thought she heard him laugh. "I'm a full-blooded Sarondaki, Zabeth, which means there's fire magic in my blood. I'm as powerless near water as Skrike." He sighed and rocked back, looking up at the sky. "No, I knew eventually they'd find me. The best strategy was to diminish my effectiveness for them and hope I could break Soowooli again."

Zabeth stared at his profile for a second and thought that maybe it wasn't all that strange that Buckle revered Roduct.

"The only part of my plan that didn't work was getting cleanly out of Delamer. I was seen before I could dispose of the body. I certainly didn't want Buckle to follow me."

"Lord Roduct," she said. "He never even hesitated."

There was a scrambling beside them and a messenger, one of Roduct's new Sarondakis, appeared beside them.

"Something's happening in the castle. Kebble wants you both to come."

Zabeth acknowledged the message curtly and reached back into her tent to grab her buckler as the warrior scrambled away. Roduct stood up and watched the bulk of the castle. While sheathing her sword, Zabeth glanced at it too. Something caught her eye, just a wisp of white light playing about the parapets.

They ran to where Kebble and Bindle stood watching. From their vantage point they could see more. Flashes of sparkling white raced along the walls and up the towers. Dimly, on the thin desert air, came what might have been screams.

"Look familiar," asked Bindle, casting a look at her.

"Woolimen," whispered Zabeth.

"Are you sure?" asked Kebble. "Bindle thought they were Woolimen too. You two are the only ones who've ever seen any."

"I'm as sure as I can be at this distance and I don't want to get any closer," said Zabeth.

"If Skrike's learned how to control Woolimen..." said Bindle.

"Of course Skrike knows how to control them," said Roduct. "He used them in his conquest of the west six hundred years ago." He took a few steps forward. "These don't look like they're under control though. If they were, they'd be on their way east or toward us."

Suddenly a red glow started to emanate from the walls. It vibrated and grew into a dome completely encasing the castle. The patches of white squirmed as the translucent sphere pushed them away from the walls. Finally they broke off and scattered in all directions. The red glow vanished and the next instant and all was dark and quiet.

"What was that?" whispered Bindle.

"I think," said Roduct, "Skrike just exorcised his house."

Kebble turned to Zabeth. "Get some of your men. Tell them to get some breakfast and then to ride out to the castle. See if we can find out what's going on."

"Right." Zabeth ran off to get Keruct and Tiacin.

26

"What was that?" said Buckle, his voice sounded high and strained. They cowered in the entrance of a cave. Just a minute before they had emerged from the cave to look upon the ominous outlines of Castle Skrike. Buckle thought that even if he never saw Methliana again, he could live a happy life so long as he never had to enter another cave or tunnel. The strength of this feeling surprised him. He hadn't realized how disappointed he had been to have had escape snatched out of his reach when they had emerged into the caverns. But there had been Shacknel to bury.

This last tunnel had only been a couple hours walk. It began in one of the caverns Buckle and Yazzle hadn't gotten around to exploring yet and ended a couple hundred feet from the castle wall. Buckle and Yazzle had to push a large heavy door open. Once outside, Buckle noticed the outside of the door was fashioned to look like a cliff side.

When they stepped out of the entrance to the cave, the world exploded into chilling cold and a brilliant glittering white. Krinseth had pulled him back into the cave and all four of them watched as the white glowing things cast weird flickering shadows through the entrance. Then came the vibrating red glow that grew in intensity and bathed the outside in crimson until it vanished.

"Didn't you recognize it, Buckle?" said Krinseth.

"Woolimen," whispered Buckle. Out of the corner of his eye, he saw Yazzle shiver. Lathel looked from one companion to another, not understanding.

"You told me of the fire you started in the urn archives? Your plan seems to have worked."

"That wasn't my intention."

"No, not yours, perhaps," she said. Her usual smile was tinged with a little wistfulness. "Nevertheless, the castle is probably less defended now than it was a moment ago."

"So we can go home?"

Krinseth smiled. "Hardly, the red glow was Skrike driving the spirits from his castle. There are plenty of Sarondakis left alive and more importantly Skrike is alive too."

"Oh," said Buckle.

"We should hurry," she said, bending over. From a crevice beside the cave entrance, she produced a canvas bag which clanked as she lifted it. She carried it out the door, saying, "We need to be in the castle by dawn." They followed, reluctantly.

At the foot of the wall they stood as Krinseth handed the clanking bag to Yazzle. "You're probably the best climber, so you go first."

"What's in here?" asked Yazzle, opening the bag to look inside.

"Spikes," replied Krinseth. "To get us up the wall."

"Won't they hear us hammering spikes into their wall?" asked Buckle.

"You don't hammer them," she said, slipping the water sack off her shoulder. "Give me a spike." Yazzle got a spike from inside the bag and handed it to Krinseth.

She dipped it into the water sack and then applied the tip to the black marble of the wall and pushed. It went in without resistance. Buckle grabbed the spike and tugged, thinking maybe there was a hole already there. It held firm as if it had been hammered in.

"We haven't much time," said Krinseth, handing the water sack to Yazzle and motioning him up the wall. The lad worked his way upwards, first dipping the spikes into the water sack and then pushing them into the wall. After a while, he became quite efficient at it and they made good progress.

Krinseth climbed right behind Yazzle and Buckle was behind her. Lathel brought up the rear. Buckle had been afraid that Lathel would pull the spikes out, canceling the magic that held them in the wall. But apparently magic was only necessary to get the spike into the wall. Once in, it held on its own.

They climbed in shadow. Buckle had to feel for each hand hold and foot hold. The castle itself sucked up light and the moon, low on the horizon and partially obscured by ragged clouds shone silver on the sand and rock far below. Buckle tried not to look down, but the view below held a morbid fascination for him. His vitals quivered with unreasoning fear. His imagination brought up vivid scenes of his body lying broken on the rocks below. He imagined what it must feel like to fall, screaming and then to hit, bones crushing, the jagged ends piercing vital organs. Buckle held on to the spikes even tighter.

Suddenly something wet and pliable hit his face and bounced off, blinding him for a moment. Forgetting where he was, Buckle let go of the spike he was holding with his right hand to wipe his eyes. Only when his balance began to shift backward did he remember. He grabbed the spike again and hugged the wall harder than he'd ever hugged his mother.

"Skrike's Hell," said Yazzle, using an unaccustomed curse.

"What happened?" said Buckle, once he had swallowed his heart again.

"I dropped the water sack."

"Good thing you didn't drop the bag of spikes," muttered Buckle. "How far are we from the top?"

"We're only about two thirds of the way there."

"We'll have to go back and get it," said Buckle, not without a certain amount of relief.

"No, there's no time," hissed Krinseth. She pointed to the eastern sky. It was brightening. "Dawn is coming."

"Then we'll just send Lathel down."

"Still not enough time. We'll have to go on."

"How?" asked Yazzle.

"Lick them," said Krinseth.

"What?"

In the gloom above him, Buckle saw Krinseth lick the palm of her hand and then grab Yazzle's foot.

"Put a spike in your mouth to get it wet. It'll work just as well."

"Well, all right." Yazzle didn't sound convinced. "It doesn't taste very good."

"I imagine not," said Krinseth.

"It works though," Yazzle announced and soon they were making progress again.

The light in the east was bleeding into the rest of the sky just as they pulled Lathel over the edge. Buckle looked anxiously around for any sign of a guard. Krinseth strangely enough, didn't seem to expect any and indeed none showed up.

"Come," she said. "We'll find a place to hide. Then we'll rest until the storm hits."

Storm, thought Buckle, looking at the still dark western sky. He shrugged. No storm could ever get over the Barriers.

And yet, he thought his ears could pick up the low rumble of distant thunder.

The wind lashed the tent canvas unmercifully, causing it to flap so loud the speakers at the table inside had to raise their voices. Ever since dawn, the wind had been sweeping across the desert, blowing up dust and sand. It provided a break from the heat. Nittle had had to reprimand more than one fool who thought it would be a good idea to stand naked outside to cool off. That is until they started choking on the dust and the sand started scouring their eyes. There were no serious casualties, however.

To Nittle's senses the wind had a taint of moisture in it. Last night he had watched the western sky, as storm clouds and lightning battled to get across the Barriers. They had made it. The sky was clouding up and Nittle could see low thunderheads rolling towards them. In a way it made sense. Of all the storms that had been hammering the west in the past year, it was only logical that one should be strong enough to get the Ratog wet. He knew that in the desert it only rained once a decade or so. But it did rain.

And it would rain today. That was certain. Nittle smiled grimly when he thought of how the Sarondakis would react when they saw that the storms which had drenched them on their miserable campaign in the west were now following them to their dry and dusty homeland. If Nittle hadn't known his enemy so well he'd have said the coming storm made victory certain.

Of course there were some here who thought the victory was already won. Fazzle drummed his fat fingers impatiently on the table. With his other hand he nervously popped small chunks of meat into his mouth. His eyes flashed resentfully at the two kings beside him.

"Well, now that we've finished our meal," said Tetwell, pushing his plate away and taking a sip of ale, "let's hear some reports." Nittle grabbed the half biscuit still left on his plate and pushed it into his mouth. This had been the best food he'd had in months.

Nodwick took a drink of his ale and surveyed each of the five new counts in front of him. Everyone had finished eating except Fazzle who'd had a second helping.

"You first Lord Nittle," said the Goswickian king.

"Yes, Your Majesty," said Nittle, downing the biscuit in a big gulp. "Marduct disengaged yesterday afternoon, about an hour's march from here just outside of Zaron."

"Do we hold the city?" asked Tetwell.

"No, Your Majesty, but my scouts tell me it's deserted."

"A trap?" asked Nodwick, putting down his cup.

"Possibly, Your Majesty, but I don't think so," said Nittle, taking a quick sip of ale. "You see, Marduct's been splitting his forces, sending away tribes to live off the desert and harry us."

"Are you sure they're not deserting?" said Fazzle, rolling back in his chair and wiping bits of food out of his mustache. "They are beaten after all."

"We've already had trouble with them, Lord. A few attacks, mostly at night, similar to their strategy before Marduct's invasion. They've also made communications, uh...difficult." Tetwell and Nodwick hemmed and hawed, exchanging knowing glances. There had been some question of Nittle's disobeying orders when the messages ordering him to disengage kept getting lost. He had been leading the army, battling Marduct's fierce rearguard action and driving deeper into the Ratog than the two kings and the Delamerian lord before him had intended. Fazzle hadn't wanted to enter the desert at all. Nittle had heard that Fazzle was close to pulling his troops out of the alliance.

"And while it's true, Lord that they are beaten," said Nittle directly to the Delamerian nobleman, "this is a defensive strategy designed to make it too costly for us to remain in the desert."

"More than that, Lord Nittle," snapped Fazzle. "If we do follow Marduct he will simply hide behind the walls of Castle Skrike while his partisans cut us to pieces at night and make a shambles of our supply lines. We should pull out now." He banged his fist on the table.

Nittle kept his face expressionless, but inside he was seething. He wanted to grab Fazzle by the neck and scream some sense into him. Instead Nittle sat across from the Delamerian, seemingly cool but not daring to respond.

"Well now," said Nodwick, "It takes time to prepare for a siege. If we hurry, we can attack before he gets settled in."

"If, if," muttered Fazzle.

"What concerns me," said Tetwell, leaning back in his chair, "is that while we have done a commendable job of driving Marduct out of the west, we really haven't destroyed his power base. If we pull out now we may find ourselves in this position again next year or the year after."

"Nonsense," snapped Fazzle. "We've bloodied their noses. They won't be back for a while."

"What's to stop them?" asked Nodwick. "We haven't decreased their fighting population by much. They still have weapons factories in Castle Skrike and Raganorth..."

"Mostly manned by prisoners from Goswick and Joswell," added one of the counts down the table from Nittle. The comment drew a sharp look from Fazzle.

"And most importantly, Skrike is still alive. With fear and Soowooli he can raise an army this size or even larger in a year's time. And he'll start as soon as we leave."

The Delamerian lord's face displayed the distaste he felt for that argument.

A messenger came to the door, out of breath and clutching a pouch.

"Message, Your Majesty," he said to Tetwell.

"Let me see it," said Tetwell, raising his hand. The messenger, dusty from the road, walked gingerly around the table, obviously unused to being in the presence of so much royalty. He handed the pouch to Tetwell and made a hasty exit.

The king opened it and pulled out a wrinkled and stained sheet of parchment. Nittle could see on the back of it some other message that had been crossed out. The king read the contents of the note silently. Nittle watched closely as a thin smile played on Tetwell's face. It grew as he handed it to Nodwick. Nodwick read the note and also smiled as he handed it to Fazzle.

The counts were looking at each other, wondering what the news could be when Fazzle crumpled up the message, threw it on the table and banged his fist. The fat Delamerian lord pushed his chair back and got up. His face looked as red as a beet. He crossed to the exit.

303

"Lord Fazzle," barked Tetwell. The nobleman turned, breathing fire. "Are you with us?"

"Yes. I am not totally unaware of history." And with that he left. If you could slam a tent flap, Nittle was sure the echo would still be reverberating.

The two kings looked at each other in relief.

"Uh, Your Majesty?" said Nittle.

"Oh yes," laughed Tetwell, looking at the perplexed faces of the counts. "You'll want to know what was in the message. To put it simply, Kebble has, on his own initiative, raised an army and is attacking Castle Skrike, possibly even as we speak. His message asks us for help."

The counts cheered.

"I can be on the road in an hour, Your Majesty," said Nittle.

"I too, sir," said another and the others agreed.

"Good men," said Tetwell. "Mount up and ride. We're going to Castle Skrike."

27

The sound of thunder awakened Buckle. He had only been dozing and the sharp crack brought him up from his half slumber, completely alert. Once the blood stopped pounding in his ears he could hear the constant slapping of rain on the stone walls of the castle.

They had hidden in an abandoned guard tower on the battlements. It had been undisturbed all day, although a couple of times they had heard footsteps rushing past and voices chattering in the consonant filled Sarondaki tongue. Obviously some catastrophe had struck the castle and its defenders were in a panic. Buckle didn't want to believe that it had been the woolimen he had unleashed.

Krinseth had kept them in the tower through the long day. She suggested that they sleep, although she herself sat cross-legged on the floor and stared forward with unfocused eyes. Only Lathel, whose understanding of the situation was limited, was able to comply readily. Yazzle laid on his back most of the day, staring at the ceiling. Buckle was saddened. At the beginning of the journey, the lad could have slept anywhere at any time. Now he could barely sleep at all. He has too much to think about, thought Buckle, too many things to remember.

His eyes found the sword of Dalmar, Lathel's hand resting on the hilt. Krinseth had told the youth that he must keep in bodily contact with the sword at all times. The only time Krinseth stirred all day was when Lathel turned over in his sleep and his hand left the hilt. She quickly broke her trance and replaced it. She gave Buckle a knowing look before going under again.

The same thunder which had awakened Buckle brought her out of her trance. She stood and walked gingerly to the door and peeked out.

She looked back at them. "We must leave now. You'll get wet."

Yazzle rose stiffly and Buckle gently nudged the still sleeping Lathel. The youth groaned and looked up at him with bleary eyes.

"Time to go son," said Buckle, and then with a look at Krinseth, "Bring the sword."

"Yes sir," he croaked and got unsteadily to his feet.

Krinseth took one more peek out the door.

"Be careful where you walk," she said. "It could be icy."

Buckle shuddered at this last advice and followed her as she dashed into the storm.

The rain pelted them furiously as they ran toward the staircase that led down from the battlements. Krinseth forged onward relentlessly so it was up to Buckle to make sure Yazzle and especially Lathel kept up.

When they reached the marble floored courtyard Buckle could see Krinseth systematically trying doors. When one opened she looked inside and then waved them forward.

Lightning flashed and thunder exploded almost simultaneously. The group hurried and Krinseth held the door open, motioning them through.

Once inside, they stood still, letting their eyes adjust to the darkness and listening for activity in the halls that stretched away from them.

In the gray milky light, Buckle gradually began to discern shapes. They were white and perfectly still. Streams of water trickled from them as the bodies thawed. There were five of them, sitting in wooden chairs along the hallway, still holding their swords.

Buckle looked at them, unable not to until Krinseth nudged him.

"Skrike's throne room is this way."

She led them into the castle.

28

Zabeth could barely see the castle through the sheets of rain pouring from the sky. She stood on a ridge with Kebble, Bindle and Roduct, as they tried to decide what to do. Rissle stood behind them, ready to offer information. A couple of Roduct's scouts stood beside him. Everybody, even the non-Sarondakis looked miserable in the rain.

"We haven't encountered any scouts?" shouted Bindle.

Kebble nodded. "Do we have any reports about Marduct?"

Rissle stepped forward. "No Kebble, the last report was the one you heard. A thousand or so men marching up the castle road."

"That was this morning. They should be here by now."

"Maybe the rain slowed them down," shouted Zabeth.

"If we don't get into that castle,' said Roduct, "Marduct will crush us."

Kebble nodded. Everyone was watching him, waiting for his decision. "I wish I knew if the castle were defended."

"I haven't seen a sentry on those walls all day," said Rissle.

Zabeth leaned over and shouted into Kebble's ear. Rain from his helmet fell on her face. "You're committed to this, Kebble. We can't turn back."

A messenger stumbled up the ridge and whispered something into Rissle's ear. The sharp eyed scout turned to the group and shouted, "Marduct's been spotted on the castle road about five hour's march at most. He shows no sign of stopping."

Zabeth saw Kebble's jaw tighten with resolve.

"Mount up," he cried and they scattered to their divisions. Zabeth exchanged a look with Roduct. Both of them knew they might be on the verge of freeing Buckle.

She sprinted down the ridge to where her men were huddling under their horses to get out of the rain. Keruct, Tiacin and Vorkle were grouped together, no doubt talking about how they expected to die. They looked up when Zabeth splashed past them.

"We're going in," she cried. "Mount up."

Her comrades swung into their saddles in seconds. The rest of the division stirred into action. She had about five hundred Sarondakis in addition to her three from the original partisans.

In this rain, a signal was impossible so Zabeth urged her horse, a sleek Sarondaki stallion, bred to the desert and pure white in color, onto the nearest outcrop of stones. The beast's hooves slipped and stones clattered down the pile as it climbed. Once atop the stones, Zabeth watched and waited. A flash of lightning, accompanied by a splintering crash of thunder, illuminated the gloom long enough for Zabeth to see Bindle's, Roduct's and Kebble's forces were moving.

"Forward," she shouted and she kicked the stallion's flanks. It leaped off the outcrop and galloped along the road that spiraled up the mountain toward Castle Skrike. Behind her just under the din of the torrential rain, she could hear her men following.

With as fierce a war cry as uttered by any Sarondaki, she kicked the sides of her horse and urged it to go faster. She felt the thundering of the great beast through her bones. Even louder was the beating of her heart as the excitement of impending battle took her. She rode wildly up the road to Skrike's door, catching glimpses of, alternatively the desert and then the mountains, depending on which side of the mountain she was on. She could tell the men around her were caught up in it also. Keruct had a bare-tooth grimace on his face and Vorkle had a wild-eyed look that was the last thing many Sarondakis had seen. Even Tiacin was smiling.

When they neared the top of the mountain they found that the army was backed up in front of the main gate. The warriors waited by the black marble walls, throwing glances upwards. They expected a rain of arrows to mix in with the downpour. Boiling oil was unlikely in this rain but surely Skrike wasn't going to let them just walk into his castle.

By the time Zabeth had threaded her way to the front, Kebble had men scaling the walls. She watched as five went up hand over hand, grasping slippery ropes. Finally they disappeared over the parapet. Zabeth rode up beside Kebble. He glanced over at her.

"I almost wish somebody would fight us," he said, shouting over the rain. Zabeth nodded.

A figure appeared over the wall. "Back up. We're opening the gate."

"See any of Skrike's men?" shouted Kebble, as he backed his horse and motioned to the others to do the same.

"Two," the man cried, "they got Gruct and Terble just as they cleared the wall. We killed one. The other got away."

"Keep an eye out then." The man nodded and vanished behind the wall again.

With a clank and a grinding, the gates, huge and ornate with gold scorpions worked into the three foot thick wood, lumbered open.

As soon as there was room, the archers fired a volley of arrows through the gateway. Everyone brought up their shields, expecting return fire but none came. Kebble motioned to two men who sat on horses close to the gate. They dismounted and entered the castle, crouching, ready for anything.

After an anxious moment of fingering weapons and nervous glances at Kebble one of the men appeared.

"All clear," he shouted.

Kebble reined his horse around and shouted orders.

"Hurry men. In five hours Marduct and a thousand Sarondakis loyal to Skrike will be standing in this very spot." He looked up.

"Dridwell," he shouted.

"Yeah, Kebble," shouted the man who had opened the gate.

"Man the gate, I'll send a few more men up there to help." Kebble looked over at Zabeth. "You ready?"

"Show me to the dungeons and then to Skrike's throne room."

He nodded and kicked the sides of his horse. Zabeth rode behind him into the castle.

After a few anxious moments in the sally port, they emerged into the courtyard. The floor of the courtyard was made of polished black marble with flecks and swirls of white. The walls were made of the same material, as was the castle which towered before her. It was a huge spired behemoth, ornately carved, as far as she could tell, during flashes of lightning, with slithering scorpions which were outlined and highlighted with gold tracery. Skrike may not have been Sarondaki, but he knew their symbols and how to use them.

Suddenly the warrior riding next to her, one of Roduct's Sarondakis cried out. When Zabeth looked over at him an arrow protruded out of his chest and he rolled sideways off his horse. Zabeth ducked, putting up her shield and tried to scan the castle for the archer. She thought the arrow had come from in front but didn't know exactly where. The soldiers around her were doing much the same thing.

"Where?" she demanded, pulling her bow off her back. But she wasn't answered as another arrow struck home in Rissle's shoulder. The scout grabbed the shaft and screamed. This time Zabeth saw it. And a flash of lightning confirmed it.

"Two," she cried. "In the window above the door." Instantly, a rain of arrows flew into the opening and a body fell out, peppered with feathered shafts. A Sarondaki jumped from his horse into the window, his legs disappearing last. After a few seconds he popped his head out and signaled that the other archer had been killed also.

"Get all the troops inside," shouted Kebble. "Fan out. Bindle take your men and head left. Secure the walls. Roduct and Zabeth, circle the walls to the right. I'm going inside."

"Let me go inside," yelled Zabeth.

Kebble shook his head, causing the rain to fly off his helmet and nose. "I'm going inside."

"But Buckle..."

"We secure the castle, then we take care of personal business."

"They could be killing all their prisoners even as we speak," roared Roduct. He presented an imposing figure even in the rain with his war paint running and his body armor dripping.

"Do as I say or I'll relieve you both of command and leave you here under armed guard." He kicked the flanks of his horse and turned away abruptly. "Open that door," he shouted to the Sarondaki still squatting in the window.

"I'm going in," said Zabeth to Roduct. "Are you with me?"

"Don't do it, Zabeth," shouted Roduct.

"What? I thought you..."

"I do. But Kebble's right. Buckle will either be dead or he won't when we get to him. But if we let Marduct breech these walls he'll die for certain and we will too."

Zabeth screamed in frustration and hit her saddle causing her horse to rear up on two legs.

"Zabeth," barked Roduct. "You're not a drudge in my kitchen, anymore. You're in an army. That means you're under discipline. Do what you're told."

Zabeth swallowed and looked around her. She happened to catch Bindle's eye. He broke contact, looking downward with a slight frown and then continued to organize his men for their mission.

"Yes, Lord," shouted Zabeth. "Shall I take the wall and you the courtyard?"

The tall Sarondaki nodded and rode off to his men.

"Dismount," shouted Zabeth to her men. "We're securing the wall."

Her men grumbled but obeyed, sliding off their horses and limbering up their bows. More men were pouring through the gate and the courtyard filled to overflowing. Zabeth realized that if the castle defenders caught them right now, there wouldn't be room to fight.

"Hurry, you dogs," she shouted. "Get those horses inside the gate house."

A huge squealing sounded across the courtyard and Zabeth looked around to see the black castle doors opening. A Sarondaki warrior pushed at them with all his strength.

A cheer went up in the courtyard as the portal opened wider. Rain fell on the ornate tiled floor behind the door. The warrior gave one final heave and shoved the doors wide open.

And then suddenly three arrow points appeared in his chest. He spat blood and crumbled to the ground.

A hideous war cry split the air and suddenly wild Sarondakis poured out of the doorway. They swung axes and swords, hacking away at Kebble's army who were still too tightly packed to effectively fight back.

From her viewpoint halfway up the stairs to the ramparts, Zabeth could see Bindle and Roduct practically whipping their men to get them out of the courtyard. She turned and saw her men were heading down the stairs, their swords out and murder in their eyes.

"Stop right there," she barked. "Turn around and get up that wall."

"But..."

"You heard me. The next person who comes down another step tastes my steel." She stood soaking wet, hand on the hilt of her sword. She felt her heart pumping fire and an animal calm enveloped her. The men clattered up the stairs like leaves in the wind. She turned and motioned to the others to continue filing beside her up to the ramparts. They clanked past, soaking and wary of getting too close to her.

Zabeth looked back at the courtyard. She couldn't see much in the rain filled darkness but she could hear the clashing of swords and grunts of combatants. Kebble, still mounted, rode under her by the stairs. He hacked a Sarondaki warrior, cutting him deeply in the shoulder. The defender screamed and dropped to the ground, trying to hold his arm onto his shoulder. Kebble paused, looking over the scene.

"Need help?" cried Zabeth. Kebble looked up, blinking at her in the rain.

"Just get your men out of here," he shouted. "And..." He motioned to the door out of which Sarondakis were flying.

Zabeth nodded and slipped her bow off her back.

"Pruct, Redwick," she shouted, grabbing two of her men from the stream heading up to the ramparts. The tall Sarondaki and the dark Goswickian stood watching her as she took an arrow out of her quiver.

"Three volleys into the doorway," she cried and watched as the two soldiers nocked their arrows. "Now," she shouted.

Three arrows shot into the darkness of the doorway. Zabeth definitely saw one Sarondaki fall. The next volley got two as they came screaming out. And the next landed three arrows in the lacquered finish of the doorway. It would be a few minutes before any Sarondaki got up the nerve to venture into the courtyard.

"Let's go," she cried, as she shouldered her bow and bounded up the stairs. Her fellow archers followed but couldn't keep up.

On top of the ramparts, with the wind to drive it the rain fell even harder. It stung Zabeth's cheek and got in her eyes as she ran along the crowded parapet. Keruct had deployed the men well, two every fifty feet or so. Other men were scampering along with her, bending forward against the wind.

Ahead she saw a clump of men breaking the symmetry of Keruct's deployment. Picking up her pace, she came to the back of the pack to find the men milling around, leaning on their bows or spears or against the parapet.

"What's going on here?" she roared. The men looked at her, bewildered. She grabbed one man who was sitting on the wall and threw him onto the stones. The men formed up quickly under her angry gaze. Down the line she could see the word being passed and the mob became a proper line.

She stuck her nose into the face of the nearest warrior. He was a Sarondaki. "What's going on?" The warrior looked at her with dark eyes and then started babbling in Sarondaki. Zabeth cut him off and pointed at the Sarondaki next to him. She thought she had heard this one speak Dernian before. "You," she barked.

"We don't know. There's some kind of delay but news of it hasn't reached us." He kept his eyes forward.

"Skrike's Hell," she muttered. "All right, everybody listen. Marduct's scouts could be watching these walls right now. If you stand near the edge they can pick you off. Stay away from the edge. Pass the word to the newcomers."

Already the line stretched back as far as she could see. "You are responsible," she yelled at the warrior who spoke Dernian. "If I come back and find another mob scene, I'll have you beaten until I can see your backbone, understand?"

"Yes," he said.

"Good." And with that she raced ahead.

At the head of the line, she found Vorkle and Tiacin crouched low behind a bend in the wall. Their eyes rested on a guard tower that reared above them and every so often they sent a group of two or three soldiers across the section of wall below the tower.

Zabeth came up behind her two comrades and crouched beside them.

"What's going on?" she shouted.

Vorkle turned to her and replied. "There are five archers in that tower. They can't see anything unless the lightning flashes but they know we're crossing. So they are firing a volley every five seconds."

"Where's Keruct?"

"He's ahead, placing the soldiers that we send through."

Suddenly a figure sprinted across the gap, coming towards them from the opposite side. It came up to Zabeth and her two comrades and proved itself to be one of the Sarondaki soldiers, a youth.

"Vorkle," he said, in the dark, "I have a message for Vorkle from Keruct."

"Tell it to me, I'm Zabeth." The boy looked at her with widening eyes.

313

"I humbly apologize for..."

"Never mind that nonsense," she snapped. Out of the corner of her eye she could see Tiacin and Vorkle grinning. "What's the message?"

The boy swallowed and recited the message. "There's about twenty of the enemy holding us at bay two hundred feet beyond the tower. We need more men." He looked up at her in fear of a reprimand. She turned away from him and toward her men.

"That settles it," she shouted. "We have to take the tower. We can't wait till they run out of arrows." The others nodded their agreement.

"Anyone been in one of those towers?" she asked.

"I peeked in one on our way here," said Tiacin. "It's a spiral staircase, leading up to the guardroom."

"Curves to the left as you're going up?"

"Yes."

"Then you'll go up first, Tiacin."

The man from Tern gave her a thin-lipped grin and drew his sword with his left hand.

"What are the doors made of?" asked Zabeth.

"Oak," said Vorkle, his beard dripping and scraggly in the rain, "but far from solid, or at least the ones so far have looked old and rotten to me."

"That doesn't sound like Skrike to ignore his defenses."

"A secondary defense, Zabeth," lectured the fat Goswickian, "and as it has been three hundred years since Skrike has had easy access to oak..."

"So you think you can get through?"

"Of course," he said, hefting his mace, "one way or the other."

Zabeth nodded and then turned to the messenger, thinking to give him a message to carry across to Keruct but she changed her mind. On the boy's right side hung his sword. The lad watched her with wide eyes.

"What's your name, boy?" asked Zabeth.

"Nuct, Mistress," said the youth. He was tall for his age, dark like all Sarondakis and muscular. Only his smooth face and lack of war paint and trophy jewelry betrayed his age.

"Are you left-handed?" asked Zabeth, pointing to Nuct's sword.

"Yes, Mistress," said Nuct, his eyes fluttering downward.

"Good you go in beside Tiacin, here." She pointed to him. "These stairways can be pretty tight and even though your left-handedness gives you more room there won't be a lot of space to maneuver in. So jabs and thrusts," she said, demonstrating the moves to the youth. "No swipes or cuts, understand?"

"Yes, Mistress."

"Good, I'm behind you and ..." She looked around and finally settled on the first three men in the line. "You men follow me."

When the group had assembled in the proper order, Zabeth shouted. "Charge."

Zabeth crossed the black paved space to the tower. The drumming of the rain drowned out her war cry. As she ran, it seemed incredible to her that she could move with the oceans of rain pouring on her, the wind driving it into her body. She imagined she'd be blown off the wall at any second. But somehow she remained and the dark hulk of the tower loomed before her.

Vorkle hit the door, shoulder first like a boulder rolling down a hill. The wood must have been more rotten he'd guessed, because the door shattered, the planks buckling and breaking in two. The giant Goswickian tumbled forward with a startled yelp and wound up in a heap at the foot of the stairs, the ruins of the door scattered around him.

Instantly Tiacin leapt over him and shot up the stair. The boy, Nuct did the same. As Zabeth was sidling around her rotund companion, she couldn't resist saying, "Vorkle, this is no time for one of your naps. Get up."

"Lady, please," he protested but Zabeth bolted up the stairs.

The stairs were lit by torches ensconced in the wall every twenty steps or so. About halfway up, Zabeth heard the sound of swordplay ahead of her and she rounded a turn to find Tiacin and Nuct pushing three wild Sarondakis slowly up the stairs. The boy was acquitting himself well, making difficult parries in the enclosed space with an economy of motion rare for someone so young. He lunged forward continually, taking advantage of every opportunity the enemy provided. Tiacin of course was a master and drove back two of the Sarondakis who looked like older warriors, probably of the castle's garrison.

At one point, the Ternian drove his two past Nuct's one so that Tiacin was even with the Sarondaki fighting Nuct. With a flick of his wrist, Tiacin clubbed the old man with his hilt. The Sarondaki tumbled down the steps. Nuct danced out of the way and pressed himself against the wall. Zabeth caught the warrior and finished him off with her dagger.

She and Nuct rounded the corner just in time to see Tiacin slip past the parry the other warrior and plant his blade into his vitals.

Tiacin stepped out of the way and the Sarondaki tumbled forward, rolling down the stairs. Zabeth stood aside to let the corpse pass. It stopped rolling about five steps below. A pool of blood grew on the step under the corpse. It looked black under the rippling yellow light of the torch. The pool expanded to the edge of the step where it cascaded down to the next one.

The third defender turned and ran upstairs. Zabeth caught the motion out of the corner of her eye. Instantly, she bolted past Tiacin and pursued the warrior. She could hear the others behind her, even Vorkle's wheezing as he struggled to catch up.

She rounded the last corner just in time to see the Sarondaki's legs disappear through a hole in the ceiling. A crude ladder led up to the trapdoor entrance of the guard room. Zabeth leaped, her feet landing on the fourth rung of the ladder and braced herself as the door slammed onto her shoulders.

A tremendous pressure then bore down on her, and in spite of using all her strength the door slowly closed. Zabeth could feel her vertebrae starting to rub against each other. She turned her head to peer inside the guard room. With a glint of silver, a sword struck out and bit her in the forehead. Blood gushed downward and Zabeth watched in horror as the blade pistoned back for another strike.

Than an arm blocked her view, and the ladder creaked with a heavy weight. The pressure on her shoulder's disappeared and her head snapped back depositing a rush of blood into her eyes.

"I can't see," she cried as her hands flailed in the air and she could feel her balance shifting.

An arm encircled her and lifted her up. Then she was flung sideways where she rolled until she hit a wall. She tried to wipe the blood out of her eyes but it was gushing too fast.

"They've blinded her, the dogs," shouted a voice that might have been Vorkle's. The sounds of fighting closed in on her, grunts, the swish of steel, and the sound of sharp edges cutting through meat and bone. Screams of terror from unfamiliar voices told Zabeth that her side must be winning but it wasn't until a few moments later that she was sure. The screaming ended and a hand grabbed her knee.

"Zabeth, Zabeth, are you all right," said Vorkle, an edge of panic in his voice.

"I'm fine," she said, wiping her eyes to catch a glimpse of Vorkle's face. "Get me a bandage for my head and some water."

She heard the sound of cloth ripping and then someone tilted her head forward and tied a strip around her head. A water skin was passed to her, which she used to cleanse her eyes of blood.

Blood was splattered all over the room. The beamed ceiling, the walls, the inhabitants, living and dead, as well as Zabeth herself were covered in gore. The bodies of the three Sarondakis lay about on the floor. A fourth was stuffed into the thin slit of a window, his skin, peeled from his body by the abrasive stone puckered around the casement. Vorkle knelt beside her and Tiacin stood in front. Nuct poked his head through the trap door entrance. She could hear the other three below. On the wall a torch hissed and sputtered.

"We thought they had blinded you," said Vorkle.

They looked like boys caught doing something wrong and trying to explain that they had had the best of intentions. Zabeth didn't know what to do. The brutality of the scene before her was in reaction to what had happened to her. Her wound or what they imagined it to be brought out Vorkle's and Tiacin's protective instincts. Somehow, Zabeth couldn't imagine them doing the same thing for Kebble or at least not with the same enthusiasm. There were differences, she thought, and there always would be. Like Kebble, she knew she had their loyalty. But there was something else there she knew, something sexual, even though they all knew none of them had a prayer of bedding her, and would have denied ever having seriously entertained the thought. Still, they thought of her as a woman and women needed protecting. Zabeth sighed at the irony. She had proved herself more capable of protecting herself than most of her men. She had in fact protected them numerous times over the last six months.

But this was loyalty, not something every leader enjoyed, and if there was something else in it that she didn't particularly like, she supposed she'd have to live with it. She couldn't make herself into a man.

"Nuct," she snapped. The boy came to attention. "Go tell Keruct we're on our way."

"Yes, Mistress." Nuct dropped out of sight. Zabeth pushed against the wall and worked her way to her feet. Stars began swirling before her and she almost toppled over.

"Are you hurt, Zabeth?" asked Tiacin.

"No, I just got up too fast."

"Kebble should probably sew up that cut," said Vorkle.

"I think Kebble will probably be busy for the next few hours don't you?" she said sharply. The stars cleared but Zabeth still felt weak; like her body was some kind of cart which she traveled in but wasn't a part of her. But she could feel the shock wearing off already. She shuffled over to the open trap door.

"Get some men up here and have those bodies thrown over the wall. The ones downstairs too."

She climbed down the ladder, ignoring Vorkle's outstretched hand.

29

Buckle pressed against the wall and slowly inched his face around the corner. The smooth marble felt cold against his skin and he tried hard not to shiver. But the wall was dry. This deep into the castle everything was still dry.

Around the corner two Sarondakis were arguing. A young one, barely more than a boy was trying to get past an older warrior. The boy's eyes were wide with unreasoning panic and it was all the old one could do to hold him back and deliver a cuff on the ear now and then. Their harsh words echoed down the hall; the boy's loud and shrill, the old man's throaty and harsh. Of course it was in Sarondaki and Buckle couldn't follow most of it.

Buckle looked back at his companions, lined up against the wall in the darkness. He held up two fingers and shook his head. Krinseth breathed an impatient sigh and motioned them to stay put. She padded back down the hall.

Leaning back, Buckle sighed quietly and massaged his eyes. Beside him, Yazzle did much the same. Only Lathel didn't seem fatigued. He stood in the darkness, eyes looking around, fingering Dalmar's sword. Not for the first time Buckle wondered just how reliable the boy was. His state of mind frequently changed seemingly with no pattern. One minute he was still in the dungeon, having to keep on alert for guards and Bruct. And then sometimes he was with them here and now. Lately he had spells where he believed he was on his father's horse ranch. But up to now he had spoken little and always did what he was told.   Buckle wasn't sure, however, that would continue.

The trek through the castle had been difficult. Not that they had encountered many guards. Indeed the castle was in a complete uproar. The outbreak of Woolimen the night before and the storm, which they could still hear, even this far inside, had scattered and demoralized the few remaining troops in the castle. And from what Buckle could tell the castle seemed to be under attack. They had spotted a few groups of warriors, armed and ready, hurrying through the halls.

The problem, at least for Buckle, had been what they'd seen along the way. Their path had led through the garrison barracks. They passed row upon row of white glistening warriors, frozen in postures of terror. The sound of water dripping pervaded the deadly silence and the smell of mold and mildew forming wafted up from the soggy floor. Buckle had hurried them through, as much to avoid one of his attacks as to get away from the awful sight. Strangely enough, however, his breathing didn't seem to be effected.

But he was affected in other ways. Every corner they turned, brought another horror, another white corpse dripping water. Once in a while, they'd find a "regular" kind of corpse, a victim of the confusion that reigned after last night. Death had been in this castle, wild, howling, uncontrollable death and Buckle couldn't escape the feeling that he had loosed it. Granted, he was following the sphere's suggestion and hadn't realized what the consequences would be, but did that really absolve him? What bothered him the most though, was that the carnage all around him reminded him of why he was here.

More and more he found himself staring at the sword in Lathel's hand, or when they were on the move he could feel it, an ominous presence behind him. He reflected that killing in the heat of battle was one thing, as was letting loose a terrible scourge. Both acts were removed, somehow impersonal. Once again, when it came to actually walking up to someone and plunging a sword into his vitals, Buckle didn't know if he could do it.

A mournful wailing echoed through the halls and the argument between the two Sarondaki guards stopped. Buckle heard receding footsteps. The old guard shouted and ran off as well.

Peeking around the corner, Buckle saw that the hallway was deserted. He motioned his companions into the intersection. They sneaked to the next hallway and Buckle poked his head around the corner. It too was deserted. He leaned back against the wall.

"What do we do now?" whispered Yazzle.

"Wait for Krinseth, I suppose," said Buckle.

"Should I go and water the mares?" Lathel spoke in an everyday voice as if he were in a stable yard on a breezy summer's day. The loudness of it startled them.

"No," said Yazzle, hushing the lad. "We need to do this first."

"All right," agreed Lathel, his voice lower. "But it's been a long time since they've been watered and I bet they're thirsty."

"We'll get to them before it's too late, I promise," said Buckle. The boy nodded his head.

"There you are," said a voice. Buckle and Yazzle swiveled around to see Krinseth standing in the torch light. She pushed past them and started down the hall in the opposite direction from the way in which the two guards ran. "Hurry, we haven't much time."

"What happened to the guards?" asked Buckle as he struggled to keep up.

"I distracted them. Rather easily too. They're all still frightened after what they went through last night." Buckle looked downward, deliberately not thinking about it. "I...questioned one of them briefly. It appears the castle has been taken."

"What?" Buckle nearly stopped. Yazzle had to quickly sidestep him to avoid a collision.

"Keep moving," snapped Krinseth. Buckle jogged a few paces to catch up.

"The castle's been taken?" he asked.

"A desert partisan called Kebble raised an army of rebel Sarondakis and is now manning the walls."

Buckle felt a bubble of excitement rise in his throat. "Then we've won."

Krinseth cast him a glance, her blue eyes dark enough to remain blue, even in yellow torch light. "You mean the war? Apparently that hasn't been in doubt for the last few months. But as you know, we're not here to win the war."

"But surely this Kebble person will take care of Skrike. All we have to do is lay low for a few hours until they secure the castle."

"That would be to underestimate Skrike. Even now, he may be escaping. Besides..." She stopped and planted a finger in Buckle's chest. "There are only two things that can kill Skrike: You and that

321

sword." The gold colored blade flickered in the torch light. Buckle's hopes of escaping his burden died.

"And one more thing," said Krinseth. "The boy I questioned mentioned that in Kebble's ranks there was a mighty female warrior from the west."

Buckle stood for a second until that bit of information came to the attention of his conscious mind, driving out thoughts of killing Skrike. He ran to catch up to Krinseth again.

"Zabeth?" he asked.

She shrugged and continued waking deeper into the bowels of the castle.

30

The staircase spiraled downward into inky blackness. The torches lining it had long since burned out and the only light came from the barred peepholes in the doors which appeared at regular intervals. Roduct peered through one of these as Zabeth kept watch on the stairs. This would be the fifth level they had checked since getting permission from Kebble to search the dungeons.

The walls of the castle were now manned with partisans and rebel Sarondakis and most of the castle itself had been secured. What was left of the garrison was a demoralized rabble. Zabeth could understand why. She and Roduct had passed through the barracks on their way down here.

Skrike had yet to be found, however.

They didn't have much time to find Buckle. Even now Marduct's troops were encircling the castle, preparing for an out and out attack. And of course Kebble had gotten no word from the armies to the west, not even an acknowledgment that they had gotten his last message. So no one knew if reinforcements were on the way or not.

Kebble had given them two hours.

"Looks clear," growled Roduct who stepped back from the door and pushed up the bar holding it shut. With a loud scream the old door opened and Roduct stepped through into the dingy torch light of the dungeon. Zabeth, right behind him, watched the light play along the edge of the battle-ax Roduct had brought along for the more stubborn doors.

A rag tag crew of men, presumably prisoners, skidded around the corner, brandishing a couple of rusty swords and some broken table legs. They saw Zabeth and Roduct and stopped, unsure what to do.

"It's a Sarondaki," cried one.

"And he's got a white woman with him," said another voice. There were a few cries of outrage.

Zabeth drew her sword and stepped forward. "I'm looking for a certain prisoner," she said.

"Just step away from that sand eating dog behind you, missy and we'll show you all the prisoners you want."

Zabeth halted and held them all in a sharp gaze. "Roduct, a lord of Delamer stands behind me."

"Wha..." came the confused mutterings of the small rabble. The faces, lined with black coal and greasy beards, looked at each other for answers.

"You are all free, gentlemen." said Roduct, his low voice rumbled through the halls. He pointed to the door behind them. "The door stands open and no guards stand beyond."

"How can this be?" A prisoner, taller than the rest and carrying a sword, stepped forward. "Last night we heard horrible screams from above. The guard's shift change didn't come and they started deserting. We overpowered the rest." Zabeth nodded. It had been much the same on the other levels they had checked. The prisoners had control and no guards were left alive. "Tell us, Lord, if that's what you are, what happened?" More of the scarecrow figures started congregating around Roduct and Zabeth.

As he had done four times before, Roduct briefly described the situation. Zabeth listened impatiently, wanting to get on with the next step in this routine which was questioning them about Buckle and then a quick but thorough search of every cell on this level.

"I know you men are weak," concluded Roduct. "But the situation is desperate. Marduct can probably retake the castle. You have a choice. You can stay down here in darkness for the rest of your days or you can go upstairs where there are plenty of weapons and places along the wall to defend. You may die but you'll die free."

There was a pause while the broken men considered this. They all seemed to look to the tall one who chewed his lip in concentration.

"Well," he said, eyeing Roduct. "I reckon my life down here is about worth a breath of fresh air. I'm going upstairs."

The others muttered agreement and began to follow the tall man as he made his way to the door.

"Wait," said Zabeth. "We're still looking for a prisoner."

"Who?" asked the tall man, poised at the door.

"His name is Buckle. He's a Delamerian about forty years old, brown curly hair, going gray and bald spot on top. He may have been with a tall blond man about twenty and named Yazzle."

"Now Yazzle I remember," said the prisoner. Zabeth's heart pounded and her attention focused on the man's face. "He's the one who killed a scorpion on the way through the desert. And come to think of it there was a man in Yazzle's gang who answers your description."

"Where are they?" Zabeth wanted to grab the man by the throat and shake the information out of him.

"Can't say," said the man. "Yazzle's whole gang disappeared right after the cave-in we had oh...I don't know how long ago. There are no calendars down here. But it was awhile. Some say they escaped. But the fact is..." He eyed them both. "They were probably killed, either when the mine caved in or during the riot that followed. They didn't have many friends here."

Zabeth looked at Roduct who cast his eyes downward and for the first time she saw the lines that creased his face. The torch light from the walls seemed to etch the lines even deeper and the shadows moved like writhing snakes on those stone features.

"They were kept on this level then?"

"Yes, Lord."

Roduct looked up and down the halls and then said, "All right, you men head upstairs. Zabeth and I will search this level."

The prisoner shrugged, seemed about to say something, but then decided not to. He turned and led his band through the open door. Zabeth stared at the door after they had left. She felt numb but at the edges of that numbness swirled a torrent of emotion like rising water on the outside of a dam. She had been honor-bound to protect him and bring him home to his beloved Methliana. But beyond that, he had shown her kindness and understanding. He had believed in her abilities more than any man save Grazzle. He didn't deserve to die in this place.

"I can show you where his cell was," said a voice from behind her. It was a high-pitched voice and when Zabeth turned around she

325

found it belonged to a diminutive man, dark-skinned but of western extraction. His eyes glistened in a not altogether pleasant way.

"Do you remember Buckle and Yazzle?" Roduct regarded the man suspiciously.

"Yeah, I remember them." The man turned and walked down the hall. Zabeth cast a look at Roduct and set off after their guide.

"Do you know what happened to them?" asked Zabeth. The man didn't answer.

"Well do you?" repeated Roduct.

The man stopped and looked back at them.

"Do you want to have a nice conversation or to see his cell?"

Roduct waved him on impatiently.

Only about half the torches lining the walls were lit, making a irregularly checkered pattern of darkness and light. The doors lining both sides of the corridor were open. Zabeth peered into each cell. Most were empty. Some had a few bodies lying on the floor. And a few still had prisoners in them. These stared at Zabeth and Roduct and their surly guide as they passed. They all had vacant looks. Zabeth wondered what would happen to them.

Their guide turned a corner and walked to a cell in the middle of the corridor. He stood by the door and motioned them in. Zabeth looked at the man and then at Roduct, whose face remained impassive.

She walked into the cell. Once she cleared the threshold, the door clanged shut. A slight swishing sound and glint of steel gave her warning as she dropped and turned, pulling her sword out just in time to stop the attacker's blade. It hung only a thin finger's length in front of her eyes and slowly descended.

"Come back here," she heard Roduct shout and then footsteps echoed down the hall.

By instinct Zabeth was able to parry the next stroke to her side while jumping up into a crouch. Then came a series of lighting thrusts and cuts that drove her toward the corner. She dived to her left, feeling the wind from a vicious cut aimed at her neck.

When she regained her feet she finally had time to identify her attacker.

"An unannounced attack from behind, Deruct?" she gasped. "There's hardly any honor in that."

"I don't owe you honor, whore," he growled. In a single cat-like motion, he grabbed a thick wooden dowel, obviously brought for the purpose and jammed it between the door and the floor.

Zabeth tried a thrust while his guard was momentarily down. But his blade flicked it away easily. With his other hand he clopped her on the side of her head, sending her rolling sideways.

Zabeth rolled into a crouch and came up with sword extended in time to parry two quick thrusts. She then aimed a kick at his knee, forcing him to hop out of the way. This gave her room to circle to her right and assume her en garde.

"Damn you," he spat. "I almost died in the desert on the way north. Most of the warriors who didn't betray me did perish. And when I got back, Skrike stripped me of honor, forced me to serve in the stinking castle garrison. But I knew you'd come. Some of the prisoners we caught when we were chasing you told me about you and this man Buckle. So I knew just where to lay my trap."

"Where is Buckle?" said Zabeth.

"Dead," he said, watching her with glee. "Undoubtedly. The guards told me he and his large companion and three other prisoners disappeared through that hole in the wall there." He pointed to a large hole just opposite the door.

"Then he could be alive."

Deruct shook his head. "No, there are miles of tunnels down there, all completely dark with unseen pits and the danger of cave-ins. They'd never be able to find their way out."

"Zabeth," said Roduct from behind the door. "What's happening?"

A cold wind of hopelessness blew over Zabeth. She thought of the last time she had seen Buckle. She had cursed him for staying behind to find his useless herbs. If only she had insisted on his leaving or stayed behind herself. She and Bindle might have been able to fight them off. Half of her pondered these questions. The other half just wanted to kill. She gave reign to the latter.

"I'm trapped, Roduct. Use the ax." She turned to Deruct. "You better hurry, if you want your revenge. It's going to be two on one in a minute."

But instead of waiting, she made the first move, a right hand thrust that drew her toward the door. But he lunged to his left, cutting her off while parrying her thrust. He answered with a series of thrusts which ticked in rapid succession off Zabeth's parrying blade as she retreated across the cell floor. She heard Roduct chopping the heavy oak door.

Her foot hit the back wall, stopping her retreat. Deruct kept on coming, his face distorted in a grimace of fanatical hate. The muscles in Zabeth's right arm felt like they were on fire and she feared they'd cramp up.

The door bowed inward and Zabeth caught a glimpse of the ax blade as it penetrated the wood.

"Is this the best you can do, Deruct?" she gasped between clenched teeth. She noted the fatigue in his face and his blows were just a little slower. Not surprising, since he'd been raining them on her for about two minutes straight. Her comment renewed his efforts but the thrusts were sloppy, enabling her to catch him and envelop his blade, driving him to her left.

She scooted to her right and spotted an unprotected knee. She snapped a kick towards it but missed. He charged her, knocking aside her blade and hammering her face first into the wall. This knocked the breath out of her.

With Zabeth pinned to the wall, Deruct grabbed her left hand and forced it straight out. Zabeth struggled but she couldn't free her sword arm. Her left hand, tan and callused, hung in the air like a tree branch, ready to be clipped.

"First, I'll cut off your hands."

"Zabeth," cried Roduct.

"Hurry," she said, trying to put a little panic in her voice.

"Now the she-wolf begins to show the proper fear."

She felt rather than saw his blade go up for the mutilating cut. With a strength born of desperation, she snapped a backwards kick. It caught Deruct's knee. He gargled a satisfying yell as his grip loosened.

Zabeth yanked her left hand out of danger and freed up her sword arm. Then she pivoted around, squatting low so that his attempt to grab her failed. Behind her back she transferred the sword to her left hand and in one motion brought the point home right into his gut. She heard a clink and looked down to see his blade touching hers. He'd parried just a split second too late.

Encountering a little resistance at the back of his rib cage, she twisted and thrust the sword in up to the hilt. Deruct coughed, spraying blood and finally crumpled.

Zabeth stood over him, her sword, still in her left hand, dripping blood. The door crashed open and Roduct ran into the cell. He relaxed after a quick examination of the situation.

"Buckle's not here," said Zabeth. Her voice quivered in spite of her efforts to stop it. "He's dead."

After a pause, Roduct said, "We should be getting back to Kebble soon."

But they stayed for a while. Not saying anything but with the same thoughts. Zabeth looked at the grimy darkness surrounding her and thought of Buckle and Yazzle, knowing that Roduct was doing the same.

When the moment passed, they left.

31

The doors to Skrike's throne room, at least as far as Buckle could tell, were made of solid gold. The hinges and the frame shone brightly in the torch light. The panels were coated with some kind of lacquer which made them completely black. The two doors towered over Buckle, being about twice his height.

"Maybe he's not in there," said Buckle. "If I were Skrike I'd figure the throne room would be the first place they'd look."

"You don't know Skrike," replied Krinseth. She stared at the door, distracted by it. "He's arrogant and thinks he has nothing to fear."

Yazzle put his hands on Lathel's elbows. "Now Lathel, do you remember what to do?"

The youth's eyes popped wide as if he'd been startled. They focused on Yazzle. "I think so, sir."

"Repeat it."

"I go inside the room." He pointed to the large doors. "And lay this sword at the feet of the man in there."

"Very good."

Buckle turned away, worried. There were in fact many things wrong with the plan. Buckle didn't think Lathel was flexible enough. What if there was more than one man in the throne room? They wouldn't be able to coach Lathel once under Skrike's direct scrutiny. With his magic aided senses he could hear the softest of whispers clearly. Only he couldn't hear, see or sense Lathel with magic. Krinseth assured them that Skrike had been dependent on magic for so long that he probably no longer used his normal physical senses. Probably.

Buckle's stomach churned like a paddle wheel in a cataract. There were too many things that could go wrong. Not the least of which was his nerve. He kept thinking about driving the sword into Skrike's body, feeling it pierce the man's viscera.

Krinseth leaned over and said gently into his ear. "I don't think it would be a good idea to knock. Why don't we just go in?"

Buckle smiled at that. "Perhaps we should look for someone to announce us."

She lifted an eyebrow and chuckled. "Yazzle, I think these doors are a job for you."

"Yes, Matron." The lad pushed open the doors.

As they walked into the throne room, the first thing they noticed was the throne itself. Huge, it dominated the whole room. It was a six legged throne fashioned into a giant gold and ebony scorpion. The beast's back was arched so high the tail was able to serve as the back of the chair. The sting hung just over the head of whoever usually sat there, presumably Skrike. Now the throne was unoccupied.

In front of the throne was a brazier on which roared a fire. Made of black cast iron with gold plate around its beast-like feet, the brazier squatted before the throne like a burning toad. Lining each wall was a black velvet arras with a slightly longer red one behind it.

Imbedded in the ceiling, maybe fifty feet over Buckle's head was a star shaped skylight. Buckle watched in fascination as the pounding rain swirled and beaded on the glass.

Then a movement caught his attention. Buckle looked toward the opposite end of the throne room where there was a cluttered desk. At the desk sat a man dressed in black. He dipped a quill into a jar of ink and then wrote on a paper.

Krinseth snapped her hand into the air and instantly lighting struck the skylight, shattering the glass and letting the wind and the rain swirl into the throne room. The fire on the brazier hissed as drops of rain fell into it.

"Yes Cousin Zalphlyn, I know you're there," said the man at the desk in a deep voice. "Just let me finish this last sentence...there." He laid down the quill and held up the document by the corners and gently blew on it to dry the ink.

"Yazzle stay by the door. Keep a lookout for guards," said Buckle. He and Krinseth approached the dark man who now stood up.

"It won't be necessary to post a sentry," he said. "My garrison is, at this moment, entirely engaged in this losing battle against Kebble." Lathel walked beside them, the sword held out in front of him at an awkward angle. His eyes were trained on Skrike. Buckle's heart beat faster every minute as Lathel got closer and the time drew near.

Skrike stood up while folding the paper in thirds. He was about a foot taller than Buckle. His hair was black and slicked down with some kind of oil so that it formed a sort of skull cap. His face was clean-shaven and his jaw was square, perhaps a little large.

"Since my warriors are all otherwise engaged, perhaps you would be kind enough to deliver this note to Kebble when you've finished your business here?" He held out the document.

"How can you say that when you know perfectly well what my business is?" said Krinseth levelly. Lathel took a step closer to Skrike, moving slowly and looking to Yazzle for help. The lad studiously ignored him just as Krinseth had instructed them.

"Come now cousin, surely you don't think you can kill me. Where's the sword? I don't see it. I don't sense it. And the champion? I know it's not you and neither of your companions look strong enough to wield an epee, much less Dalmar's broadsword. Admit it. You don't have the sword. So you may as well deliver my offer to Kebble."

Krinseth chuckled like a street vendor who'd just been caught with his thumb on the scales. Lathel took a few halting steps forward to bring him just outside the circle of light cast by the lamps standing around Skrike's desk. He hovered there, wanting instructions or encouragement. Buckle's arm itched to just wave him on. But he didn't dare.

"What's the message?" asked Krinseth.

Skrike smiled an ugly smile and said, "It's an offer really. He can have the castle in exchange for my safe passage out of it."

"Why offer him that? He can't kill you." Lathel edged into the light a step. He watched Skrike's face closely. Skrike gave no sign of having noticed. Lathel moved even closer.

"No, but he can bind me. Immerse me in water, things like that. And unlike most westerners, this man is not a fool. He defeated

332

one of my best young chieftains during the war. He'd know the techniques for properly binding a master of fire magic." Lathel stood three paces in front of Skrike who literally looked through him.

"So you're leaving like a rat abandoning a sinking ship."

"Your maritime images are wasted on me. No even as we speak, Marduct is surrounding the castle and because Kebble has few men and has to protect his rear, Marduct will very soon be over the walls and through the gate. Kebble knows that."

"Then why leave?"

"Because if Kebble manages to bind me, I can't quite trust Marduct to unbind me."

Lathel bent slightly and leaned to one side to put the sword on the floor. Buckle tried to swallow but the back of his throat was too dry. His arms and knees shook and his forehead was damp with sweat as the blade got closer to the floor.

But it stopped inches from the black marble. Time, at least for Buckle, stopped also.

"Bruct?" said Lathel. And all hope drained out of Buckle. Lathel was back in the dungeon under Bruct's tyranny.

Skrike, however, didn't hear him. "Zalphlyn, there are more similarities between us than differences. We both have little patience with these mortals."

"Why are you ignoring me, Bruct?" Of all the things Buckle had gone through in the last year this standing and waiting for Lathel to be caught seemed like the worst. He could feel a scream of fear and frustration building up in him.

"True," said Krinseth. "They are a tiresome lot. But if you dislike them so, why don't you just go back to the homeland and be done with them. Then I could do the same."

Skrike laughed.

"Don't laugh at me Bruct. I've got a sword." Lathel brandished Dalmar's sword and it flashed in the light. Buckle held his breath. Surely Skrike had seen that.

"As bad as these humans are, cousin, Tenaryans are worse. Besides, they tried to kill me. I don't think I'd be welcome."

"Well, Bruct," said Krinseth.

"Bruct." Lathel spun around.

"Why do you call me by that strange name?"

"Kill him, Lathel," she said as calmly as if she were asking him to pass the salt. The youth's eyes traveled to Yazzle and, looking back, Buckle saw him nod his head.

"What's going on?" said Skrike.

Lathel wheeled around and thrust the sword of Dalmar into the abdomen it had been made so long ago to pierce.

Skrike's reaction was one of puzzlement. He looked down at the sword sticking out of him and then up again. After blinking his eyes a few times he focused on Lathel.

"A magic blind boy," he said, more in curiosity than anger. He put his hand up to turn the youth's face. Lathel, shaking, his eyes as wide as dinner plates, stood before the tyrant. "Wherever did you find him?"

"In your dungeon, as a matter of fact."

"Really?" He glanced at her and then continued to study Lathel's face. "And what were you doing in my dungeon?"

"What else? Looking for the sword."

Skrike looked down again at the pommel sticking out of his stomach. "And did you find it?" He pulled the sword out of his body as easily as if it had been in a sheath. He examined the blade which was shiny and new despite its recent resting place.

"No," lied Krinseth. "That's a replica I had made in Masillay. I cast a few spells on it but apparently that wasn't enough."

"Apparently not," he said, tossing the sword to the floor.

This is it, thought Buckle. Krinseth will distract him and I'll rush in, grab the sword and kill him. Buckle thought his knees would give way, he was shaking so much.

"Well unless you intend to kill poor Lathel there, we'll be on our way."

Skrike cast a hard look at Lathel. Buckle almost moved but something in Skrike's face held him back.

"The boy's mad isn't he?" Skrike chuckled. "Yes, he definitely has the look of someone who's been in my dungeon. I'd be doing him a favor if I killed him. So I think I'll let him live. He'll wind up as a beggar in some filthy alley somewhere. Assuming he has wit enough left not to starve."

"Good enough," said Krinseth. "We'll take your message to Kebble. Buckle would you get the sword please?" Buckle looked at her, trying to keep the fear out of his face.

"Stop," barked Skrike, holding up his hand. He smiled evilly at Krinseth. "Zalphlyn, how do I know you aren't lying about the sword?"

Krinseth shrugged. "It didn't kill you did it?"

"No, but wielded by a magic blind, who knows...I'll just keep the sword."

"Skrike, it has no magic powers. It isn't even a very good sword. The balance is all wrong..."

"Nevertheless," he said, "I want it. Call it a souvenir of our little chat." He walked over to her and handed her the parchment. It was all Buckle could do to keep from running toward the door. "You realize Zalphlyn. One of these days I'm going to have to kill you. Just as I killed your sister."

The skin around her eyes tightened but she smiled. "But not today."

"This damn rain. Your doing, I suppose?"

"My son's actually."

He nodded and walked back toward the throne. "Tell Kebble there's no need to answer. Just leave the north gate unguarded and I'll slip away."

Buckle looked at Krinseth as she turned to go, having been dismissed by Skrike. She glanced at him and her eyes pierced him like he was a rotten peach, slicing through the blackened, rotten fruit to the hard pit inside. For what he saw in that glance was defeat. Skrike had out-maneuvered her. And disappointment. Buckle's moment had come and gone and he hadn't had the strength she'd said he'd had after all. Buckle was torn between begging her forgiveness and reminding her that he himself had told her there was no strength there.

But all of a sudden, he knew he wouldn't be able to live with the memory of that glance. Behind it was not only the despair of Zalphlyn of the Lakes but also that of Methlyn of the Woods and Dalmar the Great, whose sword was even now in the hands of Skrike. He held it by the blade and was carrying it away from them to his desk, the pommel toward Buckle and Krinseth.

Under the weight of the expectations of history, Buckle found himself to be insignificant. In a split second he commended himself to Dalmar and to the ancient Dernian Gods whose names are forgotten and he charged toward Skrike's receding back to fulfill the quest he suddenly realized he was on.

335

Krinseth remained silent and motioned Yazzle to silence also. Buckle's flapping bare feet didn't echo in the throne room. Skrike's arrogance kept him from hearing the sound, Buckle guessed, or perhaps it was one last bit of help from Methlyn. Skrike didn't turn until Buckle was almost on him.

The sword rested in the Tenaryan's hand, flashing gold in the torch light. Buckle dived for it, grasping it by the blade. The edges bit into Buckle's fingers as the sword was yanked out of Skrike's hand and Buckle painfully hit the marble at Skrike's feet. Knowing he was done for, Buckle cringed, waiting for a bolt of magic or a dagger in his back.

Instead Skrike screamed and staggered back. Buckle looked up and saw the tyrant hunched over, one hand on his desk holding him up, the other was pressed hard into his stomach. Buckle saw blood oozing between the fingers of the second hand.

Buckle looked at the sword and where a second ago it had been new and gleaming, now it was covered with gore, soaked with black blood.

"You?" Skrike's deep voice quivered with pain. "Dalmar chose you?" He fell to his knees, his supporting arm knocking a ream of papers off the desk. Blood sprayed from his mouth with every word. "I am...insulted." He collapsed to the floor.

Buckle got shakily to his feet, holding the sword by pressing it between the thumb and fingers of each hand. He was about to cast it away when Krinseth came up behind him.

"You better hold on to it for a little longer," she said in a gentle voice. He looked at her uncomprehending but didn't drop the sword. After a few seconds Skrike convulsed, spat a little more blood and fell silent.

She walked over to the body and spat on it. Steam rose from where the spittle landed. She waited for another shudder from Skrike and repeated the process. Nothing.

A tight-lipped smile covered her lips. "He's dead."

The sword slipped out of Buckle's grasp and clattered onto the floor.

"Did you know that was going to happen?" Buckle's voice was weak and rasping.

"I thought it might. But one can never be sure when magic blinds are involved. Did it occur to you?"

336

Buckle shook his head. "I thought I was going to die." He was wrapped in a cocoon of numbness which only now was starting to fall away.

She put her hand on his shoulder. He looked at her and saw there was an unspoken question in her expression.

"I'll be all right. Can we go home now?"

She smiled and hugged him. She was about to answer when five soldiers ran into the doorway. They were not Sarondaki.

They drew their swords and the lead one shouted. "Who are you? Is this the throne room?"

"It is indeed the throne room, sir. Are you of Kebble's army?" asked Krinseth.

"Aye," said the man, the point of his blade dropping, "but I repeat, who are you?"

"This," she said, "is Buckle of Delamer. Over there lies Skrike, tyrant of the Ratog, slain by this man's hand."

The soldier motioned to one of the men who ran over to Skrike and knelt next to him and examined the body, pulling the head up.

"Well?"

"That's him. I only saw him once from a distance but I'm sure this is Skrike."

The leader looked at Buckle and with a confused expression and asked, "How..."

"I escaped from the dungeon," answered Buckle.

The man pointed a finger at him. "And your name is Buckle of Delamer?"

"Yes."

"Sir, my name is Tiacin and with my company is a warrior woman named Zabeth..."

"Zabeth is here?" Out of the corner of his eye he saw Yazzle look up from ministering to Lathel, who had apparently fainted.

"Even now she is defending the walls from Marduct."

"Can you take me to her?" Buckle stepped forward.

"My intention, exactly, sir. For she thinks you are dead."

"Yazzle," said Buckle, almost laughing, "Zabeth is here."

"Yes Master Buckle, I heard."

"We're all alive," said Buckle, unbelieving. "Let's go."

"Immediately, sir," said Tiacin. "Jakwell, get the tyrant's head. We'll have something to show Marduct and his troops." The soldier beside Skrike's body nodded and drew his sword. Buckle hurried out of the throne room, Yazzle beside him, leading a groggy Lathel. Buckle stopped and turned to face Krinseth.

"Are you coming?"

She smiled. "I'm with you, Buckle."

The soldiers led them to the embattled walls.

32

The rain was slackening, along with their hopes it seemed. Zabeth leaned against the gate tower, taking advantage of a brief respite as the fighting swirled around her. She massaged her head which had been aching and feverish for the last two hours.

Two hours of butchery, of almost constant battle. It had begun shortly before she had returned to the wall, when Marduct ordered an attack. Zabeth had returned to find Sarondakis scaling the walls on tough, almost un-cutable rope made from hemp imported by Skrike from somewhere in the east, beyond the desert. The ropes were tied to spiky grappling irons which were as difficult to grasp as porcupines. And the spikes were coated with an unguent that irritated open wounds and caused the hand to swell and stiffen.

So there were Sarondakis on the walls. Now the strategy was to keep them away from the gate house and the giant gears that opened the large gate. At first, the combat had been a relief, almost a joy, and certainly an escape from thinking about the empty cell in the dungeon and the hole in the wall through which Buckle had crawled to his death. That thought brought forth a cascade of feelings which she quickly shunted aside.

But now the fighting was tortuous. She was exhausted and her head pounded like it was going to explode. She knew she was in serious danger of making a fatal mistake.

She looked at the men fighting in the distance through the gray veil of rain and envied them their huge powerful bodies. They could club away at each other all day and if they missed a cut or parried badly, chances were they could take a wound and keep on fighting. Not

Zabeth. The reserves in her slight body were few and dwindling fast. She had argued about this with old Grazzle many times.

"I can't teach you to be big," he'd told her, "and you're as strong as you can be without giving up any quickness. Speed is your only advantage. Just don't get into any long fights."

Soaked, dirty, and in her third hour of continuous battle, Zabeth snorted at the irony of that memory. The drops of rain hanging from her nose spiraled out in front of her. The rain had now almost stopped and the pre-dawn air felt cool and wet in her chest. Whenever she breathed in, she tasted the metallic tang of blood.

She heard a clank and next to her a grappling iron appeared. She could see its metal spikes glint in the distant torch light from the castle as it jerked back and forth when the warrior at the other end of the rope pulled on the line to test the hold. Then it rocked back and forth in earnest as they began climbing it.

Rest is over, thought Zabeth as she struggled to her feet. Her body rebelled as it seldom had before. Another thing Grazzle had warned her about, the aches and pains that almost crippled old warriors. Those lucky enough to be old warriors that is.

"Over here," she cried and squatted against the parapet, watching the dark air above the iron. It was a hand that appeared first. It groped for a hold along the wall.

Zabeth swung her sword hard and separated the hand from its fingers. Then in almost the same motion, she stood and stabbed downward over the wall. The blade bit into flesh, the throat Zabeth judged. She heard a gurgling cry and then a thump far below.

She dropped to the floor just in time to avoid being peppered by a rain of arrows. They whistled over her, some clearing the wall, others skittering harmlessly on the black marble.

"Good work. Can I have the next one?"

Zabeth turned and saw Bindle crouched next to her. She motioned her assent and he took a place across from her. He was soaked of course, his black curls plastered against his skull. In his hand he held a mace, gore clinging to its spikes. His leather armor hung in ruins and his tunic was ripped and damp with blood, a darker heavier dampness than the rain. He followed her gaze to it.

"Just a scratch," he said. "How's your head?"

"It'll be all right," she said, returning her gaze to the wall.

"Look Zabeth," he said, "Roduct told me about Buckle. I'm sorry. I liked the man. He helped me when I was down."

Zabeth nodded but said nothing.

"And as for...the other matter." He looked down for a second. "I just want you to know that...well..."

She stopped him with a look and a curt nod. "I understand. But Kebble's the one you should tell."

He nodded, swallowing. "I just thought that we, you and I, could be...well comrades in arms."

Zabeth looked at him strangely. "What is it that you think we're doing now?"

He smiled and opened his mouth to reply but was interrupted by the looming figure of a Sarondaki warrior, pulling himself up over the wall. Quick as a striking bear, Bindle swung the mace and smashed the warrior's jaw with a vicious upper cut. A light push sent the Sarondaki hurtling backward to the ground below. The arrows shot over their heads again.

"Time to get rid of this," mumbled Bindle. He got up to his knees and brought the mace back and then swung it, smashing the marble of the wall. He did it again and again. Black chips of marble flew outward, making Zabeth shield her eyes. Finally the grappling iron lost its purchase and fell to the ground.

Zabeth nodded her approval and stood up to rejoin the fighting.

"Good luck," said Bindle. Zabeth him a strange look.

"Back, retreat." It was Kebble's voice. "To the gate house."

Through the murk of night and rain, Zabeth could see their men disengaging from the Sarondakis and running toward the gate house. She jumped up and pushed open the door. Standing beside it she hurried them inside, silently checking to make sure none of Marduct's men tried to sneak in.

The Sarondakis were approaching closely on their heels, and Zabeth could see Kebble and a few others fighting a rearguard action, giving the men time to retreat. She bolted forward to stand beside him, attacking a warrior who wielded a broadsword. She feigned a high cut and then came in low below her opponent's guard, slipping her blade between his ribs. She had no sooner pulled it out then another took his place. But he stumbled over his comrade, making it easy for Zabeth to dispatch him with a slicing cut through his throat.

She retreated one step at a time, trying to keep in step with Kebble so as not to expose his flank. The blades kept popping up before them like vicious weeds in a garden.

Eventually her back foot encountered the wall of the gate house. To her left she could see the open door. Keruct and Bindle stood in the doorway, blades flashing silver and crimson.

"Kebble you go in first," shouted Zabeth.

"No, you go," he said.

"I'm not going to argue, Constable," she said. "Get in there now before I knock you out and drag you in."

After a pause he said with a sardonic laugh, "Yes, Mistress." And he was gone. Zabeth moved over quickly to fill the gap. She sliced open a warrior's face. He screamed and staggered back, his sword clanging to the pavement.

"Door big enough for all of us?" she asked Bindle and Keruct.

"I think so," shouted Bindle. "On three..."

"Pray Bindle, tell the enemy when we plan to make our move. Now," she shouted, spinning and pushing her two comrades through the door and rushing through after them. She reached back and pushed the oak door to slam it shut. Only it wouldn't close. An arm blocked it. The arm held a sword which cast about blindly for some flesh to cut.

Keruct swung his blade and hacked the arm off at the elbow. The warrior screamed and tried to pull the rest of his arm back. Bindle and Keruct jabbed and hacked at the stump and even through the gap in the threshold. Finally the Sarondaki escaped.

Zabeth pushed at the door but it still wouldn't close. She looked down and saw that the warrior's forearm had somehow gotten wedged in the door.

"Keruct," she cried, motioning to the arm. The dark haired soldier kicked at the limb until the fingers were smashed and mangled and it slid out the door in its own blood.

The door slammed shut and Zabeth threw the bolt home. Gasping for breath she leaned her head against the jamb and closed her eyes. How nice it would be, she thought, to sleep now; just to lie down in a corner and let unconsciousness overtake her. She could imagine her aches and pains falling away as she descended into a warm blackness.

The door rattled.

"They're using axes," shouted Keruct.

Zabeth reluctantly turned around to watch Kebble who had moved to the middle of the gate house, shouting, "Who's still got bows?" About six men raised their hands. He looked at the group and then at Zabeth who leaned against the stone wall.

"Rondle, give Zabeth your bow and arrows. Then go up to the roof. It'll be dawn soon. Keep an eye on the road leading to the castle."

"What am I looking for?" asked Rondle as he scurried up the stairs and handed his bow and quiver to Zabeth.

"Our only hope," said Kebble. Zabeth looked down, a little hope dying to see Kebble reduced to relying on questionable reinforcements. "Archers to the battlements. Keep the ax-men away from the doors."

Zabeth nodded and ran to the ladder leading up to the next floor. The gate house towered three stories above the parapet. Below them the ground floor held the mechanism for opening the gate. It squatted on the floor, all pulleys and gears. Men were down there now trying to find effective ways to block the ground floor entrances.

Zabeth, after climbing the ladder, stood on a ledge that lined the walls. There were several entrances outside to stone battlements. Above was a rickety catwalk that led to the trapdoor in the ceiling. Zabeth glanced up in time to see Rondle's legs disappearing through it.

When Zabeth reached the outer parapet, she quickly deployed the archers, saying, "It's still dark and we don't have many arrows so be sure of your targets."

She leaned over the side and saw the keen edge of an ax glinting in the yellow light as it swung back. She loosed an arrow and the ax clattered to the ground. Then she had to move quickly to avoid a storm of arrows that sailed past her.

The archer who had taken this side with her was a Sarondaki. Zabeth thought his name was Pharuct. He was small for his race though half a head taller than Zabeth. She didn't even know if he could speak Dernian.

The chopping resumed. Zabeth approached the wall but was restrained by Pharuct. He pointed to his chest, saying something in Sarondaki. He popped up over the parapet and fired the next shot but failed to avoid the return volley. He screamed in agony and his twisted body slumped into the crenel. It was feathered with arrows. Zabeth watched the silhouette in horror. Slowly the bow rose up and Zabeth realized that Pharuct was trying to save it from falling to the enemy before he died. She rushed up and grabbed the bow and threw it to the stone floor.

"Farewell. You die like a warrior," she whispered. He didn't understand a word but seemed to grasp the sense of her meaning. He grunted in satisfaction and closed his eyes.

The chopping resumed and this time the Sarondakis laid down a covering fire. Volley after volley zinged over her head.

"Mistress Zabeth," piped a voice from behind her. She turned to find Nuct, the left handed Sarondaki youth who had helped her and Vorkle take that guard tower so long ago. In his grasp was a handful of arrows.

"I picked these up when we were retreating to the gate house."

"Good man, Nuct." The boy visibly brightened at her compliment. "Pick up the ones that fall back to the floor. They're firing a lot of them."

"Yes Mistress." He handed her the arrows and then began scrounging for more. Zabeth returned her attention to the body of Pharuct, pulling it off the parapet and onto the floor. She loosened the chin strap of his metal helmet and slipped it off. It proved a little big for her but with the chin strap tight, it would stay on and not impede her sight. She then cut the straps to Pharuct's quiver and placed it on the floor leaning against the parapet.

She sliced through the laces holding Pharuct's leather armor and peeled it off him. She had to pull the arrows out to remove the front. These she put in the pile Nuct had given her. Then with all her might she hoisted Pharuct back up to the wall and, lowering her voice as far as she could in pitch, she screamed the worst curses she knew in Sarondaki.

Instantly the warrior's body was re-peppered with arrows. Zabeth had time to fire off five before they regained their wits and started firing at her. Each arrow thudded home in a Sarondaki's chest. The ax clattered to the ground again.

Zabeth slid down against the parapet. Nuct came up to her, both his hands bristling with arrows.

"They're shooting a lot aren't they?" he asked. Zabeth slowly nodded. The boy looked over at Pharuct's bow. Was it getting lighter? Zabeth cast a look eastward and sure enough the sky was brightening to a dark gray.

"I can shoot arrows," said Nuct.

Zabeth opened her mouth to protest but then realized that if the Sarondakis got into the gate house they'd kill this boy as surely as any soldier. He deserved the chance to defend himself.

She pointed to the corner of the parapet to her left. "Over there. I'll be opposite. We'll try to divide their fire. Be careful. It's getting lighter. They can see you."

The boy nodded and grabbed the bow and Pharuct's quiver. He dumped a fistful of arrows into it and then ran doubled over to where Zabeth had stationed him. She nodded approvingly, an intelligent lad.

The arrows started flying overhead again and the chopping resumed. Zabeth took her position and signaled to Nuct. Her first arrow planted itself in the new ax-man's chest. The second and third found their ways into warriors stationed nearby to pick up the ax if their comrade should fall.

Nuct's arrows confused their archers for a moment. Zabeth saw in the increasingly bright light that they were positioned in a semicircle extending some twenty feet around the door. There were twenty of them. She aimed quickly and got two before the returning fire got too heavy and she had to duck behind the parapet.

Looking over at Nuct she saw him sprawled across the stones three arrows in his chest and one in his eye. On the black stones beside him was the bow. She closed her eyes and bowed her head slightly.

A cry cut through the din of battle, reaching Zabeth's ears faint but clear. "Skrike is dead." It was repeated and all movement seemed to stop.

Zabeth scrambled to her knees and looked over the parapet facing the castle. In the doorway to the castle stood Tiacin, holding up a severed head in his hand by its jet black hair. Zabeth could see the confusion spreading among Marduct's troops. Some stared in disbelief, others began arguing and denying, and some stood still, eyes focused inward, examining this new free will that had suddenly been thrust upon them.

Inside the gate house the defenders burst out into wild cheering. Zabeth could hear them calling up to Rondle. "Who killed Skrike? Do they know? Was it Tiacin?" Zabeth looked up and saw Rondle, leaning over the edge, squinting his eyes to see Tiacin and the shadowy figures that stood behind him in the doorway of the castle.

"Get down," she bellowed.

The sharp-eyed lookout jumped and then disappeared, hunkering down below the parapet that lined the roof of the gate house.

"What's Marduct doing?" she demanded.

"I...ah...I don't know," he called back.

"Then get over there and find out."

"Yes." He scrambled over to the other side of the roof. After a minute he shouted back. "The storm's completely blown over. The sky's clear."

Zabeth looked over at the west and saw that indeed blue was tingeing the sky. She hadn't even noted that it had stopped raining. She could see stars in the western sky.

"It's hard to tell but I think Marduct's forming his ranks for an assault. There's a whole line of ax-men. I think he's going to attempt to chop his way through the gate."

Zabeth wondered what that meant. It was a pretty desperate move, considering that it was only a matter of time before he took the gate house. Maybe it meant that Marduct thought he was running out of time. Could that mean there was an army chasing him?

"Anything happening on the road?"

There was a pause. "No, it's empty." Rondle's voice sounded his disappointment. The danger wasn't over yet. No reinforcements. Zabeth sighed. Given a little thought, it made sense. Marduct wouldn't destroy the outer gate, if he thought he would have to defend the castle against the western army in a few hours. The Sarondaki warlord probably feared his troops would mutiny if they dwelled too long on what the death of Skrike meant.

"Sarondakis, people of the desert." The voice came from below in the courtyard. Zabeth looked down and saw that it belonged to Roduct. He stood, surrounded by about twenty of his Sarondaki recruits. Her former lord waved his sword over his head and shouted in the brightening dawn.

"We are free. Kill the traitors who collaborated with the tyrant Skrike. Kill the chieftains who led us into this disastrous war with the west. Skrike is dead. Kill Marduct."

In the seconds after Roduct's cry, the noise level grew from a murmur until the courtyard, the walls, everywhere exploded as Sarondaki turned on Sarondaki and the battle turned into a riot.

Instantly arrows started flying again over her head. Zabeth rolled to her right and came up shooting. The arrow was headed straight for the ax-man at the door but Zabeth was rolling again before it arrived. Three times she popped up in different places along the parapet and fired an arrow. The third time she stood and a sharp pain in her shoulder knocked her back against the wall of the gate house. Her bow rattled to the marble surface beneath her and she slid down the wall. She looked down and saw the shaft of an arrow sticking out of her right shoulder. Blood bubbled out around the shaft and pain radiated from the wound in excruciating waves. Her vision became spotted with dark blobs and her breathing became shallow.

The chopping continued. Zabeth tried to get up but her vision dimmed as the pain tore through her, causing a small yelp of agony to escape her lips. She sat still until the pain subsided.

"I need an archer over here," she called. Nothing happened. "Hey, they're getting through the door." Still nothing.

With a curse, she leaned over on her left side and then scooted away from the wall to lie on her back. This put her head just beyond the corner. When her vision cleared, she turned her head and saw Medwell's body lying on the black stones, two arrows in the middle of his chest.

"Damn," she murmured, her voice high and quivering.

Suddenly there was the crack of splintering wood and the sound of triumphant Sarondaki war cries.

"They've breached the door. They're inside," shouted a voice from the gate house.

"Damn it to Skrike's Hell," mumbled Zabeth. With every movement ushering in new levels of pain, she slowly sat up, turned and then lay down on her uninjured shoulder. She crawled on her side, fighting the pain by clenching her teeth so tight she thought she'd grind them into powder. But her vision never dimmed completely.

From within came the sounds of a desperate but losing battle. Steel clanged against steel, and the cries of both victory and deadly anguish made up the din. It filled Zabeth's ears as she pulled her way through the door and onto the second story ledge.

The gate house swarmed with fighting Sarondakis. They poured through the remains of the door below her, screaming and wielding swords and axes. She could hear a couple of Roduct's Sarondakis trying to stem the tide but were slowly being beaten back. The rest of the defenders, led by Bindle, were holding the wooden platform on which the mechanism for opening the gate stood. A horde of Sarondakis were cutting their way up the steps to the top. Bindle scurried around the platform, haranguing his troops and cutting down any Sarondakis who tried to climb on to the platform. Morning sunshine poured in through the upper story doorways.

She looked up and saw Kebble across the way, holding three warriors at bay. Her heart raced as she tried to will her broken body into action. But the pain reminded her that she couldn't answer the call this time.

Kebble seemed to be holding his own anyway. With a deft envelope he disarmed one warrior and then disemboweled him. Parrying an over hand cut to his head from the second, he flicked the blade to the side and then lunged, shouldering the big Sarondaki into his partner. A sword clattered to the flagstones and with a quick thrust Kebble made short work of the warrior.

His partner frantically tried to disengage himself from the body but Kebble's blade slashed sideways through the Sarondaki's throat. Blood geysered from the wound as the warrior slumped backward. Every surface seemed soaked with blood as the gate house turned into a charnel house.

Kebble stood for a moment, wiping sweat from his eyes and gasping for breath. Blood and sweat made his body glisten in the sunlight. He looked up and saw her.

"Zabeth, you're hurt," he shouted.

Weakly, she waved, trying to indicate that she was all right. Then she saw a Sarondaki behind him, coming through the door. Painfully she forced air into her lungs and cried in a voice higher than she liked. "Behind you, idiot."

He spun sharply, catching the Sarondaki's blade just in time. Then he grabbed the warrior's wrist, stepped back and flipped him over the ledge into the melee below.

Suddenly a grinding noise rent the air. Zabeth looked down and saw four Sarondakis turning the giant capstan that opened the gate. Of the defenders only Bindle survived. He scrambled up the steps to a second platform next to a massive gear assembly which turned as the Sarondakis labored at the capstan.

With two mighty swings he chopped a two foot length of two by four out of the railing and rushed to the closest point where two gears were grinding together. Two Sarondakis were on him in an instant. Bindle swatted away thrusting swords with both his sword and the plank. One warrior felt the bite of Bindle's steel. The gears whirled faster and faster as Bindle climbed the steps one at a time, parrying numerous blows. He now held his body sideways in a classic fencer's stance, using his higher ground to good advantage. In his left hand he held the plank out straight away from his body, its ragged end nearing the spinning gears.

With her good hand, Zabeth reached behind her and pulled out the hackbut she had found in the depot by the scorpion's lair. Awkwardly, she looked into the barrel to confirm that it was still loaded. Then she laid it in front of her and retrieved her flint and steel from her small pack. With an effort that caused stars to shoot across her vision, she moved her bad arm so that her hand was in reach. Then, working through the pain, she put the flint into the numb fingers of the hand, clenching them as hard as she could. That done, she took the cord and laid it next to the flint. After that she picked up the steel and struck the flint. There was a spark, but it didn't catch. The steel bit into her knuckles. She tried again but it failed. On the fifth try the cord began to smolder. She laid down the steel and grabbed the hackbut.

Looking down, she saw Bindle was running out of time. The plank wavered in the air just inches away from the spinning gears. With his right hand, he fought off a half dozen or so Sarondakis. Fortunately the steps were narrow and only two could get at him at a time. Still, he was mostly parrying, not thrusting. His sword point sagged and he began to get sloppy in his technique.

With a little cry of half pain, half defiance Zabeth pointed the hackbut toward the scene below her. Then, holding the weapon in her good hand, she forced her bad hand to pick up the smoldering cord and move the red tip to within an inch of the touch hole. It wouldn't have to be a great shot, just good enough to distract the Sarondakis and give Bindle the time to jam the gear works with the plank. The only thing she needed to worry about was not hitting Bindle.

Waves of pain rolled out from her shoulder as she held the cord above the touch hole and waited for her head to clear so she could aim. When the colors stopped wheeling in front of her, she saw Bindle pierce a Sarondaki and send his body tumbling back down the steps. This allowed Bindle a second to glance backward and thrust the plank into the gears. But his foot slipped on the top step, pitching him forward. The plank fell to the ground and the spinning apparatus ate Bindle's arm up to the shoulder. His screams tore the air, replacing the sound of grinding gears. The mechanism stopped.

A Sarondaki ax-man vaulted up the steps and raised his weapon to finish Bindle off. Zabeth lowered the cord to the touch hole and suddenly the world exploded both inside her head and outside. The hackbut kicked back and smacked her in the eye. Then it bounced forward and fell over the ledge. Through the stars and whirling comets crowding her sight, she saw the ax-man with half his head gone topple off the platform.

She rolled onto her back. Barely heard were harsh Sarondaki voices and then she felt a couple of people climbing the ladder up to her level. They were coming to finish her off. She hardly cared.

Then she felt something sail over her. She opened her eyes and dimly saw Kebble, crouched in a fighting stance, with his back to her, facing three Sarondakis.

"You bastards will have to kill me before you even touch her."

Rondle's voice cut through the air. Zabeth could see him through a red tinged haze, leaning over the open trap door to the roof.

"They're coming. There's three divisions of cavalry riding hard down the road and a huge army behind it. Marduct's sounding retreat and placing his defenses outside the castle."

Sure enough Zabeth heard the sound of retreat being blown on the long wooden Sarondaki horns, a low mournful sound. It was the last sound Zabeth heard before pain and fatigue plunged her into darkness.

33

The injured and dying cluttered the halls and foyers of Castle Skrike. Both westerners and Sarondakis were among them. Buckle followed Kebble, as he threaded his way through the hallway. Holding a tray of bandages, Buckle tried not to step on anybody. The stink of putrefaction threatened to overwhelm him and he had to concentrate just to keep up with Kebble as he raced from one patient to another.

It was a grisly business, and almost as tiring as all the trudging and marching Buckle had done in the last year. Buckle hadn't slept for twenty four hours, ever since the western armies had demolished Marduct at the gates of the castle. In that time he had helped perform four amputations and was on his way to a fifth, the toughest one left.

"Bindle's over this way," said Kebble, his jaw tight. This had to be especially though for the young constable. After all he and Bindle had apparently been friends. Other doctors had volunteered to do it but Kebble insisted.

"Most of these army doctors don't recognize the importance of keeping things clean. Look at this mess." He waved his hand around at the impromptu hospital. Blood soaked the floor along with urine and offal. Severed limbs lay rotting where doctors had thrown them in their hurry to get to everybody.

"Bindle deserves better."

Buckle had taken an instant liking to this brilliant young soldier. Initially it was out of gratitude for his deliverance from danger. Then Buckle discovered that he and Kebble had a lot in common. They had the same gentleness of nature, rare in an estate steward, even rarer in a soldier. Most of all though, they shared concern for Zabeth. Buckle

351

could still picture her, lying on a makeshift pallet, twitching from fevered dreams. She hadn't come to since the end of the battle.

Kebble's face and the way he stroked her cheeks and forehead betrayed his feeling towards her.

"She'll always have that scar on her forehead," he'd said.

"Well, she never cared much for her looks," Buckle had replied.

"She's beautiful, absolutely beautiful." Kebble never took his eyes off of her when he was in the same room.

They came to the corner where Bindle was laying. A dark shape hovered over him. It looked up as they approached. Krinseth greeted them with one of her tight-lipped smiles.

"Are you a nurse?" asked Kebble.

"Ah, no," interrupted Buckle. "This is Krinseth. She's a witch."

"Fire?" asked Kebble suspiciously.

"Water." The young soldier relaxed. "So you're Kebble. When we spoke to Skrike, just before Buckle killed him, he seemed genuinely afraid of you. High praise."

"From a low source," said Kebble. "Matron, I don't have time for this. You probably know why we're here."

"Yes, and it won't be necessary." She turned back to look down at Bindle.

"What?"

"I saved the arm."

"How?" asked Kebble, kneeling and pulling down the blanket that covered Bindle. "The swelling's down and..." he poked at the arm. "The putrefaction's gone away. I don't understand."

"There's still quite a bit of moisture in the air from the storm, and as he was a former traveling companion..."

"Thank you Krinseth," said Buckle. "You didn't have to do that."

"Since I've been with you, I've done a lot of things I didn't have to do." Her smile turned inward and became almost wistful. "Anyway the arm still won't be the same. I could only do so much." Kebble looked up at her. "He won't be able to move it as easily and he'll have trouble grasping things."

Kebble nodded and looked down at Bindle who groaned and opened his eyes. Buckle could barely recognize the young man. His face was darker from time spent in the desert sun and his black hair hung in greasy ringlets on the pile of straw that served as a pillow.

352

"The battle..." murmured Bindle.

"We won," said Kebble, grabbing Bindle's good arm. "Thanks to you."

"You owe me."

Kebble laughed. "That I do." Bindle tried to laugh but it caused him pain.

"The company...how many left?"

"Fifteen."

Bindle looked away toward the wall.

"That's fifteen more than we figured would come out when we started," Kebble said. Bindle nodded.

"Zabeth?"

"Alive. Hurt but alive...for now."

"She'll live," said Krinseth. All three men looked at her.

"Another old traveling companion?" asked Buckle.

"I didn't have to do a thing. The will to live is strong in that child." Kebble smiled and it seemed to Buckle that he visibly relaxed at the news.

"Uh, Kebble," said Bindle, his voice weak. "About Zabeth...and you. I just thought you should know that...well..."

"Yes?"

"Well, we're not gonna let a woman come between old friends like us are we?"

"Not a chance, my friend. Hey..." He reached into a pouch that he had set on the floor beside Bindle and pulled out a metal flask. "I was here to...well you don't need the operation, as it turns out but there's no reason why you still can't have some of the painkiller."

Bindle smiled and took the flask with his right hand. He tasted it and then looked up at Kebble.

"I thought you ran out of this stuff down in the desert?"

"I found a supply in one of the store rooms." He shrugged. "Always the first thing I look for whenever I take a castle."

"There you are," said a voice. Buckle looked back and saw Tiacin standing behind them. He wore a bright livery and looked very uncomfortable in it. Buckle had heard that he'd been drafted as a messenger for Fazzle and the two western kings. Yazzle was with him. "They want to see both of you."

Buckle groaned and Kebble stood up and patted him on the shoulder.

"Come on Buckle. It's a soldier's duty."

"I'm not a soldier."

"Tell that to Skrike." He turned to Bindle. "Get some rest. When we get things organized, we'll move you to your own room." Bindle waved the flask at him.

"How's Lathel?" asked Buckle.

Yazzle shook his head. "He still hasn't talked, Master Buckle. I'm worried. He's worse than when we escaped."

"He'll pull out of it...or if not we'll find a place for him on Methliana."

"Yes, Master Buckle," said Yazzle but the lad wouldn't meet his eyes.

Buckle put his hand on Yazzle's arm and went off to follow Kebble and Tiacin, who were leaving.

Buckle followed them to the throne room, dread building in his stomach. When they found out who he was and what he had done, they would begin to shower honors on him. All Buckle wanted to do was go home.

The throne room was being used as the headquarters for the western armies. Thankfully it had been cleaned up. The gold doors stood open and a small crowd stood in the hallway. As Tiacin, Kebble and Buckle approached, a stout man with short dark hair emerged from the room. Buckle thought he looked familiar.

"Nittle," cried Kebble.

"Kebble, I've been meaning to get down to the hospital and see you but I haven't had a chance." The two men embraced with the easy informality of comrades in arms.

"I see you survived the war," said Kebble.

"And prospered. I'm a count now."

"You outrank me."

Nittle shook his head. "Not for long, my friend. They're handing out titles in there like they were candy. Even Fazzle's in a good mood. And if they ever get their hands and the fellow who killed Skrike, they'll honor him to death."

Kebble nudged Buckle's arm. "Maybe you'd better run while you can." Buckle was seriously considering it.

Nittle looked puzzled.

"Oh, I'm sorry," said Kebble. "Nittle, may I present Master Buckle of Methliana, slayer of Skrike the Terrible."

The stout soldier bent low in a bow and said, "Forgive me, I didn't realize..." He looked up at Buckle with a puzzled expression. "Do I know you?"

"Last year on the Main Road. You were leading a troop of injured men..."

"And I met you and your group heading east." He barked a short laugh. "Master strategist that I am, I tried to talk you out of going."

Kebble exploded with laughter. "I'm glad you didn't."

"I wish you had," added Buckle, which put both men into gales of laughter. Buckle though, couldn't quite bring himself to laugh. He wasn't unhappy exactly, although the oppressive atmosphere of the hospital still clung to him and he was worried about Lathel and Zabeth. More and more his thoughts turned to home and the situation there. The date he had to be back to legally claim Methliana was about a month away. If he started back now he'd just make it. But if, as Nittle said they wanted to "honor him to death," he may have to sit through weeks of ceremonies and endure tortuous parades on the long journey back with the triumphant armies. Buckle had heard rumors about what they had planned for him. That was why he'd been trying to hide. Now though, there was nothing for it but to explain his situation and beg off all the pomp until the estate was securely his.

"I suppose we'd better go in," said Kebble.

"There's still one more in your audience yet to arrive," said Tiacin, casting a significant look at Kebble.

Kebble smiled and glanced at Buckle in a curious way. "Yes of course. Has he been told?"

Tiacin shook his head. "He and his Sarondakis have been scouring the castle, destroying all the Soowooli urns they can find."

"And we got most of them too," said a familiar voice from behind Buckle. His knees became watery for he was sure the owner of that voice was dead.

Kebble grinned and motioned for Buckle to turn around. When he did, he saw Roduct standing in the hallway, dressed in flowing sand-colored robes, his cowl pulled back over his shoulders. At his side was strapped a huge sword. On his face was a look of shock and recognition that mirrored Buckle's own.

"Lord," said Buckle and he started to drop to his knees but before he could get even halfway, he found himself crushed to Roduct's chest and lifted off the ground.

"Buckle," cried Roduct. "We thought you were dead. Zabeth and I." He held Buckle out at arm's length. "Is it really you?"

"Yes Lord, I..."

"Wait." He cast a look over at Kebble and Tiacin. "It's been said that a Delamerian slew Skrike. By any chance..."

"You are holding the slayer of Skrike right now," Kebble informed Roduct.

Roduct looked at Buckle for an instant and then let him go. He took a step back and then dropped to one knee.

"Lord, please," protested Buckle.

"Why not?" said Roduct, "Not only are you the Skrikeslayer but you're also an estate lord now yourself..." His head snapped up. "That's right. We've got to get you back home don't we? You leave tomorrow. If the kings in there won't provide transportation, you'll be escorted by Sarondakis."

Buckle could feel his eyes beginning to water. "But...but Lord, can't you come back. Can't things..."

Roduct stood up and put his hands on Buckle's shoulders. "I'm sorry...son. I'm a Sarondaki. This is where I belong, in the desert. These are my people and they need me."

Buckle nodded his head silently, not understanding but knowing that understanding wouldn't change things. "I gave up on you," said Buckle to the floor. "I saw them...take your blood...and I thought you had gone over to the other side."

"I did," said Roduct simply. "But I broke Soowooli."

Kebble cleared his throat and said, "I saw him do it and believe me Buckle, it's a tough thing to do. I didn't think it could be done, and I know about these things. No one can blame you for despairing."

Buckle looked sideways at Kebble and then over at Roduct, trying to gain confidence from their encouraging expressions.

"Buckle," said Roduct. "I see no transgression here against me on your part. But I know what you want to hear. You are forgiven."

"Thank you, Lord."

The powerful lord slapped Buckle on the back, sending him jerking forward. "Enough of this 'Lord' business, Buckle. We're peers now, at least. From what I hear, those kings in there are ready to make you a national hero second only to Dalmar."

"Can't I just slip away right now and not bother with all this?"

"No, no," said Kebble, grabbing Buckle's elbow and drawing him into the throne room. "We all have to pay for our mistakes."

356

He turned. "Nittle, find me later. I found a stash of passable brew."

"I figured as much," said Nittle. "Count on it and good luck in there."

In the middle of the throne room, a long table had been set up. Behind it sat Fazzle and the two kings. The Delamerian lord sat to the left of the other two. All three seemed to be in good humor, talking amongst themselves and the aides and clerks that bustled to and from the table like flies on a horse's back.

The one sitting in the middle looked up and said, "Ah, Kebble, good to see you again."

"Thank you, King Tetwell."

"How are things going in the hospital?"

"Still a little disorganized but we're making progress."

"Good, good," said Tetwell as he searched through the stacks of papers in front of him. "Now where is that report...here it is. If you could just give us an oral report now?"

"Yes, Your Majesty." Kebble proceeded to relate all the events leading up to and including the siege of the castle. He described the parts played by various members of his army in glowing terms, especially Zabeth, Bindle and Roduct. When he had finished they looked at each other and nodded.

"Very good Kebble. After due consideration, this is our decision," said Tetwell. He glanced over at a scribe who grabbed a quill, dipped it in ink and held it over a flat sheet of parchment. "The woman, Zabeth will receive a commendation, and in an action unprecedented as far as I know, will be offered a commission in the Barrier Scouts at the rank of constable. How is Bindle doing?"

"The arm was saved, Your Majesty," said Kebble, "but it will be weak."

"I see," said Tetwell with a sigh. "Bindle will be given a commendation and be promoted to constable also. He is welcome to stay in the Scouts and perform whatever function he can. If, however, he finds it necessary to retire, he will receive a full pension. The surviving members of your original force will be promoted one level and the families of the dead will receive pensions."

"Thank you, Your Majesties," said Kebble. "That is more than fair."

Tetwell leaned back and crossed his arms. "As for you constable..."

"I'll make it plain sir," interrupted Fazzle. "I still have doubts about our orders telling you to withdraw not getting through." Buckle thought Kebble looked somewhat uncomfortable for the first time. "But as it turned out, I suppose I should be glad they didn't. I have decided to overlook possible insubordination and vote with my colleagues."

"Kebble," chimed in Tetwell, "pending due ceremony, you are appointed Duke. A suitable estate in eastern Joswell will be found at a later date. In the meantime, as there is no westerner that I know of who knows more about Sarondakis and their ways, I wonder if you would care to participate in the coming negotiations with the tribes."

Kebble smiled sweetly but Buckle detected something like despair in his manner when he bowed and said, "It is an honor to accept your title and suggestion, Your Majesty."

"Lord Roduct," said Tetwell. "I'm sure I don't have to tell you that there is a commission and a commendation awaiting you, should you choose to accept them. But I gather from your recent activities that you have other plans?"

"Yes sir, in the past few days I have solidified my position as the leader of the Free Sarondakis."

"The what?"

"The tribesmen who rebelled against Skrike. Without them Kebble could never have taken the castle."

"That's very true, Your Majesty," said Kebble.

"The Free Sarondakis are ready to negotiate," said Roduct.

"Hmm," murmured Tetwell. "What do you think Lord Kebble?"

"From what I hear in the wind, Your Majesty, the Free Sarondakis have the upper hand. I think any treaty we sign with them will hold."

Tetwell nodded and said, "Very well. We will open negotiations as soon as possible. Were we able to find the Delamerian who killed Skrike?"

"Ah, he's right here, Your Majesty," said Kebble, motioning to Buckle. Three pairs of eyes turned their gaze on him.

"This...gentleman is the Skrikeslayer?" Nodwick spoke for the first time.

"Yes Your Majesty," said Roduct. "This is Lord Buckle of Delamer, my former steward and now Lord of Methliana."

The three noblemen, after looking at each other, stood up and bowed stiffly at the waist.

"Lord," said Tetwell. "The west owes you more than it can ever repay. Anything...anything that is within our power to give is yours. You have but to name it."

Buckle, fighting all his instincts, stepped forward, swallowed and said, "Your Majesties, I accept your thanks and in turn offer my own. Were it not for your timely arrival, I surely would not have lived to be standing here." The two kings smiled and exchanged glances. Out of the corner of his eye, Buckle could see Kebble and Roduct looking on approvingly. "Under other circumstances your kind offer would perhaps fill my head with thoughts of grants of fertile land or jewels and wealth beyond my poor imagining. But right now I just want to go home. Not only because I haven't been there in almost a year and I've suffered much but because if I don't get home quickly, I won't have a home to go to." He went on to explain the circumstances under which he left Delamer.

"Yes," said Fazzle, rubbing his chin. "Lord Roduct's sudden departure last year has left the ownership of Methliana in some doubt. But surely you know, Lord Buckle, that simply by saying so you can have any tract of land in Delamer you wish?"

"I suppose you're right, sir. But Lord Roduct's...or rather my estate is where I grew up and...and well it's home."

"Then, Lord, we could simply override the machinations of this Erklin and give you the estate," said Nodwick.

"Not without violating several basic principles Delamerians hold dear. If I must become a Lord and enter politics, I do not wish to begin with such an arbitrary act."

Fazzle nodded his agreement and even approval.

"Very well then," said Tetwell. "You leave early tomorrow morning with an escort. But Lord, once you have established your ownership of the estate, you must come to Tarion and let the people of the west honor you properly."

Buckle sighed and closed his eyes, giving in to the inevitable. He suddenly felt the need to sit down, and even more for some of Kebble's liquor.

After the audience broke up, Buckle followed Kebble back down into the hospital, thinking to pitch in again. But Kebble shoved some bedding into his arms and pointed to an empty room.

"Things are under control. Get some sleep," he said.

"You need it more than I do," replied Buckle.

"Maybe so but I'm not leaving tomorrow. Go." Buckle could see there was no arguing with him so he plodded into the room and laid out the bedding before a huge empty fireplace. A single narrow window provided the only light in the room, a hard shaft of yellow sunlight.

When seemingly a second later, Buckle was awakened by Yazzle, the shaft of sunlight was gone and the window was a black rectangle set in the wall. Buckle groaned and pulled his blanket tightly around his shoulders against the cold.

Yazzle shook him again. "Lord Buckle. They sent me to wake you."

"What is it? Time to leave?"

"No, Lord. Zabeth is waking up."

Buckle's eyes snapped open and he sat up, ignoring the aches in his back. "Is she all right?"

"They think so, Lord but Kebble thought you might want to say good-bye."

"Yes of course." He got up, refusing to groan as his body protested and followed Yazzle to the room where they had moved Zabeth.

There was a crowd there, Roduct, Kebble, and the three soldiers who seemed particularly devoted to Zabeth, Vorkle, Tiacin and Keruct. All were standing around the cot they had found for her, obscuring her from view.

"And that's how you saved Bindle's life," Kebble was saying.

"I did it just to keep the gate from opening, not for his own sake."

"I don't know, Zabeth, I think you kind of like him. Maybe I should be worried." Kebble smiled.

"If I could get out of this cot, I'd kick you." The others laughed.

Kebble looked up and caught Buckle's eye. With a mischievous look he motioned Buckle nearer. The others looked back and then cheerfully made room.

Zabeth lay in bed scowling up at Kebble. She looked thin, almost bony. There was a blood-stained bandage around her head and her arm was in a sling. Her looks weren't helped by the homicidal expression on her face. When the others laughed, she looked around dangerously and saw Buckle. Immediately her expression changed. Her eyes grew wide and her mouth dropped open.

"Oh I'm sorry," laughed Kebble. "Didn't I mention that Buckle was still alive?"

"Buckle," she shouted and sat up, her good arm extending. Pain, however, wracked her face.

"Whoa, lady," cautioned Kebble, gently pushing her back down, "you're far too weak to even think about getting up for at least a couple of weeks."

Buckle knelt down and kissed her on the cheek and then took her hand and gently pressed it to his shoulder. He could feel his insides convulsing. "I'm glad to see you made it through Zabeth," he said. He leaned back and looked at her.

"How?" she asked and Buckle gave her a brief description of his adventures. When he had finished her mouth dropped open and she said, "Then you killed Skrike?"

"Please, not you too," said Buckle. The room broke into laughter. He smiled down at her though. "So how are you feeling?"

"I'm fine," she said, emphatically, though the effort caused her to wince in pain. "If Kebble weren't such a worrier, I could be up and helping instead of..." She stopped when Kebble put his hand over her mouth.

"Maybe we should move on to another topic? Ouch," he said when she bit his hand. He yanked it away and waved it frantically in the air. Everyone else in the room laughed.

"You're lucky I can't move," said Zabeth.

He looked over at Buckle. "I think she's going to be all right. I don't know about me." He sucked his hand. "I think you drew blood."

"Good," said Zabeth.

Buckle looked back at her. "I'm leaving tomorrow, Zabeth."

"What, so soon? You'll need an escort. I can..."

"You'll stay on that cot until I tell you different constable."

"I already have an escort, Zabeth, from King Tetwell."

"But I swore an oath to your brother..."

"I release you." He smiled at her. "Go and live the life you choose. I'm the Duke of Methliana now, or will be if I can get home in time. I also release you from your fealty."

Zabeth looked up at Kebble, hope in her expression. He nodded, smiling.

361

Buckle grasped her hand. "Try not to be too hard on poor Kebble, all right?"

The beginnings of a smile played at the edges of her mouth. "Depends," she said.

"Well," said Kebble, starting to motion people out. "Let's leave them alone to talk since Buckle's leaving. But only a couple of hours, Buckle. You both need rest." The group crowded toward the door, each saying good-bye.

Buckle and Zabeth talked all night.

Dawn was breaking the next morning when Buckle climbed onto the horse they had found for him. The captain of his escort assured Buckle that the horse was one of the most docile in the cavalry. Still it was a cavalry horse and a bit more spirited than Buckle liked. He had one of the men hold it for him while he mounted.

The sunlight showed golden in the blue sky, making even the black walls of Castle Skrike seem full of goodness and promise. The cool of the desert night still hung in the air and Buckle could see his breath as well as that of the horses and other men.

Yazzle sat on his horse beside Buckle. He seemed anxious to get going. Lathel was on the other side of Yazzle, staring blankly at the deep blue of the sky.

"Are you ready to start, Lord Buckle?" asked the captain of the escort. Buckle motioned for one more moment and turned to have a last look. Most signs of the battle had already been cleared away, though Buckle could see the gaping black rectangle where the door to the gate house had stood.

A lone figure rode out of the gate and toward them. A dark blue hood covered its head, and the steam from its breath jetted out of the darkness beneath the hood. It stopped within a few yards of the escort and reached up to draw back the hood. Krinseth squinted in the bright sunlight. It brought out the red in her hair. Her blue eyes seemed to glow. He hadn't seen her since the day before and had feared she'd already left by her own mysterious means.

"Would you care to have one more in your company?"

"Not at all," said Buckle. "How far are you going?"

"I find myself with a wish to see this Methliana you're always talking about." She looked toward the sun. "That is if I'm welcome."

"Always," said Buckle, loud enough that only she could hear.

"I should warn you," she said softly. "I am Tenaryan. Soon I shall have to sleep the hundred year sleep."

"How long till then?"

She shrugged, still scanning the western horizon, "We don't have much time...twenty, maybe thirty years." She looked at him and smiled.

Buckle laughed. "Captain," he cried.

"Yes, Lord," said the young man.

"Take us home."

34

A sky full of stars hung overhead, glowing spectacularly across the Delamerian sky. The moon was a thin sliver and its silver light couldn't compete with the blazing stars. Familiar sounds surrounded them, the rustling of the leaves, the night calls of crickets and the clopping of hooves on the soft Delamerian soil.

They trotted along the drive to the manor house. After pressing as hard as they could for a month—early starts and late camps—they had arrived one year to the day they had set out. It didn't seem possible to Buckle. Surely years had passed.

Buckle didn't have it in him just then to worry though. Elation, which had been growing ever since they had left Tarion, now threatened to take control of him. He wanted to dance, to take Krinseth who was riding beside him and wheel her through the cornfields as if they were at a dance on a Saturday night. The air, fresh with the smell of good soil, was like wine to him and he never tired of taking long deep pulls of it. He was glad it was dark and his companions couldn't see the idiot grin on his face.

Buckle reined in his horse just before the manor house. It was completely black, not a light to be seen. Tying the horse's reigns to the post, Buckle grabbed two leather pouches out of his saddlebag and bounded up the steps of the porch. His heart seemed about to explode with excitement. He never thought he'd see any of this again.

He opened the door and stepped into the foyer. The others, Krinseth, Yazzle and Lathel stepped in behind him.

"This is strange," muttered Buckle. "Nobody waited up for us. Usually Bertam at least is up at this time of night." He pulled at the bell rope for the butler and turned around and smiled at Yazzle. "Good to be home, isn't it?"

"Yes, Lord. I'm looking forward to my own bed."

"Master Buckle?" They spun around to see an astonished Yarrel standing in the hallway, his long face lit from underneath by the candle he held in his hand. He was dressed to perfection in a black tunic and a cape draped about him, causing Buckle to wonder, not for the first time, if Yarrel ever slept. How easily comfortable thoughts came back.

"Yarrel," shouted Buckle, wanting to embrace the old doorkeeper, but knowing that would be beneath the servant's dignity. He settled instead for slapping him on the back.

"We made it Yarrel. We made it back."

"So I see, Master Buckle."

"Oh," said Buckle, turning to the others. "We'll need two extra rooms, nothing elaborate and is there any food in the pantry? We skipped dinner to make some time."

"Buckle," whispered Krinseth.

"What?"

"The time?"

"Of course," said Buckle. "Yarrel, what time is it?"

"I'm not sure, Master Buckle. Around midnight I believe. I could just check the clock in the study."

"Lead the way." They followed the doorkeeper as he opened the oak doors to the study and allowed them to enter. Then he walked over to the mantle and inspected the striped candle burning there.

"I regret to say, sir that it is after midnight."

"Are you sure?"

"Yes, sir. It is not long after, only a few minutes, but definitely after."

Buckle deflated, his head dropping of its own accord. "Damn," he muttered.

"I'm sorry, Master Buckle," offered Yarrel.

"Five minutes," said Yazzle, unbelieving.

"Well," said Buckle. "Maybe Bertam will have some ideas. Is my brother up, Yarrel?"

The old man cleared his throat. 'Once again I must apologize that I am the one to tell you, Master Buckle. But Master Bertam died last winter."

"Died," echoed Buckle, sinking into the nearest chair. He felt Krinseth's hand grasp his shoulder.

"Yes Master Buckle, Master Bertam suffered a rapid decline in the fall. It was a very bad harvest with the storms and...other things and it was a very tense time. I think that is what killed him."

Buckle's head was reeling. After all that had happened in the last year, the imprisonment, the battle, everything. He'd always thought that if he could just make it home, everything would be all right. But he hadn't been home five minutes and already he'd lost the estate and his brother. He wanted to weep but there were no more tears left in him.

Yarrel cleared his throat. "Master Bertam wrote a letter to be delivered to you upon the event of your return. Shall I fetch it?"

Buckle looked up at the butler, the candlelight playing over the many cracks in his face.

"Yes, of course."

"Very good, Master Buckle." He left.

When the study doors closed Krinseth sat next to Buckle, not forcing unwanted sympathy on him, but there if he needed her. Buckle thought of the night they spent in an inn on the East Road during their hurried trip back. Buckle had fallen into the habit of having a late dinner with the captain. He had been returning to his room after such a dinner when Krinseth stepped out of the shadows in the hallway. Not saying a word, she'd taken his hand, opened the door and led him inside. They had spent every night since together, although Krinseth never slept. He'd wake in the night to find her sitting at a window, staring outside. Still, it was good having her around, especially now.

"What do we do now, Lord Buckle?" said Yazzle. His youthful face was scrunched up in worry.

"I don't know. I suppose I could wait and see who gets the estate and..." Buckle paused and sighed in exasperation. "Great Dalmar, I didn't even ask Yarrel who was made caretaker. Where is my brain?"

"Don't be hard on yourself," said Krinseth. "You have reason to be scatterbrained."

"I guess I won't be needing this." He held up one of the two pouches.

"I wouldn't despair of losing the estate just yet."

"What? You saw the candle."

"Yes," she said, standing up and crossing to the mantle. "But I've been thinking. We were in the house at least five minutes before we got around to checking the time. Plus the ride from where you said the estate lands started was at least fifteen minutes even at our pace."

Buckle thought for a moment. "Obviously you're right but without a reliable witness like Yarrel pinpointing us here before midnight I don't think it will hold up."

"But any reasonable person can deduce..."

"Yes," interrupted Buckle, "I agree. But Erklin would not have left important details like that up to chance. You can be sure that whoever serves as magistrate in this case will have received a large bribe and...Wait a minute." Buckle stood up and paced to the opposite side of the study from Krinseth.

"What is it?" she said.

"I have a plan." They were discussing the details of it when Yarrel returned to the study, bearing an envelope with Buckle's name on it.

"Yarrel," asked Buckle, taking the envelope and breaking the seal. "Is there a magistrate coming tomorrow?"

"Yes, Master Buckle. Sir Nazzle is due to arrive with the sheriff and the neighboring lords to preside over the transference of the estate at about eleven in the morning. Then there is a celebratory luncheon planned."

Buckle flashed an encouraging smile at Krinseth. "Thank you Yarrel. It sounds as if you have a big day coming up tomorrow. Why don't you get some sleep?"

"Thank you Master Buckle, the rooms you requested are being prepared." He paused significantly. "In the west wing."

"Thank you, good night." The old doorkeeper bowed and left the room. "Good old Yarrel, sly as a fox."

"How so?" asked Krinseth.

"The west wing is where the guest rooms are, well away from the household bedrooms. They'll be no chance of running into...damn I forgot to ask him who the caretaker is again." Buckle reached for the rope.

"I'm sure your brother will mention it," said Krinseth, motioning to the letter.

"Oh yes, of course." He sat down and folded open the letter and started to read.

My Dear Brother,

Thanks to that business at Scarver's Inn the night you left, Erklin figured out our plan and quickly recruited a caretaker who was accepted over our choice. The man he chose was Torkle, the constable Zabeth crippled that night. He's got a bad limp and a disposition to match. If you get back in time don't fool around with him. I know you, brother. You'll want to offer him a job or a pension. Don't. Just send him away.

If you don't get back in time then my advice is to leave. Don't pay your respects. Don't even say hello. Leave without him knowing you were even here. Move on to the next district. You'll be a landless man and they have a way of disappearing here. It's amazing what Erklin can get away with without Lord Roduct keeping him at least reasonably well in line.

As for me, well I'm dying. That's nothing new. I had hoped to make it through the year but these chest pains have grown unbearable and I can hardly walk across the room without stopping to rest. My only pleasure in life was needling Torkle. He can't throw me out until this spring and he knows it. At the beginning I would storm into his study and curse him for being a damn fool (which he is--I've never seen nor heard of a more poorly run harvest--and with all the storm damage it's going to be a lean year.) But since I've been bedridden he has the upper hand. He pokes his head into my room at least once a day just to see if I'm still alive. I think he's actually hoping I hold on so he can turn me out in this condition.

Buckle, you damn fool, hurry back. You're too cheerful and good natured by half. But oh, little brother I'd sure like to see you one last time before I die. But if you don't make it in the next couple of days, I'm afraid I won't. Therefore I have written this letter and instructed Yarrel to give it to you before you see Torkle. Mind my warning boy. He's a bad seed and angry too. If Zabeth's with you she's in particular danger. He can't stop thinking about her. Take care.

Bertam of Delamer, Solicitor

Buckle folded the letter up and put it in his pack. He could feel hot tears squeezing out of his eyes and a lump lodged itself painfully in his throat. He looked up and saw the bleary images of the others staring at him.

"Torkle is the caretaker," said Buckle when he could trust his voice.

"Constable Torkle?" Yazzle's eyes dawned with full understanding of the situation.

"Yes, and he's none too pleased with us. Yarrel was doing us a bigger favor than we knew by putting us in the guest wing. We'd do well to keep out of sight until the magistrate and the other lords arrive. According to Bertam, there's no telling what Torkle is capable of."

Yazzle looked scared. He kept glancing at the door, as if expecting Torkle to storm in. Lathel's head swiveled about nervously as if he sensed the tension in the room. Only Krinseth seemed calm.

"I'm afraid we won't be able to sleep in our own beds quite yet. I suggest we sneak up to the guest wing and spend the night as quietly as we can. We're not home yet."

The next day, about mid-morning, Sora brought them breakfast. When Buckle opened the door to her soft knocking, she almost dropped the tray of eggs, bacon and toast.

"Great Dalmar, Yarrel said there was a surprise up here but I never dreamed..."

Buckle took the tray from her, smiling for the first time after a long sleepless night. He handed the tray to Yazzle and embraced her.

"Sora, the thing that I've missed most about this place is your cooking."

"Oh just my cooking, eh," said the old woman pushing him away. She looked older. Her hair was grayer and the wattle under her chin hung lower. The face itself had more wrinkles than Buckle remembered. "You don't miss me or any of your other poor servants left behind with that dunderheaded...caretaker?"

Buckle stood back, a guilty half-smile on his face.

"Oh now you're going to blame yourself aren't you? I swear...I..." She paused, her voice breaking. "Who are these people? Well that towheaded imbecile I know, but the other two..." She pointed to Lathel who was sitting on the bed. Krinseth leaned against the window, watching impassively.

"I beg your pardon, Sora this is Krinseth who will be lady of the house, assuming I will be the lord." Buckle was gratified to see Sora's jaw drop almost to the floor. She finally collected herself and made a small curtsey.

But the first words out of her mouth were, "You're a witch, aren't you?"

"Water," said Krinseth.

"Can you cook?"

"I can't even boil an egg."

"Good, then we'll get along."

Krinseth smiled, almost laughing.

"Yes, I think we will."

"What's wrong with the boy?" Sora turned to Lathel, bending over and peering into the youth's eyes.

"I don't know, Matron," stammered Yazzle. "He's just been this way."

"He's seen things," said Buckle, "and done things no one his age should do. He seems to be attached to Yazzle. I thought if I brought him here, there might be something he could do."

Sora pinched the boy's chin and turned his head. "He can sweep up in the kitchen if you want."

"Good," said Buckle. He sat down on a chair and looked at Sora. "How has it been here in the last year?"

The old cook let go of Lathel's chin and straightened up. "Master Buckle, I've worked here for over forty years as a woman and a girl and I never thought I'd see...this." She shook her head.

"I understand it was a bad harvest..."

"It was a horrible harvest. Thanks to Torkle we only got in a quarter of what wasn't damaged by the storms. I can stretch our food. That's not what I'm talking about."

"What then?"

Sora looked down. "The lash," she said. "He's been using the lash. First on the traveling harvesters which was why they quit, then on the permanent staff when they wouldn't pick fast enough."

Buckle's jaw tightened and he walked over to the window which had a view of the fields stretching out from behind the manor. They were a patchy green with young corn. A couple of field hands ranged through the rows, hoes over their shoulders, ready to use.

Closer to the house stood a new structure. Buckle had seen it when the sun came up, but had been hoping that it didn't mean what he thought. It was a post, about a foot taller than Buckle. Bolted to the top of it were manacles.

"Tell Yarrel to inform me when the sheriff and the lords come." The old cook bowed her head and left.

The morning passed slowly. Buckle stared out of the window the whole time and didn't touch his breakfast. Krinseth only picked at her food and then spent the rest of the time with Lathel, trying to talk to him. Only Yazzle laid into his meal with any enthusiasm. Without asking, he also ate Buckle's portion when it became apparent he wasn't hungry.

Finally there came a discreet knock on the door. Yazzle opened it to reveal Yarrel. Only then did Buckle turn around.

"The sheriff and the lords are here, Master Buckle and the meeting is just beginning."

"Thank you Yarrel. Lead me down to the study. Through the servant area please. I don't want them to be forewarned."

"Yes, Master Buckle." The old doorkeeper led the way and a few minutes later Buckle and he were standing outside the study, listening.

"And I still have doubts about awarding the estate to Torkle," said one voice.

"What is the nature of these doubts?" said an older voice which Buckle recognized as Nazzle's.

"Over the past year he has shown himself to be incompetent."

"What?" growled a voice that could only be Torkle's.

"Easy Torkle, I'll have none of that here. Go on."

"Well look at his harvest last year. He got in only a fraction of what he should have."

"I had storm damage," shouted Torkle.

"As did we all," said another voice. "But all of us still got in four times as many crops as you."

"Furthermore," said the first voice, cutting off Torkle's reply, "the extreme cruelty with which he treats his workers reflects badly on all of us in the district. I am given to understand that flogging is a weekly occurrence here now."

"You have to rule the kind of vermin who work here with an iron hand," said Torkle. "The lash improves productivity."

The second lord spoke again. "I've had several traveling workers tell me they may not come back to the district this year if Torkle is still running Methliana. Now that hurts us all."

"And are we going to let a lawless class of traveling riffraff decide our business for us?" This was Erklin. "If they don't want to come back, I say good riddance. Me and my men won't have to stop their fights in the inns or try to catch them when they steal your livestock or valuables."

"How are we supposed to harvest our crops without traveling workers?" At this point the meeting erupted into a cacophony of argument and conflict. Nazzle pounded it down with his gavel.

"Masters, Lords, enough I say." When the room quieted, Nazzle continued. "Now, I have gone over this estate's ledgers and while Master Torkle certainly has a lot to learn, I think he's done a creditable job. And as for the traveling workers, well they may stay away for a year or two, but eventually they'll be back. They need all the work they can get."

"Your honor," said the first lord. "I must protest."

"May I remind you Lord Ferkle that you are just a witness? If you will not sign the document, I'll find another lord who will." There was a rustling of paper. "Now Master Torkle, you need to sign first...right here."

Buckle gave Yarrel a nod and the aging doorkeeper pushed open the doors of the study and walked in.

"Master Buckle of Delamer," he announced.

Buckle strode in past Yarrel, gratified to see the looks of shocked amazement on the group of men, sitting around the oak table. Erklin's expression betrayed anger and there was just a trace of fear in Torkle's. Nazzle's brown eyes and wrinkled face were merely bewildered. Ferkle and the other two lords, Bezzle and Tartum stared in simple astonishment.

Buckle experienced a moment of fear, staring at the scene. His stomach turned like a mill wheel in a cataract. Suddenly Buckle became aware of his travel-worn clothes, his un-manicured fingernails and his hair, short again thank Dalmar, but cut by Kebble who could not count barbering among his many accomplishments.

But then Buckle thought about the last year. About Urgallo the bandit, Bruct and most of all about Skrike. Comparatively speaking, Erklin and his people were not very dangerous.

"Yarrel if you could stay for a moment, I'll need you shortly."

"Yes, Master Buckle." The doorkeeper stood at attention beside the door.

"If we could table the transfer for a moment I have some new business." Buckle threw the first leather pouch onto the table in front of Nazzle.

"And what is in here, may I ask?" His bony fingers pulled at the leather thongs holding the packet closed.

"Signed depositions by myself and others swearing that we located Lord Roduct and ascertained from him the reasons for his conduct in this district. His own testimony is in there also."

"I see," said Nazzle, holding up the first document and examining it. "Soowooli laws, eh." He pulled the shunt out of the pouch and examined it. "This is certainly authentic. I assume you can prove that Lord Roduct was a Sarondaki."

"The second document is the original deed to the estate signed by Dalmar the Great. I believe it mentions Lord Roduct's bloodline."

Nazzle inspected the next document. A murmur started arising from the room's other inhabitants.

"I don't know what you're trying to do here Buckle," said Erklin, "but it wasn't very smart to come back. I might just charge you with conspiracy in that murder."

"There was no murder, sheriff," said Buckle, looking at Nazzle. "A Sarondaki, under threat of Soowooli is allowed to protect himself, even if it means killing the person threatening him. Isn't that right, your honor?"

"I'm afraid it is," said Nazzle.

"What?" cried Erklin.

"It's a clear cut case, Erklin. There's nothing I can do." He picked up his gavel and tapped it on the table. "Lord Roduct is exonerated from all charges against him. Will he be returning?"

"No your honor," said Buckle. "If you look at the third document you will see that it is Lord Roduct's will which states that if he has not returned to Methliana in one year the estate goes to me."

The old magistrate pulled the next paper out of the pouch. "So it does." He looked up. "You understand, son that your ownership of the estate is still in dispute. By neglecting your duties here for a whole year, you've put it in jeopardy." Erklin sat back with a self-satisfied grin.

"What time did you get here?" sneered Torkle.

"Yarrel, if you could explain what you witnessed last night?"

"Certainly, Lord Buckle." The ancient doorkeeper related the events of the previous night.

"Not soon enough," hooted Torkle. "Close, but the estate's still mine." He pounded on the table with the palm of his hand.

"That's right son. The law's very clear."

"But your honor," said Buckle, bowing his head slightly. "We were in the house for at least five minutes before we thought to check the clock. And it is a fifteen minute ride from the property line."

"Yes but actually being in the manor house is an important distinction. As for the other, you can't really prove you were here before midnight." He rubbed his chin thoughtfully. It seemed to Buckle that he could read the magistrate's mind. The old man suddenly stopped his stroking and his eyes darted over at Erklin who caught the gaze.

"This is a decision which shouldn't be rushed," he said, still looking at the sheriff. "I'll make it later this afternoon. We'll have dinner first. Is anyone else hungry?"

The meeting started to break up as Yarrel was dispatched to organize the serving of dinner. Buckle had to gently put off the three lords who were anxious for news. He fingered the second pouch he carried and made his way toward where Nazzle still sat at the head of the table.

Torkle's immense bulk suddenly blocked his way, however. The man limped terribly and there was an ugly expression on his face.

"So where's that bitch, Zabeth?"

Buckle looked up at the man and smiled. "She's a constable in the Barrier Scouts," he said. "If you wish to go out there and look her up, I'm sure she'd be happy to see you."

He blanched at that, his eyes growing wide. "I don't believe you."

Buckle motioned him out of his way and walked over to where Nazzle sat with Erklin in conversation. "Excuse me, your honor but while you're considering my case, I have another item of business for you."

They looked up at him. Erklin's look was hostile, Nazzle's irritated.

"What is it?" snapped the magistrate.

"The patrol that escorted me westward was also charged with delivering official despatches from the army to local officials. News of the war and such. To save them time I volunteered to deliver these to you." He held out the pouch.

"Good," said Nazzle, "I haven't had official news since they crossed the mountains." He opened the documents, talking all the while. "Mind you, I've heard rumors. I know we won of course. I even heard Skrike...was...dead."

He looked up at Buckle, eyes wide and mouth open. He tried to speak a couple of times but couldn't. Finally he swallowed and managed, "My Lord, the estate is, of course, yours and anything else that is within my power...you have but to name it."

"What's going on here?" bellowed Erklin. The scene had drawn the attention of the whole room by now.

"Read it, you fool," hissed Nazzle, as he pushed back his chair and lifted himself up and then kneeled in front of Buckle.

Erklin snatched the paper and scanned it, his jaw working like a wine press. When he got to the appropriate passage, he looked up at Buckle, his eyes squinting and exhaled sharply. With a sudden motion, he slammed the paper onto the desk and stormed out.

"What's going on?" demanded Torkle.

Bezzle picked up the paper and read it. He smiled and looked at the other two lords. "It seems that Lord Roduct's peaceful and retiring steward is the Skrikeslayer."

The others mumbled their astonishment and then followed Bezzle's example when he joined Nazzle on the floor.

"What is this? This guy? Killed Skrike? What are you talking about?" Torkle limped around the room, arms flailing.

"Damnit Torkle," said Nazzle. "Kneel before you get into any more trouble."

"You don't have to kneel, Torkle," said Buckle flatly. Torkle stood in the middle of the room. One leg bent at an improbable angle. His arms were out in an entreating position. "The only thing you have to do is leave. Right now. I'll send a couple of stable hands with you to make sure you get to the property line. Your possessions will be piled onto the road by nightfall."

Buckle turned to Yarrel. "See to it, and then tell Yazzle to round up every whip, lash, cat-o-nine-tails and riding crop on the premises and burn them. Then he can chop down that whipping post."

"Yes, Lord Buckle. Master Torkle, if you will follow me please?" Yarrel motioned to the door.

Torkle stood for a moment, considering. He looked around like a trapped animal, trying to gather one last shred of dignity. Finally he huffed and limped out the door.

Buckle let go of an inward sigh and turned to see four men kneeling on the rug.

"Lords, your honor, I do apologize. Please get up." He rushed over and helped the old magistrate back into his chair. The others also sat down. "I believe you gentlemen were promised a celebratory luncheon."

"Indeed we were, Lord," said Bezzle.

"I think it is probably more appropriate now than ever and I don't know about you but I'm starving."

Over the meal, they listened to Buckle's account of his adventures.

Epilogue

He watched the rippling patterns in the water as the island men paddled the canoe toward the growing hulk of the shore just ahead. There were two paddlers in front of him and two behind. They hadn't spoken since they had left the island.

They seemed relieved though. He was leaving his island and they had immediately said yes to his request for a ride to the continent, even though they disliked the Delamerians and rarely paddled their outriggers to the mainland. It was only to be expected, he thought. Eleven months of storms had taken its toll, and they had suffered the worst of it. They were only too glad to set him ashore to make trouble for the mainlanders.

He wasn't in the mood to make trouble, though. In fact he was drained. Not tired. He wouldn't be tired for another five hundred years. Just drained, used up. He couldn't even make a spring shower now. Leaning back in the canoe he idly thought that he'd spend the next fifty years or so resting. He'd find a nice cottage near a bog or a fen and eat crawfish every night. Sautéed in a light sauce he knew how to make with garlic and red peppers, they were quite palatable. He patted his stomach, pleased at its progress but knowing it had a long way to go before it returned to its accustomed rotundity.

Or maybe he'd visit his mother first. She would be due for the sleep soon and he kind of wanted to see her. Maybe get her to admit for once that he'd done a good job. That's what he'd do, he decided right then. He'd visit his mother and find out for certain how everything turned out. Then he'd find his cottage and take it easy. It was a good plan and he was satisfied with it.

Up ahead lights were appearing on the shore. That would be Massilay, he thought. There was an inn there once that served a delicious broiled lobster tail and stocked a very fine white wine. He'd have to look it up if it was still there. He licked his lips and watched the approaching lights.

It was raining. Not the driving kind of rain that the storms had brought them the previous year. This was a gentle rain, a farmer's rain. It fell slowly and evenly, giving the soil time to drink it all in so there was no runoff, no flood. It wasn't the kind of rain one ran from either. It felt good caressing the skin. You had to be out in it a good long time to get soaked.

Buckle walked out on the porch of the manor house and stood watching it, smelling its earthy aroma, wet soil and hay, and listening to it patter on the rooftops and the ground. He took a deep breath and wondered again at how his chest was clear. Usually in the spring, his sinuses clogged and his chest filled up. But Krinseth assured him that wouldn't happen anymore.

"You have eaten the fruits of my sister, Methlyn and drunk water from one of my springs. There will be no more attacks."

Buckle lit his pipe and inhaled again deeply. It glowed in the accumulating dusk. He walked up to the porch railing and put his hands on it. He was just at the point where the spray from the rain lightly touched his forearms and face. He stood like that for a minute and then he felt a hand cover his on the railing. He looked over and saw Krinseth standing beside him, watching the rain. She glanced at him and gave him one of her knowing grins.

Lord Buckle of Delamer was home.

ACKNOWLEDGEMENTS

This is my first novel, written in those long gone days of my twenties. For years, I thought that the best thing about it was that it was finished. I had proven to myself that I could complete a novel length work, which is an important step for someone who wants to be a novelist. I recently reread it, however, and discovered that although it is a very flawed work, it is not entirely embarrassing. In fact I quite enjoyed it. I used to call it my Tolkien rip off, although I think it probably owes more to Robert E. Howard, but it could be more accurately seen as a learning experience. As I said there are flaws. There is way too much falling action; the world building is not quite right; and some of the effects I was going for didn't work. Those are lessons and I got better.

I considered rewriting it and trying to sell it again, but the fact is that I've moved on. My interests, for better or worse, do not include writing epic fantasy anymore. My current projects are more important to me. By the way I have two other novels, written later, that are much better if anybody is interested.

I'm in my fifties now and while I've had some success selling short stories, I really want to be a novelist. But getting out of the slush pile is hard. I find that I want to see a book of mine on my shelf sooner rather than later so I decided to go the self-publishing route with this one.

Many thanks go to Steve Saffel for some good advice on the chapters and outline that I gave him to read back when I was trying to sell the book. Valerie Stewart grilled me on the details of the world of Dalmar and is probably responsible for everything that works in that area. I, of course, am to blame for everything that doesn't. Joan Ferguson very kindly copy-edited the text.

This book was workshopped a couple of times. What follows are the names of the people in those groups. It is probably incomplete and some people who deserve thanks will no doubt be victims of my eccentric and apocryphal filing system. To them I offer my sincere apologies and thanks. Anyway, here's the list: Mindy Klasky, Brenda Proctor, Malcolm B. Wood, Donald Kingsbury, Jack Nimersheim, Jean Lorrah, Xina M. Uhl, Bruce Deepwood, Adrienne Foster, and Andy Frisby.

And lastly, I would like to thank my good friend Tom Van Horne, who upon reading this book, said I was a better writer than Stephen R. Donaldson. I never believed it for a second but the sentiment was and still is appreciated. Good critical advice is of paramount importance, but sometimes you just need a little encouragement.

BIOGRAPHY

Charles Ebert has been writing science fiction and fantasy on and off since high school. He has had short stories appear in Aoife's Kiss, Aphelion and Electric Spec, and has another scheduled to appear in Kaleidotrope in 2015. He won an honorable mention in a short short story writing contest sponsored by Xignals and another honorable mention in the Writers of the Future contest. He is currently a librarian in Durham, NC.

www.ingramcontent.com/poc-product-compliance
Lightning Source LLC
Chambersburg PA
CBHW060151260626
47160CB00001B/215